support!
— Steve Farrington

Rodrigo's Land

Manfariel Press
95 Vermont St.
Rochester, NY 14609 USA
manfarielpress@gmail.com

STEVEN FARRINGTON

Rodrigo's Land by Steven Farrington

Copyeditor: Jennifer Blanchard
Cover Design: Marcus Macleod
Interior Design: Paulino Brener

Published in the United States by Manfariel Press
ISBN 978-0-9906539-5-0

DEDICATION

I dedicate this book to all those who were tortured by the Spanish Inquisition, as well as to the indigenous peoples of the Western Hemisphere.

ACKNOWLEDGMENTS

I would also like to thank all those who helped me along the way during this journey, especially Jen, Dayna, Paulino, Saikat, Becky, Clotilde, Marsha, Alysse, Marcus, Marcos, Barb, and Rick.

My heart has become capable of every form.
It is a pasture for gazelles,
And a convent for Christian monks,
And a temple for idols and the pilgrim's kaaba,
And the tables of the Tora, and the book of the Koran.
I follow the religion of love:
Whatever way love's camels take, that is my religion
and my faith.

-Ibn Arabi, "Interpreter of Ardent Desires."

PROLOGUE:
BARTOLOME'S JOURNAL, JUNE 1514

I buried Rodrigo today.

They sent him to me, and I didn't want to hear what the old man had to say. He sat at my side for forty days teaching and telling, just not the whole truth.

Now I sit here by his grave, my uncle's all-revealing letter in my hand. I breathe in the salty air and try to ignore the blazing heat, as well as the pain that comes from knowing too much, yet somehow, not enough. It's only now that I suspect what it was the old rascal came back to tell me, and why.

The wind plucks the letter and carries it toward the shore. I look off in the distance of the vast, crystal-blue sea that some now call *El Caribe*, and I know how he gave me the very thing I needed most.

He gave me back my memory. He gave me back my *self*.

CHAPTER ONE

Eastern Cuba, April, 1514

"You need to think about what you are doing here," said Friar Pedro de Córdoba.

Bartolomé knew the reason for this visit: they were unhappy with him for owning Indian slaves. He studied Brother Pedro's face, which was cold as his icy blue eyes, though Bartolomé had seen him break into a broad grin before, even while reading something as serious as Saint Augustine.

Today, the monk was not smiling. "Your latest correspondence reveals your great rhetorical skills. But it shows a bias against our cause, one for which you also would work, had you a Christian soul."

From the corner of the room, Bartolomé's parrot squawked and rocked on his brown driftwood perch by the study's window. As he looked out of this, the younger man felt relieved that there were no workers in the fields at the moment.

It had been several months since his last letter to the brothers of the Dominican order in Santo Domingo, and his mind strained to remember. What was so bad it brought them to his estate on another island?

Friar Pedro leaned across Bartolomé's desk. The old monk was dressed, as were the others, in a coarse, black habit and thin, rope sandals, an olive-wood cross hanging from the hemp band at his waist. His graying black hair had just been shorn, as was Bartolomé's — "you'll have fewer fleas that way when you spend six weeks at sea!" his father used to tease. Bartolomé sank back into his creaky, leather-backed chair.

"Don't you know that the Indian is a rational being?" Friar Pedro said, lecturing him as if he was a wise teacher with all the answers. "He is born free and has dignity, Bartolomé. *Dignitas!*" he slammed his fist on the desk, knocking over Bartolomé's candelabra and scattering cold candles over a disorganized collection of letters and quills.

It was a hot day, even for this part of the world, which some called the *Mundus Novus*, a kind of "New World," or simply, "The Indies." The briny tropical breeze from the window helped a bit, but the air still felt stifling in this house of white stone and red tiles that Bartolomé had once hoped would remind him of a Mediterranean villa.

"What my brother *means*," said Fray Bernardo, gently placing a wrinkled hand on Fray Pedro's shoulder and rebuking him with a look, "is that perhaps we could talk about what's to be done about saving the Indians?"

Bernardo seemed the frailest of the three monks, a graying, balding old man who was thin as a reed, but whose black eyes sparkled with a youth that defied his advanced age.

"Yes," said Brother Francisco, the third monk, a stout man with light blond hair. He scratched his tonsured head and frowned. "You have heard the sermons of Father Montesinos, have you not?" He furrowed his bushy brow, like a professor at Salamanca.

"I have," Bartolomé replied, tenting his fingers and trying to think. "We correspond — but it is hard to send missives from such an isolated place as this, and not all of them make it through. There are far too many pirates and storms off the Cuban coast."

Montesinos. The man was a force of nature, the "voice of Christ in the desert," as he loved to boast. Bartolomé thought of when he'd seen him preach in the *Iglesia Mayor* of Santo Domingo, his voice thundering out from the pulpit over the humble flock, which consisted mostly of a motley crew of sailors, soldiers and petty bureaucrats. "Tell me by what right of heaven or earth you hold these Indians in such a cruel and horrible servitude!" he had bellowed, the sweat pouring down his wide forehead and aquiline nose. "On what authority have you waged such detestable wars against these people who lived quietly and peacefully in their own lands? Vanity of vanities, what do you gain from the toil of your slaves under the sun?"

That day, upon taking the sacrament, Bartolmé had prayed Montesinos hadn't heard about the Taino Indian slaves who worked on his *encomienda* whom one could observe from this very study, often wearing nothing but the cotton loincloths Bartolomé had insisted they wear for modesty's sake. He had almost expected the Dominican to deny him the host and wine out of spite.

Montesinos was but a member of the *Ordo Praedicarum* — the "Order of the Preachers" of the Dominicans — but he had friends in high places. He hadn't meddled with any part of Bartolomé's life — the *encomienda*, which was a payment of sorts, or his ordination…but what could he be up to now?

Sweat began to dot Bartolomé's forehead and dampen his robe. He found himself staring at a green lizard on the cracked wall of his study as the blond monk droned on. The unannounced visit by these three holy brothers kept him from lunch, and his stomach growled in protest. Outside, a *coquí* frog began his song, which Bartolomé thought odd, as the sun was out. Perhaps a storm was brewing?

"And do you agree with Montesinos's reasoning?" the Dominican demanded, pulling Bartolomé's attention once again to the present. The monk arched his bushy blond eyebrows at him before glancing nervously at the bird stalking this way and that on his gnarled perch. "Well? Speak!"

Bartolomé suddenly wished that he were anywhere else. A novice, he had come to the New World as a *doctrinero* a dozen years before, hoping to spread his faith among the Indians. He thought of his slaves. Wasn't he slow to anger, quick to forgive, only seldom resorting to the whip? Did not the Indians accept the Holy Faith easily from his lips? Yes, they still buried statues to make the yucca grow and hung icons of Mary around their necks to help in childbirth, but even so. And the good deeds he had done over the years…hadn't he taken in those shipwrecked sailors the year before last? Guantánamo Bay could be such a wretched and dangerous place, especially during the season of heavy winds. He thought of the pig the men had roasted that night, how it had turned and turned on the spit as it roasted and charred almost black…

"Bartolomé! Do you not believe that the Indians are rational men with souls?" asked Brother Francisco. "They're dying and going straight to Hell if we don't reach them before the soldiers do. If it pleased God to put His children here, then it's up to *us* to do everything we can to save them. Don't you realize that?"

Bartolomé hesitated and studied his visitors' faces for a minute. "Yes, of course," he said. At almost forty, he wouldn't be taken for a fool.

"So," Brother Francisco continued, thoughtfully stroking his chin and pacing about the room. He glanced first at the sagging mahogany bookshelf, then at a colorful *mapa mundi*, which portrayed the recently explored land of Vespucci's America, and finally back at the cluttered desk where the target of his diatribe sat, squirming in his seat. "So then. Why do you allow some of them to be treated as something *less* than God's children, created in His holy image? And worse yet, you grow *rich* doing so!"

5

"You forget, brother," Bartolomé said, rejoining the conversation, "I am not a Dominican, nor do I ever wish to take your harsh vows. I am held to a different standard."

It was true, he lived by a different standard altogether. Bartolomé had a nice estate. His mind wandered to the bedroom, the fine shutters with tying curtains to keep mosquitoes out, the dining room with doilies, and orange and green ceramics imported from Valencia and Faenza…

"Who do you think you are? Do you think you are glorifying God this way?" Friar Francisco said, grabbing a blue ceramic vase from a shelf and brandishing it as if he would dash it to pieces on the study's floor. "Have you not read in Ecclesiasticus where it is written that 'to offer a sacrifice of the fruit of iniquity is to make a stained offering?' You should be beating your breast in contrition! It's only a matter of time before that silver-tongued Cortés moves to *terra firma* eight hundred leagues to the west and it starts all over again!" He paused, seeming to search for another tactic, and Bartolomé heard waves crashing on the beach, a sure sign of a storm. "Montesinos is a powerful man with friends in high places. Don't doubt that a well-placed letter from him could have you stripped of all you own, or even—"

"What are you *talking* about?" Bartolomé bound to his feet and his chair clattered against the blue and green tiles of the floor. He could feel a pounding in his temples, an old, familiar sensation. "I am a good master, and I've never killed any of my slaves!" He felt a long-repressed howl welling up inside. "How dare you come to *me* to rail about this? I've seen what our men are doing back in Santo Domingo. I once saw a group of Indian children bleeding to death in a stream, their hands cut off by our soldiers. Their crime? Not gathering enough gold! Have *you* been there to see it? Or have you been hiding out in your little school in the hills?"

Silence descended over the room like a shroud. A mosquito buzzed in Bartolomé's ear, and he slapped at it, a violent smack against the moist side of his face.

"How dare you, Dominicans whose midnight order runs the Inquisition itself, cast your stones on the likes of *me*? Am I not an upright man? The voice of Christ, indeed!"

Friar Francisco took a step back, his mouth wide with disbelief, while Friar Pedro glowered like an angry schoolmaster unsure of how to handle an unruly pupil. For one wild moment, Bartolomé thought of chasing them out with his walking stick of gnarled wood. Instead, he righted his chair and sat, his face in his hands.

Finally, Bartolomé stared at the three monks once again. While the other two now looked at the white-tiled floor, old Friar Bernardo stood looking absently out the window, his bright eyes under gray brows perhaps gazing at the fields and sea below. Bartolomé wondered if, after his outburst, the men would finally leave him in peace.

Bartolomé heard the waves crash once again on the beach, and the *coquí* frog cried again.

Finally, Friars Pedro and Francisco exchanged a look. The latter was about to speak when Friar

7

Bernardo silenced him, and at last turned fully to face Bartolomé. Friar Bernardo's hands soon rested gently on the desk, nimbly supporting the weight of his meager body. He had a light gray beard, and what little hair he had left on his tonsured crown was completely gray as well. He had a kind smile, and it struck Bartolomé that the man's twinkling dark eyes seemed almost of the Orient. He wondered if the monk was descended from Moors or perhaps Jewish *Conversos*. He would have to write his uncle to inquire. People had always wondered at Bartolomé's lineage, as he had dark skin and eyes almost like those of Friar Bernardo.

Friar Bernardo studied Bartolomé for a moment, and then said, in a very low voice — so low, in fact, that Bartolomé was unsure if the other monks could hear:

"You know, there are all kinds of people in this world, Bartolomé, and God's love can only reach *some* of them. For many, far too many, the seeds of God's love fall on the stones of their hearts, never to have the chance to sprout. For others, a smaller number, God's love sends seeds that *do* sprout and take root, only to be devoured by the birds of evil that destroy all hope of an abundant harvest. This displeases God immensely, because so many plants could have grown had they been tended with care."

Bartolomé sat looking at Friar Bernardo as he thought of what to say. The monk's two companions were now mercifully silent as they hung back near the large pine armoire that Bartolomé had ordered from the Canary Islands three years before.

The old monk continued speaking a moment later, this time quoting Ecclesiastes. He said, "All things are wearisome, more than one can express. The eye is not satisfied with seeing, or the ear filled with hearing."

Friar Bernardo stood for a long moment, looking as if he were choosing his words carefully. Then he leaned toward Bartolomé as if the two men were conspiring in a plot, his voice a mere whisper. The younger priest leaned forward to hear what the old Dominican had to say.

"There are others," Bernardo said, weighing every word. "There are others, fewer still, so tragically few — in whose hearts there is fertile soil, abundant soil, deep and rich, in which beautiful things can grow. It is in *these* hearts that great things are possible — gifts which it is a sin not to use for the glory of God and the salvation of all."

The old monk studied Bartolomé, their eyes locked. Bartolomé felt he should respond, so he said, "Well, what is it that you want from me, then?" Perhaps if he pretended to agree, they would go away and leave him to do as he would.

Bernardo nodded and smiled at Bartolomé before saying, "Sometimes you have to lose everything before you can gain something." As Bartolomé wondered at this, the monk added, "Our Lord said that what we do to the least of our brothers we do also to him. Do not forget it."

He turned away then, and, as if on cue, his two companions followed him to the corridor. "You will soon receive a visitor, my brother," he said, half-turning as he reached the doorway. "He is an old man, poor and sick. He is, in fact, not going to last long. He has much to tell you and much to teach. Allow him into your home and into your heart. Be a Good Samaritan, and listen to his story. He is known as Rodrigo Bermejo. You will know him when you see him."

"But I—" Bartolomé began.

Brother Bernardo silenced him with a look. "*Domine vobiscum,*" the older man said in the time-honored way of taking leave, his dark, knowing eyes twinkling a bit again.

"*Et cum spiritu tuo,*" Bartolomé answered with a sigh.

It was only after the monks had left that Bartolomé realized that the weather was calm and that no storm would come after all.

CHAPTER TWO

Rodrigo Bermejo. Only that and nothing more?

Bartolomé sat and pondered this new information. Did the man have no famous family names or titles? How did he know that simple name? It was common enough, but he knew he recognized it from somewhere. Was this someone who lived here in Cuba? Or maybe on Hispaniola or other settled areas? Or did this man's memory harken back to Bartolomé's life before, a link with Sevilla, far back in the murky clouds of distant memory?

After a few days, his mind began to settle from his confrontation with the Dominicans. The indignation began to wear off, and the normal ebb and flow of life had returned, as well as what he considered the normal circulation of his humors. Indeed, he began to doubt that the mysterious visitor would come at all when, while sitting in his garden, he saw someone approaching from the distance.

He was a tiny old man perched on a burro making its way along the leafy path to Bartolomé's home. He had a wild gray beard, spindly arms and legs, long hair, and sad, brown, Castilian eyes. Under an ancient sailor's cap, Bartolomé saw that the man's hair was almost completely gray except for a few strands of red, and his face bore strange scars on either cheek. His torso looked taut, as if a lifetime of adventure and exertion had honed his body into a lean, muscular, almost feline form. He wore a frayed necklace with a red ruby and a brown shroud that was held at the waist by a sash of animal skin. On his face was a pained, melancholy expression, and Bartolomé thought that he had the look of one not long for this world. He wondered what was killing him. Sadness? Old age? Regret?

"You must be Rodrigo," Bartolomé said as the old man approached.

Rodrigo — there was that name again, that mysterious name that evoked sensations in his mind, memories and associations which formed like bubbles not quite breaking through to the surface.

"Yes, Rodrigo Bermejo, so named for the vermillion color my hair used to hold," the old man replied, looking as if he had reached the end of a long and arduous journey, and wanted to bask in the moment. "So, here you are, finally, Bartolomé. Bartolomé de las Casas."

"Yes, I am he," Bartolomé replied. He was surprised by the lack of effusiveness in the stranger's acknowledgement. Most Spaniards, upon visiting, referred to him as "Don Bartolomé," or said what an

honor and pleasure it was to meet the first priest ordained in the New World. Bartolomé sighed.

"Fray Bernardo told me you would come," he said, "And that I was to welcome you. Am I to understand that—"

"I'm dying?" He interrupted. "Yes, yes, I'm afraid so. It's only natural. I'm an old man, I have outlived my usefulness, and it's time that I return to the earth. 'A generation goes and a generation comes, but the earth remains forever.' Now," he said, getting down from the burro with difficulty, "Please show me to my room, if you would be so kind."

Bartolomé felt put off by such presumption, but he showed the man to a guest-chamber. The old man settled himself gently on his pallet as if his entire body ached from the journey. "If you don't mind, Bartolomé, I should like to sleep for a little while. I feel terribly weak from the long voyage. Yes, sleep for a little while, you won't mind…" He mumbled this last phrase as he began to drift off.

"Very well," Bartolomé said, tugging at the pallet's flaxen cover, "But first please tell me who you are and where you're from."

"Who am I? Where am I from?" He chuckled at the questions. "I am known by many names. Here, when speaking with Spaniards, I'm known simply as Rodrigo, although I was once also known as Benjamín, 'the young son.' I was once from Spain, you know, from your native Sevilla."

"You know where I'm *from*?" Bartolomé asked, suddenly suspicious. Who *was* this man?

"Yes, I'm from there too, although I have since been far and wide, all over the world and in many lands. I may be one of the best-traveled people on the face of the earth."

An idea came upon Bartolomé, and he grasped his guest's arm as he exclaimed, "Of course! You are Rodrigo, 'Rodrigo the Savage!' Aren't you the Spaniard they say lives among the Indians?"

"All that's a tale for another day, my boy. Now, I beg of you, let an old man get his rest."

CHAPTER THREE

Bartolomé's mind raced with a thousand questions as his curious guest slept. Was it possible he had a dangerous, wanted man in his home? He remembered hearing that Governor de Ovando, a man he had once met on the pier of Santo Domingo as he sent a renegade Taino chief to Spain, had offered a large reward for Rodrigo's capture, dead or alive. What could he have done to incite such rage from the authorities? Had he been among those Indians, the tenacious guerrilla warriors in the Bahoruco Mountains? Had he ever killed a man? But the very idea of the frail old man posing a threat to anyone seemed laughable.

It was true that Bartolomé had heard stories about him before, but he never took them seriously. Some said that he had run off to Moorish lands after helping the Indians and stowing away on a caravel bound for Cádiz. Some said that he was crazy, or possessed by demons. A rumor had made the rounds that he had been the first to spot land on the Great Admiral's voyage, and that he had tried to murder *Colón* for not giving him his just reward. Some thought him revered by the Indians because of his hatred for the Great Admiral. Others whispered that, because of his many years in exile with the savages, he would slit the throat of any white man foolish enough to venture across his path. The thought briefly crossed Bartolomé's mind that his being sent could be a kind of punishment.

But then he thought of the moment of sincerity that he had experienced with Fray Bernardo.

No, he decided. He did not yet understand who this man was or why he had been sent to him, but this was no act of revenge. At least not if Fray Bernardo had any part of it.

But what was it about a crime? There had been whispers, something back in Spain…Bartolomé remembered that some of the crew of that maiden voyage had been conscripts from a jail in Palos. Had Rodrigo really been among that first crossing with the Great Admiral? Bartolomé's mind strained to remember anything about this man who still seemed so oddly familiar. This Rodrigo, or what was it he had once been called – Benjamín – who *was* he, and what had he done? How could he find out more about him?

He resolved to write his uncle Juan immediately, asking him to explain this stranger. He knew that he would wait weeks or even months before he could hope to receive an answer. Luckily, he knew of a caravel nearby whose crew would take the letter. Of course, if *anyone* could shed light on Rodrigo's identity, it was Bartolomé's uncle. After all, he had recruited most of the men from Palos for that first journey in 1492, and had convinced Bishop Fonseca to let his young nephew come in the 1502 Armada to seek glory here in the New World.

CHAPTER FOUR

That evening, Bartolomé sat down to a supper of fish soup, rice, beans, sweet potatoes, cassava bread and plantains for dessert. The soup reminded him of the *boba* soup of old bread, beans and fish he used to give beggars at the gate in Salamanca during his student days, and he frowned slightly at the memory.

He had ordered his Indian house-slave to prepare enough for two that evening, and, sure enough, after some stirring from the guest-chamber, Rodrigo soon emerged. Instead of an evening greeting in Spanish, he directed an unintelligible discourse to the slave-girl. Rodrigo interspersed what he said with sweeping gestures that included the table upon which the food lay, pointing with his chin to that which she was carrying, and small, polite bows in her direction. Her eyes went wide, and she seemed so amazed to hear a Spaniard speaking her own tongue that she dropped an empty, wooden serving bowl. Rodrigo failed to notice, however, and simply continued talking. Bartolomé heard him mention the word "Colba" once or twice, and he recalled that this was the native word for this island. Then his guest called the food "choreto," their word for "many things," or "abundance of gifts."

At the end of the speech, the girl nodded an emphatic agreement and smiled before picking up the bowl she had dropped and beating a hasty retreat to the kitchen.

"The accent the Tainos have on this island is giving me headaches," Rodrigo said with a grimace.

Bartolomé could scarcely believe his eyes and ears.

"Well, now that our hostess has been properly thanked, we can enjoy our meal," Rodrigo said, smiling and sitting down across from Bartolomé. "*Then* we'll rest, and afterwards, we can talk. That, after all, is the Taino way."

Bartolomé shook his head and sat down. "I think you're mistaken," he replied with a chuckle. "*I* am lord of this hacienda, and it is to *me* you should be grateful."

To this, Rodrigo just smiled. They ate for a while in silence, and then he said, "You have much to learn, my boy. To whom did this land belong just twenty-five years ago?"

"You are right," Bartolomé said, choosing his words. He hated the fact that this stranger, like the three friars, talked to him as if he were a young man, calling him "my boy" and such things. Did they not realize that he was advanced in years, even if he looked young?

"It is true," Bartolomé continued, "But now *we* are here, and we can do great things with our discovery, once we subdue this wilderness. Of that I am sure. Crimes are being committed, but for now, nothing we do can change any of that. In light of such a task, what can one person do? Best to let go of any desire to change things. It's much easier that way."

"The Tainos have a saying," said Rodrigo. "'The wagging of the tail of the smallest tilapia fish can change the course of the entire river.'"

"What has that to do with me?" Bartolomé asked.

"We are all fish in the great river of life. Don't be afraid to wag your tail!"

Bartolomé laughed, imagining himself a man with a fish's tail in the Arimao River trying to swim against the flow. When he saw that Rodrigo was not laughing, he changed the subject.

"The friars say that you've much to tell me," he said. "Why don't you start at the beginning?"

But his guest didn't say a word. Instead, he sat and watched his host for a long while, a slight frown on his lips. "You don't have any sense of who you are or why you are here, do you, Bartolomé?" he finally asked.

Bartolomé was so taken aback, he didn't know what to say.

CHAPTER FIVE

When dinner was done, Bartolomé and Rodrigo moved outside to the waning sun of early twilight. They had settled into two hammocks that were suspended side-by-side from a rectangle of palm trees in the side garden. Bartolomé's guest finally began his tale.

***

"Rodrigo! Come to your lessons, damn you! You'll never be a priest if you don't learn your Latin!" My father yelled this from the garden of our home, but to no avail. I was running away from home, and had no desire to study Latin with yet another sad, old tutor.

Latin. I tell you, Bartolomé, Latin was both the bane and the refuge of my youth. I was pressed into studying it, it's true, but how I would lose myself in its beauty! The conjugations and cases are so logical, fitting together in endless, elegant patterns. And the ancient stories and myths, the grand drama of Virgil, the power and stories of the Bible. I was a prisoner in my own castle, yes, but one liberated by his imagination and the power of words.

Of course, I could have gone downstairs on banquet days, but I would have been met with astonished stares by my family and the servants alike, not to mention their distinguished guests. I can just imagine my brother, Alejandro, his doublet crimson and his hair oiled, turning to gaze upon me, all awkwardly jutting bones and russet curls, a simple smock and leggings my only adornment. I was fifteen years old, but looked twelve. As usual, the disapproving eyes of Saint James would have peered down at me from the painting in the foyer, his feet resting on the slain Moors writhing underfoot. Ay, *Santiago Matamoros!* I still feel he would have slain me as well, or at the very least, expelled me from Spain like Queen Isabel and her Inquisition would succeed in doing one day.

And so, I would sit placidly in my bed-chamber, my books and scrolls scattered about, my ancient tutor, or perhaps a servant, looking on, nodding or yawning, trying to stay awake. The gentle sounds of lutes and dulcimers, not to mention the clinking of ceramic and lusterware plates, drifted up to me and played off the singing of the canaries my mother kept in cages in the patio beside a gently bubbling fountain.

In those days, my other brother, Ricardo, was nowhere to be seen. He'd once been the closest thing I had to a playmate. By then, he was off training with the Berber and Andalusian lads conscripted to guard

King Enrique. Unlike the elegant Alejandro, groomed to take my father's place one day as a member of the nobility, Ricardo was lusty, earthy, and virile, a soldier to the hilt. He could always be seen with a girl on his arm or on his way to the lists, fencing lessons, or the bull-fight. Once he took me, not to meet his fencing-master as I'd hoped, but to watch the matadors train in their deadly arts.

"Don't cry, *Benja*," he said, trying to comfort me with a pat on the back and using the nickname he'd kept for me since my days with the wet-nurse. You see, even though my official name was Rodrigo, my family called me *Benjamín* or even *Benja*, as I was the youngest son.

"Don't cry, *Benja*," my brother said again. "The bulls die doing what they're bred to do, with glory and splendor. They are sacrificed for the honor of Spain. *Hispania!*" Ricardo cried, using the word that was the fashion in 1473 among so many sailors and soldiers who knew only a smattering of Latin. The ideal of a united Spain, fused together by so many rival kingdoms in our Iberian Peninsula, was barely more than a dream in those days.

"The bulls die. Like you will one day, Ricardo?" I asked, wiping the tears from my freckled face.

"Like I will die one day, my *Benjamín*," he said, tousling my hair. "If I am lucky. I am a warrior, after all, and hope to perish on the battlefield or defending our king. Far better to live well and die young than to waste away at a feeble old age. But don't worry, little one — you will die an old man and a contented priest. You'll see. It suits you!"

But my father was not pleased at all when he heard of the day's adventure. "What the devil were you thinking?" he bellowed at Ricardo in the foyer, the saint's eyes staring in disapproval. "Benja is meant for the church. He's far too weak to witness such things." He turned to face me, his graying brow furrowed in anger. "And you, *Don Rodrigo*," he said with a sneer, his voice starting to rise as he twisted his goatee with an angry finger. "Crying, my son? Such girlish foppery is a disgrace to the Vargas and Guzmán names. I am a Marquis and a member of the Order of Santiago! Never since our forebears fought alongside El Cid to wrest these lands from the Moors have we cried, and even less so in public! I don't care if you're only to be a priest…" He paused, looking at the suit of armor his ancestors had once worn into battle that now stood guard under the portrait of *Santiago Matamoros*. "Get out of my sight," he grumbled.

Not long afterward, during Holy Week, he made me do my penance. I had to join dozens of brothers of my father's *cofradía* as we carried a float of the Virgin of Macarena around the city. The men of that brotherhood had built the float of heavy oak, and the statue and hundreds of flaming candles only added to the weight. Instead of my usual clothing, I wore a penitent's garb of coarse brown cloth, and tread barefoot along the river. We started by the *Puerta de Macarena* and followed the old city walls until we reached the river. We then followed the Guadalquivir all the way to the center of town. Every once in a while, I would gaze up to see how far the tower of the Giralda stood from us, and it seemed an eternity before we reached it. One of the men whispered to me that the Giralda, now a bell-tower for a magnificent cathedral, had once been a minaret from which the Moors called their faithful to prayers. I felt a stab of guilt that my ancestors had played a part in their being chased from our lovely Sevilla, the most beautiful city on earth, or so I thought. Everywhere we went, women sang plaintive songs, weeping, and throwing us jasmines and rosemary.

After several hours, I began to feel like I could stand the journey no more. My bruised feet cried out as they scraped against the cobblestones, and my legs ached worse than ever before in my short, uneventful life. I thought of Mother Mary, *Maria Nostra, Mater Dei*, who was perched upon my very shoulders. I prayed to her, and thought of her silvery tears. Perhaps I should have told my father about the lachrymose Jesus in the parish church's stained-glass or the tears of mother Mary. Perhaps then he would have pardoned my show of weakness.

CHAPTER SIX

Bartolomé shifted in his hammock. "Is it true that you're a priest, Don Rodrigo?" he asked.

"Heavens no, Bartolomé," Rodrigo replied with a short laugh. "I did eventually become a man of the church, but that is all in the ancient past. I never quite became the sacristan my mother hoped for."

All this talk of parents made Bartolomé feel melancholy, as both his parents were long since dead.

"What was your mother like?"

Rodrigo's voice took on a bitter tone as he said, "Inmaculada Guzmán de Vargas. She was a sad woman with black hair twisted in tight curls. In keeping with the fashion of the day, she wore mostly blue, pleated dresses with golden-thread brocade or a tight, trimmed bodice, and a corset that left her short of breath. Her role was limited to the running of the household and the planning of banquets with Alejandro. However, sometimes she would take me along in her carriage when I used to serve as acolyte to the priest at the *Iglesia San Gil* or help with pageants at the cathedral.

One day, on our way back from mass, we passed through the Arenal quarter before turning right along the river toward home. Not far from there, I saw a group of boys playing during siesta in an *alameda* park I'd never noticed before. They ran back and forth between the poplars bearing flags and galloped as if on horseback yelling "Aragon, Aragon! By the wealth of Barcelona, King Fernando will vanquish all foes!"

I asked my mother why these boys were yelling these words.

She sighed, like a weary tutor explaining arithmetic to a slow child. "They speak of the marriage of our Isabel to that bastard, Fernando," she said, pulling a black-lace fan from the lower of her billowed sleeves which were crisscrossed by gold and silver threads. "They will use that sacrament to marry our two kingdoms as well. Then, one day, Castile will finally expel the Moors of Granada back to the Barbary Coast where they belong," she said as she fanned herself. "But don't worry about any of that, child of my sorrows. Just learn your Latin, and learn it well. Try to make us proud."

I smiled wanly as I reflected that, as Guzmáns, we were very distantly related to a branch of the same family as Saint Dominic of Burgos, the founder of the Dominican order and the patron saint of hopeful mothers.

27

I gazed once again out of the carriage's window at the boys frolicking in the green park between the playing fountains of the *alameda*, lucky enough not to have parents wanting to be made proud.

CHAPTER SEVEN

One morning not long afterwards, I decided that I'd had enough. I threw down my papers and quills, scurried past my mother as she handed a list to her most trusted steward, and bolted out through the tall, studded wooden doors of the servants' entrance on the side of the kitchen. My father's voice was still ringing in my ears as I dashed out of the garden of our home and along the narrow *Calle San Luis*, past the Santa Marina Church, trying not to trip on the cobblestones that lined the streets. Soon, I saw the river. I turned away from town, the Giralda barely visible in the distance.

I felt dazzled by the beauty all around me. The smell of late spring orange-blossoms, the shimmer of the sunlight on the water of the Guadalquivir — I felt like a poet whose heart and mind would burst with these sudden new ideas and sensations. I had decided no longer to be a prisoner in my own home like my mother's golden canaries. It was time to see the world, even if it was just for a few hours — and to hell with the consequences. I even left Sevilla's walls and wandered about the countryside for a time.

After a while, I realized that my father hadn't tried to follow me, and that I didn't need to run. I stopped for a time by an olive tree whose brown, contorted trunk seemed to writhe in agony, and I sat at the edge of a miller's pond to catch my breath. I watched as some large brown trout swam this way and that, snapping at the mayflies flying above the surface. How nice it would be to have such a carefree life, I thought.

Before long, I began making my way back. I passed through the city gates, along the Arenal, and toward the center of town again, hoping I would meet the boys I had seen at play, or others like them.

After some time, I turned back toward the river and walked along it, the tower of the Giralda an ever-larger beacon that seemed to call to me as it had once called the Moors to prayer. I passed by a many-sided gray tower called the *Torre de Oro*, as this was a tower where the Moors used to store their gold and other riches. I stopped for a while to admire the intricate writing of the Arabic carvings on its side, and wished my father had made me study that language as well as Latin and Greek. Time slipped by unnoticed as I studied the gentle curves of the foreign script and the lovely pictures of flowers that adorned the building.

Continuing on toward the *alameda*, I passed other haciendas or estates that qualified as *latifundias*, but none as large as my father's, as these were inside the city's walls. Most people were still sleeping or just waking from their siestas, but a few industrious and haggard-looking servants crossed my path as I made my way to the park full of poplars, where I'd seen the boys playing just a few days before.

Unused to such exertions, I soon felt winded and a bit dazed for want of my afternoon nap. I perched on an outcropping that overlooked the river. I sat for a few minutes watching the heavy flow of the current below. I was starting to doze off when I heard a noise behind me, and a human shadow stretched over me. Startled, I jumped, teetered on the edge of the rock, and fell into the river with a splash.

A flash of panic shook my body. I couldn't swim! I flailed around in the brown water, my eyes clamped shut, and wondered what it would be like to drown. In vain, I tried to reach the bottom with my feet, not wanting to swallow water. How many times had I seen washerwomen throwing lye, or worse, into the Guadalquivir? How many servants had thrown the contents of their masters' chamber-pots into this mighty river that now seemed intent on dragging me to the sea?

I gasped for air, filling myself with a lungful that I hoped would help me stay afloat. Suddenly, I felt a pair of strong arms around my shoulders. Then, slowly, someone began pulling me toward the shore. After what seemed an eternity, my feet touched a bottom that was muddy at first, then finally full of pebbles and gravel where I could get purchase.

My eyes were still closed and my mouth spit and spluttered. I felt the strong presence that had saved me guide me to the rocky shore as I stumbled and flopped about.

I lay there for a few moments, and once my breathing had returned to normal, I opened my eyes to see my rescuer.

Imagine my surprise when I saw that my hero was a girl!

"Hello. My name's Esther, Esther de Susón," the young woman said, as I gingerly took her hand. This name said something to me, but I couldn't quite place it.

She was a striking young woman, with lovely green eyes, an olive complexion, and long, curly black hair like a lamb's fleece. She wore a simple, tan smock and brown trousers. This surprised me, as I'd never before seen a girl wear anything but a shift, a skirt, or a dress with petticoats if she was from a wealthy family. I wondered if she had decided to disguise herself as a boy. My tutor had told me that such people could be put to death under church law.

I wiped the water from my face, and looked with dismay at my dripping clothes. Father is going to whip me for this, I thought. Just imagine if someone had seen me, drowning in the river and rescued by a girl. Mother would die of shame. And as for my father, let me just say that family honor was everything.

"You don't come here swimming much, do you?" Esther asked, a wry smile creeping over her face.

"Never," I said. "I don't strike out on my own," I admitted. "This is my first time ever, and it's not a success." I didn't add that people of my class never learned how to swim.

32

"Nonsense," Esther said. "It took me months before I tried the Guadalquivir. You hopped in your first day here!"

"Well, that's only because you—"

"Because I scared you?" she grinned.

"Startled," I corrected her.

"Who are you?" I could hardly believe how direct this girl seemed.

"I am called Benjamín sometimes, but only at home. My family calls me that or Rodrigo. I prefer Rodrigo, in fact."

"What do your friends call you?"

I felt heat rise to my cheeks. "I don't really have any." I thought of the boys I wanted to meet. "None yet anyway."

"And what are your family names, Rodrigo?"

"Vargas and Guzmán," I said, with some hesitation.

As I expected, Esther's eyes went wide with surprise upon hearing this news. She no doubt knew about the large *latifundia* my father had received upon his marriage that lay just outside the *Puerta de Córdoba* or the large, seigniorial mansion our family occupied *intramuros* in the San Gil parish. "Well then, what are you doing off your father's noble lands?" she asked. She began to laugh. "It's a good thing no one saw you in the river. The son of a marquis!"

"Please don't tell anyone," I said, my voice cracking.

Esther looked perplexed. "Who would I tell?" She had a pained expression, and I wanted to believe that she could, or would, tell no one.

She made a good point. I couldn't place where I knew her name from, true, but I felt certain it was not a family that had come as guests to my mother's banquets.

"There's a simple reason why you've never met me before now, Rodrigo," she said, holding my gaze. "It's because I'm Jewish."

I felt as if someone had kicked me in the stomach. I had always been forbidden to speak to Jews as well as Moors. I half-expected to see horns and a demon's tail protruding from the girl's body, the way some of the priests spoke of them.

"You're not a family of *conversos?*" I asked hopefully. New Christians, or *Marranos* as we called them then, were the lowest of the low in Andalusian society. Of course, the unconverted Jews and Moors who followed Mohammad were somehow more despised than they. I remember my father telling Ricardo how Spain should send them back to Africa where, he said, they belonged. He hoped the future queen would expel them from the shores of Iberia permanently, as they might try to win converts or, as Father put it, "tempt those weak, backsliding New Christians." And as Father Miguel said, "at least the *Marrano* swine are Christians, and thus stand a chance of making it to paradise." Not so for the Moors and the unrepentant Jews, who most people saw as little more than savages.

"No, Rodrigo," Esther said tilting her chin upward. "We won't be converting anytime soon. We are proud sons of Abraham, the chosen, the treasured ones with a special covenant. We're not about to surrender that."

I thought about this for a moment. I tried to imagine what life must be like for this girl, whom I somehow couldn't conceive of as fully human. What would it feel like if some group forced me to abandon my faith? My mind wandered to the Moors of Granada, that last little fiefdom of Muslim Spain, and I thought of how Princess Isabel made no secret of her designs. My ancestors had been in the orders of Santiago and Alcántara both, so the blood of the slayers of Moors coursed through my veins, no better than *Santiago Matamoros*.

"It wasn't always this way," Esther mused, seeming to read my thoughts. "Before we moved south, my family was in Toledo for centuries. Do you know what Toledo was once like, Benja?" she asked.

"Not really," I confessed. "One of my tutors came from there, and I know they have kind of a funny accent, but that's about all."

"Do you know what my grandfather called Toledo?" She had a trace of mist in her eyes as she said this. "He called it 'The ornament of the world,' a city of three cultures. It was a place of great tolerance and culture, a city of scholars like Córdoba or even our sensual Sevilla. I come from a long line of translators and scribes from Toledo. If it weren't for my people, almost everything Aristotle wrote would have been lost forever. Things were pretty good for us Jews under the Moors. But ever since the Christians invaded with their famous *reconquista*, everything went downhill. And now there are so few of us left."

35

"Don't worry, Esther," I said, trying to comfort her. "We believe in Jesus, and He is our example. He was a man of kindness and peace. You have nothing to worry from the followers of such a man."

The girl gave me a wry smile. "You're sweet, Rodrigo," she said after a pause. "But I don't think you're very wise in the ways of the world. So, tell me, young rich boy, where is it exactly you were going today before I made you fall into the mighty river?"

I shrugged. "I'm not really sure. I suppose I'm in search of adventure, away from the dull people who parade through my life day after day."

"Hmmmm," she said, seeming to size me up. "If what you want is an adventure, maybe you should come with me."

"Why? Where are you going?"

"Have you ever heard of Triana?"

I thought for a moment. Of course I had heard of Triana, but had never been allowed to visit the district, not even with an army of servants or chaperones. It was on the other side of the river. The *wrong* side of the river. I knew that my parents disapproved of the place, so I felt intrigued.

"Triana is a magical place," Esther said, her eyes aglow with gentle mischief. "It's full of sailors who have seen monsters at sea, the Barbary lands, and even traveled as far as Baghdad and frozen, northern seas. There are beasts there from deepest Africa, like camels, leopards, and even elephants. And, besides Jews and Moors, there are even gypsies!"

Gypsies. In the year of grace of 1473, the only people treated worse than the Jews and Moors were the gypsies. Our servants had told me stories since my earliest boyhood about keeping windows closed lest I be stolen by Jews or Gypsies and sent to live in some far-off place, never to see my family again.

I smiled at my new friend. "Let's go!"

CHAPTER EIGHT

The daylight was fading. The first stars were beginning to twinkle in the sky, dozens of points of glimmering light that would soon be joined by hundreds more.

Rodrigo's hammock creaked slowly in the breeze, and Bartolomé wondered if the old man had decided to end his tale for the evening. He hadn't said anything for several minutes, so Bartolomé ventured an idea in the hopes that he would be brought back from his distant musings.

"I, too, visited Triana once or twice in my youth," he said, hoping that this would stir some memory. "My father always forbade me from going there as well. I don't know what he was so afraid of — it seemed calm when I was old enough to go. But before the Inquisitors' court at San Jorge Castle was set up there, I hear it was quite a place."

The old man's eyes were closed. Bartolomé thought he had fallen asleep, but then Rodrigo exclaimed, "You can't remember what it was like back then, in those days, back before they destroyed it with that castle of torture. There was a kind of freedom, savage at times, yet unlike any other. But it's gone now forever. Almost everything from that world was taken away from me forever."

All Bartolomé could think to say was, "Well then, it still lives on in your mind, this magical Triana. Please, tell me more about it, so it can live in mine."

The old man looked at Bartolomé in the twilight for a long time before answering. "Are you sure?" he asked. "You know — mine is not always a pretty story."

"I don't mind," Bartolomé said. And it was the truth. He found himself interested and wondering where all of this was leading. And maybe it would help to elucidate who this Rodrigo — or Benjamín — really was.

"Please continue. Can you tell more tonight?"

"No. I haven't any energy left. Tomorrow, perhaps I can tell more. If I sleep tonight, that is."

CHAPTER NINE

We walked along the river for a while, Esther and I, past the bullring and the wharves where several Venetian carracks were moored in the flood-stage water. When we grew tired of walking, we stopped to watch some fishermen as they cast their empty nets into the river.

"Do you think they ever get bored of being fishermen?" I asked, biting into one of the apples she'd brought along for the journey.

"What do you think? Would you?" She spat one of the seeds from the fruit.

"I asked you first."

"That you did." She sat down on a nearby log, where I joined her. "I'm not sure. I know that *I* never would. I'd love to spend all day outside, getting dirty, being in mud up to my knees, telling dirty stories and singing bawdy songs — even if I had to be poor. That would be much better than the life my parents have in store for me."

"And what life is that?"

She sighed. "They already have a man willing to marry me. I'll be a dull wool-merchant's wife, no doubt."

"Who are you supposed to marry?" I asked, doubting that she could ever become a dull wife to *anyone*.

"The eldest Cansino son. Father is excited, of course. They're wealthy, members of the *consulado* and everything. Father thinks it's a good match. But I'll delay marriage as long as I can — especially with a *converso*. Besides, how could I become an adventurer if I got married?"

"I understand. I wouldn't ever want to marry, either."

"What has your father chosen for you?"

"Well, I'm the youngest, so I can't inherit. I'll be sent to the Church."

"I wish I could be a nun. But we Jews don't get to be nuns."

"And what if you are expelled from Spain, along with the Moors? What then?" I instantly regretted what I asked.

The words hung in the air, silent, heavy and painful. Esther jumped up from the log and walked away from me. I ran after her, trying to undo the damage. I reached out to take her arm, but she pulled away.

"What do you mean?" She turned and demanded, tears rolling down her cheeks. "Where'd you get *that* from? Your father? He hates us, doesn't he? You know, we could lose everything, or be killed.

We're tolerated now, but the king and queen – well, the future ones, anyway — you never know what they're capable of if the people turn a bit more against us!"

"Hush, be still," I whispered, wrapping one arm around her shoulders in an attempt to comfort her. "I don't care *what* you are, I'm not going to hurt you."

Esther shot me a dirty look when I said that.

"What's he told you about us? About *me?*" she demanded, pulling away.

I thought of Father telling the peasant children about how Jews would steal them away and drink their blood or sell them as slaves if they didn't obey their elders. No, I decided — I wouldn't tell anyone in my family about my meeting Esther.

"What do you know about me and my people?" she insisted.

"Not much," I said, avoiding her eyes. Although I had always heard my family say ugly things about the Jews, I couldn't remember them mentioning Esther's family by name. Could that count for something?

She looked at me in disbelief.

Could this be my first friend? What did it mean if she was a Jew and a girl?

"Don't worry. I won't let anything happen. I swear to God that I will never let anyone harm you." I stood for a long moment looking at my first friend, and, on impulse, I jumped on the log and cried, "The day the Jews leave Spain — that is the day that I, too, will leave this realm forever!"

"You mean it?" Her eyes probed mine.

"Yes!" I looked down at the girl who had seemed so strong just minutes before.

She smiled at me then, a big, warm smile. She clasped my hand, and we began walking once again, sharing another apple.

"You know who we are like? I mean the Jews?"

"Who?"

"The hoyl bird," she said in a matter-of-fact tone.

"The *what?*"

She looked at me as if surprised I had never heard of this. "You know, the *hoyl?*" she threw the apple core into the river. "Don't they tell Christian children that story?"

I strained my mind to think of any such tale, but with no luck. My mother was never one to sit and talk by the bedside. I shook my head.

Esther sighed as if in mild frustration. "Well, the hoyl bird was the only bird that, when Adam offered all the other animals the fruit of knowledge, refused to eat. He was wise and knew better. So, the hoyl bird was granted everlasting life." At this thought, my friend smiled. "But of course, he has to sleep sometime. And when he does, there is always danger. A fire may come along and consume him. But there is hope because there is always a hoyl egg, so he is always reborn. He never really dies, even though the flames pursue him."

"He rises from the ashes," I mused. "I like that. Like the phoenix."

"That's right. Like the phoenix."

Little did she know it, but Esther's legend would rise like a phoenix from the ashes one day and be reborn, just like the hoyl bird.

CHAPTER TEN

We walked along, crossed a bridge, and backtracked for a while to the north. I noticed many *tilo* and orange trees along the side of the river. We greeted some women dangling their plump, red-stained feet in the water not far from the vats where they had been stomping grapes. We spied the fishermen once more, and the sight of so many still-empty nets made me feel a bit sad.

But soon I was plunged into a whole other world, and I forgot all about empty nets Esther's religion. How strange that I'd lived just across the river from it, never knowing that my paradise could, on a clear day, be seen from my own parents' verandah.

We arrived at a small plaza at the start of San Jacinto Street, the main area of Triana. This section looked poorer than the rest of Sevilla, with its jaunty, yellowish cobblestones, small wells, and modest, old-fashioned stucco houses. A little way down the street, I spied a small church with a pointed arch. I later learned that this was the *Iglesia Santa Ana*.

When we arrived, a throng of people had gathered at the center by an ancient well covered in yellow and blue tiles. Men, women, children, and even old people jostled around a large, oak platform where a group of attractive, long-haired women sat on stools arranged in a semi-circle. A man stood in the center of them, patiently holding a small, Moorish guitar. Several swarthy men, ranging from strapping lads to a few with gray hair, waited on the far side of the stage.

To the left, I saw tents and yellow wagons with red symbols painted on their sides. These looked like an exploding star radiating out from a single source.

"Who *are* these people?" I asked Esther, growing uncomfortable. Running along the river for a bit wasn't much of a transgression, but coming to Triana without permission was something else.

"They're gypsies, silly," Esther whispered, her confidence apparently restored. "Don't you know anything?"

I was about to defend myself when a sudden hush fell over the crowd. Time seemed to freeze as the guitarist and one of the women on the stage exchanged a knowing glance. When the dark, almost feline face looked at him once more, a glint in her eye and one sleek, charcoal eyebrow half-raised, the stage leapt instantly to life, shredding the stony silence with intense energy. The man struck the first chords with such vigor that they resounded and rebounded all around.

We watched with open-mouthed surprise as the first dancer leapt to her feet and began to strike amazing poses. She held her hands aloft, the fingers twisting and twirling, her catlike body writhing, and her feet thumping and pounding the planks. Soon, other women joined in. As they gyrated, the fringes and flounces of their dresses danced and played. Those watching began to shout *"Anda! Anda! Olé!"* until we could barely hear the small guitar. One by one, the women followed the first dancer, some snapping castanets, some not, some seeming to draw strength as they played to the crowd, casting mysterious half-smiles at the onlookers, others dancing as if no one existed besides them and the guitarist. They were caught up in a sensual, rhythmic dance that seemed without beginning or end.

Some of the men on the left side of the stage yelled catcalls, whistling with dirty fingers in grimy mouths, yelling things I dare not repeat to the dancers. They tossed coin after coin onto the stage, where a small pile of money began to grow. One bald drunkard tried to grab a dancer, but another man, a young one dressed in colorful pants of red and brown and a kerchief about his dark curls, pulled him back. The gypsy guard gave the lout a swift punch in the belly and several more kicks as he lay writhing on the ground.

"Looks like *that* sailor went too far," Esther whispered. "They say never to try anything with gypsy women — or their men will make you regret it."

I felt a tug on my pant-leg, and when I turned, I saw a group of children with their hands out. Esther gave a few *blancas* to one shy girl in scarlet rags who wore her thick black hair carefully arranged in braids. I felt a tap on my shoulder, and when I turned, I saw an old crone staring at me with an intense gaze. She had a wrinkled face, her silver hair pulled into a tight bun, and she wore long rings of silver and amber in her ears. She and two others had approached us together.

"Do you want me to tell your *buena ventura*? Let me read your palm?" She pleaded in a strong accent, grasping my hand in one tight claw, her dark eyes piercing.

"I don't think so," I said. Who was this hag? Was she a witch? What would a priest say if I confessed to allowing her to do such a thing? I had allowed Esther to bring me to this place out of curiosity, but this was surely going too far.

But the woman would not release my hand. She turned it over and bent my fingers forward, straightening them out so she could better see my exposed flesh. I tried to pull away, but she held fast, frowning, as if my resistance were a mere nuisance. As the other two hags drew closer, I gave up my struggle, curious about what I would hear.

One bony finger traced along the broken lines of my palm as she muttered something in an unknown language. "You have a long life-line," she said in Castilian, her leathery face breaking into a smile.

"How's *mine* look?" asked Esther, pushing her hand playfully in between us and right under the old woman's face. The old gypsy looked startled for a moment, then shook her head and gazed back at me.

As she did so, she said, "I don't see children, or an easy time with love. No, you'll never be married."

"That's right. I'm to be a priest," I said in a haughty tone. Maybe this would make them leave me alone.

"Yes — well, your life will be dedicated to guiding others in *their* paths."

"What does it say about my *own* adventures? I hope it says something."

She gazed again at my outstretched hand. "You will travel much, and make stops in important places."

"I can't imagine where those could be," I scoffed. After all, my father wanted me to be a simple parish priest, and I don't think he had planned for me ever to leave Sevilla.

"The lines do not reveal that, my boy," she answered, sounding apologetic.

"What about my family?"

"It will always be with you, wherever you are, whoever you are with. You shall be at home wherever you go, or wherever you are *sent*."

"Wherever I'm sent? What — by God? The Church?" I wondered if I would go on a pilgrimage to Santiago de Compostela, or maybe even to Rome.

She gave me a sly smile before whispering in my ear, "Don't seek to understand, my boy. Only be ready to go where you must."

She deftly took a coin from my pocket then slipped away into the crowd, her friends behind her.

I turned back to the stage but saw with dismay that the dancing had come to an end.

CHAPTER ELEVEN

"This place is a marvel," I said to Esther. "Who are these gypsies, and where do they come from?" I had been kept from knowing about such things.

"Well, my brother David says that they're from far away, maybe Egypt. But Father says that when they arrived here a few years ago, they showed some of the city fathers papers from Flanders. In fact, that's why they call that dance they did the *flamenco*."

"But," I protested, "Egypt and Flanders are so far away from each other; Egypt is far to the East, while Flanders is way up north." I'd always been one to pore over maps as a boy, which was why I'd never failed a geography examination from my tutors.

"So?"

"So, where are they from? Surely they must have *some* land they can call home."

"We once did," said a slightly-accented voice from behind me. I turned around and saw that a beautiful young woman had been listening to our conversation. It took me a few seconds to realize that she was the lead dancer. She'd removed the kerchief from her neck, and now wore a red scarf wrapped in her rich, black hair.

"But that land is no longer ours," she finished.

"Really? How is it that you've made your way here, instead of remaining there — wherever *there* is?"

"You don't need to be concerned with us," she said, turning away.

"But I want to know." If I was going to be a man of God, I reasoned, I should know all about such things.

She turned again to face me. "But — you are *outsiders*." She studied my face with eyes that seemed to search mine in a way that none had ever done before. She seemed to weigh her words as she studied my motivation. "You really want to know about us?"

Esther and I looked at each other. "Yes," I said, answering for both.

The young woman eyed us, then looked away and sighed, almost, it seemed, in resignation. She ran her hand over her face and seemed to wipe at her eyes, even though they were dry. "We come from a land far away, and it is our lot to move from place to place, harming no one, belonging nowhere, yet welcome nowhere. That is all you need to know."

Her melancholy gaze fell on one of the red and yellow wagons off to the left, on which had been painted an exploding blue star. I wondered if this was the wagon, which I would later learn is called a *vurdón*, in which she had come from that faraway land.

Before I could say more, Esther and I heard a scuffle behind us. One of the sailors, this one even drunker than his bald comrade, had begun taunting a young gypsy man. After a moment, I realized that this was the guitarist who had played at the center of the platform with the female dancers.

"Hey, gypsy," the large, red-haired bear of a man slurred. "How many coins you steal today? How many kids you gonna snatch before you get caught?"

A crowd formed around the two men. The guitarist looked around with a bewildered expression, as if hoping that someone would intervene to stop this madness. He made a move to leave, but the crowd sealed him in. He seemed to abandon the idea of escape, but stood as far away from the sailor as he could, his hands on his thighs and facing downward, avoiding the other man's gaze.

The drunken sailor wore a grimy brown smock that looked as dirty as the things he yelled. His boots were black and his face as red as his beard, much like the bloodstains on his clothes. He tore off his smock, and I noticed a series of scars slashed down his arms and back that made me guess he'd been in many knife-fights over the years and had received the lash on more than one occasion.

"Hey, dirty gypsy!" he yelled, tossing the grimy smock aside. "Did you know your sister's a whore like her mother? My friends all want her, so give her up, or I'll dance on your grave as well as Ostelinda's once I'm done with the both of you!"

I could tell by the looks as the people pointed fingers that the woman the sailor mentioned was the woman Esther and I had been talking with.

I studied Ostelinda, the sister of the gypsy about to fight. New lines creased her forehead while she crossed her arms over her chest like one trying to ward off a great evil. She stood straight and taller than most, so did not need to perch on an oxcart like Esther and I to see. She began to bite the side of her thumb, and I realized that she dreaded what would surely come next.

While the guitarist and his sister exchanged a look, I saw a well-dressed man in a scarlet doublet, red hose, and a cape step forward to slip a knife into the sailor's hand, which the man in turn hid in his boot. I jumped down from the cart and bolted forward, trying to shove my way through the crowd. Someone had to warn the gypsy about that knife! When I finally made it to the front of that human gauntlet, I tried to call out, but the noise of the crowd drowned my voice.

"Give us the whore!" The sailor bellowed, shouting for all to hear. "Let us have her, gypsy boy!"

The younger man finally stood straight, and came forward, his face determined. He was at least two heads shorter than his adversary, but walked with such self-assurance that I didn't doubt who had the upper hand. He spat at the man's feet and backed up, standing erect once again. The spectators roared.

The two circled each other as the crowd cried again and people jostled each other for a better view. The sailor almost snarled, his face a mask of anger, and I could see only three or four teeth in that disgusting gob. The guitarist looked calm yet alert as the sailor drew near. The onlookers chanted louder and louder, men exchanged bets, and even some of the women and children yelled encouragement. As the large, red-headed brute closed in, the guitarist raised his fists to defend himself.

The sailor took a swing, but missed by an arm's length as the more agile gypsy danced away. Looking confused, the aggressor charged again with a roar of rage, but the gypsy feinted to the right, and disappeared around his flank. The large man turned in obvious confusion, and the crowd grew silent. The sailor spun around again, and suddenly, there came the young man flying through the air, his dark eyes wide, his palms open. The large man tried to dodge, but he was too slow, and the gypsy delivered one quick blow to the neck that sent him to his knees, his eyes rolling up, large drops of sweat flying as he slammed face-first into the dust.

Most of the crowd cheered "*Viva Manfariel!*" Money exchanged hands and some of the gypsy men rushed forward to stand around Manfariel, as if to protect him from further aggression. The gypsy simply stood there, looking spent and rather annoyed.

The crowd began to break up. A lad with a jagged scar on his cheek looking scarcely twelve ran to the side of the fallen man and frantically tried to shake his shoulders. When the large man didn't react, he cried, "Marco, they've killed Marco!"

A group of five well-dressed men shoved their way to the fallen Marco. One of them felt for a pulse, and shook his head at the scar-faced boy. It took all of them, but they hoisted the large man up off the ground and carried him to a black carriage under a chestnut tree. One of them looked my way, and although I couldn't be sure, as it was only for an instant, I thought it was one of the last people I would ever expect to see in such a place. This was the man who had slipped Marco the knife! As his gaze met mine, he squinted at me. His pointed goatee bobbed over a new white ruff around a slender neck and a doublet buttoned up over a familiar chest.

Had he recognized me?

I did the only thing I could think of at that moment: I tried to hide. I grabbed the excess of Esther's shirt, and buried my face in it.

"Hey, what the devil do you think you're *doing*?" she cried, trying to squirm away from me.

"I'm trying to hide from my brother," I hissed. "Only God knows what Alejandro could be doing here in Triana!" After a moment, I looked up to see if I could see him or anyone else I knew among the well-dressed men. All I saw was Esther's fist drawn back. Everything went black.

CHAPTER TWELVE

When I finally came to, I heard the gypsy girl, the dancer, say "it's been a bad day for keeping the peace around here."

I tried to sit up, but the pain in my face sent me down again.

"How long have I been out?"

"About an hour, maybe more," the gypsy said looking at me and then away. There was something in her manner that had changed. I could only see her through one eye, but it was enough. She seemed more distant now than before. Still, I had never seen such a beautiful creature, and I longed to reach out and stroke her cheek, caress one charcoal-colored brow.

"Oh, Rodrigo," Esther said, bending over me and wiping my swollen cheek with a cool cloth. "I'm sorry I hit you. I didn't know...I didn't realize who your brother was."

"What do you mean?" I asked.

Esther exchanged a worried look with the gypsy, Ostelinda. "Your brother, Alejandro. We didn't — I didn't — realize who he is, and why you have cause to fear him."

I tried to think of what she could mean. In truth, I knew very little of what my brother, or, for that matter, my father, did when they were away from home. I had heard whisperings from the servants, but had mostly assumed that they tended to business or went to fencing matches and jousting tournaments and the like when they weren't at home. When they were home, they treated the women in their employ like playthings. If they did come to Triana, was it to seek new women to conquer? Or did they come to stir up trouble, like that business with the drunken sailor?

CHAPTER THIRTEEN

The celebration began at dusk after we'd all eaten together around the fires of Triana.

How to describe those nights when the gypsies had their celebrations? That one would prove more colorful than most, thanks to the influx of people from surrounding towns who had come for the traditional horse fair, in which there were races, bargaining, trinket-selling and all sorts of spicy foods cooked, sold, and eaten. All day and night long, men rode their horses by and stirred up clouds of dirt that settled on everyone's clothes and hair.

The only time I'd ever seen anything like this tent-city celebration was *carnaval*, when people dressed in outrageous costumes — red, blue, gold, and some as dragons and devils — and danced around like madmen. Sometimes, they donned women's clothes, and the peasants of my father's lands wore false doublets to look like him and my brothers in a singular display of tolerated mockery. All the while, they drank despite their long-nosed and monstrous masks, banging pots together, and jangling strips of bells as they whistled and hooted and hollered — a chance to get it all out of their systems before the penitence of Lent. They never allowed me to participate in these festivities of course, as I always had to get my rest so as to be able to assist the priest the following morning in administering ashes to the foreheads of the worn-out and hung-over faithful.

There was much drinking in Triana that night, where *every* night was *carnaval.* I had never seen such a celebration.

If only I had known about the gathering storm my visit was about to unleash, I would have left running from that place.

CHAPTER FOURTEEN

We danced and sang, people played drums, and sounded loud recorders and trumpets. People pranced round and round under the light of the torches and lanterns hung from wagons and trees. First, we took one person's arm, then another's, and sometimes we all danced together arm-in-arm with many partners. There was no real rhyme or reason, we just did what felt right.

And the people! I'd never before seen such people. They were of all shapes, sizes, and colors. It was there that I saw, for the first time, many Africans all in one place — and I realized what a sheltered life I'd lived up until then. They were escaped slaves brought by the Portuguese, and, as members of the Wolof tribe, they were also Muslim. Even though they didn't join in our celebrations, they watched us as we danced and drank water from cups. There were also many Moors, and they were friendly and polite. I was surprised to see them unfurling their carpets and praying toward the East around dusk.

Since Sevilla was one of the most important ports in all of Castile, it was easy for all kinds of people, including those Father called "people of the bad life," to come and go among the shy Romany. Ships and boats of all sizes docked in Triana en route to places like Portugal and Genoa, sometimes bringing in slaves and taking out the wool for which our region was so famous. Besides, with the men on the ships being paid upwards of 5,000 Marevedis per month, they always seemed to have extra money to spend in Triana.

And people spoke different languages in Triana.

I had only learned Latin and Greek until then; but there, for the first time in my life, I heard real people saying things I couldn't understand. As I tried to dance near Ostelinda and Manfariel, I asked them how to say word after word in Romany.

"How do you tell someone that you are glad to meet him?"

"*Kosko divvus*," Manfariel said with a deep bow.

"*Kosko Divvus*," I exclaimed, much to the surprise and delight of several gypsies dancing nearby. This was the first time of many for them to laugh at my attempts to learn their language.

I wondered about what they believed, so I decided to start by asking about the word for 'God' in Romany.

Ostelinda smiled at this question. "We don't have a word for 'God' or even for 'Satan.' We have a word for the force of good in in the world — and one for the force of evil."

"What are they?"

"*Del* and *Beng*," she said, seeming surprised at speaking about such things to a Christian boy. She'd never had to explain them before. Years later, she would tell me that she'd always merely accepted these as natural forces, beings not needing, or even desiring, explanation.

"Do the Romany go to Heaven like we do?" I felt nervous about hearing the answer.

"So many questions!" Ostelinda replied, twirling me around as she tried to teach me a florid dance move.

"No, this way," she continued, raising my hands over my head and encouraging me to stand erect and to clap in time to the beat of a nearby drum.

After a moment, she smiled and seemed to remember my question. "No, Rodrigo, unlike the paradise that you Christians dream of, we have a different view. We believe that people return to life again and again, just in other forms."

"How?" I asked, unable to imagine such a thing.

"Well, that depends. Our ancestors taught us that if someone is made better during a lifetime, that person will be reborn better in the following life. If not, he or she returns as something lower. You see, for us, the soul, the spark that makes each person unique, is on a long journey, like a bubble that starts somewhere in the depths of the sea, but will one day burst free into the surface of the air."

Without realizing, I had stopped moving. I stood in awe of the beauty of this image, and I was about to ask more questions when a nearby man I hadn't noticed before grabbed me by the shoulder and spun me around like a windmill to face him.

"Hey, *busno* boy!" Why so curious about us *zincalos* all of a sudden?"

"Leave him alone, Gerinel," Ostelinda said, stepping between us. "He's just a boy."

"Just a boy?" Gerinel grumbled, shoving Ostelinda aside and placing his face so close to mine that I could smell the cheap wine on his breath. His dark eyes focused on mine, and he started speaking in a language I couldn't make out. I thought I heard him say "Alejandro," but I could have been wrong. Ostelinda started to say something in that strange tongue, but then seemed to hesitate, looking at me as one of my mother's timid canaries might eye an unpredictable cat.

Gerinel drew even closer, studying me, and I could feel his scraggly gray beard on my neck. In an instant, he buried his hands in my hair and began to speak again. This time, I made out the word "*beng*," as I struggled. As I fought to escape his grasp, I wondered if he thought my red hair proof of evil, as the Inquisiton would one day claim.

"*Basta!*" Ostelinda said, switching to Castilian and pushing my tormentor away. He wandered off toward the far end of the torch-lit clearing, near the *vurdóns*. When he was safely out of reach, he yelled, "Don't go learning Romany, boy, *or* our dances. And stay away from our women!" He took a final swig from a flagon and flung it at me, but it didn't even come close to where I stood.

"What was *that* about?" I asked Ostelinda after a moment of awkward silence.

To this, she sighed and said, "pay him no mind. The drink makes him act that way. Please understand that my people are not naturally trusting. There have been problems with your kind before."

I felt stung. Even though she surely didn't mean the words as Gerinel had, somehow having her say such things seemed worse.

"Is that why he called me a…what was it…a *busno?*" I asked, recalling the word.

Ostelinda flinched upon my use of this word. "Yes," she replied after a pause.

"And…*zincalos?*" I tried, unsure if I wanted to continue.

Ostelinda's face turned almost to a grimace. "That word is an injury that has followed us like the plague all the way from Venice," she said, looking down at the dust. "We gypsies know such hateful insults better than anyone. And that," she said, meeting my gaze, "*that* is why we should be the *last* ones to use them." The torchlight shadows danced on her beautiful face as she spoke.

After a time, we returned to the center of the celebration. Manfariel gave me more to drink, and I was feeling the effects, as it was my first time partaking in such revels. I felt almost overcome by the joy of dancing and seeing how Esther was able to move with Manfariel. My feelings of hurt had begun to dissipate when the music from the drums and tambourines grew faster and the cries for joy and laughter seemed almost to drown out the guitars and castanets. Only when I saw that everyone else had stopped dancing and many had scattered did I realize that something was wrong. Slowly, my gaze followed Ostelinda's, and I turned to face the last person I wanted or expected to see in such a place.

My father.

CHAPTER FIFTEEN

"Rodrigo!" he cried, and I knew that when he called me this, instead of 'Benja,' I was in real trouble.

His face was a mask of seething anger, and he looked like he barely contained himself. The music had stopped, and the gathering was now eerily quiet. I felt like I was about to be sick.

My father had brought armed men and a young valet who looked out of place in Triana, as he wore a shortened purple jerkin and red hose after the Italian fashion. Next to the valet stood Alejandro, and I was now sure that he had been there that day after all. He stood there looking satisfied, as if he had brought the wolves to a flock of sheep.

Father was dressed in his usual seigneurial fashion. He wore a dark brown cloak over his fancy violet doublet and mi-parti hose of red and white stripes with brown breeches gathered at the knee. Never had Triana seen such a patrician, I thought. I realized that he'd been pulled away from a feast or perhaps one of my brother's jousts or fencing matches to come fetch me.

"Rodrigo, you've more than disobeyed me by running away," he said, slowing his speech in an obvious attempt to control his anger. "You defy me by coming to this place, and you dishonor our entire family by associating with these *zincalos*." He looked around with disdain.

It was then that three garishly-painted tarts with low-cut bodices approached him, calling him by his Christian name. He brushed them aside like he might a swarm of flies, and returned to berating me. "How dare you carry on here this way, my son, as if you were one of these ruffians?"

I decided that it wouldn't be wise to tell him that, for once in my life, I felt as if I *was* part of something important, that I wished I *could* be one of them. What I did say, however, was "Father, please don't be angry. All I wanted was to see something new."

I stopped talking when my father strode toward me like a lion to its prey, his eyes aglow with anger.

"But *this* is not the place for you," he snapped. "You're to be a *priest*, for the love of God, and you're too young for a place like this. Triana is filled with things you don't need to concern yourself with."

"Like what, Father?" I said, stepping back and raising my voice to the gasps of those brave enough to have remained. "What does a man see here in Triana? How to drink or cause fights? How to pay for whores?

I would think you'd have had enough of that at home, the way you treat the peasant girls."

"Come with me now, Rodrigo," he said, speaking through clenched teeth.

"No!" I said, glancing around me, my eyes falling on the frightened faces of Esther, Manfariel, and Ostelinda. "No. I don't think I will go with you, Father. I wish to remain here. With my friends." I was as firm as I could be, my hands sweeping across the diminished crowd of gypsies and outcasts.

"Do not force my hand," my father said, reaching into his cloak. "Come back home, or I'll drag you back myself!"

"No!" I shouted, trying to sound as fearsome as a runt like me could. "You'll just try to keep me from life like you always do. And I want to know life!" My voice had taken on a tremulous, pleading tone that made me feel very small. Before I could say more, my father nodded and I felt a dull pain in my head as if I'd been struck with the pommel of a sword. Before a veil fell over my eyes, I was witness to a terrifying tableau: Alejandro, one of my cousins, and my father's valet seized Ostelinda. She cried out for an instant before my other cousin Juan clamped his hand over her mouth and waved his poniard in front of her face. It took three armed men to hold Manfariel and another two to hold Esther as Alejandro slowly lifted Ostelinda's skirts and my cousin Juan began to undo his codpiece. The last thing I heard in the now-deserted square was my brother as he said, "now we finally get to see what you've got under here!"

CHAPTER SIXTEEN

The next thing I knew, I was in a chamber back at home, although not my own. It was the next morning and I lay in a daze as I slowly began to realize where I was. The sun streamed brightly through the window. I remember hearing doves singing as they greeted the dawn. I woke up in stages — you know how one often wakes up that way? I had a horrible, aching pain in my head. Then I remembered in an instant everything that had happened. I sat up. As I did so, I saw my mother sitting on the edge of the bed. All that the chamber contained besides us and the bed was a small desk and a flimsy-looking table. I guessed that she had been there for a while, though I had no way of knowing for how long. She looked frail and unhappy, and seemed shorter in stature than usual. For a moment I imagined she had come to tuck me in like when I was a small child and we said *Pater Nosters* and sang *Salve Reginas* while the candles cast flickering shadows on the crucifix that hung on the wall to ward off the dark angel.

"Mother, what are you doing here?"

"What do you think? What do you imagine I have come to tell you?" she shifted her meager weight with a grimace and stared at me with her piercing, dark eyes.

I stared at the shadow she cast on the bed as my head pounded from the blow I'd taken the night before. I didn't know what to say.

"I suppose you know about last night."

"Of course I know, don't be foolish. Your father told me all about it. We're lucky the whole town doesn't know you were associating with those transients. It's a wonder they didn't kidnap you or steal you away with them, or use the evil eye on you."

"But mother, don't you know that Alejandro, and, I think, even Father have been there before, and—"

"Silence!" she growled, rising to her feet. "I don't care to hear about when they go off to do what men will do. That I can forgive because they are men. But *not*—" she said, pointing at me the way Father had the night before, "*not* my son who is to be a sacristan. Besides, I'm sure that they at least are discreet about what they do — which is far more than *you're* capable of, no doubt." For a moment, she seemed to soften a bit. "I'm your mother. I shouldn't have to talk to you about such things."

"You're so blind, mother. Don't you know what goes on here when you're not around? Or what

Alejandro and Father do to the peasant women who toil on our lands?"

She rushed forward and slapped me hard across my face. I recoiled in pain and surprise, tears welling up in my eyes.

"I do not care what they do," she said, enunciating every word as if I were a fool.

Her hands moved back and forth in front of her and she strode off to stare out the window. After a moment of reflection, she sighed. "Besides, they may amuse themselves with peasant girls who want to curry favor with the master, if it makes them happy and if my husband is more content as a result. You yourself may take one or several discreet concubines one day if you wish — just look at the Borgias." She added this almost as an afterthought, still gazing out the window.

"Mother, that's not at all how it is for Father and Alejandro. Do you know what they *really* do? They sometimes take the peasant girls on their wedding nights…"

"I know about that," she said turning from the window and coming to stand beside the old table near my bed. "The priests call it *jus primae noctis*. But soon, that will be a thing of the past."

"Well, not soon enough. Do you have any idea how many brothers and nephews of mine work the fields of the *latifundia* every day? Some even have red hair like mine and grandfather's."

"Stop right there, Benja," she almost shouted, clapping hands over her ears before once again gaining control of herself. She must have been surprised even to hear that I knew of such things. It's true that I was all of fifteen, and was rather naïve; I had always been closely watched and kept from things. However, I had spoken to certain servants without arousing suspicion. Breaching orders to the contrary, one of my tutors used to guide me on walks around my father's large estate so he could take in the fresh morning air.

Before, it had been easy to ignore the servants and their whispers. But in light of what had happened to Ostelinda, I could no longer dismiss what they said as idle gossip.

Instead of speaking, my mother looked grim, fanning herself now with a black-lace fan. Lines of qualm creased her forehead, and, like an angry child, she gathered her skirts and turned for the door.

I leapt out of bed despite my pain and grabbed her by the back of one of her blue skirts, preventing her exit. I pushed her against the wall and held her there so she'd have to hear me.

"Mother, I've waited too long, but if I have to keep you here all day, you are going to know the truth!" I thought about what Ostelinda had told me the night before, before they attacked her, and how I had promised to help.

"No, you can't make me!" She cried, her face now moist with tears. "You hold your tongue, don't speak!"

"I'm going to tell you, dammit!" I cried. I'd always been a weakling, but now found a reserve of strength that I'd never known before.

"Nooo!" She tried to break free.

"Yes." I held her firmly. "You are going to hear this if it is the last thing I ever say to you."

"Help!" She screamed, and I heard noises down below. The servants and Father had heard her cry. This only made me more determined to tell her what I had to say, and quickly.

"Mother," I said in a soft voice as I heard footsteps on the stairwell, "You *must* hear me. Father and Alejandro, they violate women, like wild animals attack their prey. The steward won't stand up to them and they take them into the barn where—"

She made one last attempt to break free as the footsteps grew louder in the stairwell of the tower, but I held her. "That's not all. They've killed some of them, and many are but girls or their sweethearts who did nothing but speak up. They've killed others who tried to stop them. And it is *always* while you're away. The peasants live in fear of your absence. They quake at the thought of it, especially the women and girls."

"Let me go," she whined, and I wondered if she was more upset about what I told her or by my holding her in place. "I won't allow you to sully your father's good name." She spat in my face as the servants and my father stormed into the room.

"You have to do something about this," I pleaded.

"Don't you understand? I am a woman. I can do nothing!" She sobbed as they pulled me off of her. As we were separated, my mother fell into the arms of a stocky, ruddy laundress. I thought for a moment that perhaps she had fainted, but her eyes soon focused on me. She looked less angry now than before. Dare I say that those eyes revealed sadness? Or was she simply weary of fighting?

After taking in the situation, my father turned and stormed toward me, struck me in the face, grabbed me, and threw me on the bed. He jumped on it and began kicking me like a furious animal while the servants stood by, their faces masks of horror.

"You'll learn your place, you bastard, you stupid idiot," he ranted as the blows rained down on me from his feet and hands. I cried and thought dully that I couldn't believe how a life can change in one day. What had come over me?

I curled myself into a ball, like a hedgehog, and the beating went on. "You will learn your place," he said over and over again. "You will dedicate yourself to study, and you will never leave this tower until you take orders, do you understand me?"

I gasped for air, trying to speak. "Yes," I cried, my voice choking with sobs, tears running down my face. My entire body cried out in pain. I wondered if my father's blows had broken a rib as I drew a painful breath. I knew I had crossed a line with him, and that I would never go back to the simple, easy life I'd known before. I began silently to implore the Virgin for protection, mouthing prayers I'd learned as a child.

I don't know why, but at just that moment, something the old priest I assisted came back to my mind. He had said, "Rodrigo, every person has the choice between two paths: between that which is ridiculous and that which is miraculous; between that which is easily forgettable and that which is laudable through the ages. Make your decision, for decide you must; but once you've done so, rest easy, as your course will be set." I didn't know why, but I felt a great sense of relief wash over me then, and I stopped crying long enough to look up at my father's enraged face.

I summoned all of the courage and dignity I could muster in my bruised and battered body. After all, what they had done to Ostelinda was far worse than this. After a long moment, I said, "*I am not afraid of you.*"

He looked at me for another moment. I thought he was going to beat me again, or perhaps kill me, but all he did was give a grimace of disdain as he studied me.

"As you will, Benja," he said with a sneer. With this, he turned and closed the door. I shuddered when I heard the key turn in the lock and his footsteps descending, echoing off the stones of the stairwell, growing fainter and fainter as he moved away.

I sat and stared at the bars at the top of the door. For the first time in my life, I was locked in a room in the tower, alone.

I was forbidden to leave that place for many years that followed that bright morning when the doves sang outside my window.

CHAPTER SEVENTEEN

I saw no one for two full days. My hunger and thirst became almost unbearable. There was only a little water left in a pot that I sipped from each day, as well as a basin for washing myself — but I would not cry for help or mercy. I often thought of Esther and Manfariel during those days, not to mention, of course, Ostelinda.

Then, on the third morning, as I lay splayed out and staring at the spot of light from the small window on the upper part of my wall, I heard footsteps coming up the stairway. Like a pup beaten too many times, I curled into a ball and tried to hide under the meager, rat-nibbled covers. As the footsteps grew louder, I imagined it was my father or Alejandro, coming to murder me in my sleep. I wondered how they would do it — a sword, a poniard, or perhaps they would choke me with their bare hands. I had a gruesome image of myself whipped and hung from the window tethered to a rope, and, as the keys rattled in the lock and I heard the door swing open, I could not bear to look, a silent scream rising in my throat. I heard someone breathing, and after a moment, I peered out through a hole in my blanket with a timid eye.

It was the kind old priest, Father Sebastián, standing in the doorway. I wondered if he had come to administer me last rites.

Slowly, I pulled the covers from my upper body, and I stared at him. I had never seen him outside of his holy residence or the church before, and it took me a moment to accept that he was in my room. Still, I felt far from relieved. Why had he come? Was he here to lecture me about obeying my parents or on the will of God?

"Good day," was all I could manage to stammer.

"Hello," he said with a serene smile, which surprised me further.

"What are you doing here?" My voice quavered.

"It might as well be I as another," he said, a humorous twinkle in his eyes. "How are you, young man?"

"Fine," I muttered, looking down.

I was quiet for a long moment. The priest didn't say anything, so I decided it was my turn to say something. "I am surprised to see you here, *padre*."

"As am I to have to visit you here, but here we are."

My stomach growled, and I felt embarrassed as well as thirsty. The priest pretended not to notice.

"Yes, but — why?" I asked through cracked lips. Was he here for last rites after all? If they meant to kill me, I wished they would just get on with it.

He was a thin man, and his tonsure was pure white, like the feathers of a swan. He had a pointed white beard and celestial blue eyes that danced with a spark that seemed to defy his advanced years.

"Rodrigo, your father is determined that you're to be a priest. That you know. Now—" he said, looking around and making note of my humble accommodations, "Am I to understand that you are not to leave this tower, under *any* circumstances?"

"Yes." I realized that he had probably been told *why* I was being confined to the tower. If he expected me to express remorse or contrition, I decided, he would be disappointed.

But instead of a reproach, the old man stood looking at me, studying me. Finally, he entered the room and walked toward me, coming to stand next to my bed. I backed away from him without thinking, and soon my back almost touched the wall. When he saw my distress, he pulled back a bit.

"Your father came to see me as I was cleaning the reliquaries yesterday afternoon. He asked if I would come visit you from time to time — to instruct you. And, of course, be your confessor." He looked around the spare bedchamber and seemed glad to see I at least had a meager desk.

"My tutor has resigned?" I said with a snort, thinking of all the tutors who had given up on me over the years.

"Let us say that he was somewhat put off by your choice to run off to Triana rather than study with him."

"I'm sure he was furious." I glared at the whitewashed wall and wrapped my arms around my knees.

"Yes, well, in any case, your father came to me as something of a last resort. He explained the situation, and I agreed. He despises the Franciscans, and the Dominicans turned him down as they're too busy with their studies and other business. I do have to admit, however, I have not had a student for many years. I hope to be adequate for your needs."

"So, you are here only as a tutor?" I asked, wanting things to be clear.

"Yes, my son."

"Fine," I sighed. My stomach growled again. If I agreed to this, would they let me eat something? And could I ask the priest to intervene on Ostelinda's behalf?

"Very well. I shall come to you twice a week."

"Yes," I said.

He smiled once again, and was about to leave when I decided to ask him something I instantly wished I could take back.

"Do you ever regret becoming a priest?"

He should have become angry with me for the insolence of my question. In fact, he would have had every right to leave right then and there; there was nothing compelling his presence in the first place. I'm sure I would never have asked such a thing if I'd been in my right mind and not swooning from hunger, thirst and fear. But instead of showing anger, he simply sat down on the corner of my bed, and reflected for a moment before speaking.

"You know, that's a very good question, Rodrigo. I don't usually think of things that way. What's done is done, after all, and we can never undo it."

"I'm beginning to understand *that*."

"To answer your question, my son, no, I cannot say that I regret becoming a priest. God created us to have a meaningful life, and mine is full of meaning. I take comfort from the fact that I can ease the pain of others, especially of the poor and the sick, as they face life's many travails. The core of our faith is compassion." He shifted to look me seriously in the eyes. He paused before continuing, looking up and out of the room through the window and then back. "As a priest, I am part of a tradition that has kept knowledge alive throughout the ages. I like to think that in my own, small way, I can do God's work here while I enjoy the brief gift of life."

"But what about adventure? What makes a priest's life carry meaning?" I exclaimed, thinking again of my new friends. "What we do is so *small* in comparison to the amount of suffering in the world. We can't possibly do enough to make a difference." I thought again about Ostelinda being attacked, and my stomach tightened.

"Tell me something, and I want you to be honest with me."

"Of course." Did he think I would lie to a priest?

"Would it matter to *you* if I were to try to help you become something better than you are today?" He moved closer to me on the bed as I moved as far away from him as I could.

I was too surprised to answer for a long moment. Nobody had ever asked how I felt or if something such as this mattered to me. All my life I had been told what to do, been forced to accept my circumstances without question.

"Yes," I said, realizing with something approaching surprise that I would like to work with this man. "Yes, I think it *would* matter to me."

"Well, then," he said, patting my knee before I could pull away, "That is all that really matters between you and me."

With this, he got up and moved toward the door. He went out to the landing beyond it and came back with a wooden tray. On it sat a pitcher of water, some onions, and part of a brown loaf of bread that looked at least three days old. He set it down as my eyes fell ravenously on the simple meal. Father Sebastián handed me an old gray goblet into which he poured water from the pitcher.

"Thank you, Father," was all I could manage to utter before taking a big gulp.

"Not at all, my son," he said.

I expected him to leave, but when I looked up again, the priest smiled and threw open his cloak, displaying a boot of wine and a small, round block of sheep's-milk cheese hanging in a cloth from his rope belt.

It was a long moment before I realized that I was crying, and turned away in shame.

"Our little secret," he said, setting the wine and cheese on the desk and once again pretending not to notice. "Perhaps next time, I can procure some ham or even mutton," he said. "I happen to know some shepherds in the area."

I tried to say something to thank this man, but I couldn't speak. My throat seemed choked with sobs of relief and sorrow.

"I will speak to your father about providing you with quills and papers, as well as some reading materials," the priest said, biting his lip. I knew that getting my father to give me anything from now on would be a struggle.

"I shall return soon, my son," the priest said, reaching out to touch my shoulder.

This time, I did not flinch or pull away from him.

***

The priest wouldn't visit me for more than a week. By then, I had become accustomed to a daily delivery of stale bread and water, and after a few days, I began to receive some watered down broth or beans and even, on the fifth day, some carrots and a partially-rotten apple for dessert.

As the days wore on, I began to develop the discipline of saving my food instead of devouring it right away. I would eat my food one bite at a time, savoring the salty or sweet taste on my tongue, making each bite last for as long as possible. I would keep a bit of food under my covers, so that if I woke up in the middle of the night, my stomach growling, I could eat a small morsel to make the hunger more bearable. I lost weight, and soon the last bit of baby fat disappeared from my body. Later, I would jump and tumble in my cell to keep my muscles from withering away, but at first, I just lay in my simple bed, trying to save my energy and strength.

Those were dark days for me. I think that, had I not known that the priest would keep his word by visiting me, I would have become despondent. But finally, when I felt I couldn't take another moment of solitude, I heard the turn of a key in the lock and I knew he had returned.

I stared in wonder when the elderly man of God showed me the heavy bag he'd brought. "How did you even get that up the stairs?" I asked. "And how did you get all that in here?"

"I have my ways," the old man replied with a wink.

He opened his sack and began removing things that told me that my father had surely not inspected this delivery. Instead of food today, though, he had brought me gifts much more valuable.

"Here are some scrolls, quills, and of course, some ink." He placed these items on my flimsy desk. "I will return in four days' time, my son. I expect you to have read the first part of this book." He brandished a Latin grammar. "And to have read in total this one as well." He placed St. Augustine's *Confessions* on my humble bed. To this, he added works by St. Thomas Aquinas and Plato's Republic, which had been on the top of the bag. Gutenburg's great invention had just arrived in Spain that year, although I had no idea about this at the time. This allowed for an explosion of printed books that had been theretofore laboriously copied by hand by armies of scribes.

The pile of books grew ever higher on my bed, and it contained works by many writers of antiquity: Aristotle, Euripides, Seneca, and Cicero. At last, the priest added to these a few hand-written books in Arabic, which had been discreetly kept out of sight at the bottom of the sack.

"Am I to learn *that*, as well?" I asked, remembering the Moorish Tower of Gold.

"Yes, you must. Who do you think has preserved Greek thought and given us practically all we know but the followers of Mohammad?" Father Sebastián paused. I thought of Esther's family of translators and scribes in Toledo, and almost smiled.

"For now, practice your penmanship by writing some practice letters in Castilian. And, I have, of course, brought you a ladder."

"A *what*?" I asked, my heart leaping. Did he mean to help me escape?

"He handed me a book. "It is by Isidore of Sevilla, a man of our own fair city. It is no less than a ladder of jewels which will help you reach the stars!"

I sighed. "Very well. Thank you, Father." I tried not to sound disappointed. "This is all very kind of you."

"Not at all, my son." He placed a hand on my shoulder and got up to leave. "In Granada, even the slaves are taught calligraphy and how to play the lute."

I had never thought of the old priest as one who could make music. I sighed and glanced up at the window of my lonely tower. What could any of this mean if I was stuck in this place?

"Rodrigo?" he said, hesitating at the doorway.

"Yes, Father?" I asked, turning to face him.

The old priest studied me for a long moment as if he were trying to make up his mind about continuing.

"There is something I want you to hear before I leave today," he said, his lips tight. "Knowledge — and by this, I mean the ability to read and write and correspond and think for yourself — is *power*. Even if we live in a world of titles and fighting men, and even if your family makes you learn all this for the wrong reasons…and even if it only affords you a few precious inches of freedom here," he said tapping his temples, his voice trailing off then. He sighed. "Let me say that I have too often seen the effects of ignorance, even among my own brethren. And you would find that a few inches of freedom is more than most people ever know in their entire lifetimes. So, no matter what they do to you, don't forget that what you are doing is something powerful and good for your life and your spirit."

"I won't, Father," I said, a weak, but grateful smile crossing my face.

"Don't neglect your Aristotle." He gave me a complicit smile before closing and locking my door, as I'm sure he'd been instructed to do.

***

After the priest left, I seized the quills and played with the ink, writing my name over and over again on one of the scrolls. I decided to read for a while. The printed books Father Sebastián had brought for me were not as nice as the ones with vellum covers Father kept in his study, but I didn't care. I decided to read Aristotle first as Father Sebastián had suggested, but as I opened the book, I saw a slip of paper fall from it onto the floor. I opened it and began to read. To my surprise, it was from the friend I had despaired of ever seeing again: Esther!

Here's what it said:

Rodrigo,

I hope this missive finds you well. When I saw you take that blow to the head, it made me wish I hadn't hit you so hard.

It is my sincere hope that the priest will deliver this. He is known as a just man, even to the Jews. He is even acquainted with my rabbi.

I have so much to tell you. With luck, it will be in person instead of by hand.

The hoyl bird will come to you soon.

Your friend,
Esther de Susón

I sat back and laughed until tears rolled down my face. I remembered the story she had told me about the hoyl bird. I wondered how we were to rise from the ashes? I thought again about my friends in Triana, and tried not to despair.

CHAPTER EIGHTEEN

I was almost asleep in my tower a few days after receiving the note. It was a calm evening, and the only sound besides the chirps of the crickets was the chime of the bells from a nearby monastery which the soft breeze often carried to my window. The wall opposite me was bathed in moonlight and I had begun to drift off to sleep when I heard a voice gently calling.

"Hey, your highness, look out the window!"

Not fully awake, I peered outside, my eyes searching in the dark below for my friend who I'd begun to doubt would even come at all. Could this be what she meant by the hoyl bird? I could barely make anything out in the weak torchlight from my parents' verandah.

"Over here, silly," she said in a loud whisper while waving her arms. I looked off to the left. As I moved my gaze to where she stood below my window and my eyes came into focus, I realized that she held something in her hand, and it seemed long, almost serpentine.

"What's that?" I asked, my voice cracking.

"You'll see." I could almost hear the grin on her face.

"All right, watch out." I saw her swing something. She should have given me more warning, because the end of a thick piece of rope suddenly struck my face. I felt so surprised that I did nothing as it disappeared over the edge of the window.

"Ay, ay, ay!" she moaned, picking up the rope once again. "I made it the first time and you drop it. Who knows how many more times until such a good chance?"

Indeed, it took several more minutes before I could finally grab the rope, a sturdy one with several knots along its length.

"Now what should I do?" I asked, holding my end of the rope.

"Tie it to something!" She hissed, cupping one hand to the side of her mouth. "Do I have to tell you how to do *everything*?"

"I don't think I have anything that would support my weight."

"How about a table or a desk? Find something quick, Benja. I'm coming up!"

I looked around at my humble dwelling. "I hope my desk is heavy enough," I called down in a loud whisper.

I tried to tie the rope to one of the legs of my desk. I stopped, however, as this was far too light to support either of our weights. I looked around at various objects that might be sturdy enough to make good my escape. The shutters on my window had only small holes. All I saw besides the usual trays for my meager meals and several pots was an old trunk in which I kept some clothes the servants had brought up for me. At the bottom of these were the ashes of the letter I had received through Father Sebastián.

I realized that I had nothing substantial to which I could tie the rope.

In a panic, I tied it around the trunk, removing the clothes and putting in some pots and trays. This I sat on, and decided it was the best I could do.

"I think I found something," I called.

The tug was immediate and frightening. I was suddenly pulled toward the window as she began climbing the rope outside. "No," I gasped, as I grabbed of one of the legs of the desk and attempted to straddle the old trunk like a horse. "You're heavier than me, you'll never make it, not without pulling us both out and breaking every bone in our bodies!"

She didn't hear me, but kept climbing as the desk scraped across the floor toward the window while I straddled the moving trunk. I remember feeling grateful that no one but I slept in the tower. There was no turning back now. I guessed she was at least halfway to my window, and it would do no good to tell her to go back down. She would weigh the same going down as coming up.

Letting go of the desk's leg, which I had dragged as far as I could, I found myself with my feet placed squarely on the wall below the window. I held the rope firm between my quivering knees, where the small trunk was wedged. "Hurry, Esther, fast!" was all I could croak as I strained every muscle of my body against the rope. My face was twisted into a contortion of fear and agony that I'm glad no one was there to see. My back cried out in tremendous pain, and my legs began to buckle. Sweat poured down my face and moistened my hands, and I could feel my hold beginning, ever so slightly, to slip. I tried to wrap my screaming hands better around the taut rope, but had little success. I wanted to cry out, as every move she made was like so many daggers running through me. Nightmarish visions of my flying through the window and of the both of us found crushed on the rocks below ran before my eyes, and somehow I found the strength to hold on.

"I'm almost there," she said, her voice still a thousand leagues away. My resolve was fading fast, and soon, I found myself in a kneeling position on the edge of the window, my shaking arms and elbows pushing against the wall under the window with the packed chest underneath pushing me up toward the aperture. Soon, the pulling from Esther drew me up and out toward the moon, first my torso, then my waist, with soon only my thighs and knees keeping me from falling. "Please, God, please, let my death be quick, or let me hold on, just a little while longer," I pleaded. Soon, I felt my entire upper body protruding out of the window, its edge cutting into the skin right above my knees. I stuck my right arm above me and grasped the top of the window to keep from being pulled out, but it did not seem enough, although this did buy me a crucial moment. I began to teeter forward through the opening when I felt her seize my left hand. In that instant when I thought I would fall, she somehow reached the window's edge and shoved me hard, and in I fell, gasping with pain, panic, and exertion. She joined me there in a sweaty, sobbing, heaving heap a moment later.

We lay like that for what seemed a long time. Finally, I noticed that she was looking at me with great serenity, her eyes softly reflective in the moonlight. I had the feeling that she was waiting for me to say something.

"You almost got us *killed*," I whispered, trying hard not to lose my temper. "You should have *asked* me first before doing a crazy thing like that."

"Benja, how was *I* supposed to know you didn't have anything good to tie the rope to?"

"The fact that I was flailing around and making mad noises should have been a first sign."

"Sorry, I guess once I started climbing — I had a feeling that told me I'd make it, and once I start something, I never go back. So I tried it, and here I am."

"All right, but please, *never, ever, ever* do that again."

"I won't have to," she said. She rose, took the end of the rope from around the trunk, untied it, walked three paces, and retied it around the bars at the top of the door.

CHAPTER NINETEEN

Before long, Esther and I were walking once again along the river toward Triana.

"I don't want to get you in trouble," I said. "How can you sneak out so easily?"

"The hoyl bird has her ways," she said with a smile and a wink. However, after more prodding, she admitted the truth. "My chaperone is one of our family's oldest servants, and she's a very heavy sleeper."

"How did you get around my father's mastiffs?" I asked. The dogs had been bred by my family for generations and were excellent guards.

"I gave them some choice cuts of mutton. Over the course of a week, they got to know me as a friend, and now would never bark at me."

I nodded and smiled in admiration of her cleverness.

"Have something to eat." This time, instead of apples, she had brought a loaf of bread that was only slightly stale, some goat cheese, and raisins.

"Where did you get all this from?"

"My mother hardly ever checks the pantry." She seemed to have an answer for everything.

Finally, I worked up the courage to ask what should have been my very first question:

"And what of Ostelinda?"

We stopped walking. Esther reached out to touch my arm like an old friend.

"She was taken away, off into the shadows that night," I said. "I saw that happening as my father hit me and then my cousin...what happened? Is she all right?"

"I will let her tell you herself."

***

The summer's breeze felt like a mother's gentle caress as Ostelinda and I sat by the river tucked away in an olive grove. I wasn't sure that the gypsy would even see me, but she had agreed to steal away to this place, provided no one but Esther knew of our meeting.

She fought back tears as she told me much more of that awful night weeks before than I ever wanted to hear.

"And that is when they broke Manfariel's arm, as he tried to defend me," she said. "Your brother did it. He is healing, but slowly. I doubt he'll ever play the guitar again." She looked at her feet. "If it weren't for Esther, I think he would have given up by now. She has breathed new life into my brother's broken body. She is a force of nature."

I had no idea what to say. "I am so sorry." I reached for her, but she pulled away, wrapping her arms around herself and rocking slightly.

She was so lovely, and it was such a beautiful night. And yet, she would not let me touch her, and I was too young and ignorant of the ways of the world to understand why.

"There is more, Benja," she said. I waited for her to continue, but she just sat there, not speaking, leaving me to wonder what more there could be as I studied her unchanging face.

***

I was able, with Esther's help, to steal away again a few nights later and continue my conversation with Ostelinda in the same place. That night, the moon was still almost full, and its reflection seemed to dance on the river's surface.

"I'm pregnant," she said after much hesitation. She studied my face for a long moment afterward, as if considering whether telling me was a mistake.

"Are you sure?" I didn't want to believe it, but doubted it could be any other way. "How can you tell?"

"Yes. I'm quite sure." She seemed not to want to dignify the second part of my question with an answer. What did I know of women's bodies?

We sat once again in the olive grove, down the river from Triana. We could hear bullfrogs singing in the night, and the gentle ripple of the water as it eddied and flowed to the sea. The moon shone almost full that night, and Ostelinda's black hair was stunning in its light.

"I know it seems too early to tell, but I know my own body. Besides, I know that your cousin Juan…" she said, then stopped, as if unable to continue.

"Ostelinda, I'm so sorry." I moved to sit next to her. She seemed to relax, and allowed me to sit close by her this night without pulling away. "If I hadn't disobeyed my father, none of this would have ever happened."

"True," she said, looking up and forcing a smile. "But I will survive." she leaned back and watched the river and the moon's reflection on the water. "I always do."

I tried to imagine what she could be feeling, and how it must be to have something growing inside you that would remind you of the violence visited upon your body.

"Are you going to, ahem, rid yourself of it?" I asked, looking away. "Or do you intend to keep the baby?" I fully expected her to slap me or turn away for my asking such a bold, impertinent thing. But I believe that Ostelinda had consigned me to the status of something like a silly, harmless child in her mind. As such, knowing that I never sought to harm, she in turn never seemed to take offense at anything I said.

"Yes, I will keep him," she said after a while. She surprised me by taking my hand and forcing a smile. "It would be easy for me to get some strong herbs from one of the old women of Triana and make a tea to force a false delivery. I did it once before."

"Why is *this* time any different?"

"This time — how can I explain?" She tossed a pebble into the current below as she searched for her words. "Because before I could do so, I had a vision in a dream sent by Del, a message about this boy. He *will* be a boy…and *this* one will be different. I would feel as if I were killing an important part of myself and maybe part of *you*, too, Benja. He carries, after all, your blood in his veins. But he will be different, good. That's why. My grandmother used to say that, after a great evil, there often comes a great good. I feel that this is such a case. I'm connected to this one. This one is coming for a reason."

"But…what if he were to end up like my father, or my brother, or my cousin Juan?"

"No, he won't. The fortune-tellers agree with me, as well as my spirit guide."

"But—"

"Shush," she said putting a finger to my lips and peering purposefully into my eyes before saying something that I would not understand for many years to come.

"No. Not this time. They won't get *this* one. We won't let it happen. We must not let that happen."

We sat for a long time without saying anything then, and I slowly turned so I could lie down while watching the night sky. As my friend caressed my hair and face, her hands became wet with the tears I shed. Tears of sadness and of fear for what lay ahead and how small I felt in the big, mean world.

CHAPTER TWENTY

Weeks later, I decided to sneak out again, and wandered around the *judería*, the old Jewish quarter, with Esther before heading to Triana. This neighborhood was created under King Fernando III, who was actually a real friend to the Jews, and had invited the Hebrews of Toledo to help populate the quarter after he conquered the city in 1248. You might know this neighborhood now as the *Barrio de Santa Cruz*, which is what they call it since the Jews were expelled and the Inquisition wanted to name everything after the Cross and Christ, in whose name they pretended to act. The area had been in decline since the riots of 1391 that targeted the Jews of our city and destroyed their main synagogue.

After the servants of the neighborhood had extinguished the hanging oil lamps on every corner, Esther and I set out to explore the cobblestone streets where her people used to live in large numbers. My friend had brought a taper for each of us so that we would not be in total darkness as we walked about. The neighborhood had a strict curfew, so we crept about with great care, hoping not to be discovered by sentinels who patrolled the area.

Each stucco house there was whitewashed and protected by a heavy oak door or thick, wrought-iron gates. However, we were able to peer in on some homes around the gates and spy gardens and patios, some of which had softly flowing fountains. The smell of jasmine and rosemary wafted to our nostrils, and I thought I could hear the gentle chirps of canaries in some of the homes. This reminded me of the birds that my mother kept at home in her gilded cage.

Esther showed me the home where one branch of the Cansino family still lived, and she implied that they had not been pressured to leave the quarter thanks to their conversion to Christianity. It was a large house with great tile-work, an elaborately detailed metal lattice grill protecting its lush garden, and a series of fountains whose water played in a way that was most pleasant.

"This could be my home if I marry Enrique Cansino," my friend said.

We kept walking, and we explored an alleyway that Esther said was known as the *Callejón de Adobadores de Libros*, as it was here that some of her poor relations had once worked at "pickling" books, turning skins into parchment, sheets, or scrolls by soaking them in brine and then sewing them together slowly, by hand. I was glad for Gutenberg's invention when I listened to Esther's description of this unpleasant process.

"And this was once the Synagogue where my great-grandfather worshipped." We stood in front of a church, *la Iglesia de Santa María la Blanca*. As she said this, I didn't know what to say, so I said nothing, and we continued our walk. We walked along the walls that had kept the Jews in for centuries, past the *Plaza de Refinadores*, until we reached *Calle Pimienta*, as this was the street where some of Esther's family had lived selling spices and pepper.

"See this home?" Esther motioned me to step closer to one of the houses on a narrow street, the one nearby that would one day bear her name. Her green eyes flickered like the candle she held close to her bosom as she told me about how it was the place where she had been born and spent the first part of her childhood.

"We'll get it back one day," she vowed. "King Enrique won't last forever. Isabel will be queen soon, and she and Fernando have big plans." Her voice revealed the excitement she clearly felt.

I decided not to mention that my mother had talked about the future queen's plans to rid our country of the Jews and the Moors. "What plans are those?" I asked, trying to look past the ornate blue and green tiles around the iron gates of the house.

"She's going to send men across the Ocean Sea!" she said, the glee causing her voice to rise. I tried to quiet her, but she kept talking. I had no idea where she could have heard such a thing, which sounded like madness to my young ears.

"And when she does, I'm going to disguise myself as a man and go on that trip. And you must come with me, Benja," she said, although by now I had clearly explained many times, too many to count, that I preferred to be called by my given name, Rodrigo. But alas, my nocturnal friends had met me as Benja, and it seemed that I could never outgrow that silly nickname now.

"We'll see the lost city of Atlantis, and Ultima Thule where the Vikings went, and maybe even India or the Land of Sind where the Great Kahn and Prester John reign!" she exclaimed, apparently curious to see where our gypsy friends came from and apparently confusing it with China or Cathay. I, however, had no such desires, having just read the Travels of Marco Polo and found them terrifying.

Lights had come on in several of the neighboring houses, and I heard the bustling of servants in one of the patios. Soon, I feared that the constable or guards would be called and we could be in severe danger.

"Let's run!" I cried, and we took off toward the river and San Telmo's Bridge that led to Triana.

***

That night, the people of Triana danced and celebrated like they had the night I was discovered by my father and the others, and I tried my best to join in the feast of sardines, garlic chicken and pepper soup. I had glared at Father's closed window as we passed it on my way to Triana with Esther. How I hated him that night! I loathed him from the other side of the shutter, despite what I had been taught by my new teacher about how I should repay kindness for cruelty, and hold only love in my heart for my enemies. I had heard from one of the servants that delivered my tray of food that Alejandro was away at a feast in Carmona, so I felt sure that I wouldn't see any of the men of my family that night. Besides, I suspected that my tirade had made Mother suspicious of my father's actions, and that perhaps he and the others would stay away from Triana, at least for a while.

I know, however, that had I seen them there that night, I would have taken up arms with the gypsy men, attempting to wield a sword or whatever else they might place in my hands. I was a young and foolish boy in those days, and I still believed in my heart of hearts that I was immortal, impervious to any harm. I'd heard that several of them had sworn revenge on my family, and were angered by my presence that night. I can't say, even today, that I blame them. After all, Ostelinda had forever been tainted in the eyes of her people by the forbidden — if unwilling — contact with the *busno*, and would have faced certain ostracism had their *voivode*, or chief, not intervened on her behalf. As for me, the dancer had reassured them and vouched for my character, the way she had with Gerinel, so it seemed that my presence would at least be tolerated for the time being. I could now sneak away from home to visit Triana any time I pleased.

If only they'd known then how much a brother I would one day become to them all.

CHAPTER TWENTY-ONE

In addition to the biblical texts I read for Father Sebastián, I was also expected to read the writings of the great philosophers of the ages. I usually read texts in Greek, especially from Plato and Aristotle, and Arabic texts, which were supposed to make me able to reason and construct more logical arguments, especially having to do with theology and spiritual matters. Of course, my teacher allowed me to read most of the more difficult texts in Castilian. As Esther never tired of reminding me, it was largely thanks to the Jewish and Muslim scholars of Toledo that these texts had come to me in my language. Sometimes, though, I couldn't quite understand that which was supposed to be so clear for me. I remember one such lesson on a hot summer's day.

"I don't understand, Father," I said.

"What's so difficult about it?"

"It just doesn't make sense. How could St. Thomas Aquinas accept both the teachings of Aristotle — who was almost an atheist, if I understand correctly — and yet still be considered a Christian scholar?"

"Well, now you're *really* on to something. You see the nature of the conflict," he said, leaning back and folding his hands on his chest and staring at me for a while before speaking. "He saw both reason and faith as gifts from God, Rodrigo…"

"Yes, but how can such different things be in harmony with each other?"

"Do you remember our discussion of Averroes, the Muslim philosopher from Córdoba?" he asked, trying another angle.

"Yes."

"Do you remember what his basic conclusions were about the Aristotelian teachings?"

"Yes, they claim humans are capable of reasoning and knowing without divine intervention, and that God may not even exist." I looked in my notes for the exact selection from his work, entitled *Harmony of Science and Religion.*

"Correct. Now, that is *one* way of looking at things. Reason and logic are tools, and it is important not to discard them as valid ways of knowing. You know, the Jews have a whole literature, the "Commentaries," or Talmud, based on a reasoned study of their sacred texts. So you see, using the mind is an important thing when thinking of things spiritual."

"How can you still believe in God if you do?" I was still confused. "Doesn't all that thinking get in the way of faith?"

"The other extreme is the idea that a literal reading of sacred texts is the *only* way of knowing anything. Remember what Ibn Arabi, the Muslim philosopher also from Córdoba, said: "If one were to listen to the jurists, relations between God and man would be nothing more than those of master and slave. Faith and philosophy begin where *their* arid laws end.""

I thought about the many conversations I had had with the Romany about their traditions and religion. Was that also a valid way of knowing things?

"So, what *can* we believe?" I wanted to know.

"Perhaps *everything* you learn has a grain of truth in it," my teacher said. "Even things that seem to be in conflict with one another."

"*Everything?*" I exclaimed. "How could that be? *Something* has to be the best."

"Are you sure?"

"Quite," I said, in my youthful self-assurance.

"But what if," he said with a smile, "human reason is a gift from God, so that we may know the world all the better? And what if revelation, and other traditions and forms of gaining wisdom for that matter — like intuition — can help answer some of the questions that reason can't even postulate? Without the 'un-moved mover' as Aristotle called what we call God, how could the world and all of Creation have come into being in the first place?"

"I still don't know. I think that reason and faith are just different ways of looking at the world, and I think that they'll always be at war with one another."

"Factual knowledge is a fine thing, Rodrigo, but it can only go so far. People have been wondering about this for thousands of years. There's nothing new under the sun. Maimonides warned us against taking the scriptures literally, as we risk forgetting their eternal meaning when we do this. Remember, mere facts can't give richness and meaning to life. We are granted life so that we can discover its meaning. You need to examine the traditions of wisdom and — perhaps more important, look inside your own heart — for the answers that matter most." He paused. "As Averroes pointed out all the time, the most important lesson we can take from holy texts is that God wants us to work things out for ourselves. It's wonderful advice for those who follow Mohammed, and good too for a Christian, my son."

CHAPTER TWENTY-TWO

On another day, around the time of Candlemas, Father Sebastián appeared with a friend with whom he had been in correspondence for many years in theological matters and other subjects. His name was one that, as I understand it, has become very famous in recent years, thanks to the books he's written on grammar and philology. His name was Nebrija.

Father Sebastián wanted me to meet him, I think, because he was one of the luminaries of our time — and he wanted to inspire me to become one of them as well.

When I met him, this Nebrija was in his early thirties, a handsome man who crackled with enthusiasm for the work he was doing. We talked about Aristotle, Latin poetry, Plutarch, the Italian arts of different types of which he seemed fond, and the history of language and its role in society. I heard that he was put to the Inquisition years later, as well as many other writers and thinkers.

"That's right," Bartolomé said, feeling a bit ashamed, although it wasn't his fault. The fury of the grand inquisitors, Juan de Guzmán and his goon Torquemada, seemed to know no bounds.

"It's also ironic," Rodrigo said, ignoring him, "That so intelligent and peaceful a man should see his grammary of the Castilian language, something that initially was a purely intellectual pursuit, become the instrument of conquest."

"I agree," said Bartolomé.

"Bartolomé, did you hear what Queen Isabel's first reaction was when she learned of Nebrija's work?"

"What on earth is *this* good for?" the queen asked several years later when the book was presented to her, or so the story goes.

"Language," said the bishop of Avila to Her Majesty in 1492, "is the perfect instrument of empire."

And so it was, Bartolomé. Once the reconquest of *Hispania* was complete, Isabel would turn her attentions to consolidating her power and using the Castilian language as a tool to help her do so.

CHAPTER TWENTY-THREE

Just a few days after meeting Nebrija, I returned to Triana. I sat with Ostelinda by the fountain near daybreak and tried to carve a flute out of a long stick that was a gift from Manfariel. I had decided to heed his advice and learn to play at least one musical instrument, because music, as the fortune-tellers used to say, is "the cosmic dance of which we are all a part." Up until then, the only thing I had ever played were the bells at Christmas Mass, when I was very young, too young even to help Father Sebastián.

I did my best, but the knife caught on little knots in the wood. Ostelinda looked over at me, and coaxed the instrument from my hands, the corners of her mouth rising at my clumsy efforts.

"Here, let me show you another way," she said.

I surrendered my project to her, and she began to shave the wood in long, smooth strokes.

"You must love the wood, Benja, and you have to caress it as you cut. You mustn't fight it. It is more than technique, it is a *feeling*. A sort of mindfulness and finesse you need as you act in all things. It is a kind of *duende*, or spirit. Just like how I dance, you know, with soul and exuberance. Try to feel the spirit of your task enter you."

I began again, and decided to ask her something I had been wondering since Father Sebastián's lesson. "Ostelinda, what do you think about intuition? You spoke of it the other day — a feeling you get about what you should or shouldn't do sometimes."

"Yes, what of it?"

"Well, I was wondering, how can you tell when you have that feeling?"

"I just know," she said.

"But *how*?" I demanded, slipping on a knot in the wood and accidentally cutting my right hand, the one in which I held the wood. I cried out in pain, and began to suck on the wound, hating the taste of blood. Ostelinda scooped up some mud from the base of the fountain and took a leaf from a plant in her pocket. I held out my hand to her, and she took it and caressed it gently, like a mother might.

"It's not deep, it will heal quickly," she said, her voice smooth and comforting. The bleeding eased as she put some more mud on the cut and massaged my hand with the leaf from her pocket. "Don't worry, Benja. You'll be all right."

After a few minutes, my hand felt better and I was able to imagine that I would be able to climb up the rope to my room later that morning upon returning home.

We hadn't spoken in several minutes, but I knew that Ostelinda was watching me, and I suspected what she was going to say.

"There's a lesson in this, my friend. When you try too hard to understand — or when you're not mindful — you can cause harm, and the smallest things can have huge consequences. That's why you must always be vigilant and not fall prey to the traps the world sets for you. You must instead be in tune with what nature or *Del* tells you. You must learn to trust your instincts, because most of what the world shows you in terms of temptations is illusion and mindlessness. So be mindful, very mindful."

"Is that how the Romany live — mindfully?"

"That's only the beginning, Benja," She said, continuing her work. "You don't have to prove yourself to anyone or for anything. Does the free bird have to justify itself to the hunter who stalks it? Of course not. The beautiful lilies you see in the fields don't have to be hard-working or wise for God to love and clothe them, and neither do you. What you should do is try not to worry. Let your life sing with a beautiful, simple sense of balance and purpose. Everything else will take care of itself. You'll see."

This made me think about something Father Sebastián had told me on the second day he worked with me: "If you follow your true path in life, it will save you. If you do not, it will destroy you."

CHAPTER TWENTY-FOUR

"This is all very interesting, Rodrigo. But when are you going to explain how you got to the Indies and why you've come to tell me all of this?" Bartolomé said.

"You must trust me, Bartolomé," Don Rodrigo said as he creaked gently in his hammock. "You need to hear what I am saying. It is more a part of you than you realize."

"Why?" Bartolomé asked, putting the squawking bird back on his outdoor perch.

To this, he said nothing more than "I hope that you'll understand one day soon."

CHAPTER TWENTY-FIVE

And so it was that I spent several years that way, locked in the castle's tower by day, sneaking out and running off to Triana by night. What things I learned! I was eventually able to play the guitar with Manfariel, having decided that the incident with the flute was some sort of sign. What's more, despite the fears of a few, I began to learn the language of my adopted tribe. Esther tried too, although she was much slower than I. I learned how to play chess, Turkish draughts, how to tumble and run, train monkeys to do tricks, and even to charm snakes out of a basket with the help of an old, thin man who had dedicated himself to that art. I learned to fish by the light of the Andalusian moon, and even to dance the flamenco with Ostelinda, my hands always resting skillfully on my hips which were never still. The people of Triana even began to say that I could dance with *duende* — that special feeling and spirit — and this was a real compliment coming from them. One of the old women even made me a lightly-jeweled belt to wear while I danced with Ostelinda.

What a pair we made as we sang those ballads and *sevillanas* with our guitars and castanets! Sometimes we would perform special dances while Manfariel, whose arm had finally healed, played the chords that struck into us like knives. We sang soulful ballads based on the early chants the Romany had sung since time immemorial. I sang, "*N'aviom ke tumande o maro te mangel, N'aviom ke tumande kam man partir te den,*" which means "I did not come to you to beg for bread, I came to you to demand respect." Another favorite was one that went, "*Andr oda taboris, ay pahres buti karen, mek mariben chuden,*" which means, "Do not hit me, do not beat me, or you will kill me. I have children at home, who will bring them up?"

I learned many things from my Romany friends in those early years. But I also learned much with Father Sebastián. It was a curious double life, you know — dancing to the songs of Triana some of the time, and then studying the writings of some of the greatest thinkers who ever lived at other times. Somewhere amidst all of that I must have slept and eaten enough to stay alive; but then, I was so young and fit in those days.

Sevilla in the years leading up to the Inquisition was an enchanting and sensual place. Isidore of Sevilla's poetry praising our city seemed to echo from every corner and stone for me. Living there then was like waiting in the quiet moments before a storm, I realize now.

Sometimes, Esther and I, concealed in our special black capes which were gifts from Ostelinda, would allow ourselves to get lost in the moonlit city when we found ourselves with a bit of time to spare. Those serpentine streets, lanes, and white one-story houses were the source of endless curiosity for us. We still never grew tired of peering through the bars and trying to see patios and little gardens that harbored flowers and cool fountains. We loved the splendid arabesque arcades and the pungent smell of incense, orange blossoms and oleander that would make us ache to believe that the Moors had never really been expelled and held only Granada. We liked to pretend we still lived in the city of Al-Geber who, Father Sebastián taught me, had not only designed the beautiful Giralda tower, but had also been a brilliant mathematician. I would often picture the two of them playing chess in the orange grove by the Alcázar.

I loved how Sevilla was a city of shopkeepers and apothecaries, and had enjoyed as a boy strolling among the birdcage and pottery shops, always noting the prideful smiles on the faces of the people displaying their wares there and at market. Even today, I miss seeing the blue and green tiles on every wall, as well as the quiet courtyards with frilly, horseshoe-shaped arches. I adored the old cathedral by the Dominican college, where I would spend some of my later years. This is where I rang bells as a child, and had once seen boys luckier than I chosen to dance before the altar on special holidays. It was then that I truly believed the old saying, 'To the man God loves, He gives a house in Sevilla.'

Later, I would walk Esther back to her home, which was well into the new Jewish quarter. Here, I could smell the cooking of goose grease and the roasting of chickpeas that the poor had to feast upon. During the day, if I were lucky enough to sneak out, I could always hear the pounding of the silver-and-blacksmiths in their shops, and smell the dyes of the people who illuminated ancient manuscripts in their little studios.

"What are those silver things on the doorposts with that strange writing?" I once asked Esther.

"Oh, those. They're called mezuzahs. They contain scripture, so that we're always reminded of the importance of knowing the Torah," she said.

It was a place where her family lived and I didn't feel welcome. As such, I never entered her home until much later than that day.

Sometimes I would spy in at her home on a Friday night before heading to Triana. On most nights, Esther could sneak out, but *never* on Friday nights. It was during that time, the *Seder*, that her family insisted on her being there for the prayers and the bread that I heard was like a flat, flaky biscuit, as it was made without yeast. On other nights, I sometimes heard them singing, at the hour of sunset, "*Shema, Yisrael, Adonai, Eloheynu Adoni, Echad*" before a Shabbat Meal.

I remember that once, during a *Seder* during Passover, I stole up to the window that looked in on the family's small courtyard. I could hear voices inside as well as see candles and oil lamps flickering and the play of shadows on the wall. I saw the entire De Susón family sitting in their salon, around a table adorned with a white damask tablecloth. Their eyes were closed, and they prayed in a tongue that seemed just as foreign to me as the Romany tongue once had. I later learned that they were singing *piyyutim*, or chanted psalms of the synagogue. On the table next to them sat a wooden cylindrical chest that I later learned was used for the storage of the sacred texts from which they read.

Suddenly, Esther's father, a man with a long, gray beard and a prayer shawl, took one of the bits of biscuit, held it up for everyone to see, and said:

"Behold the *matzo* bread. We ate it during our slavery under Pharaoh, and we eat it to remind us of the poor and suffering everywhere in all lands. We eat it and pray that all peoples may have liberty, justice, and peace."

As I studied the faces around the table that night, including Esther's, I yearned to understand what they said, especially during the prayer that followed. I thought about *my* prayers, the ones I had learned from Father Sebastián, and the incantations I heard from the Romany to their deities.

What can this all mean? I wondered.

It was then that I noticed Esther's eyes on mine — and I disappeared with shame into the night.

***

Any doubts I had about whether Father Sebastián suspected the double life I led disappeared one day in June of 1474. I had come home much later than usual, had neglected to untie the rope from the bars on my door, and forgotten that my tutor was coming early the next morning. I heard his key turning in the lock. I awoke with a sinking feeling of dread as the door swung open. The old man stood there looking at the rope, a knowing smile dawning on his face.

"You'd better clean up your messes before your tutor visits you each week, Rodrigo," was all he said, his eyes twinkling like an accomplice caught in some minor mischief.

The priest seemed to read my thoughts, because he then quoted one of his favorite Bible verses to me:

"Go, eat your bread with enjoyment and drink your wine with a merry heart; for God has long ago approved what you do."

We never spoke of it again.

CHAPTER TWENTY-SIX

"The old king Henry IV — nicknamed 'the impotent' because of his lack of sons and the rumors he was a sodomite — died that following December. Isabel and Fernando would finally unite our new nation of *Hispania* soon enough, but for now, Isabel was crowned Queen of Castile in Segovia by popular acclaim, and this began a long struggle for power against her sister in Portugal. A civil war ensued, of course. I received word that my brother Ricardo, one of the dead king's highest-ranking guards, had been sent to fight on the side of Isabel in the royal militia, mostly in Asturias and Extremadura. Father Sebastián assured me this was a prestigious organization, and that I should be proud of my brother. I didn't care; however, that year was when Ostelinda had her baby, a boy whom she named Pobea."

"*Pobea?*" Bartolomé asked, the word seeming, like Rodrigo the day he had first seen, oddly familiar.

"Yes, that was it." Rodrigo stared at him with a curious sideways glance.

"And what does that name mean?"

"In the Romany language, it means 'redeemer.' She may have chosen this name to offset the fear that the fair-skinned child was tainted by white blood, or that she had forever brought *madine* — shame — upon her entire tribe for her actions. Ostelinda tried to think of her baby — the one she had dreamed about — as a kind of redemption for the violence which had been visited upon her, and hoped he would bring joy and happiness to the world. She always believed in balance, and she felt that this child would offset some of the evil done by my family."

CHAPTER TWENTY-SEVEN

The people of Triana loved to tell stories. But one stands out in my mind that illustrates why I loved them so much, and why I had so much in common with them.

"Do you want to know why the Romany sell horses, and don't stay anywhere very long, Rodrigo?" asked an old man as he sat on his straw mat beside the fire. They would often tell this sort of story concerning their past late at night when most of the other *gadje*, or non-gypsies, had gone elsewhere for the night.

"Back in the Land of Sind, there once was a red king," he began. "He had three sons, and one of them was very smart, another was average, and the last one was not looked upon as bright. The first two had always been admired by the king and all his court for being so practical, but the young one was always looked down on for being a fool and a dreamer."

I wondered if the old man was trying to make me feel bad about myself by starting the story this way.

My family had always ridiculed me by saying things like 'Benja is just a foolish dreamer.'

"Now, one day, all three of them set off to seek their fortunes. The first one thought he'd make his money on something worthwhile — so he decided to work as a moneylender. But he made a bad deal with a corrupt man, and was soon chased out of town without anything to show for all his hard work. That's how the Romany learned always to live free of debt, and do simple jobs, like fixing pots or selling things at market.

"Now, the second one, he was still pretty smart. He was good with wood, and he became an expert carpenter. This was fine until one day, a swarm of hungry insects descended upon the town where he lived, and destroyed all the trees and wood all around. So, he had to leave that place because he couldn't make a living any longer. From this, the Romany learned that you shouldn't put all your eggs in one basket, if you can forgive the common expression. It's good to have lots of things you're good at.

"Now, the third son, the dreamer, hadn't gotten very far. In fact, he'd just sat by a fence near a field where a stream flowed and a herd of horses grazed. The boy sat there for such a long time that the horses got used to him, and came over to have a better look.

"Now, these horses had been kept by an evil old lady who never rode them and didn't love them. So, one day, the lead horse said to the boy, 'If you want us, you can take us with you and keep us and sell us. But you have to be good to us and treat us with kindness. It doesn't matter where you take us, because horses have a carefree spirit.' It was also they who taught us that, even in a world full of cruelty and anger, where everyone wants to humiliate and degrade us, our people were made to be beautiful children of heaven and friends to all living creatures everywhere.

"And so it is that the Romany have loved horses ever since, and love to wander with them."

***

"Esther, will you teach me about your religion?" I asked. After all, it was not just the Romany who had sparked my curiosity about things of the spirit.

I had come to stand by the tall hedges outside of her house earlier that evening, waiting for the first three stars to appear, which signified the end of the Jewish Sabbath. Somehow, she had managed to sneak out that night without her new chaperone.

She smiled at me, and I felt myself blushing a bit under the lantern lights. "You saw me watching you that night." I silently reproached myself for my eavesdropping.

"Spying on your friend Esther," she said, before admitting that she had been watching me as well.

"But will you teach me?"

"Of course," she tossed her head, her long hair cascading down her back. She really was becoming a beautiful young woman, and Manfariel and I were not the only men in Triana to notice. She had even begun dyeing her fingernails with henna on occasion.

"I can never really feel entirely interested in the prayers anymore, so sometimes I look around during them," she said.

"Is that the only kind of prayer your family does?" I asked.

"What a thing to ask. No, we say many others, of course."

"Such as what?" I asked, snacking on some almonds and aubergines she had offered me after I'd complained of being hungry.

"Well, let's see," she said, taking out a prayer book full of Hebrew writing. I stared at the characters on the page and yearned to know what they said. "There's this prayer here, which I wish other families didn't have to say. It's called the *Kol Nidre*, and it means — it's kind of like a way of telling God that 'we didn't mean it,' that we didn't mean to take the cross by day in order to protect ourselves. I, on the other hand, don't care and would never pretend."

I wondered if this is what people meant when they accused *conversos* of "Judaizing" by night. I decided that I couldn't really blame them, as Jews were weighed down by every restriction possible — and things were getting worse. They couldn't join certain guilds and professions, they had to live in certain places, and couldn't trim their hair or beards — all of which just made them stand out that much more. If Jews — or at least, unconverted ones — broke any of these rules, they could be fined or even get a hundred lashes on their backs.

"Why don't those old *Seder* prayers interest you anymore?" I asked, changing the subject back.

"Oh, I still *like* them," she said, smiling wistfully. "I don't know. I used to feel fulfilled with what I took from the whole thing — almost as if the entire tradition of my people were there with me as I prayed. I also felt that Yahweh — God — was watching me, and had a very special role just for *me* to fill in His plan."

"And you no longer feel that?"

"Yes and no. I'm proud of my people and my tradition, but I wonder if there is *more* to it out there — you know, more than just *my* people."

"And you'd really never consider being one of the *conversos* like some of your family's friends?" I realized as I said this that this was a delicate question for her, who was as stubborn as a burro, and would resist converting just because that was what some people expected her to do.

"You must be joking with me," Esther said. "There is no possible way that I would do that."

"Well, how do you know? Wouldn't that make your life easier?"

"Benja — you don't believe *everything* you're told, do you?" she asked, her voice heavy and accusatory.

"No, of course not," I said with a scoff. I wondered where she thought I got my news of Sevilla from in those days besides her. "Why don't you like them?"

"For one thing, did you know that most of them are not converted to Christianity at all? That's hypocrisy, not to mention foolish and unsafe. Everyone hates them, you know that!"

"Yes." I remembered all the times I'd heard guests at my parents' feasts criticizing *conversos* as they sat in the alcoves talking amongst themselves, thinking no one overheard.

"And did you know that they still recite their Hebrew prayers, most of them anyway, just as my family does? Most of them go to the cathedral on Sundays and then the synagogue on the following Saturday. And do you know what?" She leaned over closer to me and whispered, although there was no one within earshot, "Many of them make traffic with the African slave trade."

"*Oh.*" I couldn't think of anything else to say. I knew that there was such a trade going on with the Portuguese and some of their colonies in Africa. But I had never stopped to wonder how the whole system worked, nor who financed or benefitted from it. I supposed it had something to do with the Medici bankers who had become powerful in our city in recent years.

"Well, maybe they're just doing what they feel they have to do to survive," I said.

At this, Esther merely scoffed.

"What is it that your father calls them? He said a prayer for them one time. The Anu-something."

"The *Anusim*," she clarified, her voice heavy.

"And what does *that* mean, exactly?"

"It means 'the forced ones.' He calls them that too charitably, because he thinks that conversion is what they *had* to do."

"Well," I said, taking a swig from a wineskin, "this isn't exactly the easiest time to be Jewish."

125

"Yes, but they still *do* have a choice, and no one's put a lance to them to force them to abandon the faith of our fathers."

"So," I asked, after a minute of awkward silence, "even though you don't want to convert, you still wonder if there is more out there?"

"Yes, of course," she said, then paused. "What do *you* wonder about, Benja?" she asked.

"I wonder what lies at the other end of the Ocean Sea." This was the first time I confided this to anyone. I looked west and thought of a letter by an Italian named Tuscanelli that Father Sebastián had assigned me to read. This man held that the East, as well as all its treasures, was indeed reachable by ship. People thought that perhaps seven hundred leagues west of the Canary Islands lay another *Terra Incognita*, full of gold and pearls, known as "Antilia," or maybe even the lost world of Atlantis.

"Of course, according to Eratosthenes…" I trailed off, as I saw my friend raise an ironic eyebrow at my verbosity. It was true that I had perhaps spent too much time studying alone in my tower, and I wondered if all that was drying out my brain.

"I think that maybe your idea was a good one," I said. "Perhaps we *should* try to go on that first voyage, whenever it leaves."

"But aren't you afraid of falling off the edge of the world?" Esther asked, her voice gently mocking me. "I seem to remember a scared boy not long ago who claimed that there might be monsters or fires out there. Besides, you know what Esdras said, you know, the prophet we read last month. He posited that only one-seventh of the world is water. If he was right, you'd never get seven hundred leagues across the sea. Wouldn't that be too far?" Her eyes shone with the laughter that lay just behind her words.

"True, but I was talking to some Italian sailors the other day, from Genoa, who said that everyone knows the earth is really round, like a ball. And that we could maybe go to the Indies or a place called Cathay. Or maybe a whole other world."

"Ay. I bet they were drunk when they said that," she said with a laugh. "I could see traveling to India, though," she said, stroking her chin.

"Yes, they were rather drunk," I said, laughing and remembering how one of them had slurringly confessed that his friend had gotten in trouble with some of the local whores, or "public women" as they sometimes called them.

We were silent for a long while until I ventured to say, "My father always used to call Jews, even those who converted, heretics and Judaizers. He said that Spain would be better off without them."

"That's usually how the Old Christians see us. They hate us if we don't convert, then they mistrust us if we do. But, you're different somehow. Why is that?"

"I don't know. I can't decide for myself why I'm different." But then I thought of what Father Sebastián had taught me, and I said, "But I do know that I want to learn, I want to take it all in as much as I can. I want to travel, and I want to go far away from here one day to discover what's on the other end of the earth — or die trying if I have to. I mean, don't you still want to try that, Esther?"

"Ay, ay, ay," she said with a sigh. "I bet once you get there, you'll want to go even farther — it won't be far enough for you." We chuckled, both knowing that she was right. "You know what your problem is, Benja? You're a wanderer. I don't think that you'll ever be happy staying *anywhere* very long without becoming bored and wanting to go somewhere else. It makes me think of the story of your namesake — he was the youngest son of Jacob who had to form his own tribe down in the South of Palestine. The lost tribe of Benjamin. Yes, you're a wanderer and a roamer, all right."

"Like my fortune said I'd be," I mused.

"*Which* fortune?" Esther asked.

"The one the old woman gave me the day we arrived in Triana — what's her name? Mauda?"

"Yes. Mauda."

"And do you know what *your* problem is, Esther?"

"What, *you?*" she asked, mocking me.

"No. Well, yes. But your problem is that you can never go without *fighting* and making some kind of trouble!"

CHAPTER TWENTY-EIGHT

"All right, no one's here!" Esther said, turning around and motioning me to come in through the gate and doorway in her family's home. "Everyone's left for the market, just as I thought."

My heart pounded as I stepped over the threshold and onto the tiled floor that felt cold to me through my soled feet. Once inside, I sniffed the air of the house, curious about what a Jewish household would smell like. I faintly detected the scent of saffron and unfamiliar spices in the pantry. Soft light filtered in from a window high above the table, and I could hear birds twittering. Unlike so many families in Sevilla, this family chose not to keep small birds as pets by the windowsill.

"Are you sure this is safe?" I asked for probably the tenth time that day. "What if your parents were to come back?"

"Look," Esther said, holding up her hand, "We've been through this. When they go to the market, they take *everyone* with them — the servants, my brothers, everyone. That's how they get the metals they use for the smelting, the products we need from day to day, and the food to eat and prepare it the way we must." She paused, and her mood lightened a little. "Now, you *do* want to see it, don't you?" she asked, a playful smile on her lips.

"Of course," I said, brightening.

"All right, then — sit down here." she indicated that I should place myself opposite her at the table. Once I had done so, she went over to a closet and took out a small bundle wrapped in a white cloth, which she placed on the table between us. My eyes grew wide with amazement as she removed the cloth and revealed what was underneath.

Before me stood the elaborate silver cup I had seen Esther and her family drinking from that night when I had spied in on them!

"It's called a Kiddush cup," Esther said, beginning her explanation. "We put wine in here for the Seder dinners." She indicated the top part of the finely-wrought and bejeweled goblet. There were designs of Jerusalem on the outside of the cup, or so my friend told me.

"What are these parts here for?" I asked, pointing to what looked like two chambers on the stem of the cup.

"Those are spice boxes." Esther began spinning to remove the top of the structure and reveal the chambers where cinnamon and cloves were stored to keep the wine and ceremony full of flavor.

"We often use these spices in the blessings and prayers," Esther said, then removed a smaller cup from the larger, the first one, which, she explained, was set out for Elijah every time there was a dinner.

Further down on the stem of the goblet, I saw some of the same Hebrew letters that were on the mezuzah on the entrance to the house. I knew the Torah was very important to her people, yet I couldn't help but feel struck by how different all this was from how things were done in my home. We never had things from Jesus's parables etched into the structure of our house. The closest thing we had was a set of religious triptychs from Flanders that hung opposite Saint James, Santiago de Matamoros.

"What about *that*?" I asked, as I pointed to something stuck down further in the stem of the goblet.

"That," she said with a smile, "is something I am personally very proud of. Have you ever heard of a Megillah?"

"No," I confessed. "What's it for?"

"It contains a special piece of parchment that we read aloud during Shabbat." She pulled out the little metal box and gently tugged on a little edge that was attached to the parchment of which she spoke. "Can you tell me what this is?" She asked as she set it before me, a playful smile on her face.

I studied the Hebrew characters for a long moment, but could not decipher any of them. I felt embarrassed, as I had been studying the language for weeks, and should have been able to read at least *something*.

131

"What does this word mean?" she asked, pointing to one of the words on the far right part of the script. "Can you tell me what *this* is, at least?"

I studied the word, and thought that I wouldn't be able to capture its meaning when suddenly recognition flooded into my mind. I sat up straight in my chair and smiled.

"It's 'Esther.' It's your name!"

"Exactly," she said, leaning back in her chair. "So, do you have it yet?"

"Yes!" I exclaimed. "It's the book of Esther you've got there!"

The late afternoon light was fading a bit, so Esther found a taper to read by. Then I sat back and listened to the story of the brave Jewish queen who was my friend's namesake. I let the beauty and complexity of the ancient language wash over me as she read the parchment. As she told of how Queen Esther had used King Ahasuerus's favor to save her people from their enemies, I wondered if Esther and her people would be able to protect themselves from the storm-clouds gathering about them in our country.

***

Not long after Esther showed me the cup, and on a day my brother Ricardo was off putting down a rebellion in a small town of shepherds and wells, I was able to witness a very important part of the Jewish year. It was the moment where the rabbi puts all the sins of his community on the head of a goat, which then is to run far, far away, thus cleansing the people of all their wrongdoings before the eyes of God.

They all stood in a large semi-circle on one of the hills just outside of Sevilla, a bit of scrubby brush and a carob tree the only thing blocking me from their sight. I decided not to show myself, although this time Esther had, in her own way, invited me there. Some of them were dressed in the same prayer shawls I'd seen that other night, and they closed their eyes as they said another prayer, as always, in Hebrew, which I was starting to understand better all the time. It was, without a doubt, the hardest language I'd ever studied.

At the end of one prayer, the old rabbi came toward the goat held on a rope by one of the boys who wore a prayer shawl, whom I'd seen lighting the long tapers during the Seders. The rabbi continued with another prayer with such a seamless transition that I marveled at his oratory skills. He placed both his hands on the goat's head and spoke his incantation that asked for God's forgiveness for his people, laying all of their sins upon the beast's head.

With a quick movement, he freed the goat, and the animal bounded off into the distance. As he did so, the people's eyes slowly opened, and I felt moved by the stillness and the sense of relief as I felt all of their sins wiped clean and put onto the animal that receded from sight into the distant hills.

After all these years, all I can say is that we Spaniards would need an entire herd of such goats and an entire army of such rabbis or priests if we were to ever wipe out even a small part of the sins we've committed on the Tainos. May God forgive us.

CHAPTER TWENTY-NINE

Bartolomé sat for a while by himself that night thinking of a time that he himself had tried to learn about the ways of a people foreign to him. When his father had come back from Colón's second mission in 1495, he brought with him an Indian slave who had been baptized and christened Juanito. The boy had lived with him in Salamanca as he continued his studies at the university, and they only seldom returned to Sevilla to see friends and his uncle, under whose tutelage the Indian was officially placed. It was during those visits that they would walk about the city, past the wharves and the Giralda, past the Colegio San Miguel where Bartolomé had studied as a boy and along the cobblestone streets where he used to skip lectures to walk and think. Bartolomé told Juanito stories about his life, so that the boy would know him better. He told him how he had been the best student in his class and had not needed all those lectures, how his classmates used to call him a dreamer, and how his father had always gotten him the most eccentric tutors, even if he couldn't always pay for them. But despite Bartolomé's best efforts to know him, the boy rarely shed his reserved way of speaking. He learned Castilian quickly, and, despite a slight accent that he never lost, he impressed most people by his fluency after the first couple of years.

Bartolomé was a curious young man, so he would often spend long evenings posing all kinds of questions to the boy in order to learn more about his land and people in the New World. He remembered one conversation they had on the banks of the Guadalquivir one evening, the breeze wafting through the nearby orange trees.

"Who is your king in the New World?" Bartolomé asked.

"There's no king in Quesqueya, the mother of all lands," the boy replied. "I have a *cacique* — it's like a kind of chief — named Guarani, who is wise and takes care of me and protects me. He is, in this way, like our medicine men, who ward off the evil *zemis* and the Lady of the Winds who lashes our land each year. But we have no king — not like here. And why do you call *mine* the 'New World?' How can you be so sure that *yours* is so much older?"

"That's easy," Bartolomé said, shaking his head. "*Yours* has just been discovered."

Juanito looked at him as if he was the biggest fool he'd ever met when he gave that answer.

Bartolomé thought about how some were calling that new place the "Novi Orbis," literally, a "new world" of islands off the coast of China. He always wondered what life was like in such a faraway place. His father had said in one of his letters that the people there were so godless that they went about naked as the day they were born.

"Don't you believe in God or Jesus Christ as the redeemer and savior in your land?" he wanted to know. Bartolomé had never been allowed to go to the trials of the Inquisition as a boy, but he wondered what Torquemada would have said about such a sinful way of living.

"You mean like Yucahu and Atabey — or the good *zemis* — the spirits of my ancestors?" Juanito asked, touching the small, triangular amulet he always wore as a necklace. Bartolomé had this removed not long afterward for fear of its being a pagan temptation.

"Yucahu and Atabey? No, I'm talking about *God*," Bartolomé said, exasperated. How long had the boy been living with him in Spain and still couldn't understand what he meant at times like these?

Juanito was silent for a while, and Bartolomé felt ashamed for snapping at him. He really needed to learn to control his temper.

"I believe in God, only we give him different names, that's all," Juanito finally replied. "But, for us, you see, God isn't an old man in the sky." He frowned slightly then, and looked away, studying the river that could, in theory, take him home at any time.

"For me, it's the spirit of the yucca harvest, and the mother goddess of water, tides and fertility. There's god-spirit in the land and the sea, the earth and the moon. There are gods in the wind and the rain and the sun and the stars, as well as the forest *zemis* who live in the trees and under rocks. The spirits are in the song that the men of my village drum to and sing as they go out in their canoes to fish...and in the lullaby mother used to sing to help me fall asleep while she wove and the evening air would rock my hammock." His eyes were cast downward then, as if avoiding Bartolomé's. "Now, it's the nearly-silent voice that speaks to my heart, and tells me that all will be well."

Bartolomé was startled to hear the boy speak this way. He couldn't recall another time when he had talked so long and said so much. He tried to think of a way to respond then, wondering what he could say that could convince him of the truth of his faith — but the words would not come.

"You Spaniards," Juanito began again to Bartolomé's surprise. "You talk so much about your savior — *San Salvador* you call him. You love him so much you named an island after him. Well, if you really want to help, don't let wolves count you as a friend. Pray that a *real* savior will come to save my people one day."

CHAPTER THIRTY

Bartolomé, did I ever tell you about Father Sebastián and the lessons he gave me on the Bible? One of his favorite parts of it was the book of Matthew, especially that part about turning the other cheek that Esther had such a hard time with.

"All that ever gets you is two sore cheeks!" she once scoffed.

Sometimes, when we had finished my other readings, and before chess, Father Sebastián would read me parts of our holy book and we would talk about its lessons and meaning.

I remember one day when he read me the part of a rich young man who had kept all of the Old Testament commandments, and Jesus told him that, if he wanted to be perfect, he should sell all of his possessions and give the money to the poor. But the man did not want to do this, because of the attachment he had to his wealth. "It is easier for a camel to go through the eye of a needle than for a rich man to enter the kingdom of God," Jesus had preached afterwards.

I thought about this for a long moment, and then said, "Father, if that is what the Bible says about wealth — well, so many of the nobles, like my family, for instance, claim to be such good Christians, yet are wealthy. The two don't go together."

He smiled at me and asked, "What do you think you can learn from this lesson?"

"I don't know. Perhaps not everyone who claims to be a follower of Jesus really is in sincerity?"

"You're getting there. What else? What can be said about hypocrisy?"

"Well, for one thing," I said, "I don't think God cares much for all of the shows people put on for him. It seems like they're just going through the motions, but aren't really trying to love their fellows or follow God's plan for them."

Father Sebastián closed his eyes then and recited from memory something from the book of Amos:

"Take away from me the noise of your songs; I will not listen to the melody of your harps. But let justice roll down like waters, and righteousness like an ever-flowing stream."

I thought for a long moment of all the feasts my mother and brother had held and of the money Father had dedicated to our parish of San Gil. The only things they seemed incapable of giving anyone were justice and righteousness.

And love.

"What does this lesson teach you about people who only look at certain parts of the Bible and neglect the other parts — the parts that talk about how they should act toward one another?" Father Sebastián asked me.

"Maybe that people use certain parts of the Bible for their own purposes; they ignore some parts and use others to prove themselves right? Like when someone claims to be a good, but wealthy, Christian?"

Father Sebastián smiled slightly as I said this. It didn't occur to me until much later that my teacher was, indeed, quite uncommon in his thinking.

"What does the book say about people like me? Those who *aren't* strong and rich and powerful?"

The old man moistened his index finger and turned to a place a few pages away in the old, musty book and began to read:

"Blessed are the meek, for they will inherit the earth

Blessed are those who hunger for righteousness, for they will be filled

Blessed are the merciful, for they will receive mercy

Blessed are the pure in heart, for they will see God

Blessed are the peacemakers, for they will be called children of God."

And finally:

"Blessed are those who are persecuted for righteousness's sake, for theirs is the kingdom of Heaven."

I never thanked the old man, but it was on that day that I began to formulate my own beliefs based on the Bible — but not *solely* on it. What if, I thought, the Bible is one way of knowing the truth — whatever *that* was — but not the only way? What if the lessons I could learn from the Jews, the Muslims, the Africans, and the gypsies were all a part of the miraculous puzzle? Was I not living the joy that these words — called the *Beatitudes* — spoke of when I brought bread from my meals to the hungry gypsies and the escaped slaves? Was I not meek in all that I did? Were not my compassion and my persecution things that were leading me to the Kingdom of Heaven?

I thought and prayed more about this. I was happy the way that I lived, and I felt at peace with God. I loved the world, I loved God, and I loved my fellow people. Hadn't Jesus reduced, in that same book of Matthew, all the commandments of God to these simple things? The people I knew who were the most miserable were my parents, those who possessed and desired so much — and yet would never be happy.

It was then that I had another thought, one that scared and exhilarated me at the same time: Maybe Jesus wasn't talking about a literal place called Heaven where we would all go after we died. Maybe he was talking about having and making a Paradise for ourselves while we *lived*. Maybe Hell is what people like my parents create for *themselves* while they live. Maybe they do this not knowing how to break free as they torture *themselves* — and everyone around them.

CHAPTER THIRTY-ONE

Despite all the sufferings and fond memories I have of those years, I remember the events of one day more than any other. This was when Pobea was still a very small boy and had barely begun to walk, to the great joy of his extended family in Triana — a place that the gypsies liked enough to consider staying longer than usual.

The war had been going on for probably about three years. It was fought with land troops and corsairs on the high seas — but that had not affected *us* very much, except that we had more soldiers and refugees than usual from surrounding places like Trujillo and other parts of Extremadura. In our little corner of the kingdom, however, it was simply the morning after a particularly lively celebration.

I'd stayed the night in Triana, as I knew that I would not be missed until at least midday when my food would be served at home. It was also not one of the days I expected Father Sebastián, and I felt sure that no one would see the curious rope hanging from my window in the tower that morning.

The sun shone beautifully on the river, as it was a memorably sunny day. I had fallen asleep in one of the gypsy wagons, a Moorish guitar by my side. I felt sick from all of the wine I'd drunk the night before. Several coins lay in my pockets, gifts from a thankful crowd who had rewarded the music I had played to accompany Ostelinda's sensual dance, to the usual hoots and hollers of the sailors, soldiers and escaped slaves. But best of all, there was a troop of traveling troubadours who had been among us for the better part of a week.

The only troubadours I'd ever met before then had been a group of French *jongleurs* who sang the story of El Cid. They relished the tale of the crafty, side-shifting *hidalgo* and his battles with the Moors. *They* had held the favor of the king when they came, and this made all the difference in the world in the Castile of those days. I'd seen that show as a boy during a sumptuous feast my parents hosted, and I remember feeling dumbfounded that anyone could learn so many verses by heart. Their repertoire, however fun and witty, contained none of the racy or bawdy things that *these* troubadours visiting Triana sang of.

I had become fast friends with one of the actors, Lorenzo. He was an Italian boy my age who sang like a lark of the exploits of old miser Pantalone whose servant, Arlecchino, had stolen his money and cuckholded him by seducing his young wife. He was exuberant, so full of life, that I forgot myself and my meager problems whenever we were together.

Lorenzo's skin was the color of olives, and he had dark, chestnut curls as well as light brown eyes that fascinated me. His great confidence and charisma made him the natural leader of his troupe. I loved watching them improvise, night after night, acts that were never quite the same as the night before. They had a basic story to follow, but took cues and even insults the crowd called to them. These they wove into their play, often tumbling, juggling, and striking each other while singing in rhymes, sometimes improvising on the spot. I still remember one verse Lorenzo sang while wearing his mask and multicolored costume as Arlecchino:

> *Old Signor Vecchio,*
> *Sad man Pantalone,*
> *Where will you go now, signore?*
> *I have taken your money and also your wife,*
> *Drunk all of your wine and run off with your son*
>   *To the palazzo where we'll drink and dance*
> *And not come back till the moon has gone home...*
> *What say you, oh sad Pantalone?*

These troubadours had performed all over Europe, and I begged my new friend to tell me his stories and teach me something of Italian. I ached to hear all about Tuscany, France, the green hills of the Basque country and of Catalonia.

He regaled me with stories of his youth, and how he'd once worked in Florence in something he called an *atelier*. He explained that this was a French word for a kind of workshop where boys our age modeled as older men made sculptures after them. He told me of his friend Leonardo, a wild character so gifted he could never concentrate on one project at a time, but rather filled notebooks of sketches and a multitude of ideas his fevered mind imagined. "Some of those machines were for flying," he said, holding his arms out at his sides and running down toward the river, and then sweeping back up to where I stood laughing and clapping my hands. "Come on, do it with me!" he cried, and we swept down to the bank of the river and back again, flapping our arms and pretending we could fly to the moon, or at least to the land of Sind. On that day, Bartolomé, I really did feel that I could soar, so high was my spirit, full of a feeling I'd never known before.

He told me how he had been forced to flee the city of Florence under great secrecy because of the allegations of a jealous and violent lover. He had then, quite by accident, met the troubadours and an enterprising man in the university town of Bergamo and traveled with them all over Italy, France, and our peninsula playing the part of Jupiter in their play and the part of Jesus in the passion and mystery plays that they also performed before adopting the story of Arlecchino and Pantalone.

He told me grand tales as we stole through the city in capes, mine a black gift from Ostelinda, Lorenzo's a royal blue. As we drank sweet wine from stolen bottles, he spoke of Petrarch's Laura, courtly love, and fleeting, noble ladies whose men were off waging wars. These women hosted elaborate dinners and revered the troubadours for the songs they sang about how knights were supposed to demonstrate their love. The troubadours, with their talents, were the intimate friends of these ladies who lavished gifts on them and held great banquets to celebrate their role as liaison-makers and confidantes.

How I dreamed of so many things during those days! I dreamed of joining the *Commedia dell'arte* that my friend talked about in nearly every breath. As we walked along the river together, I dreamed of leaving with him and his friends to see the world. I imagined myself helping him before a performance, choosing his costume and masks, powdering his face, trimming his well-groomed beard and helping him learn songs in a foreign tongue in a distant land. Perhaps it would be the mysterious court of Kublai Kahn that Marco Polo had described in the account of his travels, a book that I had finally come to embrace for the fascinating adventures contained therein.

Yes, that was what I wanted! I dreamed of Lorenzo and me, a famous, inseparable team dressed in the finest silks and ermine to perform for emperors of the East. I saw us feasting on ambrosia and pomegranates. I imagined myself doting on his provisions as he sang in his melodious voice, a voice that would make the kings love him and maidens weep and angels fall for their love of us.

"Rodrigo, Rodrigo, wake up!" the voice came, jerking me out of my reverie.

I opened my eyes slowly, still wanting to believe that my dream was real, and I opened the flaps of my wagon, my eyes blinking in the already bright sunlight. Esther and Ostelinda stood before me, glancing behind as if pursued by wolves.

"What is it? Where's Lorenzo? He said he'd wake me this morning so that we could—"

"He's fled, and so have the others," Ostelinda said, cutting me off. "Something's happened, so come quickly — to the fountain on San Jacinto Street!" They shot nervous glances over their shoulders as they talked, and left me to wake other sleepers as fast as I could.

I began to dress myself, my head aching from the festivities of the night before when Lorenzo and I had danced arm-in-arm around the fire and drunk wine after my performance. We'd downed so much that his lacy white shirt was stained red in several spots. What could have made him leave like that, without taking me with him, I wondered. And why did Ostelinda say he'd *fled*? Fled from *what*? If he didn't come back soon...

I walked to the well in the center of the square Ostelinda and Esther had directed me to, a place where the men and boys used to sell their wares at a makeshift market. But on that day, a strange sight lay before us. The members of our unusual community, many barely more awake or coherent than I, were standing in a group, blocking the main attraction from my view. As I began to push my way through the crowd, I asked what the commotion was about.

"It's the *queen* who has made a visit to Sevilla, and, for some reason has decided to stop in Triana," someone said.

I stopped with fear when I heard this. I had never seen a member of royalty before, and I didn't know how one should act in the presence of such people. I crept close to the front of one side of the crowd, and stood behind some of the other men, looking between various heads at the scene before us. There stood the queen as well as a small army of her royal entourage.

What I saw of our monarch that day surprised me. She was a beautiful woman with auburn hair and grayish-green eyes, looking like a princess from the north thanks to her Plantagenet ancestors. It's funny to say it now, but her confident and independent bearing reminded me of Esther. In those early years, Isabel wasn't nearly as pudgy as she became after bearing her children, and she was considered quite attractive. She sat mounted on a white steed that looked bred especially for her, such was the ease with which she rode him. *She* didn't have to apply for a permit like we do for mules during this accursed war, I thought.

Although her clothes were elegant — she wore vestments of gold and purple, richly adorned with large gems — she didn't seem preoccupied by her looks or royal trappings. Rather, she sat with the cool confidence inspired by the knowledge that her authority would be respected no matter how she appeared, and that her every need would be attended to while in our midst.

One thing I found odd was the fact that, instead of a scepter, she held a white embroidered cloth in her right hand that she used to cover her nose and the lower half of her face. I had to think for a second before realizing that it must have been because Triana smelled badly to her, or she feared we would somehow make her sick. If Triana smelled, I thought, *I'd* never been able to notice, and it had certainly never made *me* sick. But then again, I was hardly a queen.

"Good people of Triana," she began, addressing us all. "I am your queen, Isabel, and I have come to view Sevilla today." She looked like she wanted to get this part over with quickly. "I have heard that Sevilla is a city in need of order, and that this has become a place where sin and mayhem have ruled for far too long."

She stopped and looked at the faces around her. I remember thinking that she was wasting her time with the people of our quarter; we, after all, were not involved in violence against the *conversos*, the brigands who conducted highway robberies and made towns and roads unsafe, and had nothing to do with the battles that the Duke of Guzmán Sidonia, a distant relative of mine, and his enemy, Ponce de León. These two had fought for years, nearly embroiling the region in civil war. We in Triana kept to ourselves and bothered no one, besides the occasional sailor or nobleman who got his pockets picked upon arriving in our port on his way to Triana's many tabernas.

"What is the principal activity of this place?" she asked, bringing me back to what was going on.

We looked at each other, hoping to find an answer, but then a sailor's voice from behind us rang out, "Drinking wine and dancing, Majesty!"

"I see," she continued, forcing a smile while trying to ignore the comment. "Am I to understand that many of your community are gypsies?"

"Yes, that is true, we are Romany, your Ladyship," said a voice. Every head turned to see who had spoken. It was Manfariel.

Isabel turned and trotted her white horse over to the side of the circle where he stood. He held his ground and did not seem intimidated. She sat for a moment regarding him, as if trying to choose the right words before proceeding. She wrapped her petticoat a little more snugly around her torso and said, "When you arrived some time ago, the people of our country looked upon you with interest, fascination, even. You were a new and exotic people in our midst."

"Yes?" Manfariel put forth in a respectful tone. I sensed a slight nervous edge to his voice that I hadn't heard before.

"One might now begin to wonder why it is that you are still here. What are your intentions in Castile?"

Manfariel looked confused. I felt sure that no one had ever asked him such a question before.

"I can't speak for all of my people, but myself, I hope to have a safe place to live, a place we're not chased out of, like how we were chased out of our land of Sind so long ago—"

"Your land of Sind?" Isabel sneered, cutting him off. "Spare me. You never came from such a place." For a moment she sat without saying anything, letting the feel of her authority permeate the air. "You're nothing but the banished sons of Cain. You were the treacherous villains who made the nails that crucified Christ at the hands of your friends, the Jews. Then you were banished to roam the world forever, no better than them or the worshippers of Mohammad, those Moorish Idolaters."

The queen was wrong, and, because of that, I felt laughter welling up inside of me. As much as I tried to stifle it, a chuckle burst forth.

The queen turned toward where I stood, and moved in my direction. Amazingly, my first thought was of how relieved Manfariel must have been that she had stopped tormenting *him*.

"Who is that laughing?" The circle parted to reveal me as I tried, once again, to suppress my laughter. She stood in front of me, glowering down from the horse, as the crowd held its breath. The cavaliers and the ladies of the entourage watched me with apparent surprise.

"Why do you laugh?" She shifted nervously, her voice cracking. "What is so amusing, boy of flaming hair?"

"I'm so sorry," I began. "It's just that you are *wrong*." Could it really be that her tutors had been inferior to my beloved Father Sebastián?

"*Wrong*? Wrong about *what*?" she crossed her arms over a gold-thread bodice and arched her brows.

"For one thing, about the Moors. They don't worship idols. In fact, they're forbidden to do so. They worship God, whom they call Allah, but they do not worship Mohammad. If you study our Tower of Gold here, left by the Moors, you will see no images or idols."

151

I paused, wondering if it was wise for me to continue. One of my problems as a youth was that I couldn't stop my tongue once it began wagging. This time, speaking required prudence.

"Mohammad was the prophet they believe brought and completed God's message," I said, choosing my words with care. Who was *I* to lecture Her Majesty? "But they don't think he's divine, as Jesus is for Christians. That's why their art has no human imagery — its designs alone are to give one a feeling of the infinite." My education was really beginning to pay off, it seemed.

I saw smirks among our party, and I glanced at a man I knew who was Muslim, a Moor whose name happened to be Mohammad, a common name among his people. I pictured a crowd worshipping my occasional chess partner as he stood on an altar, his turban tall and a perplexed look on his face, and this made me chuckle again, even as I tried to stop. As I laughed, a few of my friends began to join me, while others looked on in horror as the scene unfolded.

I really should have stopped then, but something made me continue. "There's no need to feel any animosity toward the Muslims as a Christian. Do you know what Mohammad once said to his followers? That they should say unto the Christians, 'Their God and my God are one.'"

Now, even some members of Isabel's party were smirking discreetly at how she was being shown up by this ragged boy. There were ladies, knights, and prelates leaning on crosiers, and even one man dressed with the red and gold embroidered overcoat of a royal herald. One of the *caballeros*, a confident-looking man I later learned was named Pulgar, said, "The boy speaks the truth, m'lady. The Moors do not worship any idol."

I thought that, if she had ever employed Moorish guards as her brother had, she would have known all this. She had only to study our Castilian history as well; Alfonso the Wise once said, "Let the Moors live among the Christians while preserving their own faith and not insulting ours."

Isabel studied me for a long moment, obviously trying to gain back some of her dignity. I nearly felt sorry for her, as she looked hopelessly embarrassed. I wondered what she would have said if she had known that my ancestors had helped her ancestor, Fernando III of Castile, expel the Moors of Sevilla over two centuries before.

She looked to her left, and her gaze settled on Esther and Ostelinda. They had not given in to the temptation of laughter, but rather stood by stoically, waiting for the party to leave us and continue on to the city's center. Esther wore one of her simple, nondescript outfits that made her look like a boy, the kind that made the nocturnal escapes from her home easier. Ostelinda held Pobea close to her, a protective hand on his shoulder.

The queen leaned forward in her saddle. As she approached my friends, she crossed her arms over her chest again and said to Esther, "You have the face of a *Jewess*." I wondered at this accusatory tone and her harsh words, as I had heard that she had many Jews and *conversos* at her court — and that some were even among her favorites. Besides this, the Jews really were good citizens, having reaped the benefits of hard work as moneylenders, merchants and artisans for generations, despite all of their hardships. During those years, I heard that the Jews even contributed over 1,500,000 gold ducats for the war against Granada — no doubt against their wills, for fear of expulsion or worse. Spain is no doubt the worse off for their loss.

"Well," said Esther dryly, "Perhaps that is because I *am* one."

Fresh laughter rolled from the Triana community at this impertinent retort. Esther never was one to mince words or fear reprisal.

Queen Isabel's face turned a deep shade of crimson then, and she looked at Ostelinda and spat at the dust before her feet. "I would not have your children here, woman. This rat-infested gypsy slum is unfit even for *your* offspring." And with that, she turned and rode on to cross the bridge to Sevilla, her entourage following close behind and trying to keep up.

CHAPTER THIRTY TWO

Her arrival in the city, unlike that of Triana, can best be described as triumphant. I guess it was as different from El Cid's entrée into Burgos as it could be. From what Father Sebastián told me, the people were happy to see — or at least to appease — the young queen, sending some blackamoor slaves dancing wildly out to meet her dressed in all kinds of colors, and nobles and rich *conversos* accompanying her in her route throughout the city. Apparently, people who had known about the arrival of the queen, whose intentions were to "cure Sevilla of its wickedness," had lain out rich tapestries and awnings in addition to those usually stretched from roof to roof across the narrow streets to block the sun and hold in the cool air each morning. They threw jasmines and roses from their gardens in her path and put out their most decorated statues of the Virgin as a sign of warm welcome — and perhaps, I imagined, a subtle, almost servile plea to be gentle.

My parents were among the high nobles and *conversos* — many of whom, like one of Esther's estranged uncles, were members of her court — to accompany her in her cortege. It led from the *plaza de toros* to every quarter of Sevilla, and, eventually, to the cathedral where she prayed at length in front of the Ivory statue of Our Lady of the Kings which, according to legend, her ancestors had carried into battle. From the sounds of it, the procession was almost as elaborate as when she had been crowned in Segovia and anointed with ancient Visigoth oil. She rode on a fresh white stallion wearing all sorts of jewels and royal trappings that day, and the Sword of Justice had been carried before her.

CHAPTER THIRTY-THREE

"Father Sebastián, why is it that you take the time to teach me?" I asked my teacher one day. "You must be so busy most of the time, so how is it that you come to me every week without fail?"

"As someone wise once told me, sharing your knowledge with another is the best way to attain immortality," he said.

It was an exceptionally sunny day, and as the light shone in at a slant on my floor, I was reminded of the sunny day when I had first been banished to my tower several years before. I couldn't believe how quickly the time had passed.

"Father, why is it that there are powerful people in the world, when most of us are so weak?"

"You want to know about the powerful?" He put down the book he'd been consulting. "Does this have anything to do with the queen's visit?"

"Yes — the servants tell me she's here in Sevilla. But I mean — how do leaders like her justify their positions?"

"They usually don't have to. You've read enough of the philosophers to know that. They're the leaders, and others simply follow them," he said. I had learned very well by then that he was the kind of man who would subtly draw someone out to elicit certain reactions, thus leading the conversation the way that *he* wanted it to go. He was very clever at this, and it had taken me at least a year before I began to figure out when he performed this rhetorical dance of which I was just now learning to be a willing partner.

"But surely they have some kind of justification for *why* they lead?"

"Sometimes they do, but usually not." He corrected with his plume some error in my penmanship, which still often left much to be desired. "Have you heard of Manrique?" he asked. It was not uncommon for him to ask me random, unrelated questions when it struck his fancy.

"No, padre, I haven't," I said after thinking for a moment.

"Really? I have been remiss in my duties then, haven't I? I've been so busy filling your head with all the wisdom from ages past that I've neglected the best of your own time." He made a *tisking* sound to himself under his breath as he searched for a book in his satchel, which he soon produced. Finding a page, he read me a poem written by a man who had been preoccupied with death since losing his father. I remember it to this very day:

"These powerful kings
whom we see through writings
now past
with cases sad, crying
had good fortunes
disrupted and lost;
so it is that there's no strong thing,
popes and emperors
and prelates of ranking
thus treats them Death
like the cattle-herder
who has nothing."

I sat contemplating this poem for a little while, considering the fact that death, for all its sadness, was at least a just thing that made no distinctions of class or station.

"Padre?"

"Yes?" He put this book aside as well, perhaps sensing that I wanted to ask something difficult, and that he would have to enter into a complicated explanation to indulge my curiosity — which he always did without complaint, unlike my old tutors.

"Father, is God truly all-powerful?"

The old man smiled a bit then, and I guessed that this was a question he had either often asked himself or been asked by others.

"If I were to tell you 'yes', would you then ask me how it is that evil exists also, and that an omnipotent God could allow such a thing?" He folded his hands in his lap.

"Yes — how did you know that I was going to—"

"Because, Rodrigo — you are so much the man I was at your age. I'm not ignorant of the things you must wonder about. I was once young, too. Remember, there is nothing new under the sun."

"So, what is the answer, Father? If he can't destroy evil, it means that he isn't all-powerful. And if he *will* not—"

"Then he isn't all good," he said, interrupting me.

"Well, yes. And if he *does* exist, which I don't doubt Father, but — why would He want us to worship Him?"

"You know..." he said, biting his lip, "Sometimes I can't explain *all* of the answers to you, my boy. Sometimes you will need to allow yourself the chance to live with the questions for a while so that you can find your *own* way into the answers."

I gathered my courage and continued. "If I may ask, Father...what is it that *you* believe?"

He smiled at my persistence, which often, I admit, bordered on the irritating.

He took a breath. "I can tell you what I was *taught*. I was taught that, after the fall from grace, those who rebelled against God were destined to live in the misery of their sin and their separation from Him. I can tell you that Satan is the master of all those who are tempted and fall into wickedness, and that all of mankind lives in the eye of God, that History is but the blink of His eye, and His eternal fury and damnation will soon bring about the second coming, when He will punish the sinners and call His servants home, as He revealed to Saint John...."

His voice trailed off, and we sat in silence for a long time as he paused and looked at me wearily, his lower lip quivering a little, almost as if in fear. It was, I guessed, the fear of being found out, the fear of being tricked into some kind of confession.

"That is what you were *taught*..." I prodded.

"Yes."

"Is that what you *believe*?"

The old man looked very tired then, as if a whole lifetime of teaching, learning and thinking had worn his spirit out, and he had wasted away to a shell of his former self because of the struggle. I remember thinking that this was the first time my tutor had truly seemed old, or anything other than *ageless*, for that matter.

"I think," he said finally, the color faded from his usually jovial face, "that things are going to become very interesting now that the queen is here. I think that she means to *stay*."

CHAPTER THIRTY-FOUR

And so I waited.

I waited for the answers to my questions, but I also waited for Lorenzo to come back for me. I used to dream that he had climbed the rope to my room while I was asleep and we had already left for the East together. I even left it out for him at times, half-hoping that, despite whatever he had to fear, he would take the chance to come back and try to take me with him.

I never shared this hope with anyone, but I think Esther and Ostelinda both knew why I sometimes would slip away from the evening dances, a melancholy look on my face and a bottle of wine in my hand as I sat by the olive trees. I would sometimes walk along looking up at the moon, wondering if my friend saw the same moon as I in some far-off land as he performed for beautiful ladies in luscious courts or other rowdy crowds of gypsies, sailors and runaway slaves — all without me, his dear friend Rodrigo.

But he never came back, nor did any of the others of his troop.

And so I waited, and slowly grew into manhood. I still remained a prisoner of my invisible father; a prisoner, that is, except when I could escape for a while to the freedom of my stolen, raucous nights on the outside, still too afraid to free myself completely from the fear and safety of my own tower prison.

It was the longest, hottest summer of my life. And, as always, Father Sebastián was right. Queen Isabel remained in Sevilla.

CHAPTER THIRTY-FIVE

She soon established herself in our city in every sense of the word. Soon after her arrival, the number of her knights and assistants — who had strange accents and often complained about our "inferior" and "singing" Andalusian way of speaking — was expanded several times over. There was a real question on everyone's mind of how best to handle this new influx of secretaries, prelates and cavaliers. The servants told me that Father had insisted — and Mother had at length relented — on allowing some of the ladies-in-waiting of the young queen's court to be billeted in our home, down below and across the corridor from the glazed, *azulejo*-tiled banquet hall.

I pitied them for having to put up with, as I imagined it, Father's constant harassment.

There was a palpable difference in the mood of the town since the arrival of Queen Isabel. When I would walk about at night, my cape concealing my identity, I sensed none of the relaxed sensuality I had

felt before when stealing through the streets with
Esther or Lorenzo. Where easy laughter had once
wafted on the fragrant evening breeze in the narrow
streets among the pink houses and dog rose, I now
sensed a guarded reserve.

Her Majesty held several audiences with the
people of our city, much like the ones that would
come to Hispaniola years later at the behest of her
husband, who wished to investigate all the abuses
there. Father Sebastián told me she was concerned
about what she called the 'moral situation of the city,'
as well as the many conflicts which had arisen out of
the so-called 'disorderly' years leading up to her visit.
According to what I heard, the plaintiffs who claimed
that they'd been wronged would make their way past
the portcullis and the large, marble columns to the
throne room in the royal *Alcazar*. It was there that the
young queen sat on her large gold dais, dispensing
judgments.

After having subdued other parts of her
kingdom, she wanted to stabilize the life of the cities
of Spain. I heard through friends that she wanted to
begin dispensing her own brand of justice to make
what she considered some 'necessary changes.' After
another visit to Triana — which, thankfully, I was not
there for — and many complaints about the vices that
she had observed there, as well as more complaints
about the Jews and false *conversos*, she decided to take
her quest one step further than a simple hearing of
pleas from the provincial gentry. Soon, she would call
upon none other than the venerable bishop of Cádiz,
Don Alonso de Solis, whose task it was to help her to

investigate and decide what to do about the 'wicked Sevilla' which caused her so much anger and loss of sleep.

I didn't like the sound of that one bit, and neither did anyone else in Triana.

CHAPTER THIRTY-SIX

Now, I don't mean to say that *all* of the monarch's intentions were misguided; that would be far too facile a thing to say. Like anyone, she had her good and bad qualities, and who am I to judge her? The human heart is a deep enigma, a very deep one indeed. It may be said that even after the great expanse of the earth is fully explored, and when there is nowhere *anywhere* to be discovered — why, even then, the heart, with all its hopes and desires, will still remain to us a hopeless, impenetrable mystery. As Father Sebastián always used to say, "The individual is ineffable."

I believe, even after all these years, that she truly thought that what she was did was right and for the general good. Or maybe I'm just a foolish old man to think that.

But who could blame her? She had, after all, just finished codifying the laws of the kingdom. As such, she saw the world through the eyes of an ingenuous jurist who, looking up from a book, can't imagine a world that doesn't fit the rules he'd spent his entire lifetime faithfully writing.

However, all else aside, it soon became apparent that her strictness was having a disastrous effect on the city. I believe that not a single house in all of Sevilla was spared some accusation of wrongdoing. Even my father, a Vargas connected in marriage to the house of Guzmán, was accused of having pilfered money in some of his dealings with powerful merchants. It was a horrible time for many, and even some of those who had nothing to fear left Sevilla under the cover of night. From what I heard from Esther, who had heard it from someone else, the city lost something like four thousand people in just that first week of judging alone. People had their fortunes wiped out and their lives destroyed by one swoop of the pen at Isabel's court.

What the queen didn't grasp is that the commercial life of Sevilla, as in many places, rested upon a complex system of informal agreements and unspoken dependencies. For example, if the wine-maker couldn't pay the money he owed the cobbler or the weaver in the summer, he would agree to pay later in the year, perhaps with silver or perhaps with wine. The problem that the queen failed to realize is that life and people — I mean *real life* and *real people* — do not conform to the easy ideals set down on paper. It is also important to remember that her brother, Enrique, had almost bankrupted the royal treasury thanks to his decadent lifestyle, so people mostly bartered instead of using the currency in circulation. So, as in the case of the winemaker and the cobbler, some were made to pay enormous sums for the fact that the queen just happened to have arrived in the *summer*. As you can guess, at least half of the people were unhappy with her rulings.

The people of Triana were largely unaffected — and if truth be told, perhaps a bit *amused* — by the events set in motion by Queen Isabel. It all seemed such a mad circus to us, and we were not concerned because of one simple fact: Triana folk were not, for the most part, property owners. Things could be disturbed, and land redistributed to the royal heart's delight for all we cared. Nevertheless, we agreed when the Bishop of Cádiz, who had been implored to visit Sevilla by many wives, children and family members of the fugitives, made an impassioned plea for Her Majesty's clemency. He pointed out that God metes out justice along with mercy, and that Her Majesty would be wise to do the same. "If not, Sevilla will soon be completely depopulated," he said.

Ah, justice and mercy. The duel between these two was not confined to Sevilla, as I was to find out. I doubt, in fact, that the struggle will ever be closed between those who favor justice and harsh punishment and those who are merciful until the end.

This time, the plea for mercy did not fall on deaf ears. Even Isabel was smart enough to realize when she was bested. Her pride was not such that it prevented her from discerning which battles were worth fighting and which best left for another day.

If only we could have seen what was coming, the people of Triana would never have laughed the way we did when the queen relented on her quest to try every case in Sevilla.

She would now, it was announced, focus her energies on a different, more elusive problem, the only one, in fact, to which she had not granted amnesty.

The problem of heresy.

CHAPTER THIRTY-SEVEN

Apparently, Isabel was concerned with finding out who was a sincere Christian and who was, in her words, a 'heretical, backsliding, non-believer.'

But all that was to come later.

In the short-term, she was involved with various kinds of intrigue between, of course, the Duke of Guzmán Sidonia and the Marquis of Cádiz, Rodrigo Ponce de León, both very distant cousins of mine. Both men hoped for her support, but she played them off each other, sending them on missions to help regain lands and fortresses the royal family had lost under her brother in his struggles against the moors or the Portuguese. I must say that Her Highness had a way of making things turn her way. Also, her husband, King Fernando, was to join her soon. The two hoped for a male heir, as it became apparent that the queen was with child.

They were, I would realize later, methodically plotting to grow their strength in Europe after consolidating their power in the Peninsula.

The people of Sevilla breathed a bit easier that fall and winter, as the queen had decided, at least for the moment, to relent on her campaign to rid our city of its so-called "wickedness." A pregnant woman, the queen turned her attentions now toward her family, and she began to teach her daughter, also named Isabel, to be a patroness of the arts. A certain man of the cloth, whose renown was considerable, was chosen to be her tutor and to meet with her almost daily. His schedule, by royal decree, allowed him little time to do anything else, including visiting a certain lonely boy in a certain lonely tower.

The queen was soon to be disturbed, however, by the knowledge that the Portuguese were becoming rich by a method I would soon find out about the hard way, as I yearned for adventure, discovery, and a chance to escape the confines my father had placed on me.

The time had come. I no longer had even Father Sebastián to guide me. I had become a man, and it seemed that I had to do something *then* or *never*.

And events fell together all too well.

CHAPTER THIRTY-EIGHT

"Do you love him?" I asked Esther.

"Who, Manfariel?" she said, knowing that each of us knew whom the other meant.

"Of *course*, Manfariel. Who else?" I asked with a laugh.

Esther and I walked along one of the paths that meandered along the river, hand in hand as always under the cool, moonlit sky — two old friends between whom there could be no secrets. The sounds of the guitars and castanets of Triana were barely audible in the distance, and we heard no crickets singing in the still air.

"Well...let's just say that he's the most tenacious of the men in my life," she said.

"Only the most tenacious? Nothing more than that?" I asked, squeezing her hand and teasing her.

She smiled at me, and the gentle coyness of her green eyes told me that her secret had been found out.

"I thought we'd been discreet. How did you know?" she asked.

"Oh, come, Esther. It's always been clear that you care for him. And when he looks at you—"

"What *about* when he looks at me?" She turned and asked abruptly. I wondered if she had a difficult time interpreting her lover's feelings.

I grinned then, and said, "When he looks at you — I can easily see that he loves you."

She looked relieved, and for the first time of our friendship, I saw her make a lighthearted laugh — or almost a kind of girlish giggle. I thought about when I had first met her, and how much of a woman she had become since then.

And how much of a man *I* had become as well.

"Yes," she confessed, "I love him. It's so strange, you know — I never thought that I *would* fall in love. And I never thought it could be with a gypsy."

It's true. Whenever I saw them, they seemed like a pair of turtledoves, like the ones mother kept in her chamber by the window.

"Does it bother you that you're of different peoples? Your family would never agree to a marriage with a non-Jew…and the Romany might not allow it, either — even with *you*."

"No, they never would. My family still wants me to marry Enrique Cansino. But that will never happen. He's even paid me the necessary courtship visits, but I've always done my best to ignore him. I shan't stand under the wedding canopy with him."

"Why not?" I asked, already knowing the answer.

"Have I *ever* let my family dictate what I would do, Benja?" she said.

"No. No, I suppose you never have," I said.

"The Talmud tells us that woman came from the rib of man on his side, so as to be his equal, under his arm, to be protected, and from beside his heart, so as to be loved. And Enrique doesn't make me feel any of those things."

"Oh," I said.

"Besides, I would never marry a *converso*. You should know that more than anyone."

To this I offered no reply, knowing that the less said the better.

"I've found my true family among the Romany, Benja. I will always remain a Jew, and a proud one at that. But — I have learned that I could never live without both worlds. Does that make any sense?"

"Oh yes. I have grown quite accustomed to living a double life as well," I said.

I stopped speaking and realized that she was looking at me in that quizzical, knowing way of hers. I tried to change the subject, but she took my arm and fixed me with a steady gaze as she asked, "What about *you*?"

"What about me *what*?" I felt sweat on my back and palms, knowing what she was going to ask.

"Well, you have known so many people in Triana. Whom do you love? I know that you love Ostelinda, but as a sister, much the way you love me...but tell me, my dear friend, you must have loved, and longed for something more than the travels you're always talking about. You must have. Come, you *must* tell me."

I stared deeply into her green eyes, but could not bring myself to tell her the truth, the secret that I'd kept to myself for so long, unable to reveal.

I tried for a moment to say something, but only a pathetic sound of embarrassment escaped my lips.

It was then that I was saved — or perhaps condemned — as a man's deep voice spoke from behind.

"Is it adventure you crave?"

We turned around, stunned, to see a tall, dark man emerge from the shadows. I realized after a second that he'd been following us.

Esther's hand protectively tightened in mine as she asked, "Who are you? What do you want?" in the most threatening voice she could muster. Our palms were so wet together that I wondered which one of us was more afraid. By holding her hand, I could feel her pulse beating like the heart of a small bird, strong, confident and steady, like the day we had met four years before when she'd pulled me to safety.

"Easy, easy, no need to be alarmed," the man said, approaching us with his hands held up in a peaceful gesture. I could tell by the lilting and slightly nasal way he spoke that he was Portuguese, and probably a sailor.

"Why have you followed us?" Esther demanded, trying in vain to frighten this unwelcome intruder who had so rudely interrupted our conversation.

"No reason, really. I just wanted to speak to your friend," he said in a voice smooth and confident.

"Go sing it to the goats," she said, using a phrase we'd picked up from the gypsies. "We were in the middle of something," she said with more than a note of defiance in her voice.

The two stood there, nose to nose in an absurd showdown about who would have the chance to speak to me. I looked back and forth between Esther and this mysterious man. Where had I seen him before? I tried to think...

Of course! I remembered when I'd been playing a moving song a few days before around the fire; the bottle of wine passed back and forth between Manfariel and me as we sang a song to which Ostelinda had slowly danced. It was a song we had composed about Marco Polo and a young man's desire to retrace his famous trip to the East. My thoughts wandered to Lorenzo that night, and as Manfariel plucked at the strings and I sang about adventure and kingdoms and beautiful, far-off queens, I had noticed this man sitting across the fire from me, alone, his eyes locked on mine.

I'd tried to look away, but I couldn't avoid his steady, blue eyes that had made me squirm and miss a few notes of the song. Manfariel had turned and glanced my way, knowing why, and hadn't said anything. He was the only one to see.

"Don't worry, Esther," I said, then turning to the man and speaking in broken Portuguese. "I'll listen to what you've got to say," I said, trying to sound steady and sure of myself.

CHAPTER THIRTY-NINE

Long before the rumors of my death began to circulate, two women sat side-by-side by the river, talking. The conversation was relayed to me many years later, and went something like this:

"I didn't know who he was, and I didn't trust him. He said that he was known as Francisco, and that he *had* to talk to Benja right then. He claimed it couldn't wait — it was something about going to India or *the Indies*. What could I do?"

"Did you try to leave with *Benjacito*, leaving the man behind?" Ostelinda asked, her dark eyes focused steadily on those of her friend and using one of the nicknames the gypsies used for me.

Esther shifted uncomfortably. "No. It's hard to explain. He was just *overwhelming*. He had a hypnotic voice, and it was hard to refuse him. I felt that he could have whatever he wanted, just by asking for it in that smooth way of his." She looked at her companion, ashamed that she hadn't been stronger. "That doesn't sound very logical, does it?"

Ostelinda put her hand on her friend's arm. "No, it doesn't. But I understand. I *know* how men can be."

She could empathize all too well. But that didn't make her feel any better about having left me with that mysterious mariner she didn't trust, the one who'd been roaming all over the earth — the one who'd made her clasp my hand so tightly it almost hurt.

She'd known that she would lose me to him that night. She had sensed that he would exert his will over me, and that nothing she could do would stop him.

"I was, however, able to give him one thing that I meant to before Francisco went off with him," Esther said. "It was the reason I asked him to go on that walk with me in the first place."

"And what was that, dear one?" Ostelinda asked with tears forming in her eyes.

"I gave him a necklace that held a ruby — a red gem that my grandfather gave me when I was young. He told me that, one day, I too would give it away to someone special, and that it would bring courage, strength and protection. Now, no matter what happens to him — he will never forget me — or *us*."

The older woman drew her closer then, and held her as the tears poured forth from both of them.

CHAPTER FORTY

"Jump, damn you, boy!" Francisco yelled.

"I don't know if I can."

"Of *course* you can. Do it."

Francisco and I had been up all night long, and we had drunk several bottles of wine. I felt sick all over.

"You want to know about the world, don't you Benja?" he had asked me, his teeth showing in the moonlight as we walked along by the river. His arm was around my neck, and he spoke with his face close to mine. "I've heard you speak, and I've heard your songs. I know what it is you dream of."

"Yes, I *do* want to hear about the world," I had said meekly, not knowing what else to say and confused by his sudden attention. Most people didn't pay me much attention, after all.

"Well then, I shall tell you stories!" He cried, jumping atop a rock that lay on the path by the river. "What do you want to know? I'll tell you stories about everywhere I've been: Rome, England, Constantinople. Why, I'll even tell you all about *India*."

"*India?*" I asked, trying to hide my surprise. "Have you really been there?" He knew how to get my attention, that Francisco. He was a clever man.

"*Been* there?" He still stood on the rock, and began to wave his arms wildly. "Of *course* I've been there. I've ridden elephants there taller than me on this rock." He jumped up to show me how tall the elephants were in that distant place. "Not only that, but I've seen entire cities where the cupolas of the houses were made of gold. I've seen emperors with harems and a hundred servants and ladies with a dozen lovers. I've seen all these things and many, many more. It's a land full of expensive Calicut spices, exotic goods, and aloes that could make our fortune."

I wondered if he had seen Lorenzo during his travels, but I dared not ask him that. "Have you been to the Kingdom of Sind?"

"*Where?*" he asked, sounding confused and annoyed at the same time.

"Never mind," I said.

"I don't know of that place. But I bet I can do better than that," he continued. "I have seen enough to become rich. *Very* rich." Then he jumped down from the rock and took my hand in his. He looked straight into my eyes and said, "Benja. Do you want to be rich, too?"

I didn't know what to say to him before then, but I felt myself pulling away. I had never much cared for wealth or possessions, and I certainly didn't want to become like my parents.

"Not so fast," he said, holding me tight. "I know you, Benja. I know you better even than you

181

know yourself." I wondered at what he had just said, but I stopped trying to escape his grasp and decided to listen.

"I know you," he continued, relaxing his grip. "We're of the same breed, you and I. I've been watching you, paying attention if you will, noting the little things. Yes, I was once like you. You, my young friend, can never be happy in a place like this. Am I right?" He looked at me and waited for an affirmation before continuing. I nodded, and began to imagine some of the things I could do if I were wealthy.

"You can never stay in one town, even if it *is* Sevilla with Triana right next door. No — you were *born* to travel, *made* for grandeur and adventure. I'm making you the offer of a lifetime, Benja. I need men, and *you* must come with on my next trip. You can't throw your life away on the *priesthood*."

"How did you—" I began, dumbfounded. Only a few friends knew of my family's desire for me to take the vows. Just how closely *had* this mysterious stranger been scrutinizing me? I somehow slipped free and began walking, then *running* away from him. He ran after me, yelling, "Just think about it — you could come back here years from now filthy rich, in a ship full of gold and pearls. Imagine what your family would think *then*."

Then he said something that finally made me stop:

"You wouldn't need a *rope* to get home then."

No one knew about my rope. No one except Esther, and, I supposed, Father Sebastián.

And, of course, Lorenzo.

But I couldn't guess how Francisco could have known about it. Unless—

He nodded slowly in the dim light.

"Yes. I have been following you, my boy. And I have cut down your rope, cut it down with my knife. There's no way you can go home now." With a feral smile, he took out a dagger he had kept concealed in his cloak. The polished blade shown in the moonlight and I wondered if it had ever been used to cut human flesh. He held it up for me to see, and then he brandished it in front of me, daring me to try to flee again.

He smiled a carnal smile as he knew that he had me right where he wanted me. He threw the dagger into a nearby log, and dared me to answer his challenge by picking it up.

After a moment's hesitation, I bent and plucked it from the wood.

"Then we leave tomorrow morning!" he said, rubbing his hands in anticipation.

After I agreed to go with him, he put the knife away and smiled.

"Tonight we celebrate, my young friend!"

Then, we drank wine, and I became drunk as I tried to forget the dread I felt.

I decided to make the best of a bad situation, and began at first to chuckle, then to laugh, and finally to howl out loud. Perhaps this was, in fact, a blessing; I was going to travel like Marco Polo! I was finally going to leave my home, and do what I wanted to do — go out and see the world. I began to believe that this was a good thing, and that now was finally my chance —

perhaps God's will for me, then or never — to leave, and have my *own* adventures in a far-off land.

So, why was I hesitating now that he had brought the boat around to where we'd slept and was asking me to jump?

I couldn't refuse now. I had no clothes, as he had scooped them up with him as he left to fetch the boat from the shipyard. I lay in the early morning sun on the thick branch where we'd slept after a late-night dip, even though I still couldn't swim. I suppose I could have run off naked and barefoot to Triana where my friends would have laughed and taken me in; But even if that worked, what then? It could only be a matter of time before the servants would report me missing and Father would tear Triana apart looking for me. And if he found me in Triana, he would surely kill me or beat me, not to mention harm my friends.

I closed my eyes and thought about the time that Father Sebastián had told me that if only my faith were as large as a mustard seed, I'd be capable of moving mountains.

I tried to pray, but the only thing I could think of was that verse from Ecclesiastes that says "All streams run to the sea, but the sea is not full."

I whispered a sad farewell to my friends — and then I jumped.

CHAPTER FORTY-ONE

Once we met up with Francisco's crew, we made our way along the Guadalquivir, slowly heading south and west. We passed town after town as we moved away from Sevilla. We passed numerous fields of onions and small, isolated farmhouses where men who worked at cutting and piling brush with their hoes would sometimes stop and wave as they wiped the sweat from their brows.

As we went on, my trepidation was replaced by an exhilaration that words can't describe. I was free, finally free! Of course I'd miss those I loved back home — but such was life. After all, as Francisco had said, I would go out and have my *own* adventures and return a rich man.

If only I hadn't been so horribly naïve.

***

It didn't take long to reach the sea — I only remember it taking a day or two. I remember waving to shepherds as they tended their flocks and called, "Riu, riu, chiu!" to each other to say that all was well. When we reached the sea, just past the port of

Sanlúcar de Barrameda, I remember seeing the swirling, foamy waters of the river as it met the sea. I was afraid we would capsize in the violent currents and riptides that rocked our little frigate. But as I should have expected, Francisco and his little crew, of which I had become a part, got through this without a problem. After all, I'd learned by then how to position the sails to catch the wind at the appropriate times. He taught me how to tell time with an hourglass, and this helped me to navigate with some of the old charts he kept in a leather satchel.

He'd even taken care of all of the provisions, so I didn't go hungry. We feasted on beans, salted mutton, apples and pouches of watery wine during those days. We tacked the sails, and began to sail south and east along the Andalusian seacoast. We saw places like the bustling port of Algeciras where Moors did active commerce with Christians, and the mighty rock of Gibraltar, which the Moors had called *Jebel Tariq*, and the Pillars of Hercules which stood like lonely guards at the end of the world.

Besides advising us to be on the lookout for Barbary Pirates, Francisco said he needed to make several stops before going to Lisbon and then departing on our journey.

Lisbon! I could scarcely believe my ears as I heard the word. I was going to visit a grand city — and a capital, to boot.

I would sit on the bow of the ship sometimes, my fair skin burnt and my hair an even lighter red than usual. Francisco would sometimes have to come up and make me come to bed at night as I lay watching the sky. I was unable to sleep, such was my excitement and anticipation about going to the East.

"Will I really be rich, Francisco?" I asked him one night as I lay staring up at the stars by which I was learning to navigate with the help of a compass that found Polaris without fail.

"Richer than your wildest dreams, my friend. But you will have to do exactly as I say. Do you trust me, boy?"

"Yes," I said, trying to sound sure of myself.

"That's good, that's as it should be. Because, if you don't, you'll die on your own, like a lost pup."

***

The other men on our ship, mostly a gang of ragamuffin Portuguese sailors, didn't associate much with me. Barriers of class, language and age separated us, and when I did speak, they often scoffed at what I said. Nevertheless, they'd sometimes speak to me very slowly in their language, which I had learned to speak — although, like the Italian dialects, not without mistakes.

We arrived in Lisbon, the capital of what Father Sebastian had called 'the most advanced country in all of Europe.'

CHAPTER FORTY-TWO

The splendor of that city was unlike anything I'd ever seen.

It was full of shops, merchants, and tradesmen. There was a bustling sense of activity I'd never known growing up in my beloved, lazy Sevilla. I'd seen quite a lot of things in Triana, but this was something else altogether.

I was first impressed by how organized the seafaring Portuguese were. For example, Francisco had to show a detailed manifest before docking, and the port inspectors seemed bent on finding anything wrong. This they did without a problem, and ordered my friend to scrub his deck and get rid of the boat's vermin. This took several days for us to do, and I had to scrub with the rest of the men.

On land, there were parakeets, monkeys, bananas, and plants brought from the islands Portugal had recently claimed, like Cape Verde, Porto Santo, the Azores, and the Madeiras islands. I also saw, for the first time, very rich and very poor people living side by side. I saw newly-rich men dressed in the finest clothes, with rich red robes and long beards, attended by up to a dozen servants and slaves. They went from bank to tavern, passing by wrinkled old men who held out their hands for silver coins. At Rossio plaza, a place bordered on all sides by an arched palace, I saw an old beggar whose face was bubbled up and disfigured beyond recognition. He held a painted picture of himself as a young man, his sad eyes imploring me to be generous. I gave him two *cruzados*.

"What'd you do *that* for?" asked Francisco, shaking his head.

"He looked like he needed some help," I answered.

"*Don't*," he reprimanded. "That was too much. Besides, it only encourages laziness and roguery."

I walked around the city for an entire day while Francisco said he needed to take care of some business at the port. He gave me a few coins that were to last me a day and a night.

"Have some fun, amuse yourself, and later — find yourself some whores," he counseled me as I walked away. "And don't forget to be here at the port tomorrow morning when we weigh anchor."

I promised I wouldn't forget, and would amuse myself, though not the way he had in mind. Instead, I set out to explore the city.

I walked along beside the far side of the port, by large, single-decked lateen-rigged caravels. In a place known as Tanoaria square, I came to a large building with three parts through which I saw lots of people entering and exiting. I saw an old man, a beggar, standing by one of the wharves. I asked him what the building was.

"It's called the *Casa dos Escravos*," he said in a thick Lisboan accent. *The Slave House*. "When the ships come in from Africa, that's where the slaves go first to be dealt with. Look over there," he said. I looked where he pointed to, and spied a newly arrived ship at the dock. "The Blackamoors — the ones that survive the trip here — go into that first area. They're inspected, recorded, fed, and kept there until a sale day."

"When are *those?*" I asked.

"You're in luck. There's one this afternoon, if you want to watch."

"I don't think I want to," I said. It all seemed so brutal to me, the act of capturing the Africans and bringing them to our shores only to sell them off.

"You should come anyway. It's a real sight. The selling goes on in that square right over there, near where the carracks and the galleons are moored."

***

The selling was brutal, as I knew it would be. Prospective buyers came up and pried the Africans' mouths open to inspect them, grabbed them, felt them, made them bend over and jump up and down, made bids for them, then haggled over the price. The slaves screamed and sobbed at being separated from their friends and relations, yet there seemed to be no regard for such ties as they were auctioned off, one by one. I thought about how my teacher would have been furious to witness such an affront to human dignity. The ones no one wanted — the sick, the dying, the old and the young — were sent back into the Slave House to await another auction or their deaths, whichever came first.

I thought of those escaped slaves I knew in Triana. They'd slipped away from masters in Sevilla and other areas of Andalusia and Iberia. I thought of their stories — the beatings, the toil, the anger. Had they all been brought to this place, too?

I walked the streets until nightfall when I finally chose a small tavern not far from the port. I drank a few tankards of rotgut and brandy as the men sang seafaring songs and exchanged stories, always, of course, in Portuguese.

I wanted desperately to go home. I wanted to see Esther and Ostelinda. And, of course, Father Sebastián. But I knew that it was too late now. There was no turning back.

And besides, tomorrow, I would be on a marvelous voyage to the East.

So why didn't I feel excited anymore?

***

"*Senhor*! *Senhor Rodrigo*!" the voice rang out. "You must get up, sir. Your boat — she'll leave without you!"

I had slept too late. I jumped out of bed and grabbed my small sack, which I slung over my shoulder. "You must go now, sir," he said to me in broken Castilian. *El capitán* has sent for you—"

"Yes, I know. I'm sorry," I grumbled in annoyance, not recognizing the attempt to speak my language, and tossing the innkeeper three *cruzados* and

191

the rest of the *maravedis* I had in my purse. I tried to shake the headache away, but it was no use.

"Thank you sir," he yelled to me as I ran down the stairs and out the door into the street of the Moorish quarter.

I heard later that he'd bet a gold coin that I would never come back alive.

He almost won his bet.

***

"Benja, where have you been? The ship — she's about ready to set sail. Jump aboard."

Francisco was standing next to one of the caravels, pointing to the narrow plank they used for boarding.

"But is this one of the ships used for—" I began to protest.

"Don't be a fool, Rodrigo. Would I ever lie to you? Do you remember what I told you about following my orders exactly?" he asked, gripping me by the shoulders and holding me in front of him. "We have special permission from Alfonso, *the King of Portugal*, to use this ship for our expedition."

"Really?" I asked, hesitating.

"Yes. Now *get on*, for the love of God. *Deus meu!*"

He let go of me, and I had to walk across a quivering plank in order to board the ship. Once I was on, the plank was pulled aboard by a dark, heavily scarred man I hadn't seen before, and the last of the ropes was unmoored. A graying man with a thick book and several ink quills who looked like some sort of clerk jumped out of the ship at the last moment. We began to move.

"What about you?" I shouted.

"Don't worry about me. I'll be along on the next one!" he yelled, cupping his hands to his mouth.

I looked around at the port as we pulled away. I didn't see any other ships being readied for voyage.

I looked at Francisco again. He was just standing there with a loathsome smile on his face. I looked at the man who had just pulled the plank aboard, who was wearing a stylishly embroidered silk shirt and a turban that covered some of his curious head-scar. He looked away from me, but nodded at the man on shore who had jumped out. This man pulled out his purse and began to count out to Francisco what looked like a lot of money.

I wandered about the ship, which was breathtakingly large. Everywhere, men were at work hoisting up sails and lugging heavy sacks from place to place. Finally, an older man I recognized as the captain approached me. He wore a white sailor's smock, brown, billowy breeches, and a red-feathered cap that set him apart from other men on board.

"*Bom dia*," he greeted me in his native language. "Good morning. We're going to be working together, you and I."

"Oh?" I asked, sounding less than enthused at the prospect.

"You are to be my *pagen*...em, *cabin boy*," he explained in Castilian. "That is, until you become a fully-fledged *lanzado*. Until then, you will work with the scrivener and Kinjay, the interpreter."

"This boat isn't headed to the Indies, is it?" I fought back tears as I finally realized what was happening. I couldn't swim, so there was no hope of escape.

At this, the captain bellowed a deep, hearty laugh. "He thought he was going to *India*," he yelled to the men working around us. "I bet you thought you would get to be a Chinese king, eh? And be able to get around the damned Ottomans. Hey, Alberto — Francisco tricked another one with that stupid story!"

I turned away from the men, and tried to keep calm. The saltwater spray pricked at my eyes, and I told myself that my tears were but drops from the sea. I couldn't believe I had let Francisco fool me, and that I had been so pathetically naive. I wanted to jump overboard and try to make for land, but I knew better. I would surely drown or be attacked by big fishes if I attempted such a thing.

"Cheer up, laddy," said one of the sailors, sauntering up to me. "You'll be able to have any darkie girl you want as a *lanzado*. Trust me, you'll have your pick down there."

"Your *pinto* will get lots of use in Guinea!" cried one of the grommets, a dirty, bearded man with no teeth who called down from the rope on which he balanced. He pointed at me, grinned, and then gyrated his hips as one grimy hand grabbed his crotch and he made a toothless grimace. This brought howls of laughter from the men around me, including the captain. I was the only one not in on the joke.

I felt sick. I wanted to go home. I would have given anything to have Esther there with me to defy these men and their brutish ways. She would have known what to say or do.

But there was no one there to defend me this time.

I was all alone, and I held the ruby necklace that Esther had given me under my shirt as the boat headed out to sea and the white sands of Lisbon grew to no more than a speck.

CHAPTER FORTY-THREE

"In nomine patris et Filii et Spiritus Sancti."

Bartolomé broke the bread and gave communion to the Indians of his *encomienda*. It was Easter, and he had just delivered a sermon about the passion of Christ, his death and subsequent resurrection. He spoke about how Jesus had been tried before Pilate, and how he had been persecuted and crucified. But the words felt hollow. They were well-learned passages from pages that had long since failed to stir the priest's heart or move his soul with joy.

After drawing the service hastily to a close, he was soon on his way down the stone-lined path which led to the house where Don Rodrigo sat waiting in his hammock, his breakfast long since finished and cleared away.

"So where was I, Bartolomé? Oh, yes, I was on my way to Africa, against my will, and there was no turning back..."

***

We spent a long time at sea. It seemed to me like several weeks, but I doubt that it could have been *that* long.

I was aboard the *Santa Lucía*, but she was nicknamed the *María Luisa* after the bastard daughter of the captain, Joao. It was one of the single-decked lateen-rigged vessels, as were most of the Portuguese slave-trading ships in those days. This triangular-sail design, I was soon to find out, was the best for navigation, handling especially well in waters where the wind changes quickly.

"She's a hundred tons of fine Portuguese work, my boy," the dozen or so *marinheiros*, or able seamen, bragged to me. "She can carry up to a hundred-fifty slaves easy," said one man. "Two hundred if we really cram 'em in."

Besides the dozen *marinheiros*, there was about half that number of lesser-ranking grommets — who were usually seamen-in-training-as well as the captain. Then there was the pilot, a quiet, thoughtful man who spoke little and, I soon realized, was far more respected by the crew than even the captain while at sea. There was the scrivener, a precise and dull man named Jerome, Kinjay, the African interpreter, and then, finally, there was *I* — the captain's cabin boy and, against my will, *lanzado*-in-training.

I spent most of my time doing undignified chores for the captain, who was a boorish bear of a man in whose cabin I also had to sleep. I tried to keep out of everyone's way, and not to fall too sick, as I had

197

not yet gotten my 'sea legs' and the rocking of the ship kept me in a constant state of nausea. I was to spend at least one hour a day with Kinjay, whose job it was to teach me some Wolof, his native language, and train me in the art of being a *lanzado*. I think they must not have known where to place me for a while, because Wolof was not going to do me any good where I finally ended up, except years later in the *real* Indies.

A *lanzado*, as I learned, was a white man who lived among the Africans. It would thus be my job to live as they lived, learn their language or languages, and, most important, to organize the buying, selling and assembling, of slaves to be picked up by caravels like the *María Luisa*. For this, I would be provided with guns, although strictly none of these were to be sold or traded to the Africans. I'd also be given things with which to trade, a small prison, and, of course, some monetary compensation. And I would probably be allowed to live, and perhaps, one day, return home.

"The secret is not to become too soft or to care too much," the captain said one day as I was helping with the rigging of the foredeck. "Caring makes you weak and, worse yet, *vulnerable*. You'll have to be stronger than the darkies, faster than the darkies, and, most important, more *clever*. You'll have to learn how to play them off each other — to sell themselves, and each other. And they *will* do that, and very well," he laughed. "That's the only way that you'll get ahead, or *survive*, for that matter."

***

Kinjay and I sat side-by-side on the bow of the ship one morning after I'd said my five Hail Maries and eaten my ration of onions and salted bread. The rocking wasn't quite as bad as some of the other days, when I felt like I was almost going to die. The sun felt nice as it reflected off the water and shone on my face. We'd already made a stop in the port of Madeira for more supplies and, I was to learn, spices, textiles and trinkets to be traded for gold in a place called the "Gold Coast" — far along the southern coast of Africa, near where Marco Polo called a passage to *Terra Incognita*. Just a few years before, the Portuguese had discovered that gold could be traded freely for almost anything at all, and this was making the Portuguese tons of money. During each of these stops, I had been locked down below to prevent escape. On this day, Kinjay had decided to tell me some of the history of the Portuguese slave trade. Sometimes it was hard to understand him as he spoke a pidgin Portuguese which had a large amount of Wolof and Spanish in it as well, a dialect known simply as the *fala da Guiné*, or 'guinea-talk.' This is what I was able to make out:

"Well…back twenty years ago, the Pope passed a Bull — that's like a law — called the *Romanus Ponti-Ponti-factus* or something like that. That gave control of the Slave Trade, at least way further south, to the Portuguese. But they've gotten all the way to Cape Verde and beyond like that. There's an island near there called Santiago, sort of a base for all trade with Upper Guinea — not that you're gonna see that place. I think you're gonna work at a post which is much, much farther south, closer to Prester John — who's a very big king. It's called the Bijagos Islands. Almost no white men been down there like that. That Santiago — that where I was sent when I was first captured, and then away to Portugal like that."

"Kinjay, may I ask you a question?" I said.

"Ye-e-s," he answered guardedly, as if trying to guess what I was going to say.

"Why it is you're helping the Portuguese? I mean, as an interpreter. I don't understand."

"We-e-ll, after four such trips, I earn me free." His eyes seemed to twinkle at this thought. "Joao — that man my master, you see. He gets a free slave to be sold in my place by the crown every voyage I serve him like that. After two more time, I be free, a free man like that."

"But doesn't it bother you that you're helping them to enslave more and more people? Do you know how those slaves are treated in the land of the White Man?"

"That not *my* problem," he said, looking away with a scowl. "Why should I care about them? They'd do me to get ahead just as I do today!" I could tell I had hit upon something he did not like to think about. Still, I pressed him further.

"What will you do once you've earned your freedom — go back to your home where they must hate you? Or will you attempt to live in Castile or Portugal where, even if you *are* free, you'll always be despised, the lowest of the low?" The only place that I knew for him to go would be Triana.

"No. It's not *like* that," he retorted angrily, tears forming in his eyes, as he jumped to his feet. "I don't need to tell it to you. What the *caray* do you know about Kinjay and what I want like that? White men, all alike, all dirty, filthy dogs!" Then he went away cursing in Wolof, and I felt almost sorry for him.

We didn't talk much more during the rest of that day. I can't say that I much blamed him.

***

Not very long after that day, we stopped in a port known as Arguim. As we entered it, I saw on the starboard side what looked like an enormous fortress. After we had anchored and moored the *María Luisa*, I was once again locked in the captain's quarters, although I could see out of his window. I saw the captain, the scrivener, Kinjay, and a few of the able seamen go down to where a small delegation of white men and some Africans dressed in white-and-gold colored over-shirts and baggy white trousers were standing. They conferred for a few moments, and suddenly they broke into loud, uncontrolled laughter. They laughed deep belly laughs — especially the Africans — at the mysterious joke, and they clapped each other on the back and shoulders as tears rolled down their faces.

Soon, they started to calm themselves. I, of course, could understand none of what they said. I noticed that one of the white men — all of whom, I observed, were dressed like the Africans — had produced a ring of rusty keys. Still chuckling from their joke, the group began to walk down the wooden wharf where the ship was moored and towards the entrance of the fortress.

While some of the crew loaded ivory, gold dust and malagueta pepper on the main deck, what looked like the main door of the fortress opened, and I noticed a few more white men, all of them dressed as the others. The one who had been holding the key ring went in, and soon came out with a few more guards, some of whom were armed with swords. Then, to my amazement, a long chain of Africans, all attached to each other, began to follow them out of the imposingly large structure which looked not unlike any building one would see in Europe — or, for that matter, the tower in which I had until so recently been imprisoned. The slaves were led out, and they walked with a stoic resignation I'm sure that *I* would have been completely incapable of had I been in their place. There were more men than women, and more adults than children and youths; but they all had a resigned look that told me that they had accepted their fate, whatever the voyage they were to undertake would hold for them.

They were marched along the wooden wharf to the entrance of our ship, all the while guarded by the white sentries. The few who dared defy their captors were quickly driven onward by the sticks and scabbards the sentries brandished. By this time, I noticed that there were not one but several partitions to what I had perceived as one whole and uninterrupted length of chain. As they arrived at the hatch of the *María Luisa*, other members of our crew were there to meet them and lead them to the ship's interior.

I, of course, did not observe the process of chaining up the ship's human cargo, remaining as I did in the captain's quarters. But I heard the cries from below, which made the skin on my arms turn to gooseflesh. The protests coming from the Africans were met with sneering insults from the grommets and seamen. These men cursed in Portuguese as they installed the slaves in the hold. These were attached to, I assumed, the large wooden shelves that stood row upon tight row down there, with less than half a man's arm-length separating one shelf from the next. I'm sure that the sight of this helped to evaporate the stoicism of many of the captives. Somewhere down there, a woman screamed and cried out, a young child's voice yelled something back, and the sound of a man's sobbing could be heard above the din.

I looked at Kinjay as he stood alone on the wharf, a bit apart from the other men. Tears stood on his cheek, and he turned away when he met my gaze.

I have never forgotten the look of shame and remorse I saw in his eyes that day.

CHAPTER FORTY-FOUR

The day after our stop in Arguim, I began to feel horribly sick. By this, I don't mean the way I had felt before; now I felt dizzy, I began to shake with fever and diarrhea, and I had to vomit almost constantly.

"You've got the bad air — what the Genoese sailors call the *mal aria*," Joao informed me. "It must be because of all the damn darkies — they bring bad luck and bad air with them everywhere they go."

So I was locked in a special room below for nearly a week, and all the windows of the cabin were shut up and none of the 'bad air' was allowed in, which, the men believed, would make my already precarious condition even worse. I wondered if I had too much or too little blood, phlegm, or bile that was causing such an illness. The captain gave me a vile medicine called theriac for my fever, but this did nothing to help. In fact, it made me want to retch every time I took it. I was refused water, as the men thought that liquid would make my illness grow worse.

I grew delusional, and for hours or days at a time, I kept to that bed in the cabin suffering from the fever and haunted by visions, images of Esther being run through with a sword by Queen Isabel, of Father Sebastián with worms in his rotting eye-sockets, and of course, of Lorenzo running away from my tower into the night, not hearing as I called after him, over and over and over again, the calls trapped forever in my desperately-parched throat.

CHAPTER FORTY-FIVE

Rodrigo had gone to bed, and Bartolomé sat in his hammock watching the waves rolling gently in from the sea. He breathed in deeply the warm, salty Caribbean air, and stretched his arms and legs in relaxation, glad not to be in a situation like the one his guest had just described. It was then that he heard Rodrigo again talking in his sleep; the priest crept to where the old man lay, and, to his horror, this is what he heard Rodrigo say:

"No! So much mess, I never wanted to come here…too many bodies into the sea. No more into the sea!"

***

Throughout that voyage, I can think of very few moments that gave it any kind of feeling of redemption or meaning, Bartolomé. I befriended one of the many gulls that followed our vessel, a majestic bird I named Carlos. How beautiful he always looked flying high in the sky. I'd rescued him from the torments of the grommets one day as they jabbed and poked at him while he lurched about on the deck of our ship, and since then, he'd always seemed to know that I'd give him whatever leftover scraps of food I could find, as well as keep him out of harm's way.

But of course, after we'd picked up the slaves, I was mostly occupied with cleaning or taking care of them in various ways, in addition to the unpleasant task of disposing the occasional body into the sea.

By and by, I learned that my final destination would be, without a doubt, the Bijagos islands, to be reached *after* a further trip to the Gold Coast. I would be dropped off there after the ship took on as much gold as it could carry, and then the vessel full of that, spices, and human cargo would return to Lisbon where Joao would see more riches added to his already impressive store.

But I was not to see or remember this leg of the voyage, as I suffered another bout of the *mal aria*, and once again was locked away in the small cabin where I had been banished before. For yet another ten days, I was later told, I tossed and turned in a delirious frenzy, lingering close to death, always screaming out for Esther and Lorenzo, my blanket soaked through with sweat and tears.

Then, finally, my fever broke, and I was declared healthy enough to brave the night's air once again. So I sat on the foredeck of the ship, and talked with Kinjay about the Wolof people, of Guinea, and its gold. After a while, the African told me a funny story of a spell a witch once had put on him that made him fall in love with one of his uncle's wives. I asked him to tell me another story from his land, and he agreed on the condition that I would sit in a special way: my legs had to be crossed, my back straight up, while he told the story the way an old griot had related it to him. He began with, "There was a story...our legs are crossed...it happened here...it was so...." Then he said, under his breath so no one but I could hear: "*Alhamdulilai Rabil Halamina*, Praise be to the Lord, Allah."

The story he told had an interesting twist and a lesson. It was about a hare who wanted to be smarter than he already was, so he went to Allah, who promised to grant his wish if he would bring him three things: a bag of blackbirds, a calabash of lioness's milk, and an elephant's tusk. To get all three things, the hare had to deceive or bring harm to other animals. He had to trick the crows to fly into a large sack, had to lie to the lioness to convince her to give him her milk, and had to make a mighty elephant trip and break off his tusk in order to obtain the last item of his list. When at last he went before the great Allah, he showed him the fruits of his efforts, to which Allah replied that he could not give him more intelligence, as what he had was more than enough; if he had any more, he would entangle the world and destroy it.

We talked until the sun came up on my last morning aboard the *María Luisa*. For the first time since leaving Lisbon, I had begun to feel almost good. Then I saw that we were navigating our way through an archipelago of small islands. Finally, we approached what looked like a large island. I saw a coast dotted with mangroves and a patch of land covered with palm trees and thick, dense, verdant forests which I later found to be mostly of acacia, or thorntree.

"Where *are* we?" I asked, fearful of the answer, as I realized that we were readying the ship for mooring.

"Hey, *amigo*, you don't know where we are like that?" asked Kinjay, hitting me playfully on the shoulder. "Welcome to your new home, my friend. You in the Bijagos Islands. You gonna live on Big Bolama Island!"

***

The men soon tied up the mooring of the ship, and my few possessions were quickly fetched from down below.

"Come now, boy. We're going to go and introduce you to your new home," Joao called to me from the other end of the ship.

I looked out across the bay where we had come to rest, and I saw a long house made of felled trees with a trail leading into the jungle behind it. Next to this, I spied a place where a campfire had recently been burning.

"Old Paolo must be asleep or off somewhere," muttered Joao to no one in particular as he approached where I stood. "Antonio, fire him a warning shot so he knows we've come."

The grommet carried out this order, firing a shot from the bombard on the aft deck. We studied the forest for a long minute. Maybe there's no one here after all, I allowed myself to hope. Maybe they'll forget about this madness and let me go home.

Suddenly, a great piercing howl came from a ridge on the hill above the house, and I saw a stocky white man, nearly naked except for a loincloth, some painted markings on his body, and a long stick in his hand running toward the shore waving his arms like mad.

"Very well, he's here. Let's go, Rodrigo."

"No, wait," I said, holding onto one of the ropes of the main mast. "Could we — I'm not sure I want to do this."

"Nonsense, you *have* to go. Besides, this is going to make you rich. And with the mind you've got for languages, you'll do well for yourself. Come now, he's waiting," the captain said, coming closer, grabbing my thin arm and pushing me forward.

I had no choice but to get off the ship and meet the strange man who was waiting down below. I'm to be on *land*, I thought as walked along the bouncing plank. I'd almost forgotten what it felt like to be on solid ground after all that time at sea.

CHAPTER FORTY-SIX

"Paolo, this is Rodrigo, your new *lanzado*-in-training," Joao said. Only Kinjay had accompanied us to meet the *lanzado*, perhaps to have a chance to say goodbye. "Now, he's a very ambitious and hard-working young man, and, moreover, he's *smart*. How many languages is it you speak, now, lad?"

I counted on my fingers: Romany, Portuguese, a bit of Italian, French, Castilian, Arabic, and a few phrases of Wolof. I wondered if being able to read Latin, Hebrew and ancient Greek counted. I decided they did, so I said, "Ten. I speak ten languages, so *far*." I decided to ingratiate myself by seeming willing to learn new ones. What was it that Father Sebastián said about knowing languages — that the conquest of the best knowledge is achieved through them? I would eventually learn over a dozen, but I hoped that the conquest of my trip home could also be achieved that way, too.

The strange man, Paolo, just laughed. "Well, boy, you'd better learn *Balanta* now," he said, his green eyes full of laughter. "That's about all we speak around here."

The word sounded so strange to me — *Balanta*. In fact, the people among whom I would be living mostly called themselves the "Bolama" people, named after the island they inhabited. They were a small tribe of the larger Balanta people, whose name, I would discover, meant "those who resist" in their language, and for good reason. Over the centuries, the Bolama people had developed their own customs that were sometimes at odds with their Balanta cousins. Also, their local island dialect had grown apart from the Balanta spoken on the mainland.

As I looked about me, and studied with a sideways glance the apparent madman standing next to me, I couldn't believe that I was really about to be left here.

"Let's collect your slaves first," Joao said, "and then we'll talk about Rodrigo some more."

We walked up to the wooden house I had seen halfway up the ridge, and Paolo lifted a latch on the door upon which the design of a big fish was carved. He apparently didn't have keys to his doors like they did in the great fortress I had seen before. A shaft of sunlight fell on about a dozen Africans who squinted at us as they sat squatting on the earthen floor. They were attached to a long chain that connected each person to the others.

Joao barked out a command in a strange language. That must be Balanta, I thought. The men and women got to their feet. He yelled at them again, and they began to shuffle out of the little building with a look of fear I hadn't seen on the faces of the people at the first stop we'd made.

I wondered how they would fit in the ship's hold, and where exactly the crew was planning on putting them.

"How is our little Kinjay, eh?" said Paolo, putting out his hand and squeezing the man's upper arm, even as the African flinched and tried pulled away from him.

"Doing his job like a good one, eh? I can remember that day I got a captured boy from one of them war raids up the banks of the great river. I could've sent ya down the Nile to Prester John straightaway. I remember it like it were yesterday. Not long to go 'til you earn your freedom, eh boy?"

At this, Kinjay just looked at the ground and shook his head.

***

The *María Luisa* was gone, and I was left alone with the strange man who was supposed to train me to do what he did — to become like *him*. I had a hard time believing this could be possible.

I'd watched the ship leave early in the afternoon, after the new group of slaves was brought in and a place — *somewhere* — had been found for them. Soon, all of the provisions had been taken care of, and Paolo had been given fresh supplies and trading materials. At other times, there would be red cloth, glass beads and hawksbells like later in the Indies, but I didn't see such items that day. Instead, they gave my new master some stale biscuits, chains, tools, and other supplies, and some birds and monkeys were brought aboard for the men to sell back in Portugal. The old *lanzado* had been paid handsomely with a bag of coins for his slaves. Soon, the moorings were drawn up and the ship began to move. Some of the men waved goodbye to me, and I waved once, but not at the grommets. I waved at Kinjay, who stood on the aft deck and forced a smile as he waved back.

When the ship passed out of sight, a profound sadness fell upon me, but there was nothing to do but follow Paolo back and prepare for dinner and my new life in this strange new place.

My life as a *lanzado*.

***

I went back with my new master to his thatched cabin, the place where he lived, slept, and conducted his business. "I try to live as the Blackamoors do," he told me, "but I sure don't live *with* 'em."

He prayed for a long time to the cross that hung on his wall, above a small stone statue of the Blessed Virgin. Then he began to prepare our dinner, which consisted of rice, spiced vegetables, roots, beans, roasted beetles, and oranges and bananas for dessert. I walked around the meager habitation as he jabbered away incessantly about life among the Bolama, and about the Portuguese presence there.

"This place has only been known about for, oh, less than twenty years now. It was discovered by Cadamosto on his second voyage down to these parts. I'm the first white man to be down here as a *lanzado*. You know, further inland, on the mainland, the other Balanta people are being edged out by some of the

214

other Africans, like the Fula, the Mali Empire, and the Mandinga. The Mandinga — I sure hate 'em for the Mohammadans they are, but I got to respect the empire they've made for themselves. They're an organized bunch, they are. Not like *these* primitives. They'll overrun and absorb the Bolama if we don't first."

He went on to tell me about the Portuguese king, Henry the Navigator. This king had held symposium after symposium on Cape St. Vincent to learn the arts of geography and navigation. Soon, they'd begun to explore, while we in Castile had been embroiled in wars and our provincial politics. The Portuguese, however, had kept sending men further and further south and east along the coast.

"Let's hope we reach India soon, by the breath of God!" Paolo shouted more than once.

"And don't you Spaniards go thinking you're so bloody great for havin' the Canary Islands." He pointed a grubby finger at me, as if accusing me personally of having snatched them away from his countrymen. "We could've had 'em if we wanted, but Portugal had bigger fish to fry. You can have 'em and rot there for all I care, by the Virgin's spit!"

As he talked, I wandered out to the patio of his compound. I had already observed the pallet on which he slept — a pile of grubby rags thrown in one of the corners of his rectangular room. The structure was made of thin, local trees and thatched on the top with what looked like so many palm leaves woven together into long, stringy braids. I assumed that this must work fairly well, as a light rain had fallen the night before, yet the interior of the home seemed perfectly dry. Out on the patio, I observed a long cloth that had been hung by both ends to sticks at either side of the outside rafters. Years later, while living among the Tainos, I would observe a similar sleeping tool known as the *hamaca*. But of course I had never seen such a thing before; it was used for sleeping, and my host noticed the quizzical look on my face upon seeing it. "That's called an *ufudo*," he told me. "The people here often sleep on 'em, especially on hot nights when the inside of the hut gets too stuffy and hot. That's where you'll be sleeping, my boy."

"Thank you," I heard myself say. I didn't know how else to respond. I was thinking about the mosquitoes and other insects, and wondering how I was supposed to protect myself from them.

"So, now, as I was saying," Paolo continued, "Cadamosto was a great man..."

***

I learned many things about the gentle, shy Bolama people over the next few months, some from my mentor but much more from my daily interactions with the people themselves. I worked with them in the rice-fields — with both women and men, which surprised me-and this helped me to learn their language bit by bit. Sometimes, we would sing songs beautiful in their complexity and imagery, which served to lend rhythm, joy, and a sense of inspiration to our labors. One of my favorites went like this:

"Goddess of light, Goddess of love, give us your rice, give us your rice

Goddess of light, Goddess of love, give us our rice, for we have worked hard

We have worked hard, worked hard, worked hard,

Since the cock's cry, since the moon took her sleep

Give us your rice, give us your rice

Goddess of love, of earth, give us your food

So we may be strong and praise you some more

Give us your food, give us your food

Goddess of earth, give us your rice,

So the sons of the earth can praise you some more..."

I discovered during this time that the kind of language I learned was different from that which Paolo spoke; he'd learned the phrases of utility, of business, trade, and obligations. He would often bark orders or questions eliciting specific responses, usually barely waiting for a reply. I noticed that, despite all the time he'd spent among the Bolama, which was about two years, he still spoke haltingly and the people looked at him with curiosity when he addressed them, so little, it seemed, did he understand their ways. He spoke to explain the wares brought from Europe, and he negotiated the trade of various animals and spices. By being cunning and manipulating, he convinced some of the greedier members of the island to do something insidious: sell or trade him their children or servants, many of whom were considered lost causes anyway. Some had been accused of witchcraft, theft, or worse yet, dishonesty or disrespect toward their elders. In addition to this, the *akidmo*, or medicine man, would sometimes prophesy that a child would be unlucky or evil as an adult, so such children would also be sold or traded to Paolo, who was a specialist in the language of such exchanges.

I, on the other hand, remember that the first words I learned were about a whole other side of life — health, sickness, happiness, sadness, fatigue, and words that pertained to living and dying. I learned as I sat with the people and ate with my fingers from their wooden bowls. After only a few months there, Paolo needed me to interpret for him on the rare occasions he wished to express ideas of this nature. I made an effort to learn the names of the people by whose side we labored, even if they could never pronounce my name well. When I had learned enough to converse and be understood, I was even invited to a tribal council meeting, which had been called to discuss the tribe's future. I felt honored because I knew that Paolo had only ever been invited to dance with the men around a fire at *kussundé* festivals where the Bolama beat drums and reenacted wars while wearing fearful wooden masks. He had never been included in such an important event, and was not invited to this one. This, as you can guess, made him insanely jealous, and he pouted in his compound the entire evening because of the snub.

***

One of the most interesting things about the Bolama was their lack of social classes, something I had always known in Sevilla, and only too well. I quickly learned from my rice-harvesting partner, Kuja, that they did not even have a king or a chief, a fact that left me nearly speechless at first.

"But how do you keep order among your people?" I asked. "How do you decide what can be done and what is forbidden?"

He set down his *tebinde,* which was a kind of tool used to prepare the earth for planting crops, and we took up our woven baskets in which we carried our rice and millet. We began walking back to our compounds, but on the path that led back, my friend sat down on the large protruding root of a *fo* tree, and began to tell me about his people.

"Now I don't know how you do it there in the land of the *nassari* —" this was their word for whites — "but here, we revere those who have gone before us, those who possess the wisdom and the power of the gods, and even talk to our distant father god who lives far away across the sea."

I thought of how I had been taught reverence for the saints by Father Sebastián — how he held them up as shining examples of wisdom and virtue through the stories he told me. They were folks who, he claimed with a smile, were "a bit closer to God than the rest of us."

"You know about our ancestors." At this, the young man took a few small, carved statues out of the pouch he kept by his loincloth, his only clothing, and caressed them with care. "We adore our ancestors, as they're closer to the earth mother than we are." I was struck for a moment by the parallel words of the two men. "This one is my mother," he continued, kissing the statue. "And this, my grandfather, a strong, wise man, and a brilliant hunter of the clever hare."

"He's still here, you know," he said after a contemplative pause. "You see, *Rod-ee-go*, we Bolama know that our ancestors and their spirits are always with us, protecting and guiding our ways and our actions. They're everywhere around us right now. I can feel their love and wisdom. Can't you?"

We sat in silence for a long while, and I admired the simple beauty of the birds as they swooped by over the immense *bolanha*, or floodplain, which was now rich with silt deposits which helped give a rich rice harvest. Unlike the Tainos, the Bolama didn't need to build *conuco* mounds or burn off their brush at the end of every season to replenish the soil.

I tried to listen and feel for the spirits of the Bolama to speak to me, but at first, all I could hear was the distant bellowing of the hippos.

I continued to sit and listen, and I felt the breeze as it gently caressed my face like a soft, gentle lover seated at a window might. It was then that I thought that, perhaps, I had heard something, a message in the wind brought to me by the departed souls of the Bolama as they whispered from across the ages.

"All of this was given to us by the gods as a gift!" Kuja cried, suddenly bounding upwards. "This tree, that rock, this rice-plain, it is all alive and has a spirit, and is all a part of the bounty we're given from the gods. May they — and the spirits who are always around us — be praised forever."

CHAPTER FORTY-SEVEN

It wasn't easy to get quick answers from the Bolama, I was soon to learn — that just wasn't their way. When I would ask something, they'd usually change the subject, or tell a joke, or perhaps answer with a riddle.

"Who is the leader of your people?" I would ask time and time again.

"Does the snake need a head still to crawl, my friend?" They would ask, to the laughter of all those present.

"I don't know," I would reply, perplexed. "Yes, I think it does." Questions and answers like this only amused my friends all the more, and they would often slap my shoulder playfully as they laughed at the riddles I could never quite comprehend.

"Why should the oldest, wisest part of the snake not rule? Has the snake not shed that part yet for a reason? It is still good, yes?" This came with more jovial laughter as they watched the confused look on my face as they explained that the eldest member of the tribe automatically served as its chief. And it didn't matter if that person was a man or a woman, he, or she, ruled a special council of elders that made decisions regarding almost everything about the life of the tribe.

They would sometimes ask me, "How many wives does your father have there in the land of the *nassari*?"

"One. He has only one, as that is all God will allow," I said, deciding not to mention the women my father pursued like a wolf in heat.

The people seemed to read my thoughts. "And if he is a bad man, can your mother put him out of the house and take a new husband?" one older woman asked.

"Certainly not!" I responded, almost wishing that my mother had that right.

"Oh, then your country is very, very bad, *Rod-ee-go*," they would say, clicking their tongues and shaking their heads in disbelief. "And your God is very cruel indeed." It was at moments like these that I could not tell if they were being serious or if they were simply trying to play games with me.

***

But life wasn't all work and talking for me while I was there. I also learned to play the drums during my stay with the Bolama.

Many of the men of the island played a kind of instrument called a *kusundé*, a hallowed out gourd with three strings that reminded me of the lutes the servants played on feast days back home in Sevilla. But since I was only considered a *nugayé*, or young, unmarried man with no prospects, it was decided that I would only be allowed to play the drum. This was better, however, than what the Bolama thought of Paolo—a spoiled, dirty overgrown child not capable of making any music at all.

One morning, one of Kuja's cousins, a tall, thin, serious boy named Firofa, came to get me quite early, not long after the sun had come up and while fruit-bats still flew about.

I'd been expecting Firofa, as I had asked to learn how to play. People told me that before I could play properly, I would have to make my own drum. According to Bolama folk wisdom, a person couldn't just play any instrument that might be lying about, because there was none of his or her soul in it. No, I'd have to go out and find a tree that spoke to me and asked me to carve from it if I ever expected to play it well. This reminded me of the time that Ostelinda had tried to teach me to carve a flute.

We walked along a path that ran parallel to the floodplain and one of the streams that fed into the bay. I tried to make conversation with Firofa, but he would have none of it — he was there for a purpose, and he wanted to hear nothing that might distract him from this most important of tasks.

"You've got to *listen* to the trees," he told me in a loud whisper. "Listen to them very well, and one of them will speak to you, and ask to be cut — that's the one you'll cut down and use to make your drum." Apparently, it didn't matter as much which animal the hide came from to stretch over the drum's shell.

STEVEN FARRINGTON

Imagine — a tree that was to speak to me! I
tried to keep from laughing at my guide, who seemed
completely serious about the fact that I needed to keep
my ears open for such a message. I wondered how
exactly "my" tree would speak to me, and in which
language it would do so.

We took a small raft to the mainland and hiked
for a few hours into the forest. The acacia trees grew
taller and thicker as we walked further away from the
water. Soon, we came to a small savanna, and so we
stopped for a small break. Firofa, who had been silent
for hours, finally spoke some more to me then.

"*It will* speak to you," he said. "*Your* tree, it will
be there when you look, if you keep your heart open
for it. Open your mind, and you'll feel the voice and
the message."

It was all I could do to keep from chuckling as
I envisioned a tree with a big mouth calling out to me
to chop it down. But I somehow kept my doubts to
myself as we began walking again and entered the
forest. Soon, we reached the river Geba, which was so
wide I could barely see across it. We turned right along
an established path. Taller trees stood everywhere,
acacia, palm, and others I had no words to name.

We continued on, and I didn't hear anything
from any of the trees we passed.

Firofa finally insisted that I shuffle along while
kneeling, in order to draw closer to the earth and the
trees' roots. But after a few minutes, my knees began
to hurt, and I began to consider the possibility of
pretending to hear something from one of the trees we
passed so that I wouldn't have to continue on this way.

224

Finally, my guide stopped and turned to face me. His look showed his disappointment in my efforts. "Look," he said in a reproachful tone, "this isn't working for you, yes?" His dark, perceptive eyes studied my face for a moment, and then he said, "You're not trying hard, are you? I don't think you believe in the message of the tree. Am I wrong?"

"No, you're right," I admitted. "But how are trees supposed to talk to me and ask to become my drum? Forgive me — but this just seems silly."

The young man looked annoyed. "Sit down right now, here," he said sternly, indicating a dry place beside the river.

I did as he directed, and he arranged me the way he thought I should sit in order to be most receptive. It reminded me of the way Kinjay had sat on the boat when he told me that story about the hare so many months before.

"Now," he said with great firmness, putting his hand to my forehead and pressing hard with the middle finger, "I want you to let your mind hold nothing. Don't think of anything at all."

After a moment of tranquility, I did feel that I had emptied my mind of everything, including the desire to find a tree.

"Now," said Firofa softly, sensing that I had achieved the desired mental state, "is your mind cleared of all the things that filled it before?"

I nodded gently.

"All right," he said, removing his hand from my head. "Now, you can't try or think much about this, but, just let the image of a tree come into your mind. Don't look for it — simply let it appear to you."

Before long, a picture of a tree appeared in my mind, as if by a miracle. I let out a little gasp when I had the image, a clear portrait of a tall acacia with a thick, gnarled trunk.

"You have it, now?" Firofa asked with satisfaction. "Open your eyes once the sight is there in your mind's eye."

When I felt that the tree was well enough imprinted in my mind's eye, I opened my lids.

"We keep going," the youth muttered. I felt disappointed in his reaction, since I felt that I'd finally done what he expected, and wanted to enjoy the moment.

After a time, he snapped still and said, "Here." He rose and ducked into the brush, and I had to jump up suddenly and almost run after him, despite the numbness in my legs, so as not to lose him.

But then, abruptly, he stopped, a wide smile of satisfaction finally dawning on his face.

We were standing under my tree — and it was exactly as I'd pictured it!

***

A few nights later, I sat around the fire with my drum, the one I'd made from *my* tree.

We'd used some sharpened *tebinde* and one of the steel hatchets the Bolama had gotten in trade for slaves and parakeets. It might have been just my imagination, but I thought I heard a sigh when the tree collapsed to the ground.

I'd spent the afternoon hollowing out the widest part of the trunk, where the dried calfskin would be stretched. It was a slow and tedious process, but I enjoyed it. I felt as if I was forging a bond with my tree, which would later be burned at the evening fire, and my drum, which was supposed to give me spiritual insights when I played it. As if the feeling of satisfaction I felt as I carved were not enough, Kuja and some of his friends came and sang to me as I worked, and I felt a sense of unity I hadn't known since leaving Triana. I found it interesting how the men in this country were happy to sing and hold hands together at all times, never fearing how people might think of them. I still today wonder if giving women more power than men in their society had the unexpected result of freeing the men who lived there in ways Spaniards could scarcely imagine.

I started out drumming with some of the others, who'd begun soon after the sun went down. Broad grins stretched nearly from ear-to-ear as we drummed, and I noticed that many of the men enjoyed making different faces and moving their arms differently than the others, even as they kept the same beat. Special bracelets, tortoise shells, spears and wooden masks had been brought out for this event, some depicting warriors and even lions, cows, bulls, and other animals. Still other masks were of old women and men, painted in fanciful colors and grimaces that made me laugh. As the evening wore on, the young men tried on various masks and took them off again, and I couldn't see any reason or pattern for how they did so.

Some of the drummers got so caught up in the rhythm that they stopped playing and stood up, needing to dance with their entire bodies. Fortunately, there were plenty of drummers, and as they got up to dance and twirl joyfully around the fire, others arrived to take up the playing; in this way, the sound was never diminished by those who left their drums to dance.

I allowed my eyelids to close once I'd established a beat of my own, and my mind felt numbed into a sense of calm as my hands kept a constant cadence that matched the beat around me.

Soon, a vision appeared to me, as I'd been told by the medicine man, or *akidmo*, would happen. He said that it would be symbolic, an example of what was happening in my life, and that I should learn from the message that the Earth Goddess would send me.

In my vision, I saw a red bull. It was prancing around at first, and then it seemed to be dashing about, with no rhyme or reason. As the red heat of the fire burned on my eyelids, I saw the bull thrash about in anger, as if it were ready to break free from its ring and smash anyone in its path.

Suddenly, it broke free, and I let out a gasp. The beat of the drums seemed to grow louder in my ears as the animal ran madly through my mindscape. In horror, I realized that the animal was bent on destruction and mayhem. I gasped again as I saw it chasing people — people of the Bolama that I knew and loved, like Kuja, Firofa, and the *akidmo*'s old and fragile mother. The bull was running across the floodplain and stomping on all the rice, and people were jumping out of the way as it charged them. It entered the village, and knocked down the compound of Winnoka, the elder who served as the Bolama chief at that time. It turned over rice-baskets and drums and everything else it could reach, and knocked over walls and pots and stone hearths. I saw in my vision that Paolo was cheering the bull on, and even tried to mount it and ride it for a while, but was shaken off.

Then the bull was mysteriously in Sevilla — in Triana, to be exact. Only this time, Triana was in flames and people were running back and forth and screaming for help. Still, the bull ran this way and that, knocking over wagons, tables, tents, and Ostelinda's stage. In my vision, I saw Pobea running away from Ostelinda's flaming wagon, and somehow I knew that he would be safe, that I would save him eventually. Then, the bull ran down San Jacinto Street to the Church of Santa Ana, where, for some reason, Father Sebastián was giving mass. He looked up from the Eucharist he was about to serve the faithful, and slowly waved his finger back and forth while making a scolding click with his tongue.

Now, the bull was once again mysteriously transported, but this time it was across the river to the *plaza de toros*, where, it seemed to me in a detached kind of way, it ought to have been all along.

But it wasn't alone. In the bullring also was a matador who was dressed in a long and flowing cape, which was green and red and laced with gold thread. He wore luxurious silk stockings and a doublet made of the finest red silk, and he wore his hair pulled back in a tail under the best kind of matador's cap. When he turned around with a flourish the small stands had been made enormous, like the coliseum of Ancient Rome. This stadium was now full of people, guests of my mother's banquets, and as he flashed his sinister smile at them, I realized that the matador was none other than my brother Ricardo.

The booming of the crowd in my vision grew greater and greater as the drums of the Bolama grew louder and louder with every passing second. I could feel the men dancing near me, and it seemed that they were dancing madly, furiously, and angrily. I could smell their sweat.

In my vision, I saw the crowd, and, in what seemed like the middle of the arena, there sat my parents and Alejandro, all of them dressed in their finest clothes. Sitting behind them silently were Lorenzo, Esther, Manfariel and Ostelinda, now holding little Pobea on her lap. They were all staring helplessly forward, as if they were bound at hand and foot to prevent escape.

Suddenly, I noticed that there was a special platform in the stadium, upon which sat the queen and her family. As the noise reached a fevered pitch, she stood and stuck her thumb downward, which made the crowd roar ever louder.

At this, Ricardo made one swift, almost feline movement in which he produced a dagger from somewhere deep in his embroidered cloak. He danced forward and brought it crashing down to the top of the bull's skull as the animal grunted and died instantly. A victor, my brother removed his dagger, wiped it on his cape, and then cut off the animal's ear, which he held aloft for the crowd's thunderous approval.

The drumming became an insane, screaming roar as the beats merged into one loud blur and my own anguished scream as I saw that the bull's face was *my* face, and there was a gash of blood across it.

CHAPTER FORTY-EIGHT

The weeks went by, and I slowly began to forget the horror of my vision.

I grew to tolerate the crunchy beetles roasted over an open fire, and even to enjoy playing dice with Paolo, a game we introduced to the Bolama, who would gamble small trinkets and bits of food instead of the coins that we usually played with.

I was never able to have what I would call interesting conversations with Paolo like I'd been able to do with Father Sebastián or my friends in Triana. I tried to make him see the light of logic many, many times, but as the old saying goes, "Don't waste your time throwing daisies to pigs."

One day during the dry season, however, my master went too far in what he was willing to bet me.

He had drunk the last of a bottle of *porto* which had been left him by Joao, and he was feeling wilder than usual.

"Bet me your stupid necklace, you scamp," he croaked at me, slurring his words. "It must be worth something. Ay, maybe it could go toward your freedom money and your wages if you won something against it."

"No," I said, getting up from where we sat on the dusty platform of his compound. "This is out of the game." I tucked the ruby under my shirt. "Don't ever offer me such a thing again."

"No, no, my boy," he crooned to me softly. "I want your ruby. I want you, too," he said, lunging for me and falling down by the opposite wall.

"No!" I yelled, running out of the building and toward the village. "Never!"

Paolo and I never discussed that evening again. I kept my necklace hidden from then on.

***

We saw a few more Portuguese caravels and rigs as they passed by, and some of them stopped to buy the slaves and the merchandise my master wished to sell. Some of the Portuguese asked me questions about the Bolama. Although I tried not to lie, I sometimes found myself talking in circles, much like the Bolama themselves, so as not to give away too much.

"How many swords, muskets and men would it take to conquer them completely and take them all as slaves at once?" a sailor once asked me.

"I couldn't say for sure," I replied. "They can be like a snake sometimes, you know, crafty and fast, and most of all, elusive as the clever hare."

***

The Bolama's big meeting was finally held one evening under the tree by the floodplain a few days after my incident with Paolo. People began to gather at dusk after the evening meal, while middle-aged men lit fires in the center near the compound of the high priest. The elders were gathered at the head of the assembly, and the rest of the tribe — including me — were scattered in a semi-circle around them. The oldest men, who wore the red turbans and tortoise shells of those who had survived the initiation voyage known as the *Fanado*, and the old women of the clan sat in order of age, Winnoke, the oldest of the women, led them, and they waited for the low hum of conversation to end before the woman rose to cry out an incantation which immediately silenced the tribe:

"Brothers and sisters of the Bolama, our friends the spirits of our beloved ancestors, we humbly ask your guidance for the struggles we endure while we pass through this world."

"*Rah!*" The clan cried in unison.

"Brothers and sisters of the Bolama, we ask that the spirits of the animals of the earth and all of the trees and rocks bring us the fruit of their wisdom as we walk among them."

"*Rah!*"

"Brothers and Sisters, I ask for your patience and your forbearance regarding all that we will discuss this night."

"*Rah!*"

"Brothers and sisters, I ask for you to have the strength of the great lion and the cleverness of the sly hyena to solve our problems with strength and intelligence."

"*Rah!*"

With a look of satisfaction, Winnoke took her seat upon a stool made of carved *fo* wood. There was a long moment of silence, which I presumed was meant to allow the power of the prayer to sink in, and for the members of the Bolama to gather their thoughts. Then, without rising again, the old woman began to discuss, casually, affairs of the clan. She brought up, one at a time, subjects such as the state of the year's harvest; it was good because of the rains that had come in full force, and Timafi, the rainmaker, was praised. They talked about the food that was needed and who needed it most, and the animal sacrifices, especially of cows, to the ancestors and to appease the earth goddess. I understood what they said for the most part, but there were some words that were beyond my grasp of the language.

Soon, the talk moved to more serious matters. Some Mandinga emissaries had appeared from the mainland, and had demanded bribes to avert an attack. The Bolama, unsure of what to do before a clan consensus could be arrived at, had yielded to the harsh demands for food and animals in order to appease their aggressors and buy time. The tribe's members discussed this development with tones of dismay, and I tried to follow the complexities of what they said.

My ears pricked up, however, when they began to speak of the *Nassari*, and started looking pointedly at me. They spoke of the frequency and number of ships that had appeared in the bay in those months. I heard Louhah, a man whose daughter had been taken on the *María Luisa* when I arrived, say something about a voyage, but then Winnoke started speaking quickly and angrily to him, her eyebrows furrowed as she delivered an angry lecture. The man was muttering some words of apology when Winnoke suddenly turned to me.

"Where have the sons and daughters of Bolama been taken?" she asked.

I felt surprised. I had become used to the easy-going indirectness of these people, and this sudden, blunt question threw my attention. I didn't know what to say, and I stammered something incoherent to them in Castilian.

"The old, odd *Nassari*, Paolo, he asked for our sons and daughters, the ones that were bad and wrong — he said that they would be taken away, but he swore on his ancestors that they would be brought back soon. For us, it is a dishonor not to give that which is requested. But, where are they, *Rod-ee-go*, and when will they return?"

I felt all eyes upon me, and I broke into a sweat. I looked around at my new friends, and tried to read the thoughts their faces expressed. I knew what they believed about things like property and ownership; whatever I had asked for during my stay they had given me with a smile. Never had anything been held back or kept from me. I had also learned that, when the previous holder needed whatever had been borrowed again, I was to render it happily back to him or to her. This is how the Bolama lived and died in those days as they were being edged out of existence from every side: they gave and loved freely, warmly, without inhibition, as happy as birds in a nest and almost as naked as the first people of the Garden of Eden.

As the first people of the Garden of Eden, indeed, I thought. And I, with my spices and cloths and trinkets, am I no better than the serpent, come to open them up to the evils of the fruits of temptation. Suddenly, I hated my race and my people, and this rage, this anger about what I had done and what we had done filled my stomach and made my head swim as if to swoon there in front of the assembly and its revered elders.

"My friends," I said, my throat dry and my hands clenched. "I fear that the sons and daughters of Bolama have been taken far away and that you will never see them again."

CHAPTER FORTY-NINE

One night not long after that meeting, I awoke to the sound of drums beating again — only this time, neither Paolo nor I had been invited.

Paolo lay fast asleep in his bed, and showed no sign of being disturbed by the curious, angry sound. He always *was* a heavy sleeper.

I made my way down from the compound and walked along the trail, which led alongside the floodplain, not far from where I toiled alongside my friends.

I pushed through the last of the trees and the brush and came out into the edge of a large clearing, one that I had never been to or been shown by the Bolama.

The image of what I saw there has stayed with me always, and I'm sure that, were I to live to be a hundred, I would never forget it.

There was a huge bonfire in the middle of the clearing, and it was amazingly tall, unlike the previous time. I think the pyre must have been at least twice as tall as a man.

Around this fire danced the men of the tribe — all of them, from the looks of it. The women and children stood on the edge a short way from where I stood, and played their *kusundé*, those gourds with strings like Lutes, and drums like mine, hollowed-out logs with goatskin pulled tightly over one opening.

The men were dressed in the most gruesome, frightening costumes I've ever seen before or since.

Their entire bodies were covered in dried grasses, and they wore masks, red, black and green, with frowns and snarls and grimaces painted on them. They had long noses and showed mouths full of bared teeth.

They were truly masks of terror and masks of anger.

Suddenly, a cry went up from the women, a sound the men took up as well. It was shrill and angry and hurt. Instinctively, I ducked behind a log.

With this call, the men of the Bolama yelled and screamed as loud as their lungs would permit, the drumming grew faster and more intense, and I felt sure that I would go deaf and mad with this sound. I couldn't believe that this was coming from the same drums they'd been playing joyfully not long before.

I turned around and watched them as they danced madly, warlike, rushing each other and waving their arms above their heads in anger. It reminded me a bit of the jousts I'd seen as a child, in which men seemed to be practicing war on each other.

This went on for hours, until the women and children had wearied of beating the drums and the men lay exhausted and heaving on the ground beside the dwindling fire.

***

Things weren't the same between my island neighbors and me after that large meeting and the night at the fire, as you can well imagine. The songs we sang now as we went back and forth along the watery rows of rice in the floodplain were sung with less joy and conviction; men and women smiled less, and the children were more harshly reprimanded than before for the smallest of offenses. Beatings could come from trifles such as straying too far from the village as they went gathering fruits and nuts and beetles, or for not coming back soon. And, sadly for me, I was no longer treated to the delicious laughter and delightful humor to which I had been before; now, the people looked at me seldom and spoke to me less, answering me merely in low, monosyllabic, distrustful tones.

The Bolama now knew they were bound for extinction. It makes me think of how even these peaceful Tainos were themselves being chased by Carib people as they in turn had chased out the Ciboney before the Spaniards came here to the New World. In any case, in addition to the visions the high chief received to this effect in her dreams and the revelations of the cocoa nuts she arranged, there were other signs of aggression all around: there had been more Portuguese and Genoese ships in the port lately than ever before. And, as if this weren't enough, the Mandinga kept on sending more and more war parties and emissaries into the islands which were so precariously nestled between the continent and the vast expanse of sea that led who knew where.

The Ocean Sea — what a magnificent mystery it was for me. There was flotsam that washed in from the west, some of it as carved sticks and driftwood from ships, and I wondered where it could all come from. How interesting too that the water there seemed to flow from the west instead of the other way, as it did in more northern climes. I remembered reading something that Father Sebastián had given me, written by the Arab geographer Al-Idrisi in the Twelfth Century. He wrote that the sea was full of profound darkness, high waves, storms, monsters, and violent winds — and that it was for these reasons that no sailor dared try to sail across it.

Sometimes, after a day's work in the fields, I would eat with Paolo back in our compound — after so many months had passed, nearly a year, I had begun to regard it as my own as well as his, even though I had had nothing at all to do with its construction — and I would sit in my *Ufudo* and watch the setting sun as well as the rising moon in the west.

What *could* lie across the Sea of Darkness? And why *hadn't* anyone been brave enough to dare sail it? Sometimes I'd dream of stealing one of the Genoese ships and bearing my Bolama friends off across the sea. What were monsters and high waves compared to what the *Nassari* could do?

CHAPTER FIFTY

Two more years had now passed, and the Bolama, or at least the Bolama as I knew them, were no more.

The Portuguese had learned not only how to dominate that part of the African continent all the way down to Sao Jorge da Mina; they'd also learned a lot more about sailing on the open sea. Some were even learning to study the trade winds that ran from the equator to the Canaries. Wouldn't this, some of them dared to imagine, be useful somehow for traveling west? It was almost as if we were all thinking the same thoughts in those days, and the rumbling sounds of a trip across the Ocean Sea came to all who listened.

In any case, the Portuguese had completely overrun the land of the Bolama, the other Bijagos Islands, and the rich floodplain where I'd gathered so many basketfuls of rice with my friends.

It had started slowly; at first, some sailors and caravels had come through, soon followed by scribes and cartographers. Then, more and more caravels had come, always with the intention of collecting more and more slaves to sell in Europe. Soon, the Portuguese had established a garrison on one of the islands that sat just out of sight of the bay from where I lived with Paolo. Soon, the old *lanzado* had been replaced by armed men who were better prepared for their gruesome task; one battle had been enough for them to capture and place into irons most of the local Africans. Paolo, now dressed as a Portuguese on the mainland, helped in the process, though he was overseen and outranked.

During this time, I'd largely been overlooked. When the new arrivals thought of me, it was how they considered Paolo — an antique, a leftover from an earlier time. My presence was tolerated as long I worked hard and stayed out of everyone's way. I no longer slept in the little compound I had shared with Paolo, but instead occupied a small lean — to near the new mini-fortress where the slaves were kept. It was, you see, my task to guard the slaves and to make sure that none of them escaped. Little did they know, however, that I had the tendency to be a bit "careless." It was thanks to this carelessness, as well as the skill of some of the best Bolama warriors, that a small band of the people still lived by an isolated marsh not far from the bay where I had first landed. As the Portuguese began to move inland and tried to bargain for more slaves with the Mandinga, this small group went unnoticed.

I would sometimes walk along the floodplain where the sweat of my brow had once run into my eyes as I stood bent over my rice-basket, my European clothes once again restored to my stronger and leaner back. I tried to remember the songs I had sung there as we had worked, and of how I had tried to sing along, never quite capturing the words or the rhythms correctly. The birds still sang in the branches above, and the stream by the floodplain still played a reassuring lullaby at night, but I was the only one to remember the old songs of joy and thanksgiving to the earth as I walked along and the daylight dabbled with the redness of my hair.

It fell to me at times to take the inmates out of their prison between shipments of the caravels and to oversee their work in the fields. This was mostly done to keep the slaves strong so that their muscles wouldn't go bad from the lack of use. The farming also provided food for the outpost.

Unfortunately for the Portuguese who lorded over us, I was no better a field overseer than a prison-guard.

Nevertheless, I had to enforce a certain amount of strictness if I was to hold my post. So it was that the muscles of the Bolama remained strong under the hot African sun, and enough rice was produced for everyone; enough was produced also for me to bring some to the few refugees who hid near the marsh without its being missed. Afterall, everyone was getting rich in those days, and if a little went astray sometimes, no one said much.

"Where will the sons of Bolama be taken, *Rod-ee-go?*" the people asked me time and again. I had successfully avoided such questions for a long while, but the time finally came to tell them the truth about what happened to the enslaved.

"They're taken far away, far to the North in the large floating wooden islands you see there in the bay," I said. "After a long time, they go to a place called Lisbon, or *Lisboa.*"

"*Liz-BO-ah?*" they would ask, trying to say the strange word as I said it in Portuguese.

"Yes. And once there, they have to work for the people there and in other places, like my country, which we call *Castilla.* They're sold off for money, one by one..."

"What is this *silver* you speak about?" The question came from Triera, the oldest man and a former plow-farmer. Winnoke had been killed — and I do not like to think about how — and he was the oldest of the community-in-exile, and thus its leader. It was also customary that he would voice the questions and the concerns that went unspoken by the rest of the members of the tribe. "What is it, and how can it be so valuable that the sons and daughters of Bolama can be sacrificed for it?"

I tried to think of a way to explain what I knew as the truth of my country to these simple cultivators of the land, but I couldn't do it in a way that wouldn't sound ridiculous to them.

"Why would men give small plates of gold or silver with a picture on it for another man, and how would they then keep him?" he asked.

"They would beat him if he tried to escape — or call upon bailiffs to capture him again if he got away," I answered.

"Why would they want these pieces of gold in the first place?" he wanted to know.

"Because you can obtain other things with the metal."

"What things?"

"Things such as wool, flour, food…"

"Why would you need to obtain food if enough is produced for the entire community?"

"Because, where *I* come from, people are not like they are here. They're jealous and petty and mean. They don't share, they don't help each other, and don't do things joyfully or with a gentle heart and a song on their lips like here."

The eyes were on me as I said this last phrase, and as I raised my gaze to theirs, the confused and hurt looks I saw there made me want to run far away.

CHAPTER FIFTY-ONE

"Finally, Bartolomé, things got too bad there for me, and I had to leave. I had to return home once again," Rodrigo said. The two men had been taking lunch outside on the patio of Bartolomé's manor garden.

"What happened? What forced you to leave?" Bartolomé asked.

"I don't think you would want to hear about it."

"Of course I want to hear it. Come now, what was it?"

"Are you sure?" Rodrigo asked, putting down his bowl of maize and cassava.

"Certainly."

"If you're sure, then I suppose I will tell you. I must warn you, though — it's not a pretty story."

CHAPTER FIFTY-TWO

It was a dark night, and I was lying on the sand on the beach, looking up at the stars. I remember thinking again for perhaps the hundredth time how different the night sky was in Africa. Father Sebastián had taught me astronomy from my window, and had told me what the ancients had called the constellations, using names from mythology like Cassiopeia, Orion, and the seven sisters of the Pleiades. He had also taken time to explain the stories of the Greeks and the Romans about them. Anyway, I was trying to see if I could make out all of the "seven sisters" when suddenly I heard a scream, and then, shortly after this, the sound of someone crying for help in the local Bolama tongue. I jumped to my feet and made my way over to where I had heard the sound. It had come from one of the small, wooden shacks built for the Genoese sailors who'd been visiting and buying their share of the loot that the Portuguese were only too happy to sell them.

I found a group of white men outside the hut who were smiling and laughing about something. I wanted to find out where the cry had come from, and so I asked these men if they knew anything about it.

"Oh, go back to yer own place, boy, that was only a little nothin' that ya heard," said one of the men, smelling of alcohol. I guessed that they had brought some *porto* with them, as this was what his breath stunk of.

Still, I persisted. As a self-appointed protector for the remaining Bolama, I wanted to find out more. I asked once again what it was I'd heard.

"Oh, our mate's got one of them darky girls in there in his shack, and is having his way with'er." The man slurred some of his words. I doubted if he would have been so candid with me had he not been drinking. "We're all waiting our turns here, and you can, too, if you want."

"No, thanks," I said, and sat down not far away under a tree. I needed to think.

The only girl in the fortress then, at least as far as I knew, was Wanari, Winnoke's grand-daughter and one of my closest friends. I couldn't let her be violated by these men and live with myself.

I went to the back of the shack where I would be able to spy what was happening.

Once there, I saw a horrifying sight.

There she was, Winnoke's granddaughter, and she was bound hand and foot as she lay there, naked, crying in the dust. Her face was streaked with tears as she struggled against the chords that held her. Her eyes burned with anger, hate and fear as they pleaded with me with firey intensity to do something-anything-to save her from her agony.

I've always associated the smell of a fresh rain with that moment; it had just come down that evening, and the heaviness of it filled my lungs and stuck to my skin as I tried to decide what to do.

The man, her rapist, came toward her again, seeming intent to have his way with her. She screamed and writhed like a snake under him, but this did not stop him from his carnal act; indeed, it only seemed to excite him more, and he struck her and called her his whore all the more because of it. I could see him in the firelight; he was a man with a long, narrow face and a thin beak of a nose that was framed by the ruddy complexion. When he was done, he rose from where she lay, and placed his boot on her neck.

She lay almost perfectly still then; her side still heaved from her sobs, and her cheeks had dried once more, although the lines of her tears, which she seemed to have no more of, had left long, jagged tracks in the dust on her face.

"You stay right where you are, you stupid bitch, unless you want to die tonight," he snarled before leaving.

Now was my time to move, as I knew he'd only be out of the shack a minute or two at the most before the next one would come in.

I knew I wouldn't be able to sit there and watch it all happen again.

I rose.

CHAPTER FIFTY-THREE

The two sat for a long time in silence. Bartolomé wondered what his guest had done next, but the man seemed too deep in his thoughts and distant pain to speak further. When the priest asked what happened to the girl, his guest simply said, "They caught and killed her. I was put on the first ship back to Lisbon. I was lucky to escape that hell-hole with my life."

***

Bartolomé lay awake for a long while that night, and he thought about what Rodrigo had told him about the Bolama. He thought about how this man, a Spaniard living in the New World, was perhaps the only one alive who knew anything about them, still spoke their language, remembered their old ways and dances and songs — ways which had been wiped out by the aggressive Mandinka and Portuguese.

He wondered if that could be what the Spaniards were doing to the people of the New World. Would they too soon be wiped out? Would it not be better to bring in more of these hardy Africans to do the work here, if they could brave it better than the Tainos?

CHAPTER FIFTY-FOUR

It was a long trip back to Lisbon. I don't want to talk about it. It would just sadden me too much. Let's just say that I made the journey in chains with a nasty letter for the royal inspectors.

As you may expect, the people at the *Casa dos Escavos* had no use for me, and the royal authorities didn't wish to involve themselves in my imprisonment. So I was set free, provided I left Lisbon right away.

I didn't really care one way or another. I didn't have anywhere special to go.

So, in late January of the year 1481, after three years away, I made the trip back to Sevilla sad, lonely, and penniless. The worst part is that I didn't care at all about what might happen to me upon my return. I just wanted to leave before that same group of sailors was due back at the harbor — or before I could be sold off as a slave to one of the Venetian galleys in the harbor.

Little could I have known, however, the hell I was going back to in the city of my birth.

***

The fire crackled in the hearth as the tears made their way down the old man's face. Bartolomé reached a hand out to comfort him.

"There, there," he said, placing it on his shoulder, trying to comfort him.

Rodrigo didn't say anything, but sat there lost in his thoughts.

"Those were some pretty bad years then, those that you were gone for. After the death of Fernando's father, the two kingdoms were finally joined into the Kingdom of Spain and Castile ceased to exist. The *conversos* were attacked more and more, there was the usual hunger, epidemics, and scarcity—"

Rodrigo snorted. "Those problems weren't anything compared to what I came back to."

Bartolomé took his hand once more. "Why? What happened when you got back to Sevilla?"

"It was Esther," he said, wiping away another tear. She — her whole family, her brothers — they were caught in a trap. Someone had to be first, and they were among the first ones."

CHAPTER FIFTY-FIVE

As my boat approached Sevilla, a strange feeling arose in my stomach. I remembered how I'd once thought I would return home with boundless riches, and that I would be a success. I had hoped to escape my family once and for all, and to help the people of Triana by sharing with them all I had. I suppose I'd imagined myself as kind of a notable or grandee who would go amongst my people and be heralded as a savior.

The boat docked, and I paid its captain the last *cruzados* I had left. I was now a completely penniless refugee instead of a rich savior.

Such is life, I thought bitterly. I thought that if I ever saw Francisco again, I would kill him.

I walked casually through the streets of Sevilla. Nothing much had changed there, I thought.

But *I* had changed. I had changed much, and not for the better, I thought, walking by the taverns and pottery shops I had so often snuck past in the dark of the night. I was older, jaded, and yet strangely more confident. Or maybe I was just indifferent. I felt hollow inside, and I just didn't care. The innocent child in me had been destroyed by what I had seen, and I felt there was nothing left inside of me to replace it.

Now that I reflect on those days, one thing is clear to me: I don't think I ever really recovered from the loss of Lorenzo. That is to say that I never really forgave him for just leaving in the middle of the night without so much as a good-bye. He'd left me with nothing as I sat there in Sevilla awaiting his return those years before. It had gotten easier while I'd been away to forget how he'd just abandoned me as if our friendship had meant nothing; but then, upon my return to Sevilla, everything flooded back at once, and the old wounds that had become scarred over and forgotten began to bleed once again. "Oh, well," I thought to myself bitterly. "Maybe he actually made it to the Land of Sind."

I spent a long time sitting on the edge of the fountain looking up at the cathedral. I wondered why I'd never really appreciated the intricacies of it before — the beautiful structure, and the Minaret of San Marcos, which stretched high into the sky. I noticed that the project to connect the cathedral to Santa María de Sede, begun almost eighty years before, was still incomplete. The smell of oranges, something I've always associated with being back in Sevilla, wafted gently on the breeze.

All of a sudden, I realized that the part of the city where I had been walking, near the *Reales Alcazares*, had become strangely silent and empty. I saw a few people moving excitedly toward the other side of the cathedral, and I jumped up, wondering what could be happening.

"Come and see!" cried a boy of about twelve, as he dashed by me. "They're going to burn the Judaizers!"

"The *what?*" I asked in disbelief. "*Who* are they going to burn?"

"Where have *you* been?" he asked. "They're having a fine *auto-de-fe* for the De Susón rebels who dared raise arms against God and the inquisitors. Father says they want to bring the *conversos* to consort with the devil."

"*The devil?*" I asked in amazement. A sick feeling rose in my stomach, and I began to run, no, fly with all my might toward the gathering. My indifference was giving way to panic and rage.

How could this be happening?

CHAPTER FIFTY-SIX

The *auto-de-fe* was far worse than I could have imagined. It took place not far from the cathedral, right by the college where the Dominican friars lived in their cloister. Where was Father Sebastián, and why was he not putting a stop to this, or pleading for the lives of Esther and her family?

Soon, the people of Sevilla paraded my friend and her brothers and father through the narrow streets in wagons and farm-carts drawn by burros. I tried to reach them or call out, but the streets were thronged with crowds. They made their way into the small plaza where the crowd had gathered and someone had erected a makeshift stage.

The prisoners were all dressed in flowing yellow capes and pointy, cone-shaped hats. An excited old woman in an old mantilla told me that this was the garb for those who would now plead for mercy before Torquemada and the rest of the Inquisitors' Tribunal. One of the members of that panel was my cousin, the powerful Juan Ruiz de Guzmán, the one who had raped Ostelinda.

The Jews were painted all over with red and yellow hellfire and devils without claws, with large, diagonal black crosses painted on the fronts. The lady told me that these had been dubbed *Sanbenitos*. To me, they looked like the silliest costumes I'd ever seen — Holy Week cloaks gone mad with colors of rage.

I tried to get Esther's attention by waving to her, but she looked heavenward as they were all taken from the carts and tied to the stakes. I noticed that her hair had been cut very short, almost to her scalp, and that there were bloody wounds on her head. I didn't like the angle at which she or her brothers were standing; it looked like they had broken arms or legs. When I looked closely, I realized that several of them, including Esther, had to be tied to the stakes with their arms behind them so that they wouldn't fall over. They all had injuries that had not been hidden well for the occasion. I was to learn later that they had been among the first to have their limbs dislocated by the dreaded triangular racks called *potros*. These horrific devices pull people apart as they scream, plead for mercy, and admit anything at all about Judaizing — among even the most piously Christian of *conversos*.

I looked over at the Moorish-style *Alcázar* that the Christians had dubbed the *Castillo San Jorge*, where Torquemada's minions had no doubt done their gruesome work. This castle would, in the years to come, become the headquarters of the Inquisition. Its orange, spindly spires clawed their way to the heavens like two tortured demons. Just as Saint George had slain the dragon, this castle was supposed to slay the Dragon of Evil represented by backsliding *conversos*. I turned and took a breath as if to yell something to my friends.

"Hold your tongue," the old lady warned before I could speak. "You can mock them all you want from here, but if you look like you might help them or be a friend, you'll find yourself up there, too."

I didn't care then what they might do to me. I couldn't take my eyes off of her, my true friend, one of the only ones I ever had in this world.

Once the cheering and jeering of the crowd had died down, Torquemada came forward to address the prisoners and the other counselors of the Inquisition as well as the crowd. He was a short man dressed in a white habit and a black mantle with a cross over his chest. It had been rumored that Her Majesty was thinking of gracing the proceedings with her presence that day, and that was why they had waited so long to begin. I noticed that Sir Pulgar — the one I had seen years before upon Isabel's first visit, Her Majesty's chronicler — was among the inquisitors' court as well. He sat comfortably on his wooden chair, off to the right of my cousin. Soon, my brother Alejandro would be one of my cousin Juan's most trusted henchmen in this new position of power.

The Inquisitor Torquemada began to speak. When he did, the crowd quieted down a bit; but the occasional catcalls of, "Burn the heretics!" continued from all sides as he pronounced his discourse.

"We are here today to witness the burning of these Judaizing heretics," he said, his voice thundering above the tumult. "As advised by the Apostle Paul, they have already been admonished twice and ordered to beg for forgiveness. They will now be asked a third time to repent for threatening to kill the members of our court. You all know that the arms were found at the home of this heretic, Benadeva," he said, pointing at one of the hooded men with a flourish.

A loud yell began at the rear of the crowd, and reached an almost deafening crescendo by the time it got to where I was standing. "Burn the heretics! Burn the Judaizers! Burn the heretics! Burn the Judaizers!" the crowd yelled ever more loudly. I felt more confused than I had ever been in my life. How could any of these people really think that this little band of Jews and *conversos* could have tried to kill all the members of the Inquisitorial court? But, thinking back on what happened, I suppose that the charge of "Judaizing" was probably the one that held more sway with the people. That charge, as well as their suspicion and hatred of *conversos*, was certainly more than enough to make them want to see Esther and her family burned. During those years while I was away, Jews were accused of weird rituals in which they were thought to feast on the hearts of Christian children while worshipping The Black One and conducting strange rituals commemorating the killing of Christ. They were also said to have caused great plagues by poisoning Christian wells, which, of course, was just as ridiculous as all the other lies. In those days, there seemed to be no limit to what the clerics would say to incite hatred against them. My once-lovely city was a tinderbox waiting for a spark to blow it to the heavens.

I looked around me, and everywhere I saw looks of anger and bloodlust on the faces of the people. I was reminded of the day, many years before, when I had witnessed the fight between Manfariel and that seaman Marco. I thought of how the crowd had craved violence that day as well. I had a hard time reconciling my memory of a relaxed and easy youth in this city with the reality I saw around me. I also had a hard time believing that this could all be led by a man Father Sebastián had told me was probably the wisest and best-read theologian he'd ever met. Torquemada may have been well-educated, but to me he was never more than a rabid mastiff serving my cousin, Juan de Guzmán, in his lust for blood and destruction.

Studying the legality of their actions, one might wonder why the Inquisition was allowed to persecute Jews, who were technically not under the authority of the Church. However, as I later found out, they tricked every member of this group, including Esther, to sign a parchment stating that they wished to convert to Christianity. Once they had done so, the Inquisition was free to do whatever it wanted to them, treating them all as *conversos*.

Torquemada waited a short while before continuing. Once the crowd calmed down, he exchanged confident glances with some of his council and bailiffs. Men in heavy chainmail shirts covered by white chemises covered with red crosses had appeared, and stood menacingly about. Some of them wore red vests punctuated by small studs and steel breastplates or pointed helmets. I imagine they had been ordered there by the queen to keep the peace.

"As you all know," began Torquemada, "there is the problem of the *conversos* and the Jews who tempt them here in Sevilla, as they are a problem everywhere," he said, but was forced to stop again because of the clamor from the crowd. "They're in grave danger for their very souls, and even more so when Jews try to convert them back to their godless ways and fight the Holy Office established by Her Majesty and His Holiness, the pope."

The Jews and *conversos* were the goat upon which they were heaping all of their guilt and fears. I would soon learn that the queen, through her obsession with the Inquisition, was hoping to unify her kingdom as it had been merged with Aragon. And why not? It seemed the perfect plan, after all: give the people of the Spains a common enemy and they would begin to rally together as a nation rather than as a collection of competing regions and peoples.

"That is why we now have this *auto particular de fe*," Torquemada cried. "We shall see if they won't repent. If not, they will be killed the way they once killed our lord!" At this, the crowd once again roared its approval. "They will be declared to be in abjuration *de vehementi*, and then burned — and the missing brother burned in effigy."

It was then that I noticed that one of Esther's brothers must have escaped, as there was a wax statue representing him.

Good for him, I thought. I hoped he would form an army I could join.

Some of the other members of the Inquisitorial Council — Diego de Merlo and Diego de Deza among them — had risen now and gone to the prisoners. Four large men with bulging muscles and black hoods over their faces, who carried knives and swords, stood nearby. I noticed that one of them, Pedro, was the man my father had always used as a bodyguard and torchbearer when he went on nocturnal visits to Triana.

"Diego de Susón," began Torquemada, addressing Esther's father. Esther was still looking heavenward. "For the last time, just in case you have changed your mind while languishing among the rats and the filth of the *calabozo*," he paused, and the crowd roared its approval once again.

These *calabozos*, in case you haven't experienced them, are the underground prisons they used, and still might use for all I know. In case you've never been in one, Bartolomé, and I pray that you never have — thank your blessed saints that they've kept you from such an abomination to the dignity of human life. Many a prisoner never survived the disease, the rats, and the putrid, rotting smell of human flesh wracked by plague and pox and disease. The only time you'd eat or drink was when they chose to throw some gruel or bread your way with their slop buckets.

"In case the filth of the *calabozo* has brought you to your senses," the counselor continued, "I ask you a third time to repent, and to renounce your efforts to bring the fragile, weak *conversos* back to your godless ways."

"Burn the heretics! Burn the bastards!" cried the crowd.

Diego de Susón the elder looked like he was trying to gather the last shred of his dignity. I remembered sadly how years before I saw him hold up the matzo bread and pray for things like liberty, justice and peace for all peoples. Now those thumbs were mangled, having been splayed and crushed by the screw and those arms had been broken on the wheel, in a vain attempt to extract a confession.

My mind protested again, wanting to know why this was happening, and how it was that no one was stopping it. Had everyone gone mad? Or was it that my people needed a new dog to kick now that the Moors were all but expelled from Castile, and the Portuguese had been defeated and stopped from trying to place their queen on our throne?

De Susón raised his head to speak, and the crowd quieted a bit to hear what he would say. I couldn't believe they would accept anything but the burning of this man and his family.

"We've done nothing wrong," he said simply. "We never planned any insurrection — you all are out of your minds to think so. And as to the other charge — we never tried to change anyone's beliefs. That isn't our way. We just ask to be left alone to practice our faith."

At this, the crowd howled and hissed at his meager defense. "That's not what your daughter said!" yelled out one man, whom I recognized as one of the frequent guests at my mother's feasts. "I heard she said she wanted to get *all* of them, she did."

Torquemada went to where Esther stood, as if the man had given him another idea with which he might incite the crowd. He reached up and grabbed her chin, turning it to him.

"Well, you little tart, what have you got to say for yourself? You admitted yourself that you wanted to kill all of us, and that you wished all the *conversos* would change back to Jews, didn't you?"

To this, Esther spat in his face, inflaming the taunts of the crowd even more as the man wiped the saliva from his eyes. I had to stop myself from letting out a jubilant cheer.

"I was tortured — you had me on a rack, you beat me, and you cut me with your knives," she said to him, looking desperate. "When you torture someone, it isn't hard to bring about a confession to such things and worse."

"We did no such thing," her accuser said, trying visibly to retain his composure. "We gave you a fair trial, complete with witnesses, as His Holiness has prescribed. You were found to have done all of the wretched things you are accused of, and you even signed a writ of it by your own free will," he said, holding up a piece of paper in one clenched hand.

"You knew what the answer would be before you began," she said through bared teeth. "It was a foregone conclusion — and that paper was signed under duress."

"Well, perhaps that is because we know who we were dealing with — heretics and rebellious Judaizers!" he yelled again with another flourish to the crowd, which cheered once again.

"Now, I will ask you one last time — do you or do you not renounce your heretical ways and accept the One True Faith?"

"Never," she said defiantly.

"And there you have it!" he yelled. "I believe that is all the proof we need," he finished, a satisfied smile on his beardless face.

The crowd roared louder than before when one of the executioners appeared with a flaming torch from the side of the cathedral. How sickening, I thought, that this might have been taken from one of the gently burning candles from the statue of the Virgin, and was now about to be used for a violent act of destruction. It was an act that I'm sure Our Lord himself would have opposed, had he been present.

"Furthermore," Torquemada continued, playing with her like a cat sometimes will play with a mouse, "As if this were not enough, did you not try to convert a young Christian to your evil ways, thus turning away a man from his destiny in the priesthood?"

I felt sick to my stomach, and I wanted to yell out a defense, so that they would blame me in her place. But I knew that it wouldn't do any good.

"Benjamín, I mean, Rodrigo, wanted to learn from me," she said without raising her voice. "He was the one who wanted to know about the faith of my fathers. I never forced it on him."

Not long after this, a legend was born about my friend. It told that she survived that day, like a phoenix arisen from the ashes, confessed her sins of fornication and disloyalty, and converted to serve

Christ as a nun. The legend told that she had been the one to tip off the authorities about the rebellion in the first place. Some called her "*La Bella Susona*," or just "*la fermosa fembra*" because of her beauty, thus erasing the name of Esther forever from Sevilla's memory. According to the most popular version of the tale, when my friend died many years later an old woman, her dying wish was to have her skull displayed above the entrance to her door as a symbol and warning to others not to follow her example of youthful folly. The street of the *Barrio de Santa Cruz* in which she used to live was known first as *La Calle de La Muerte*, and then just *Calle Susona*. I never found out who the imposter was who claimed to be my friend, but I never forgave the woman who helped Sevilla to forget about the true life, and death, of my friend.

The inquisitor studied Esther for a long moment. I thought he might speak again, but he said nothing more. As the torchbearer drew closer to the platform and Esther's family, I thought I would faint. As the first brother began to burn, I saw the others struggling to break free from their ropes and I even saw the beads of sweat that had formed on their foreheads. Pedro's screams of pain were soon joined by those of his brothers and their father, who, in his fear, had wet himself.

"That'll never put the fire out!" some of the crowd yelled, mocking him. "You'll have to piss a lot more than that, you dirty Jew!"

Later, masons built small ovens in which to burn the so-called "leaders" of the enemies of the Inquisition for whom special torture was reserved.

These were infamous circular *quemaderos* at the base of the stakes where the most unfortunate screamed as the flames consumed them. I'm sure that, had there been a *quemadero* there, Esther's father would have been stuffed into it. In later years, the more fortunate were mercifully strangled by garrets so they couldn't feel the burning torment of the flames — which, I remain convinced, is by far the most painful kind of death.

When the man lit the wood under Esther, I lost control. She began to scream in pain, and then an awful thing — she looked my way.

"Bennnnnnnnnnnnjaaaaaaaaaaaaaaaaaaa, help, ahhhhhhh!" she cried out in agony, throwing her face once again toward the sky.

I felt a hysterical cry bursting forth from my throat. I had lost all sense of fear for what could happen to me. I had become a wild beast, and I wanted to fight for the first time in my life — I mean, I wanted to really break bones, I wanted to attack and bite and kill the man who had done this to Esther. I wanted to fight like the crimson-colored bull of my vision.

Then, suddenly, a hand clasped itself over my mouth and someone dragged me away, trapping my scream inside my own damned, deafening ears.

I will never live long enough to forget Esther's screams of agony as Manfariel dragged me away to safety. They're echoed by the screams that were, and still are, trapped in my mind every time I wake up in a cold sweat more than thirty years and a world away from that day that the Inquisition came to Spain.

CHAPTER FIFTY-SEVEN

Rodrigo didn't want to talk much for a while after reliving the day they burned Esther. Strangely, Bartolomé also felt that he, too, had lost someone very dear, and he couldn't quite figure out why he felt this way for someone he had never met.

During those months of storytelling by Rodrigo, there had been more and more reports of Taino revolts in the islands, especially those further out from the small circle of those first settled by Spain. With every Indian and slave revolt, the wrath of the crown's representatives grew more and more fierce.

There were many things Bartolomé wondered during those days. Were the inhabitants of the New World on a path headed to extinction? Could an entire race of people be wiped out in just a few short years?

He now turned to Rodrigo with newfound urgency, hoping that somehow his stories would give guidance on how he should act.

***

"So, Don Rodrigo, what happened next?"

"Nothing."

"Nothing? What on earth can you mean, nothing?"

***

Nothing. It was at that moment that I ceased caring and trying. My heart seemed to stop its beating in my chest that day.

I vaguely remember some of what happened afterward; I remember the surprised looks of the people in Triana as Manfariel led me back there. Some triumphant return. There was a storm raging in my head that day, Bartolomé, and it rested just behind my eyes and stopped there, never breaking through. My soul was in a rage against Francisco for having sent me on that stupid voyage, which had gotten me nothing and had taken me away from the only people who had ever meant anything to me. I hated him and I hated Lorenzo for never coming back so that I could have been a troubadour and I hated Esther for allowing herself to be burnt by the Inquisitors. But most of all, I hated myself for not being strong enough to prevent these things happening to the people I loved.

Soon after I arrived among the Romany, I collapsed — or so I was told later.

I was placed in one of the *vurdóns* to sleep, and was told that I didn't wake up for several days. Manfariel had seen to it that I was placed in the same one as Ostelinda. When she had heard that Esther was to be burned, she'd felt desperate, and had somehow swallowed some poison. Not an enormous amount, mind you, but enough to make her unwell and bedridden. We were, the both of us, left alone in the *vurdón* with only Manfariel and Pobea who placed cool rags dutifully on my forehead and tried to make me eat at least some spice soup. Ostelinda and I only spoke once, and I will never forget the desperation in her voice as she spoke of the storm-clouds gathering around her family in Triana.

So there I lay, drifting in and out of consciousness. I was told that I ranted and raved, much like I had when I'd been in the bow of the *María Luisa*, and that this time no one had been able to understand what I said. Some of them thought that I'd truly been to the Indies, or possibly to the Land of Sind. You see, there really wasn't very much to hope for in those days, and when times are bleak, I've learned that people will cling to any little hope to make them happy.

But soon, I began to lose too much weight. My voice grew weaker, and my breathing grew so shallow it made the healers worry. Ostelinda hadn't improved any, either.

Pobea was sent to Santa Ana's Church, and a priest was asked to come right away. It was lucky that Ostelinda's son knew a secret entrance to the church. It could be accessed from one of the side doors, as this allowed him to enter it when most of the others were denied or simply ignored entrance because the foul old priest didn't much care for gypsies. But luckily, Pobea had enough of my cousin's blood to be able to pass as a white boy.

Soon, with the help of the priest, last rites were administered. But it didn't do any good. Ostelinda died anyway, right by my side, without my even knowing it.

***

The funeral pyre was so immense that its smoke could be seen three towns around.

All sorts of flowers and satin robes were placed about her. How beautiful she looked, like a girl again, pure and sweet and young, as if the past few years hadn't happened at all.

I sat in the entrance of the *vurdón*, my head propped up on my elbow crying as I watched the flames dance back and forth on the beautiful sight they'd built.

I couldn't believe that I had lost two friends to the flames in less than a week.

***

As luck would have it, it wasn't long before rumors started spreading that the "prodigal son" had returned. This was, I feel certain, due to the above-mentioned priest, who wasn't exactly known for his discretion.

As it turned out, my presence there was the only pretext they needed to get back at the small community once and for all, as it dared to exist in the shadow of the Inquisitorial Court.

***

It started just after the midnight call that all was well.

I heard a piercing scream, and I sat upright next to Manfariel. It was a stormy night, and I'd already been unable to sleep because of the thunder

273

and lightning that I feared could start a fire, what with all the wagons full of hay and barns ready for the horse-selling fair.

Manfariel had finally gotten to sleep after tossing and turning for hours. He was despondent over the deaths of the girl he loved and of his sister. Soon, more voices followed the scream, voices of confusion and panic, and those of men who yelled out in warning or anger.

I jumped to my feet and bounded outside. The shouts were getting louder as I spied a group of men on horseback racing through the settlement, splashing through the quickly forming mud puddles. They were carrying clubs and burning sticks they were using to set the *vurdóns* on fire. They burned brightly in spite of the pounding rain. Others were swinging maces or bearing lances. Was this the fraternal group which my brother had been a member of? I saw a man jump from his wagon, which was engulfed in flames, and run toward one of the men, screaming and bearing a knife. The man growled back at him as he swung the mace before bringing it down on the side of the other's head with a loud cracking sound. I turned away, unable to stand the ghoulish sight.

More and more of them came every minute, and I saw what was happening: the men were being subdued so that the women and children would be defenseless — so that the attackers would be able to have their way with them.

I ran at the men and begged them to stop this senseless and unprovoked attack on my friends. But most people are harmful when they can be, and cruelty is by far the rule in this world, rather than kindness, which is the rare exception. All around me, then, men were being clubbed, speared, and massacred while the soldiers called them filthy, heathen dogs who deserved to die.

As the smoke nearly blinded me and stung my throat, I choked back tears as one of the men ran Manfariel through with a lance. I held his head in my lap as the life drained out of him and he gasped Esther's and Ostelinda's names.

The gypsy women were raped in the few *vurdóns* left. Some of them were attacked in the mud around the settlement, and the children were either put to the knife or fled to the meadows and hills outside of Triana. Some of them fled to the *Iglesia Santa Ana*, and banged loudly on the door, hoping for help from the priest. But the doors of the old church remained closed as they far too often do when the innocent cry out for mercy. There seemed to be no help for anyone then, the night that Triana was sacked and the place and people I loved were destroyed.

CHAPTER FIFTY-EIGHT

My father reached up and tugged the rope that rang the bell of the ancient College of Sevilla. It clanged loudly, and a few doves flew from the belfry in fright, only to roost moments later atop the minaret of the Giralda.

The door opened a narrow crack, and a squinty middle-aged man wearing a white habit and a black mantle — much like that of his brethren who ran the Inquisition-peered out at us in curiosity. "What do you want?" he demanded, his voice heavy with suspicion.

"I've come to see the prior about my son," Father said, with a note of distaste at the man's rancid breath.

"Is he expecting you?" the man asked, licking his fingers and making a disagreeable slurping sound. "Prior Hojeda doesn't like it when—"

"Oh, let me by, you dolt!" Father said in annoyance as he pushed his way past him into the musty corridor of the cloister with me in tow. "I've got business with him, and I sent a note about it yesterday."

A few minutes later, and after the prior had been pulled out of a lecture about mapmaking, we were sitting across from him at his desk in the rectory.

"So," the man said, looking at me warily, "he wishes to be admitted here as a penitent monk?"

"It's the only thing for him," Father said with a sniff. "Ever since I had him brought back from the rabble of Triana, I can't do anything with him, and I don't want him in my home anymore. I think he'd be best suited for the confines and strictures of the Church."

"What is it that *you* want, my son?" the man asked. He was fat and auburn-haired, and smiled a lot more than I'd expected him to. How could life in such a place allow for good humor?

"I want nothing but peace and rest," I managed to say.

"And do you yearn for silence, self-denial and contemplation so that you may better serve the Lord, and that other men may be saved from darkness?" he asked, as he fingered the leaves of a thick tome on his desk.

"Yes, sir, that is what I seek," I said. "I've grown weary of the things of this world."

"The monastic life isn't for the weak of heart," he said, "or the weak of *faith*. Are you ready for a life of denial, of abnegation — of the surrendering of your own self — to the will of the Lord so that His will shall be done on earth as it is in Heaven? I hope this isn't a caprice of some sort, or a silly whim."

STEVEN FARRINGTON

A whim. I remembered when my mother had referred to it as that once, when I was a boy. "Benja, why do you love the portrait of the Virgin so?" she had said. "Why do you cry and light a candle for her every time we go to the cathedral? It's so capricious. Stop it right now, Benja, you are not a girl. What will people say?"

"No, my motives for entering this place are pure." I sighed, thinking I'd made myself clear by now.

"How attached are you to the ways of the world, boy?" the prior asked, coming around his desk. "Are you prepared to rise on the third hour every morning for confession and then toil in the garden? Are you capable of surviving on stale bread and a bit of wild honey, with meat only on the rarest of occasions?"

"That I am." I stared straight ahead, trying to look stoic.

"The life of the cloister isn't just that of prayer and meditation, but also of learning and the cultivation of the mind. Are you willing to attend dull lectures on various subjects, as well as spend long hours reading thick books?"

That part seemed the best part of the proposition to me. "Yes, sir. All that I can manage."

"Are you willing to see people sent to the burning faggots as the only remedy for Judaizing? Not to mention, shall we say, punishment for other offenses," he watched my reaction with a critical eye and looked suspiciously at my flaming locks that had grown long during my time away. The smile I'd seen earlier had now disappeared from his countenance.

To this, I could say nothing that would reassure the prior. The memory of Esther was too fresh in my mind.

"How strong is your faith, boy?" he snarled, now just inches from my face.

"It is solid, sir," I said, forcing the necessary lie. My only spiritual advisor, Father Sebastián, had died in his sleep the previous winter after a long and difficult theological fight with the Dominicans that had left him without a friend in Sevilla.

"He is, after all, a Guzmán," my father said. "That must count for something. He carries at least a drop of the same blood as the founder of your order."

The prior stood and stared at me for a long moment. Then, turning for the door, he said, addressing my father, "This boy isn't for the monastic life, Marquis. In the future, don't try to leave your whelps on the doorstep of Mother Church when it's no longer convenient for you to see to them."

Father glared at me for a long moment after the prior left, then dashed out to pursue the discussion further in the corridor.

I'm not sure how much money or how many threats were exchanged between the two. Also, considering the strength of the Inquisition and its potential for destroying anyone in its path, I'm surprised Father dared to risk inciting Dominican rage, our well-placed relatives notwithstanding. All I know is that, by nightfall, my red locks had been shorn and I had a small cell with a bit of hay on which to sleep on the river's side of the college.

CHAPTER FIFTY-NINE

Bartolomé still had a hard time believing his guest had been a monk. But he guessed that by this time, he should have been able to believe almost anything about Rodrigo. He was just that kind of man, he supposed — full of surprises.

"What were those years in the college like for you?" he asked him one night as they walked along the shore. "They can't have been happy ones for one who was so adventurous."

"Bartolomé, the lack of excitement was exactly what I was looking for. I only wished to be left alone to read, write, think, and tutor the occasional student. Adventure and the desire for something better had only brought pain and suffering, like for the bull in my dream."

Considering all that he'd told him, Bartolomé couldn't very well disagree.

CHAPTER SIXTY

I was now totally numb to what was going on around me. I was indifferent to the screams of the Inquisition that was in full swing as the years advanced. I offered a novena for Ostelinda and Esther, but became insensible to the plight of the Jews. Although they'd been tolerated before, now they confronted the choice of conversion or expulsion — and conversion guaranteed nothing. People blamed them for every problem, from interest on loans to the rats and lice that plagued them at night. Diseases like pox and thrush had even become worse, and this was also laid at the feet at the Sons of Abraham.

I also didn't much care about the war against the last stronghold of the Moors, which began again in 1481 when the caliph refused to pay tributes to the Catholic Monarchs, Isabel and Fernando. Some of my cofriars traveled to Baza and Cordoba to be with Fernando's troops for the final push on the caliph's son Boabdil the Cruel's troops in Granada. They hoped to end the seven-hundred-year-old *reconquista*, which had begun when St. James had appeared on a white horse, spurring Christians on to action in Compostela. I was sent, against my will, to Granada for a time to help set up a monastery, but I did not stay long. After the conquest, though, I spent a time exploring that city, and even though it was a hot spring, I spent a day wandering through the great Moorish palace of the Alhambra and its amazing garden, the Generalife. It was lovely, with so many flowers, fountains, and fish-ponds. It was the very vision of a Muslim Heaven-on-earth.

Everywhere I went in Granada, I saw pomegranates, which seemed to be the symbol of the city. I remembered how Esther had once told me that King Solomon had kept a pomegranate garden on his palace grounds, and that she loved the succulent fruit because it held 613 seeds, the same number of *mitzvoth* in the Torah.

It was lovely to explore Granada, but I wanted nothing but to return to Sevilla and remain alone in my cell, the soft Andalusian sun drifting through the bars between prayers, collation, and my work in the herb-and-bean garden. I was content simply to stroll between the stone arches of the cloister and listen to the birds sing their early morning greeting each day in the gray dawn before everyone else awoke for prayers and confessions.

One day, I met a shy young man there named Pedro Millán. He had been standing in the shadows, observing me for a while, and noticed the sad, almost tortured look I wore, and how I lingered by the columns and arches near the garden. He asked me to pose for him for a statue he was making of Christ Tied to the Column. At first, naturally, I resisted the idea, hoping as I did only for a life of anonymity, but the man persisted and even asked permission from my prior to use me as his model. Finally, under pressure from the prior, I reluctantly agreed to model for the man, and I spent several long weeks posing beside a column in our garden as I spied the beans that I would rather have been harvesting than standing still for that sculptor. For a few days, the man even tied a rope around my neck and wrists, and I didn't even bother to protest, such was my feeling of resignation. I was told years later that this sculpture graced a corner of the *Iglesia de San Gil* where my mother heard mass as an old widow, and seeing my likeness there brought her a small amount of satisfaction, even if it meant that I had been turned into a column of stone.

When the sculptor had finished, he asked me if he could send a painter friend to have me pose for a Saint Sebastian that he wanted to do for the cathedral. I refused, needing, as I explained to him, to return to my life of simplicity and routine.

Perhaps I should have become a Franciscan. But there I was, and the Dominican monastery gave me what my heart longed for: safety, silence, and simplicity.

But above all, I wanted to forget. I wanted to forget so many things.

CHAPTER SIXTY-ONE

There is one day, perhaps in 1486 or 1487, that stands out in my mind from that period as being what you could call, I suppose, an exciting day in the life of the cloister. In any case, it was far more interesting than the usual reading of the Song of Songs among the monks.

The famous mariner, Cristobal Colón visited the cloister that day. Not that *I* ever saw him. I only heard his voice as I turned a corner in the corridor, and he spoke with an odd accent that was as soft and soothing as it was strangely familiar. It reminded me of the Portuguese sailors' patois, only it was marked by a strange twang. The cowls of my habit blocked my face, and I never looked up to see his.

I heard all about what he said later, and saw that he easily won the monks over to his side — which isn't really surprising, since he'd always had more friends among churchmen than among any other class of people. The Church had never forgotten the humiliations of the Crusades, and the eviction of the

Christians from the Levant in the Thirteenth Century. My fellows had faith in this man who carried a Book of Hours and said all the same prayers they did.

He sat with them and broke bread and ate his fill of onions and the usual thin, meatless broth. He even tried a goblet or two of our crude wine. He told them grand stories about how he planned to use his findings to further the spread of the Holy Faith, and to smite the infidel in the Holy Land once he was made rich enough. He said he wanted to be an arrow in God's quiver, but that he couldn't do this without their unflagging support. They were only too eager to listen as he assured them that the gold he'd traded as a youth in Tunis was but a drop in the bucket next to that which he'd possess once he mastered the Ocean Sea.

"Oh yes, my brothers," he said one night about halfway through his visit. "Jerusalem will yet be awash in the blood of the infidel!"

Wasn't it Saint Christopher who had carried Jesus across the waters? he asked. Didn't the Book of Psalms prophesy that it would be he to "bear their words unto the ends of the earth?" Didn't it also say that those who went to the sea for the Lord would have His protection? Hadn't their countryman Seneca written that, "one day the chains of the ocean will fall apart and a vast continent will be revealed, when a pilot will discover new worlds and Thule," that lost, northern, ice-locked land Colón claimed to have visited, "no longer be the ultimate," the farthest-known place on earth?

For the few monks who raised their eyebrows in surprise, like Father Hojeda at first, he was always ready to make a show with the maps, charts and papers he kept in a thick satchel by his side. He used examples and quotes from Alfragan and Ptolemy, as well as from Marinus and even the Bible to further prove his case. He truly believed that God had granted him the gift of knowledge as well as the burning desire to carry out His plan.

"I'll even find Antilia!" he crowed that day of his visit, jumping up and spilling his wine on his neighbors at the bench beside him. "The lost city of Atlantis will be ours once again, and I can prove it!"

This was all before the learned men, led by Talavera, the queen's confessor, met in Salamanca and decided to recommend that she *not* finance this "ludicrous expedition," as they deemed it. But it would be the black and gray friars, and especially Father Marchena of *La Rábida* Monastery of Palos, who would sway Isabel in the end.

In the meantime, Colón was bored and frustrated by events at court. He set up a mapmaking and book shop in Sevilla — something that was possible thanks to the hundred or so printing presses all over Europe by then. But I heard that he wasn't very good at his trade — his customers always grumbled over the notes he'd scrawled in the margins, forgetting which books were his and which were for sale.

He lived off a modest stipend that the court had accorded him while the queen tried to make up her mind about him. But a few things I'd learned long before then about the Genoese is that they're ambitious, hardworking, and, most of all, stubborn. And it was never more the case than with this Colón.

Despite his keen mind and determination, people made fun of him nearly all the time. I heard that some of the fishmongers and laundresses by the river called him "dumbo Colombo," using his Italian name, for following the court from castle to castle and battlefield to battlefield, not knowing when to give up.

If only they'd known what would happen in a few short years, and how he would show them all.

CHAPTER SIXTY-TWO

You can see that this was an interesting time to be alive in Sevilla, what with the war against Granada on and Colón winning more men to his cause every day. *I* couldn't be bothered with any of it, however. As I said, I just wanted to be left alone, out of sight, forgotten old Fray Benjamín, my pains and losses my sole companions. I never even saw the Italian directly, as I always stole back into my cell whenever I heard his booming voice coming from the common dining room.

I probably would have been left alone, too, and would be an old man in one of those cells today if the stars hadn't been written so differently. If I hadn't been accused of that horrible crime, they never would have threatened my life and sent me, against my will, across the Ocean Sea as that madman Colón's slave."

Bartolomé could hardly believe his ears. His guest was finally admitting how he'd been sent across the Ocean Sea — and it *was* because of a crime after all!

"So, what was it that you did?" he asked, trying to sound casual.

There was a long silence. Then his guest said, "Bartolomé, is it really so important for you to know? Isn't it enough that I am here, and have that be the end of it?"

Bartolomé was taken aback by his defensiveness. Had it really been so obvious his curiosity in what had brought him to this part of the world?

He looked over at the old man as he sat there, rocking gently in his hammock, and tried to fake a smile.

Rodrigo cleared his throat. "You know, there are many reasons why I've chosen to come here and relate this story to you. I'd hoped to give you an important perspective on what recent times have brought us. I want you to see how the forces of hatred have led us to where we are now — and what's at stake for these natives that we're threatening to wipe from the earth before a few years pass. And all you can worry about are trivialities about my life? How dare you!"

"I'm sorry," Bartolomé said, looking down at his folded hands. "I've heard so many stories over the years—"

"Well, you shouldn't believe everything you hear," Rodrigo said, getting up and grabbing the cane he'd been using for the past few weeks. He scowled as he picked up his cap. "It was a mistake to come here. You're just like the rest of them, I should never have thought otherwise," he said, forcing his arms into his cloak with a grunt.

"Where do you think *you're* going?" Bartolomé asked, clutching at his elbow. "Do you plan to leave? Where would you go?"

The old man laughed out loud at this. "My dear boy, do you think I haven't anywhere to go? Where do you think I've been living these last twenty years? I've been living among the people of this land since you were barely more than a schoolboy, and I know these woods better than any man, black, white *or* brown."

Bartolomé loosened his grip on the old man's arm. "I'm sorry."

"Is that all you've got to say for yourself?" He gave a disgusted grunt. "After all this time and effort, I realize that all you care about is what sin they thought I committed. I could leave right now and live on *guayaro* roots, like during the famine a few years back."

Bartolomé stood there feeling embarrassed, not knowing what to say.

"No, no," the old man said, turning away. "I had hoped this wouldn't be lost on you, but you've missed the point entirely."

"I'm sorry," the priest repeated.

Rodrigo was turning to leave again, but then hesitated and looked at Bartolomé. "You know what you are?" he said, turning to face him, his fists clenched at his side. "You're *worse* than all the others, you know that? You're *worse* than the men who hanged your precious friend so many years ago and murder and rape and pillage the innocent Taino. You're *worse* than all the others combined. And do you want to know why?"

"Why?" Bartolomé asked, choking back surprise, anger and hurt. He wasn't sure he wanted to hear the answer, and he hated to be reminded of how Juanito, the slave his father had brought him, had died.

"You're worse than all of them," he said, pointing a crooked finger in Bartolomé's face, "because, unlike them, *you* have a conscience, and *you* know right from wrong. What's more, *you* have the power to make a difference — to write to people and let them know what's happening over here, no matter how desolate the place to which they've exiled you. You're a persuasive man of learning and letters — people would *listen* to you. They may have listened to me once too," he said, turning away, "but I lost that chance long ago."

"I thought I could fight violence with violence," the old man whispered after a moment. "I thought I could help them to resist like fighting men. But that's a lost battle now, and you're the only hope these people have against being completely wiped out."

Bartolomé reached out to touch his shoulder, but once again Rodrigo pulled away.

"You know who you remind me of?" Rodrigo asked. "You're like that man in the story from Matthew — the one who kept his nose clean and didn't break any of the laws, and was happy being just good enough — but he was dismayed when told he had to sell all his worldly possessions or risk separation from God forever. He loved the world too much to let go." He stopped for a moment, letting the words sink in. "You've got a great mind, Bartolomé. You've got a beautiful estate and slaves who attend to your every need. You could live out your years here in luxury and I'm sure that most people would never find fault with you — everyone else would have nothing but good things to say about you."

He paused and took a deep breath. "But I'm not impressed at all by great minds or beautiful buildings if there's no heart in it. Faith without works is dead. The way you live now — you're just an empty shell. There's so much you could have, my friend, but — you're just too attached to the illusions of this world to travel the narrow path. Remember that Our Lord said it would be easier for a camel to go through the eye of a needle than for a rich man to enter the gates of Heaven."

Bartolomé moved toward him then and tried to find the right words to say. His tongue felt very dry then, and he felt once again like a lost boy seeking his father's embrace during a thunderstorm. He looked down the hill at all that lay below him before he spoke.

"If I let it all go," he said, his voice hoarse and cracking, "if I let it all go, and become like a child in order to enter the gates of heaven, if I take the narrow path—"

Rodrigo turned fully to face him. His eyes told him all he needed to know about the ultimatum he was giving.

Bartolomé paused, then said, "If I agree to follow you down that path, and allow myself to be stripped of it all, if I were to let it all go — will you help me along the way?"

"It won't be easy," Rodrigo said. "You'll have to open your heart and stop living in the world of illusions."

Bartolomé looked again on all he owned — the plantation, the farm, the slaves, the fields. He thought of the mines just a few leagues away, and how much they could earn for him.

How could he give it all up, just like that? Couldn't he keep it and just become more charitable? How could anyone fault him? He would be doing more than most would do in his place.

He looked at Rodrigo again, the setting sun shining in the few red strands of his gray hair. The man's fiery dark eyes studied him from a face full of scars and wrinkles.

Rodrigo would never respect me if I tried to compromise, he thought. If I faltered, he'd leave me. With him, it was all or nothing, and they both knew it.

Just what was at stake here, anyway? Bartolomé wondered. And why was all of this so difficult?

CHAPTER SIXTY-THREE

It was a warm day in early August, 1492 as we made final preparations for the Great Expedition.

I'd been rescued from the Inquisition's dungeon only a few days earlier. A man had come in, and I'd thought that I was to be dragged to the interrogation room and clubbed or beaten again. I thought I would be sent to the flames. But no — an emergency permit had been granted for old Fray Benjamín, and I was transported straightaway on muleback to Palos de la Frontera.

I remember the first time I saw the three caravels bobbing gently in the harbor. It had been so long since I'd been near one. I felt the old fear of the sea and the *malaria* that I had had before. I hoped that this time things would be different.

As I've explained, Colón had to try long and hard to convince the royals of the merits of his idea. But Isabel had finally been convinced to patronize the experiment, since it was a relatively small amount to gamble, with much to gain if things went as the Italian said they would. Besides, her most trusted counselors had reasoned, if the strange mariner could bring boatloads of gold back from the Indies, it would surely be enough to smite the infidels who menaced the faithful in the Holy Land who had participated so valiantly in the Crusades. And with Dias's discovery of the Cape of Good Hope, an easterly route to the Indies had been discovered for the Portuguese — and the stakes were that much higher for finding a route there through the west for a Spain that saw itself on the rise.   But getting royal approval had only been the first of many steps. Colón had almost been driven mad and lost his then white hair by the so-called "Spanish things," the little Castilian ways of delaying and putting things off because of our inefficiency.

But even all that had been just the first step. It was much easier to finance and marshal resources for the voyage than to find men willing to risk life and limb on such a venture. Don't forget that Colón was seen by most as a foreigner not to be trusted, and rumor had it that he knew next to nothing about sailing, an eccentric full of empty boasts and promises. Needless to say, there were very few initial volunteers. Four men were offered amnesty from a local prison — a murderer and three fellows who'd been caught trying to free him. They had chosen, like I did, lunacy over a death sentence. The only difference, of course, is that I had been compelled to keep the nature of my crime to myself, as I've done for all these years.

The town of Palos was in an uproar. Not only were all the preparations being done for the historic voyage that Saint Julien's Day — but the port was bustling with Jews fleeing the realm. A royal edict of expulsion had finally been trumpeted in every town's plaza, and all the roads were full of them as they trudged along, banging tambourines to keep their spirits high. The last of the Moors had been defeated just seven months earlier as well. The great Boabdil had stopped on his famous bridge — the one that they now call "the sigh of the Moor" — to look back one more time at his beloved Alhambra on the hill with its rich fountains, cool arcades, and jasmine gardens. He'd handed over the keys to the palace, and reached through the bars of the gates to kiss the royal hands of our monarchs. Ever since then, Isabel and Fernando, as well as their troops, seemed to be itching for another, more challenging fight.

The last of the Jews had to be gone — minus their wealth — by sundown, or risk being burnt at the *quemadero*. Some of them had managed to smuggle themselves to Portugal or Navarre, but many were milling about the decks and crowding onto the last boats that would bear them to sea, risking gales, pirates, or cheating tricksters. Only Byzantium in the East seemed a beacon of hope to these people without a land, wanderers like the Romany had always been.

The Jews departing then wore nothing but brown rags and carried only a few belongings, such as the tools of their trades, with them. It seemed that besides that, the only things they could carry were their long faces and the yellow stars they'd been forced to wear. Many highly-placed Jews had converted to save their posts, and I heard that fully one third of their entire number had done so in that sad Jewish year of 5253.

Our ships were stocked with everything we would need for the voyage. Biscuits, beans, fresh water, vinegar, wine, onions, salted meat and chickpeas were among our provisions. We also brought gifts of mirrors, beads and bells for any native people we might meet. This didn't make sense to me, as I couldn't imagine the great Khans of Cathay or the people of the Kingdom of Sind wanting such silly trinkets. Marco Polo never brought such things with him.

But who was *I* to question such things? I was a man old enough to be the father of some of the sailors, a poor devil who had been stripped of his identity and forced to take his chances with destiny — all because I spoke some languages and it was rumored that I'd once been to the Indies already. The lie had saved me from the flames of the *quemadero*, and I wasn't foolish enough to deny it. I will admit to you that my biggest fear in life has always been a death by fire. I'd like to believe that there are things I am above doing to avoid that kind of death, but I don't like to lie.

We the crewmembers had to go confess and take the wine and wafers in the Church of San Jorge before boarding our ships in the late afternoon of August the second. As I slowly made my way toward the end of the dock to where my assigned ship, the *Pinta*, sat rocking gently in the water, I heard the last of the Jews in the nearby ships singing psalms for comfort. Some of them yelled and jeered at us, but most of them just watched us and silently wished us well, voyagers as we all were, bound for the unknown.

I gently touched the ruby necklace under my white sailor's smock, and thought of how many times someone had tried to take it from me. Paolo had tried to steal it from me in the land of the Bolama. I'd almost died of hunger and thirst rather than trading it on the voyage back to Lisbon. I'd been ordered to get rid of it for the monastic life, and had been forced to bury it in the putrid underground dungeon of Torquemeda — but it had remained with me through everything. It was a testament to my love and friendship for Esther, as well as all those I'd left behind. I'd had to change my name yet again because of the ignominious accusation they'd laid upon me back in Sevilla, but even still I wore my ruby necklace under that rough sailor's smock. No longer could I wear the name of Fray Benjamín, the nickname of my childhood into which I had briefly escaped. I had toyed with the idea of going by Lorenzo, the name of my long-lost friend whom I still missed every day.

Some of the men of the crew had smiled when they'd met me going into mass, and had joked that I looked just like the Marquis of Cádiz, Rodrigo Ponce de León — that crazy rascal who had sacked Sevilla when I was a boy, and had just recently died. He also had that rarest of things among Andalusians, even if some of our ancestors *were* Goths: hair so red it made one think of a campfire the gypsies burned at their annual horse fair, the Inquisition's flames which had replaced them, or the red banners which were displayed over the Holy Court's balustrade which told the eager crowds of an upcoming *auto-de-fe*.

The men of the crew began calling me Rodrigo, and at first I winced. I didn't want anyone knowing my true name, even if it was one I hadn't used in years. But then, I decided that there might be some use in such a lie, such as it was, hidden in plain sight. Rodrigo had been the name of my disastrous first adulthood, after all. But for these crude men, I had nothing to fear if some found out that I had worked in the Portuguese slave trade. In fact, this made me seem more like a man to be reckoned with.

So it was that I came again to call myself Rodrigo, even though I hated the idea of using the identity that had caused me so much suffering. Rodrigo de Triana — or, occasionally, Rodrigo Bermejo de Xerez, as my hair was still the color of vermillion and I was rumored to be from that nearby city. I denied none of the rumors the men spread about me and my roguery. I decided I was well beyond that now.

I thought about how strange it was that I was forced to change my name to survive, and that I had also reverted back to the name of my illustrious ancestor and the name my father had hoped would bring respect for our name. Never again, until now as I tell my story, would I utter the family names of Guzmán or Vargas.

As I stared at the last ship that carried away the last of the Jews, a bitter grimace creased my lips. A memory of a promise surfaced in my mind, one that had remained long-buried. I'd once promised Esther that I would leave Spain forever the day the Jews were expelled from our realm. And now, it seemed, I *was* never to return.

How strange life can be.

***

Before I knew it, we were leaving on our voyage.

Early that morning — the morning of Friday, August 3, the anniversary of the destruction of the Temple of the Jews so long ago — the glass marking four A.M. was turned over, and we were about to drift out of the harbor of Palos. Friends and families of the men came down to bid us farewell from the cliff and the monastery of *La Rábida*. Young women yelled out, "Go with God!" and, "We'll light a candle for you in the church and pray to the blessed Virgin!" Another girl yelled, "We'll order a mass said for you, and sing *Iam lucis orto sidere* as you leave, my darling!"

Needless to say, there was no one there to bid *me* farewell that day. Even my father seemed glad to be rid of me once and for all, or so I assumed.

Everything was in readiness for the voyage when a man walked up to me and clapped me on the shoulder as I stood on the foredeck of the *Pinta* looking out at the multitude on the shore.

"Ah, you must be the one they call Rodrigo de Triana," he said.

I recognized him as Martín Alonso Pinzón, the much-admired captain of the *Pinta*, which had been commandeered from a private owner for this most royal of expeditions. Strange, I thought to myself. I haven't met Captain — for he was not yet an Admiral — Colón himself.

"Yes, I am he," I said, wondering what he might or might not have heard about me.

"I haven't had a chance to speak with you before now, as my brothers and I have been so occupied with the preparations," he said, taking out a sheaf of neatly stacked papers. "*And* you're a last-minute recruit. Now, am I to understand that you've got experience as an able seaman? And you're good with languages, yes? Because if so, we can pay you the 5,000 maravedis which we'll pay to all the able seamen, plus whatever—"

"You shall pay him only as much as you'll pay a common grommet, and make him earn it like the dog he is," snarled an eerily familiar voice from behind us.

I turned to face the Captain General, the man who would soon be known as the Great Admiral, Captain of the Ocean Sea — and the blood seemed to freeze in my veins.

Standing before me, thin white hair and all, was the man from whom I'd tried to rescue Winnoke's grand-daughter so many years ago on that fateful night in the land of the Bolama as the rain fell so gently on my face.

CHAPTER SIXTY-FOUR

One after another, the anchors were winched up with the help of the windlass. To help out, I grabbed one of the wooden handles that provided leverage. It was back-breaking labor, and I prayed that we'd never have to kedge one of the ships out of shallow water. Finally, the boats pulled out from the harbor, and we readied the three caravels for the trip as we rolled from the river Tinto and onto the Ocean Sea.

I felt fortunate to be assigned to the *Pinta*, the ship led by Captain Pinzón, as he was said to treat his men well, provided they worked hard for him. In some ways, I might have been thought better suited for the flagship, the *Santa María*, or the "Sweet Mary" as the men called her. She was about a hundred tons burthen with a conventional rig. She had a mainmast taller than the ship was long and a main yard that was nearly as long as the keel itself. The mix of forty Andalusians, Galicians and others on her would have made anonymity easier — but with Colón as her captain, I thanked God that I'd been stationed on another ship.

The ninety-foot *Santa Clara*, or *Niña*, which had been given to Vicente Pinzón to captain, was slightly larger than the vessel I rode, and bore twenty-seven men. It was a family affair; two Pinzón brothers rode her out to the Ocean Sea, and no fewer than three of the Niño family, her owners, went along for the ride, stationed at various ranks.

But ours was by far the most agile of the ships. Like the *Niña*, she sported four masts, ample below-deck space and was full of rigs, ropes, rings, and pulleys. She was also what they called in those days a *Caravel Redonda*, which meant that she had square sails on the main and foremasts for sailing downwind, but lateen sails for the mizzen masts, which gave us plenty of agility. I know for a fact that Colón cursed his flagship daily, and would choose the *Niña* to be his ship of choice in later explorations.

Each of the vessels had been painted red, yellow, and blue by her crew. I couldn't see at first, but below the waterline was painted with pitch to discourage barnacles and leaking.

In any case, we in the *Pinta* ranged far ahead of the others most of the time. This was good news, for we hoped to be the first to spot land and thus win the coveted prize of 25,000 maravedis as well as a doublet rumored to be as scarlet as my hair.

As we headed out to sea, my trepidation gave way to excitement for the adventure that lay ahead. I hadn't planned this, but I was finally on my way to the Indies!

I was thankful that I remembered some of what I'd been taught as a grommet back in my slave-ship days. Even though I couldn't do a thing with the quadrant, I knew how to read a compass, how to navigate the rudder using Polaris, and could furl, hoist and position a sail with ease. I was unafraid to sit aloft in the crow's nest, lean precariously against a rail to place red-hot coals from the fire into our brazier or help fire the bombards when we had to send a message. I tarred the ropes, set out casks to collect rainwater, and swabbed the decks with seawater and brooms we'd brought along for that function. I had no reservation about cleaning the lee after the men had relieved themselves there. I cooked the broth of meat and onions in the giant cauldron every night and could lead them in prayers afterwards at Compline. I even impressed the ship's grumbling old surgeon with the work I did. I did anything I could to avoid confrontation with Captain Pinzón, the one man who'd shown that he'd give me a chance and treat me fairly. And, of course, I hoped to avoid a clash with Captain Colón. I threw myself into my work in order to avoid seeing my old enemy again while he wielded the power of life or death over me.

I used to lead the men in songs and prayers at the morning watch, and I used to sing:

"Blessed be the light of day
And the Holy Cross, we say!"

And at night, once I'd see the binnacle

lamp lit:

"God give us a good night and good sailing;
May our ship make a good passage,
Sir Captain and Master and good company."

I would even lead them in a Salve Regina, remembering my favorite childhood night-time prayer, using for once the Latin I never thought I would need:

"Salve Regina, Mater Misericordiae
Vita Dulcedo et spes nostra salve..."

Late at night as I shivered on my sea-rotten plank — or, if I were lucky enough, a dry coil of rope by the great hatch — I would practice my languages to myself as I once again watched the changing places of the stars and constellations. "*Kosko Divvus*," I said to myself in Romany, tightening the thin poplin cloak about my shoulders. "*Shalom*," I whispered in the ancient tongue of the Jews.

"*Andr'oda taboris, ay*." Don't throw me overboard, Captain. You'll need me to speak to the Great Khan when we arrive in the Land of Sind, and maybe Lorenzo will even be waiting for me when I get there."

CHAPTER SIXTY-FIVE

I don't want to bore you too much with the details of my voyage across the Ocean Sea. But there are a couple of moments you might be interested in hearing about.

First, we stopped off in the Canary Islands about two weeks after leaving Palos. Colón had decided to travel westward on the trade winds and then return at a higher latitude on the westerlies — an idea I had, of course, once considered while living among the Bolama. In any case, we on the *Pinta* had some problems with our rudder during the first part of the voyage, and I'd been afraid for a little while that the ship would sink and that we'd all have to clamber aboard the *Niña* and the flagship or drown. Captain Pinzón suspected foul play, possibly on the part of Colón, and some of the grommets grumbled among themselves that the owners of the ship had maliciously sabotaged the whole expedition. I wondered what would happen to me if we had to turn back. Would I still be punished, I wondered, or set free, forgotten in all the hustle and bustle?

We limped into Las Palmas to stock up on supplies and to make repairs while the other two ships continued on to San Sebastián, where, it was said, Colón hoped to cavort with one of his mistresses. I heard that he felt guilty about the child he'd fathered four years before in Córdoba, but he didn't ever strike me as one who was too laden with guilt to experience the pleasures of the flesh. In any case, when we arrived, Captain Pinzón contacted some of the island's toolmakers, smiths, and carpenters, and the marshal was able to commission more tar for the ropes and a new fin for the *Pinta*. After two weeks of work, we finally took sail and headed for San Sebastián.

After taking some of the boats into harbor, Colón met us at the steps of the Church, where he'd just come from a special mass with his mistress, Lady Beatriz.

"We've got to stock up a bit more, lay in more supplies of fruits, molasses and food for what lies ahead," he announced grandly. "You've got four days of leave, men. Spend them as you would."

The men hollered their approval at this unexpected gift, and soon all the brothels of the island were full of drunken sailors who'd been given an advance on their first month's pay. They spent it liberally, not knowing if they'd even survive the trip that lay ahead. The island's sheriff had his hands full with them for those few days.

I, of course, had no desire for such debauchery, and elected to explore the town and its environs, spending my money — and my evenings — in a comfortable inn where the wine wasn't watered down, the rats were few, and the noise was low.

But on my second day of exploration, I encountered, at the edge of town, someone I'd never expected to see again — much less still in the bonds of servitude.

CHAPTER SIXTY-SIX

"Kinjay?" I said, approaching the white-haired man as he bent over a beehive in the crook of a tree. "Is that you?"

He turned slowly toward me, a surprised look of recognition on his face. "But — how you—" he stammered, rising slowly and greeting me with a warm embrace. "How you know to come here?"

"I didn't," I said. "I was just here and exploring the island. How did *you* end up here? Weren't they going to free you after four trips?"

The truth dawned on me as I spoke these words, and I wished more than anything that I could take them back. No explanation was necessary. It was obvious he had been tricked.

"I be here eleven years like that," he said, his lower lip quivering. "I wanted to go back to my village and sleep by my wife. But that village not even there now, not after what they did to it, and the folks they took."

"I'm so sorry for you," I said. "Is there any way you can earn your way out?" I know, in retrospect, that this was a stupid thing to hope for if he'd been imprisoned for eleven years.

"No, no way they're gonna let me free," he answered bitterly, putting down the pot of honey he'd been collecting. "They lie. All you white men liars all the time with Kinjay."

"I'm so sorry," was all I could say.

"Well, they got me gathering honey."

"So I see. What do you think of it?"

He looked at the beehive that he'd been studying before I'd interrupted him. "It not so bad. I do it, and they never sting me. I sing, and they no want to hurt me like that." He showed me how he could put his arms into the hive and pull out a whole honeycomb. All the while there were bees buzzing around him, yet none of them stung him. He was a real bee-charmer, I thought.

"They come and go, so there's nothing bad here for them," he said. Then he asked, "How things for you, Rodrigo?"

"I'm more like you than the bees these days," I said after a moment. "I've got to go with a special group of men to the Indies, in a ship."

"Why you got to go *there?*" he asked, his brow pinched in confusion.

"Our queen wants us to go there so we can bring back lots of gold and make Spain rich, so that we can fight against our enemies."

He just looked at me and shook his head, the honey dripping from his hands into the clay pot by his side. "Kinjay never understand you white men."

All I could think of was that story he'd told me all those years before on the deck of the *María Luisa* about the hare that was never satisfied with what he had. What was it Allah had said to him? That if he were allowed the freedom to do whatever he wished, he'd entangle the world and destroy it?

Why the hell were we going on this mad expedition, anyway? Weren't we just like that hare?

CHAPTER SIXTY-SEVEN

It was October 9 — just three days before I was to see land.

The voyage had seen its ups and downs. There had been many days when we'd scudded and covered well over a hundred miles at eight, nine or even eleven knots. There were days when the air had been so still we'd barely moved on the glassy surface of a sea that was as calm as a farmer's pond. On those days — at least, on the ones when we'd not been hopelessly mired in thick seaweed and floating meadows — we'd put out the dinghies and some went swimming, the men doing flips from the starboard side of the *Pinta*, splashing each other and holding contests to see who could hold his breath underwater the longest. We also tried to catch fish that we cooked over our wooden fireboxes.

We had allowed ourselves to grow hopeful when we saw floating sticks, plants, and, occasionally, a flock of birds that swooped down on us from the heavens. We saw Jaeger gulls, the boatswain bird, and even some frigate birds. As time rolled on, we'd seen flying fish, a whale, and dolphins that jumped and played and smiled at us with their big gray faces and big black eyes.

About halfway through the trip, we saw something that scared us all a little — a shooting star tracking its way across the heavens. Was it an omen of things to come? A sign that we should turn back?

A stern wind had risen and pushed us forward, buoying our enthusiasm, but it had died again after we made a few days of solid progress. But soon, many of the days became, once again, tranquil, windless, and rainy, which melted our optimism like sea-foam. We'd already surpassed the distance Colón had said we needed to cover before reaching the Indies or at least Antilia, according to both of the journals he kept, and Tuscanelli's letter. As the editor of his writings, Bartolomé, you must know that, due to his poor estimates, the false journal he kept in order to keep his secrets safe was more accurate than the journal he kept for himself.

Many of the men grumbled that they didn't trust him to bring us back home alive. Some became outwardly defiant, saying that we should head for home before our supplies ran out. By the sixth day of October, some of the men had been on the verge of throwing him overboard with their bare hands. They would have, too, had he not lied and told them that *Cipangu* was just over the horizon.

***

The sun came up in a fiery blaze through a light rain that ninth day of October.

Captain Pinzón had told me that morning, as I turned over the first of the eight glasses that made up a watch, that Colón was a fool for not ruling his men with a stronger hand. "He's going to have a mutiny if he doesn't pick up the whip or execute a half-dozen of the instigators," he said, a bit of the morning rain dripping from his nose. "It only takes one man to start a riot, and that could spell disaster for everyone." He looked at me, and smiled. "We just need to hang on a bit more, Rodrigo. We'll see land soon enough. I can feel it. Now, why don't you paddle over to the flagship and work on your Arabic with Torres? You never know — maybe the Moors used their scimitars to beat us to the Indies while we were getting ready to send the heralds and banners of Castile and León into Granada."

So, despite the rough seas, I'd spent the late morning and early afternoon perched on the windlass of the *Santa María* with Luis Torres, with whom I was to serve as assistant interpreter if — or when — we would reach land.

Torres was an interesting man. A *converso*, he was also a distant cousin of Esther's. He was from Salamanca, where he'd studied Hebrew and Arabic, as well as a smattering of Latin, Greek and Aramaic, the language of Jesus. Whereas I spoke some Italian, Wolof, Romany, and the Bolama dialect of Balanta, he spoke fluent Catalán, French and Galician, which made him eminently useful on the flagship that boasted such a variety of men. Between the two of us we commanded over a dozen languages, since Portuguese was a given for two reluctant seafarers.

The man was exceedingly lucky that I'd held my tongue when I found him reciting his prayers asking God for forgiveness of his sins on the Day of Atonement. I had also heard the long-familiar words of the *Kol Nidre* that day under his breath.

Did he associate with impurity? Our expedition was the very definition of it. Did he presume error? One can only find error in what resulted from our foray into the unknown. He recited a *Kaddish* and a *Shema* for his faithful departed, and I ate twice my usual rations that day, thanks to his fasting.

I talked with men from many different backgrounds on the *Santa María*: Basques, Galicians, and I even met William Ayres, a boy from Galway, Ireland. Needless to say, I asked him many questions to find out about his distant, green island, and why he'd left it — but all he seemed to want to do was complain about the "damn English" who fought and lorded over his land.

He did, however, confide to me that, when Colón was on his way back from the northern trip to the icy land of Ultima Thule, he'd found, with some of the astonished fishermen of Galway, two long, narrow boats tied together with two decaying bodies in it, one man and one woman. These two had dark skin, and it had been whispered during the burial at the graveyard by the little stone church that they were from the distant land of Cathay. When William had asked Colón about them and where he thought they'd come from, the mariner pointed to the great expanse of ocean to the west.

315

"They come from there, out there somewhere. And I'm going to go there someday soon. I swear it. I've been talking to some of the old men from the icy land of Thule, and they told me legends of their Viking ancestors and the *Skraelings* they met in Vinland, near China, across the sea."

This was all that was needed to convince the young man to follow Colón on this mad adventure. When I asked him if it was adventure or riches he sought, the young man smiled and refused to answer.

William lay a hand on my shoulder as I sat watching the sun climb higher in the sky.

"Do you want to hear an old poem my grandmum used to say to greet the morning when I was a child?" he asked. "It's called 'the Deer's Cry.'"

"All right," I said. "I'd love to hear it."

The young man took a breath and sang:

> *"I arise today*
> *Through the strength of heaven, light of sun*
> *Radiance of moon*
> *Splendor of fire*
> *Speed of lightning*
> *Swiftness of wind*
> *Depth of Sea*
> *Stability of earth*
> *and the Firmness of rock."*

"That's beautiful," I said.

We had all heard or read, of course, the tales of Marco Polo, but occasionally William would tell us the stories of an Englishman named Sir John Mandeville, who'd also supposedly made a trip to the East sometime in the distant past.

"There'll be monsters and giants when we get there," he told us, raising his voice like a troubadour one day as he sat on the grate of the hold, where all the food, casks of water, gear, and supplies were kept. His hair was even redder than mine, and his skin had grown more and more freckled as our trip progressed. "We'll see folks with no heads and one eye on each shoulder. Their mouths will be full of razor-sharp teeth in the shape of a horseshoe on their chests. And they only eat raw fish and human flesh."

We all scoffed at what he said, but he'd continued just the same.

"They all have big, ugly lips that cover their whole faces when they sleep. That's why they never need pillows!"

Several of the men had groaned and pounced on him ferociously, knocking him onto the deck where a coil of rope broke his fall.

The rest of us, however, believed what we'd heard or read of Marco Polo's adventures. We knew of gold and the Great Kahn, of course, but also the province of Manji, idolaters living with all kinds of indulgences, elephants, aloes, camphor shrubs, and artists accomplished in the arts of painting and puncturing the skin with needles.

That morning on the flagship, I'd been mostly able to avoid contact with both the grumbling sailors and the Captain himself, who would probably have growled at me to do this or that, as he usually did.

So it was that Torres and I were deep into a conversation about the Hebraic meaning of the psalms and lamentations of the Babylonian exile when I heard a crash and smash from down below, where the captain's quarters were located.

Suddenly, four of the men burst through the hatch that sealed the lower deck from the main deck. Torres, William, and I rushed over to see what the commotion was.

The men had stolen some of the swords sealed below in a locked trunk. These were not intended for use until such time as we reached the Indies, but now, four of the Galicians, who were naturally feisty and less loyal to the Monarchs than the Andalusians, had gotten hold of them. A cheer went up from the men who'd been grumbling under their breath for weeks.

Before I knew what was happening, a large crowd rushed up the stairs and gathered on the poop deck at the rear of the ship. They were gathered around Colón, who'd been staring off into space, leaning on the mizzenmast after having consulted the compass down below, which he used for, as he called it, "running his westing." He'd been doing this a lot lately.

The renegade Galicians advanced on him. "That's it, you bloody Genoese," snarled the leader, a tall, stout man who hadn't shaved in weeks. "We're not going to take it anymore. We're going back! The food's almost gone, and who knows what lies ahead? If we follow you, you'll lead us to our deaths!"

The dazed captain got to his feet, stumbling a bit as he did so. He looked frantically around to see if anyone would fight on his side, but it seemed that he was surrounded on all sides by snarls and angry looks.

I almost felt sorry for him, as he looked so helpless and old.

"The food's almost gone, and so's the water," said one of the men who carried a sword. "The biscuits are gobbled through with mealworms, and the wine's all been drunk. We've seen your logs — the official one *and* the one you mean to fool the queen with. We're way off course."

"Not at all. We're almost there, I'm sure of it. It's just taking a bit longer than we thought, but we'll be there any time now," Colón said, in a weak attempt to placate the men.

"You lying son of a bastard!" cried another of the swordsmen. "You don't have any idea where we are, and we're just going to keep going until we die of starvation and thirst in the middle of this huge sea. You even switched our sails to these that won't hold a blessed drop of rainwater. I bet you're trying to kill us all!" To this, the crowd roared.

"Why would I do something like *that?*" Colón asked with a sneer. "If you die, I die too, you know. We need each other. Now, you've got to stop crying about the little things! We're almost there, I swear to God."

"You've been telling us we're 'almost there' for weeks now," said a tall blond man with a pock-marked face, advancing on the captain with his sword. "We want to turn back while there's still a chance that some of us might make it back to the Canaries alive."

The men muttered their approval of this idea, and hurled insults and jeers at Captain Colón as he backed away from them to the edge of the ship.

319

"Give me three days," Colón pleaded, trying to raise his voice over the rising din. "If we don't make it in three days, then I promise you that we'll—"

"You've had all the chances you're going to get, you filthy son of a whore!" the blond man said, advancing again with his sword. Some of the mariners and grommets had their knives out, in case he should choose to run toward them.

Was I never to reach the Land of Sind?

"Make your choice, you swinebreath scamp," the stout leader of the rebels snarled. "Be ye run through with this damask steel, or will ye jump to swim with the mermaids?"

"May God take you! I'll never jump from the ship Queen Isabel *herself* commissioned me to ride to the Indies," Colón said in a defiant tone and with a raised chin, his arrogance surprising more than just me. "You'll have to kill me here, and wipe my blood from the planks of the ship — then be tried for treason back in Palos. Now, I've come this far on my trip to the Indies and I shall continue until I find them, with Our Lord's help. It is my destiny, and yours, too! I pray you not to lose faith."

Colón was truly the kind of man who plowed ahead no matter how the winds lashed him.

"Better to risk a charge of treason than die a slow death on the Ocean Sea," the stout leader answered, as the man drew back his arm to strike him down.

"No, stop!" I yelled, pushing my way through the men and standing before the bewildered captain. "Think about what you're doing, men. How can you think of going back now, when we're so close to land?"

The leader paused, and some of the others mumbled amongst themselves, annoyed at my attempt to interfere.

"Get out of the way if ye know what's good for ye," said the rebel.

I took a deep breath before plunging ahead. "Look," I continued, "you've all seen the sticks and the plants and the animals. Why, just the other day we of the *Pinta* found a live crab on some of the floating weeds. Doesn't that tell you *something* about how close we are to land?" I could feel my heart beating faster than it had ever beaten in my life, and my chest heaved under my smock.

"Get out of the way or I'll kill ye just like him," the man growled. "How would ye like a palm of steel in your liver?"

"Listen," I persisted, trying to choose my words carefully, "we're almost there. Don't you all want to go back to Spain laden with gold and treasures?" I remembered how I'd once been lured away from Iberian shores with that very same promise, and I shuddered to think I was now making the same argument. But this was different; it was to save a man's life. I still remembered what Father Sebastián once told me: "God values the life of every single man, woman and child. Don't ever forget that as long as you live. Don't forget to show everyone compassion."

At the mention of treasures and gold, the men seemed to soften a bit, so I continued speaking. "Our captain has sworn that if we don't encounter land in three days, we can turn back. I've seen the ample supplies that we still have," I said, stretching the truth. Since I had been the one to clean the bilges not only of the *Pinta* but also of the *Santa María*, I could claim to be familiar with our stockpiles, which strengthened my argument.

"And don't forget that we supplied ourselves well in San Sebastián," I continued, reflecting for the first time of the name of my long-ago teacher and the port where we had last glimpsed land. I didn't want to let on that I'd heard from Pinzón's own lips how we'd only brought enough water casks and leaky hogsheads of wine for four weeks, and had made it as far as we had only through strict rationing. "We can still go three days more and head home with every man surviving and none committing treason."

Many of the men seemed to have stopped their grumbling and scowling, and a few were uttering agreement with what I said.

Suddenly, the *Pinta* came alongside and captain Pinzón was shouting down to us, trying to find out what was happening. Luis Torres shouted something up to him, and within moments Pinzón and a half-dozen of the *Pinta*'s Andalusians were standing on the deck a few feet away from me, their swords drawn and ready for action.

"You will continue until we reach land or another three days, whichever comes first," Pinzón said, his voice heavy with authority. "As the Captain has stated. There'll be no bloodshed today, and no more talk of treason — or else men will meet their deaths upon the first word they utter. Do you all understand? The *Pinta* and the *Niña* are going onward to land or to Hell if necessary, as Her Majesty has commanded. I will personally see to it that anyone who tries to commandeer this ship will be hanged once he reaches Spanish waters. Have I made myself perfectly clear?"

The men nodded and muttered their acquiescence as Pinzón's men collected the swords and knives, which they took downstairs and locked up once again.

This time, he posted a guard by them, just in case.

Maybe now there was still a chance I'd reach the land of Sind, I thought to myself, satisfied with my handiwork. If only I had known then what I know now, I would have begged and pleaded with them to send us back home that very moment.

CHAPTER SIXTY-EIGHT

The sea was once again rough. A gale was on the way, and the men were afraid. It was the evening of Thursday, October 11. The crew of the *Santa María* had found, soon after their near-mutiny, a plank and some green branches, and this had filled them with hope and excitement for the first time in weeks. Even during the evening worship, and during the prayers when the men should have had their eyes closed out of reverence to the Lord, many had theirs open a bit as they scanned the horizon for any sight of land that would make them rich and win them the doublet that our captain had promised.

We were moving now at seven knots, and all of the men were up. Most of them were positioned on the foredeck, but I had been roused from my sleep not long before to stand watch in the bow, where I was to do an eleven-to-three watch. I had the best view of all as I lay cradled sleepily against the ropes of the foremast.

It was at this time that Colón must have falsified his journal, because he would later say that he'd seen a thin light from his cabin window, like a candle going up and down in the wind. But everyone knew this to be impossible, as there had been no such light; all the men were straining their eyes on the foredeck of our forward-ranging *Pinta*, seeing nothing. Nothing, that is, until I spied in the moonlight from my vantage point the sight of waves crashing against cliffs on a beach. It reminded me of a place where I'd often swum in the nude when I'd lived in the land of the Bolama. With their help, I'd even learned to swim in those days as a lanzado.

I cried out, "*Tierra! Tierra!*" As loudly as I could to signal the approach of land, afraid that if we didn't come about soon, we'd be smashed upon whatever shoals may have been on the outer banks of that place.

Soon, the other ships fired their bombards in recognition, and began to come about as well. Captain Pinzón was by my side, and all around men were clapping me on the back and shoulders and congratulating me as if I were a hero.

I was the first of the expedition to spot land in the New World, and everyone knew it.

I wanted to burst forth with an "*in excelsis Deo!*" at that moment. Could this be the magical land I had so often dreamed of?

Would I find my friend here? Was he performing for the Great Kahn or the king of this far-away land? Would the two friends finally meet at long last, one having gone east and the other west?

CHAPTER SIXTY-NINE

The next day, after much celebration and drinking of the little wine we had left, we sailed about the island trying to decide what to do next. Before long, we sought an opening on the western side of it, through a reef. We anchored by land in shallow water near a beach of the smoothest white sand. Captain Pinzón declared it to be the best spot for a landing, as it was sheltered from the winds and waves of the Ocean Sea, and the dinghies would be able to move back and forth between the ships and land without risk of capsizing.

But where *were* we? We saw nothing of the cities of gold and houses with cupolas about which Marco Polo had written. Was this truly the land of the great Kahn or the Kingdom of Sind? The men wondered if King Solomon's mines could be among the treasures we were about to discover.

Before long, we saw a few very dark-brown people creep out from the forest and sit on the beach peering at us. We wondered if these were the people

William had told us about, two of whom had washed ashore in his northern land. They wore next to nothing, and their faces were painted in what seemed like strange colors. They carried long sticks with pointed ends, like lances made of wood. The only people they made me think of were the Guanches, the natives of the Canary Islands that I had glimpsed during our brief visit there.

I must admit that my first sight of the Taino filled me with fear and trepidation. Who were these people, and what would they do to us? In retrospect, I'm sure it was *they* who were more afraid of *us*, who had come in giant, floating fortresses and carried lances capable of running men through for the slightest offense. But then again, at least back then, it simply wasn't in their nature to be mistrustful. It was as if they never assumed offense from the beginning, something which I'd unfortunately had to learn to do long before then.

It was decided that a few of us would make an expedition to explore the land and meet with the natives. Although there were dozens of men who begged to accompany Captains Pinzón and Colón, Luis Torres and I were chosen to go, as well as two armed Andalusians. After all, the Captain said as he put on his finest uniform of scarlet velvet and silk, how better to claim this land for Her Majesty than to arrive with men already speaking the language of the conquered?

And so it was that, not an hour later, Torres and I sat in the front of the dinghy as the men rowed us to shore. Pinzón wore his best plumed hat as he tried to hide his nervousness with a smile as he resolutely faced forward. Captain Colón stood perched upon the very front of the boat, his right hand on his hip and his left holding the white banner with the standard of Castile. It was embroidered with a large green cross — a favorite symbol of the Inquisition — which he was to sink deep into the white coral sand once we reached land, thus claiming it for Spain and naming himself viceroy and governor of this place.

The natives came forward to meet us as the boat made contact with the hard sand of the beach. Colón, of course, leapt out first, and fell to his knees as he plunged the standard deep into the sand of the beach. Since the sand was soft and fine, the stake went deep and was buried almost up to the flag itself. He prayed for a long moment then to the Virgin and Saint Christopher for having borne him safely across to the sea, just as Jesus had been in the saint's tale. He commanded us to do the same, so we all fell to our knees in prayer and thanksgiving that our long trip had at last come to an end.

I opened my eyes as I felt a hand on my face. It was a boy, maybe the age of sixteen, wearing red, green and black paint in lines and dots on his forehead and cheeks. He wore a small loincloth and earrings of seashells. He touched my red hair, and then pulled his hand away. His friends giggled and smiled their approval. I noticed that their pointed sticks had been left back near a log at the forest's edge.

I smiled back at them. In that moment before the Great Admiral raised his sword and christened the island Guanahani 'San Salvador,' I knew that I would get along well with the inhabitants of this place.

***

So much happened in those first few days of contact with the Tainos. They were so named, I was soon to find out, because they described themselves as good, honest people — unlike the much-feared Caribs to the south, who were said to eat human flesh. Colón simply called them, as every group we'd encounter, "*indios*," as he thought we'd actually reached the Indies. In any case, those that we met first in those smaller, less developed islands also called themselves "Lucayans," from their name for that place.

But did Colón really think he'd reached the Indies? He'd ostensibly been sent on an exploratory mission to find a way to open up trade with the Indies, not to claim or enslave them. What hadn't we been told, and to what knowledge had the royals been privy? Did this have something to do with those dead bodies they'd found in Ireland in those boats?

Colón gave them the trinkets — glass beads, cascabeles and red caps like the one my mother used to wear. In later months, the natives of Hispaniola would yell, "chuck! chuck!" for these toys whenever they saw us coming.

In return, the Tainos gave us gifts of green guacamaya parrots and *nagua*, which they grew for blankets and clothing. I think it works much better than the cotton used in Europe. They got it from a tree they called the *ceiba* tree, which had a wrinkled and furrowed trunk and soft, silky bows of a cotton-like substance. It made me think of the expensive robes

329

mother had had shipped from an Egyptian trader when I was a boy.

The men were overjoyed to be off the caravels and on dry land. They splashed each other in the water, and frolicked with the Taino children who came out to play with them. Their parents would sit on the beach and watch, unafraid of these exotic creatures with red, blond, and brown hair on places like their chests, bellies and legs. At first they gestured heavenward, thinking that we were gods sent down to play with them and grant blessings upon their land. But soon they learned that we were human and perhaps not very different from them.

The men were happy to learn one thing about the guileless Taino women: that they gave themselves to them without hesitation, with many of them acting almost as courtesans after an expensive meal. The men took advantage of this, and fornication became excessive the entire time we were there. This began a dangerous trend, in fact, since the men soon became so crazed with lust that, wherever we went, they would be more bent on finding and conquering women than on trying to do God's work among the people we encountered.

Despite this, the Lucayan Tainos were excessively generous hosts. They gave of themselves without thought of recompense, as I've learned over the years is their custom. Thus, we were given to eat foods such as tunafish — we thanked God it wasn't salted like that which we'd eaten on our voyage for five weeks — roasted iguana, and meat which I later learned was *hutia* — the little rabbits they still keep as pets and in great corrals. At night, they'd use the fires to warm themselves as they lay awake, staring at our ships in fascination.

During these first few days, Colón readied the men to explore the island. They would see all sorts of things, like trees taller than the oaks of Castile, covered with masses of delicate bloom; tiny pink and red blossoms; brightly-plumed red and green birds; and colorful butterflies. I, on the other hand, sat with my new friends by a grove of trees trying to learn their language. We were near the new cross the men of the *Niña* had erected, a place of gentle shade and breezes.

I held up various objects, such as seashells, sticks of driftwood, baskets, and fruits, asking the name of each thing in turn. I pointed to myself, learned how to tell them my name, and began to learn how to say all sorts of things as we laughed together in the shade of the palm trees. I soon surpassed Luis Torres in learning the language. He sat on a log nearby, writing the words down like a good scribe should, but refusing to interact with the guileless people who sat giggling and gesturing at my feet.

"What is that thing?" I asked, pointing to one of the dug-out trees that the men used to paddle out in the sea and hunt sea turtles.

"*Canoa*," they answered. I wondered if a pair of these had swept that woman and man out to sea and then to Ireland years before.

"And *that*?" I asked, pointing to the hanging net three young boys sat in as they watched the lesson, only paying half-attention to what was going on.

"*Hamaca*," the children exclaimed, warming to the game. That might not be a bad thing to take with us when we go, I thought to myself. It would be more comfortable than sleeping on the splintery, sea-splashed deck. It reminded me of how I had slept when living with Paolo among the Bolama.

"How about *this*?" I asked, picking up one of the long, yellow bars of fruit that grew tall on a stalk in the soft soil by the stream.

"*Maize*," they said, and I became the first man of the expedition to try the strange food.

Just then, a small silver-green bird whose wings sounded like the humming of a bee flew up beside me, and stuck its little beak into a large, red, bell-shaped flower. "And him?" I asked, pointing to the bird. "What's *he* called?"

"Zoom, zoom!" they cried, and I couldn't hold back a laugh. I'd never seen anything like it before in my life.

One day after I'd learned to say all of their names, one of the boys brought what seemed like a very strange thing indeed — a roll of leaves rolled into a small stick they called 'tobacco'. They meant for me to light one end and smoke it for pleasure, inhaling through my nostrils. At first I refused, since it seemed such an odd thing to do. But as they insisted more and more, I decided that doing it just once could have no dire consequence.

They lit a stick of the concoction, and I inhaled a strong puff of it. The smoke burned my throat and lungs, and tears welled up in my eyes as I coughed and sweated. Soon, I was vomiting in the bushes as the people laughed and pointed at me, covering their mouths and running to fetch their friends to watch.

No one else in our expedition would try the stuff for weeks, until Luis Torres was goaded into partaking of the strange drug in Cuba, where he retched almost as badly as I had.

CHAPTER SEVENTY

I didn't dare ask the captain about the silk-jacket prize for spotting land during those days. I decided he must be so busy with his preparations for the exploration of the island that he hadn't given it a second thought. I only hoped to be able to return home with enough money to help the poor and the suffering people displaced from my beloved Triana. I had sometimes seen them begging for alms at the door of the cathedral on Sunday mornings or waiting for their free soup from the friars.

But Colón was not interested in giving me my just reward. He saw himself as guided by an almost biblical destiny, like Isaiah was, to conquer, enslave and take over — and he could accept no challenges or distractions that might keep him from this mission. I'm not sure if he would have honored his promise to another man, one who hadn't interrupted him in the middle of his carnal lusts years before in the heat of an African night. But in any case, it was not written in the stars that I should ever return to Europe, especially as a rich man. In any case, I doubt that the civil and clerical authorities would ever have let me receive my prize, as I was one who'd been cast out and condemned for a crime I didn't commit.

Colón soon tired of San Salvador. He and his men had explored the island and found it to be small, with a lake in the middle at the top of a plateau its only natural wonder. So it was that I soon found myself in front of him with Guamdewatku, the island's *cacique*, or chief, to serve as interpreter. Luis Torres had been unofficially demoted to scribe, which seemed to suit him well. He'd given up trying to address the people we met in Arabic and Greek, and I'd tried out my Latin, Italian, and Romany as well. It was all to no avail. This was not the Land of Sind, I had realized with no small amount of sadness.

"Ask him where we can find gold," the captain commanded, thrusting the chief forward. Unlike the natives of other areas, these Lucayan Indians didn't carry their lords about on litters, and he'd been standing next to us, suspecting nothing. All around us were men from the *Santa María* who had their swords half-unsheathed for the first time.

Torres and I exchanged a nervous look. He knew that 'gold' hadn't been one of the words that we'd learned from the natives. In fact, now that I thought of it, we hadn't seen any of the precious metal at all among these, the first people we encountered.

I swallowed hard. "That isn't one of the words we've learned as of yet," I said, choosing my words cautiously.

"What have you been doing with them all day long for the last two days?" Colón demanded. "We've got no time for playing games, Rodrigo. The kingdom of Cathay and all its riches await us, and we want to open up a trade route as soon as possible."

Captain Pinzón opened his cloak and searched one of his pockets for something. In a moment, he held out a gold ring he'd brought from Las Palmas. Indeed, it was to be a gift for his wife should he ever return to Castile.

"Ask them the word for this," he said hopefully. "Then you can ask them where we might find some more so we can load our ships with it and spices for our return."

I turned to the *cacique* in front of me. "*Daca Rodrigo,*" I said, introducing myself, and touching my chest, which the Indians often do to show respect and reverence. It wasn't really necessary to introduce myself, as my name had already spread among all of the Indians of the island as "the only white man who could speak." Soon, I was known as 'O Rodrig-ero,' a play on words that among the speakers of their language is still an honorific title for me.

I held the ring up for him to inspect, and I asked him what the thing was called. A confused look crossed his face, but then he smiled. "That is a *yari,*" he said with a short laugh.

'*Yari*' is the Taino word for 'ring,' or 'small bit of jewelry.' I shook my head and tried again, pointing to the metal which of which the object was composed. My interlocutor still looked confused, but then one of his men, who stood behind the tight circle, shouted something to him, and he smiled and nodded, comprehension finally dawning on his face.

"*Caona*," he assured me, nodding. "That ring is made of *caona*."

"And where can we find *caona*?" I asked, content that we were finally getting somewhere.

The man's brow furrowed and he thought for a moment, then he began speaking too quickly for me to understand what he was saying. I was able to understand, however, that there was no gold to be found on the island, but maybe there was some to the south or the west, where the dreaded Caribs were said to live.

"Where's the gold? Where's the kingdom of the great Kahn?" Colón asked again, angry that this was taking so long. He was an impatient one, Colón, especially when gold was on his mind.

"He doesn't know where there's any to be found," I said. "I'm not sure if there *is* any on the island."

"Oh, there *is*, be sure of that," Colón said, pushing his way past the men who had stood shoulder-to-shoulder with him and striding to the middle of the circle. "They know what it is, and they have a word for it. The bastards are holding out on us." He turned around and snatched the ring from my hands and held it up to Guamdewatku's face. "I want *caona*," he snarled at him, indicating his chest with a thumb. "Give me *caona* or you're going to get it, you stupid, heathen monkey. You'll die, by the breath of the Virgin. Tell him *that*, Rodrigo."

I swallowed hard, and tried to quell my *own* fear as some of the men began to unsheathe their swords. What were they planning to do?

"Please, captain, a little patience. I beg of you not to do anything rash. Give me some time, and I'm sure—"

"By San Fernando! You'll tell him what I told you to say, you loathsome bugger," he said without turning to face me. "Joaquín, bring me some steel."

Joaquin was a lean, mean-spirited youth who had not been among those who'd risen against him on the day of the mutiny. The boy brought him a sword made of Moorish steel, and Colón took the hilt without removing his eyes from those of the *cacique*. "Now," he said, pushing the sharp point into the soft belly of the man, making him wince with surprise and fear, "tell him what I told you to say, or I'll run him through."

The man reached out for the blade. As his hands closed around it, he cut himself and blood splattered the sand below him. He shrieked and jumped backwards. Colón nodded to his men, and two of them stepped forward and held him by his arms.

"Where is *caona*?" I asked him again, this time almost pleading as I looked at him in a way that allowed my eyes to convey the gravity of the situation. Was he really holding out on me? Every fiber of my body told me that he wasn't. "My chief, a bad man. Please, where *caona*? Please, I help you." I prayed that the answer wouldn't be *"Ita,"* for that means, "I don't know" in Taino.

The man just looked at me and shook his head slightly from side to side. "*Ita*. I don't know, O Rodrigero. *Ita*. Not here."

The people scattered, yelping and crying as he fell gurgling to the ground, the sword thrust into and pulled out of his belly. A small flood of blood covered the ground near the lake into which the *cacique* was carelessly thrown not two minutes later, the blood from his wound staining the clear water.

Thus began the destruction of the Indies. The chance we may have had to befriend these people and learn from them was forever lost in that moment of impatience, cruelty and rage wrought by a man driven mad by greed and the lust for power.

***

Colón ordered half a dozen of the Indians of San Salvador to be taken prisoner as we readied the ships to leave the island cove. He hoped to show them off in Spain, and, of course, to have them teach me their language so that I'd be a better interpreter for him in the future.

Try as I might, I was unable to shake the feeling that if I'd spoken better, I could have prevented Guamdewatku's death. I took my transfer to the flagship without question, and began to learn the Taino language as quickly as I could. So it was that after we explored island after island, and as Colón had more and more people run through with his now blood-stained sword, I worked long and hard, from sunup to sunset, to be able to become a beacon of hope between the Tainos' world and my own.

As if our captain could have been reasoned with. One would think that after I'd saved his life, he would have at least paid me the courtesy of listening to my opinion every once in a while. But in place after place — Santa María de la Concepción, where one of the captives escaped, with my help, to warn the others, and Fernandina, an oblong island not unlike San Salvador — the captain was just as cruel and demanding as he'd been the day he'd murdered Guamdewatku in front of his own people.

CHAPTER SEVENTY-ONE

Bartolomé sat alone in his hammock that evening, trying to sort through how he felt about what Rodrigo had told him about his captain. It wasn't exactly a flattering story of the man who had become to be known as "Captain of the Ocean Sea and Viceroy of All the Indies." Still, he thought, this New World had been founded upon violence, and he had to accept that.

His mind began to wander back to how it had been when he'd first arrived in Hispaniola a dozen years before, in 1502, before he had been chosen to edit Colón's journals.

"Hey, *doctrinero!*" the men had shouted at him one day as they came out of the recently thrown-together tavern. "Won any converts lately?"

"None as yet," he admitted ruefully. He felt humiliated by the fact that he had been in Santo Domingo for almost two months and had been unable to come close to, let alone preach to, any Indians.

Or, more accurately, any *live* ones.

341

Once, perhaps three weeks after his arrival, he had been invited along with a group of soldiers as they ventured out into the bush. He had seen the corpses of some women and babies, and, when he asked for an explanation of how they had died, the men quickly changed the subject.

"Why do the babies look like that?" Bartolomé was so bold to ask. "It looks like they've been chewed on, and some of them are only half there!"

"Well," said one of the soldiers, "They've got a lot of wolves around here."

"Really?" the *doctrinero* said. "I heard there weren't any, only our attack dogs." He had noticed that the Spanish dogs, most of which had been thin and bony to begin with, had been especially so lately.

"They've got to eat *something*," his friend said, before the third soldier kicked him, thinking Bartolomé hadn't seen.

He turned to the men who stood, drunk, outside the tavern with all of the cracks in it. "Why do you ask if I've won any over? What do you care if I *have*?"

"We just heard about something you might be interested in seeing," the ugly one missing an ear said. "It might be a way for you to win some souls. But if you're too busy, maybe we can just try you another day," he said, starting to turn away.

"No!" Bartolomé said, grabbing his elbow. "What is it?"

The man studied Bartolomé for a long moment, and Bartolomé tried not to look at the mangled stump that was where the man's left ear should have been. "Let's just say they've gotten creative with how they deal with prisoners captured out in the bush," he said, pretending not to notice. "Come out with us, and maybe you can save a few souls this afternoon."

"If they've *got* any to save, that is," said one of his mates, slapping him on the back. At this, they all shared a hearty laugh together.

Bartolomé did not see what was so funny.

***

Bartolomé followed the men about a league outside of town, and he felt himself feeling more and more lost the farther out they went.

"Where are you taking me?" he asked.

"We're almost there," said one of them, a gray and gruff man in a brown sailor's smock. "Be patient, mate. It won't be long now, and you'll see the best-kept secret in the Indies. If this ain't the way to make 'em convert, I don't know what is!"

He was about to ask him what he meant by this when the soldier let a branch smack him in the face for at least the fifth time that day. Bartolomé felt himself losing what little patience he had left. Why had he come on this journey if all he was going to see was diseased, bloated, and chewed-up corpses? He was a *doctrinero!* He had come to save souls.

"God's teeth!" he yelled in anger.

Suddenly, fresh laughter from all sides met his words, and he realized that they had come into a clearing in the woods.

What he saw as he opened his eyes would shatter the last illusions he had about what his fellow countrymen were doing in the New World.

There was a low gallows in the middle of the clearing, and over a dozen men hanging from it. Off to the right of this was a large heap of bloody bodies and human entrails. The prisoners were all naked, and they hung from ropes just long enough to allow their feet to touch the ground if they strained hard enough. A few of the shorter ones, whose feet were unable to reach, were already hanging lifeless from their ropes, their bloated and blue faces masks of fear, pain, and rage.

"Ah, so we've got another *doctrinero*," said the man in charge as he playfully wielded a sword. "Maybe you'll have more luck than we've had today, *padre*." He curled his lips and sneered this last word. Bartolomé hated it when people called him that when they could tell by his habits and look that he was not yet one.

"So far, no converts," the man said, swinging his sword around again. As if to underscore this point, he turned to the gallows and pointed his sword at the belly of one of the men hanging from it. His hands were tied behind his back, and he didn't kick at the Spaniard because of his delicate balance.

"Hey, savage!" the man said to him, as he held up a small, wooden cross. "Hey, you, monkey — kiss this! Come now — kiss this and become a Christian. Come on, be good. We've got a nice man of the cloth to help you." He held the cross up to the frightened man's face, and shoved it to his lips. The man sputtered something in his native language, and there was a pleading tone to what he said. But he didn't kiss the cross as the soldier wanted him to, so the soldier poked the point of his sword gently into the man's belly. The Spaniard kissed the cross and held it out to give the Indian one last chance. When he didn't kiss it, the soldier shoved his sword deep into his belly, just like Colón had done in Rodrigo's tale, and the man gasped as blood gurgled from his mouth. At this, a cry went up from the other men, although it was a weak and resigned one.

"At least now I know *that* steel works," he said, tossing it onto a pile of bloody swords and knives behind him. "Toledo still makes the best in the world!"

Things seemed to get even worse the longer Bartolomé stayed in that area, despite his many protestations to the local authorities.

As if the sword-testing torture wasn't enough, he soon realized that it was common for the men to go out into the Taino villages looking for women to rape and disembowel. He was horrified to learn that they dashed their babies' heads against rocks if they cried too much or made too much noise — that is, unless their dogs were hungry for fresh meat. They whipped, beat, or tortured the men for the most minor offenses, and Bartolomé knew that his fellow Christians even did this just for sport. He pleaded and tried to reason with them, but they would hear none of it. Sometimes one of the soldiers would let him get close enough to an Indian to try to tell him about Jesus before killing him, but he did not speak their language at first, and they spoke no Castilian. And as far as he knew, except for a few soldiers who had left the settlement to live

345

far off in the bush, not one of his fellow Christians had made even the slightest effort to learn Taino.

How was he supposed to be any good to these people under such circumstances? All his countrymen cared about was gold and sport. Most of them didn't even consider the Indians human.

After a few months of sleeping on a dirty pallet on the stinking floor of the tavern — during which time he spent most of the money he had borrowed from his uncle for the trip — he was finally taken in by a kindly Franciscan brother named Fray Antonio. For almost three years, they followed band of soldiers after band of soldiers as they swept the bush, trying to do what they could. Occasionally, they were able to save children from the wrath of the Christians or get a Taino to kiss a cross. But more often than not, they were met with disappointment. Such a day was the day a group of men, women and children from a group of rebels were burned en masse on top of one of the mountains in the central sierra of Hispaniola.

"Repent, my sons and daughters!" Antonio cried out in broken Taino. "Profess to be true Christians before it's too late!" he pleaded as the flames leapt from the logs underneath the bound victims.

"Are there white men like you up there in your Heaven?" asked the leader, Hatuey, with a look of determination.

"Yes, there are!" Fray Antonio yelled above the roar of the flames.

"Well, then — you won't find *me* there!" the rebel leader screamed back before his flesh began to roast.

It was only after they had been killed that Bartolomé recognized one of the charred corpses as that of Juanito, the young slave his father had brought back from the Indies.

He buried him alone that night, when no one but the moon was there to see it. In his grave, he placed the amulet he had once so selfishly taken from him before praying for the salvation of his soul. What was it he had called it — a *zemi*? It was supposed to be some kind of protective spirit, if he remembered correctly. For the first time, he noticed that it was of a man who was crouching and baring his teeth. He thought of how his friend had been standing upright on one of the stakes as the soldiers burned him. He had not cried out to Bartolomé the entire time, even though there would have been no way to help him even if he had.

Juanito's soul was not the only one Bartolomé prayed for on that lonely, moonlit night.

CHAPTER SEVENTY-TWO

At the end of October 1492, we reached this island, the Isle of *Colba*, which, like everywhere else we went, was covered in lush, green groves. Colón seemed convinced that this was a peninsula of the Chinese province on Manji. In fact, it wasn't so far from here where we landed after circling around for a while. Many of the guides confided to me that they couldn't understand why we'd wanted to come here, as the island wasn't much different than any other we'd seen, except perhaps in size.

Colón had seen more and more natives with gold bracelets and trinkets in their noses as we'd moved south and west. We'd seen that the farming these people performed consisted of heaping mounds of alluvial soil in rectangular rows for the planting of maize, sweet *batatas*, and strange beans and, sometimes, yuca. We also saw for the first time lots of *conuco* — big round, starchy tubers that serve as a major source of food.

Our captain, of course, wasn't interested in learning about the people and their habits, as I was. He wanted to find where the gold was. Some of the captives we'd taken from San Salvador had jumped overboard — silly me, I never *did* get good at minding captives — and had warned others about us, and how aggressive and irrational we could be. So it was that, as we went along from island to island, no one wished to talk to us. Whenever we asked about gold and the cities of Cipangu and Cathay, they just ran away and hid or waved us onward. So we traveled toward *Bohio*, and also toward *Colba*. This was where Colón told us we would find the "towns, castles, and the substantial dwellings" to which Marco Polo had so often referred in his writings. Colón also hoped to find dragon-mouthed bronze cannons, as well as lords and ladies in gold brocades everywhere strolling over bridges and small green ponds and fountains.

I was chosen, along with Luis Torres and a few others, to journey to the center of Colba to try to find the place Colón said the Great Kahn was waiting. But all along the two day's journey, all we saw were green, tall trees, black soil, and singing birds as well as lush meadows of blooming flowers and bean and cassava farmers. These men came up to us without fear, much as the gentle people of San Salvador had. None of the escapees had reached this far, I realized. Still, I said nothing when our guides whispered warnings to them about us. When they did so, they always told them, however, that I was the only one of the whole lot to be trusted.

"Are you sure that they even want us here?" I asked Colón one day as we sat lounging in our *hamacas*. Why would they even want us to teach them about the Holy Faith?

"Don't be silly," he said with a dismissive shrug. "Why, the great Kahn himself once sent emissaries to the Pope seeking teachers of the Gospel. If the infidels hadn't blocked out the entire Levant, I'm sure China would have been colonized by those loyal to the Holy See a hundred years ago, and they'd all be saved by now. His Holiness depends on us — that's why you must go with the mission to find the great Chinese leader."

When we reached the center of the island, we were received cordially by the *cacique* of that place. He wore a crown of feathers and sat on a throne of wood with a head of painted golden eyes instead of a throne of rubies, so we knew for sure we'd not reached the lands Marco Polo had written about. There was no gold to help Spain smite her enemies, but only mud and round or rectangular thatched huts, yams and prickly fruits called *ananas*, some *butia* rabbits, and rows and rows of tobacco and maize everywhere we looked. I had to laugh a little at the silliness of it all. Here we'd mounted this whole expedition, only to find kind, smiling people who seemed to be nothing but simple farmers who knew almost nothing of gold, and could understand even less why we were so bent on finding it.

It was there that I learned the meaning of the word 'Ca'n', which sounded like the Great *Kahn* we'd been searching for. This word means 'center' in Taino.

The chief had a great laugh when he showed me that the center of a prickly fruit was also called the 'ca'n.' In search of the Great Kahn, we'd traveled to the middle of Cuba — and all for nothing.

So it was that we decided to go where they told us to go next, an island which would become my home for the next two decades: the land of *Bohio*, called 'Haiti' or sometimes '*Quisqueya*' by its natives — what you know today as Hispaniola, "the Spanish island."

***

We toured around *Bohio* for weeks, finding more and more of the same things, before our flagship was smashed on that new-world monstrosity-reefs-on the northern coast. And it was on Christmas Day, of all days! Our leader had to found Villa Navidad in that place.

After our disappointing trip to the center of Cuba, some of the men had seemed to give up hope of ever reaching the riches of Cathay and Cipangu. Many of them prayed to the Holy Virgin as well as Saint Christopher — they decided that the patron saint of travelers might be a better fellow in whom to place their faith than the captain of the same name. Most of the men openly grumbled once again; more than a few had expressed their desire to return home as soon as possible, seeing nothing to gain from staying in this place where there were never more than small trinkets of gold to be found. Pinzón heard their concerns patiently, but steadfastly maintained that we should explore these lands to our complete satisfaction in order to make a full report to our monarchs once we returned home. "That's what we've been sent to do, after-all," he said at least five times a day after I returned to the *Pinta*, even after the winds lashed us with an awful storm that separated us from the *Niña* while the others worked at building the new settlement. Or at least we used the storm as an excuse, as I believe that Pinzón wanted to beat the Admiral — for that is what we must now call him — to where all the gold was to be found in our faster, more agile *Pinta*. By now, he had grown to despise our leader, as we all did, and grew less able to hide his feelings by the day.

And so we set off to explore the island of Babeque, where we'd heard the natives gathered gold by moonlight and fashioned it into bars. We saw fish and small sea turtles being roasted on *burens* — a type of griddle with four legs. This is not the usual way the Tainos cook meat, though. They roast it over an open fire with a spit, which I've grown quite accustomed to over the years — especially their succulent rodents, the *cori*. I understand people call these 'Indian pigs' nowadays, or even 'guinea pigs.'

Not long after exploring that place, we continued back to *Bohio*. We explored up and down the coast, past the peninsula the people called *Guanacabibe*, or the "back of the island," and decided to journey inland to see if we could find any sign of the others. This was once we'd reached a place we called *Puerto Blanco* in the Indian kingdom of Xaragua.

We met and spoke with some of the natives of that region, and their dialect was a little different than that of the Lucayans of San Salvador. In fact, this dialect seemed to resemble the others so little that I found myself having to ask people to speak slowly and explain various words that were beyond my grasp. They were astounded to see us, as all the other peoples we'd encountered were, and were equally surprised to hear me speak to them — with a Lucayan accent, no less.

But soon, we were brought to their village, and I gasped at what I saw there.

We were standing in front of the capital of the kingdom of Behecchio. The village was small by European standards, but it was impressively laid out — and the Taino culture in Hispaniola is — or was, in any case — the most highly developed of any of these islands. Of course, it was nothing compared to what I was to experience in the land of Guarionex, or of his father, the great Guacanagari, the one who was, even then, having vivid *cohoba* — induced visions of the coming of *Guamikena* — the white man.

We'd known that we were in for something different on our way in to the village. We'd seen immense fields of *conuco*, with mounds three feet high and at least six feet across. And mark this — all of these rich, black mounds were tended by workers who had only to dip water from the irrigation canals running in straight lines as far as the eye could see. It was the most impressive feat of construction I'd ever seen in my life, with the possible exception of the Giralda in Sevilla or the Alhambra with its court of Lions and Tower of *Las Infantas*. Even the aqueduct of Segovia left to us by the Romans seemed useless compared to this.

STEVEN FARRINGTON

The city itself contained perhaps two thousand souls and no fewer than fifty houses. But this figure is misleading, as each house contained three or more families, all related to each other by blood. They were constructed of wood and thatched, and were arranged around a central plaza. The cacique's home was in the very center and, unlike the poorly made round and cone-roofed homes that the commoners inhabited, his was rectangular and even had a little entranceway and spaces for windows built in.

Several women cooked meat on spits and men carried calabashes full of water to put into pepper-pots simmering over the fires, which they would use to garnish their meats. Off to one side, some women were finishing up their task of filtering out the poison from the cassava, with the help of baskets, pounding what was left into flour for *cassavi* bread.

When we approached them, the people stopped what they were doing and stood up to have a better look at us. I noticed that they weren't like the Lucayans or even the Indians of Cuba, who had come up to us with no fear or mistrust. The people of this island were much more wary of outsiders.

I also noticed that the dress of these people was different. Where the Lucayans had barely worn anything at all, the younger women here wore colorful headbands, and the older matrons wore skirts of various lengths. The men wore cotton loincloths, where many had gone nude on other islands, and some of them here wore elaborately decorated belts, necklaces, feathers, plugs, and hanging pendants in the form of masks which looked like they were made of *guanin*, an alloy that includes gold. Some of the babes and small children had thick bands of netting wrapped tightly around their heads, and this held a rock to their foreheads. I would later learn that this was because their parents hoped to give them a flattened forehead if possible, which was considered a noble look.

These Indians were so different from the Lucayans that I wasn't surprised to find that many of our Indian guides were petrified to go with us to meet the inhabitants of this place. They were afraid of being killed or eaten by these people, whom they probably confused with the Caribs.

Soon, the Cacique Behecchio was summoned, and the man emerged magnanimously from his house, followed by some of his servants. I was surprised to learn that his name didn't start with a 'g-u-a' prefix, as had the names of all of the chiefs whom I'd met up to then. That was what all noble words begin with in their language.

I was sorry that we didn't have any Lucayan guides with us then, as it fell to me to serve as the interpreter, which I didn't feel confident doing yet, having only studied the language for about a month. And, as I've said, the dialect changed much from place to place, and the kingdom of Behecchio was no exception.

Stepping forward, I bowed to the chief and said, "We come in peace." If only it were so! "We come from very far away, and we're looking for the Kingdoms of Cathay and Cipangu, as well as the land of the Great Kahn. We search for gold, silks and spices to take home with us, as well as our friends in two big *canoas* like the one we came in."

The chief looked at us and frowned. I wasn't sure if he would be able to understand everything I had to say, so I spoke slowly and deliberately, using only words I was exactly sure of.

"You seek spices?" he asked, speaking finally, looking toward the pots roasting on the fire. I remembered how we'd shown some oriental spices popular back home to the people we met in Cuba, but they'd only shaken their heads in confusion saying "*ita, ita.*"

"Yes, but that isn't so important," I said. "Do you know where we could find *caona*?"

"You can find it in the mines to the east sometimes," he said absently, and I interpreted this for the crew.

"May we go there?" asked Captain Pinzón, stepping forward, and motioning to me that I was to ask the chief his permission.

The chief now smiled for the first time. He looked like he had an idea. "Not right away. Tonight, you stay here for a large feast. Then, tomorrow, you will have to win in a feat of skill against the men of my kingdom. Then, if you can do that, you will be allowed to go there."

"What sort of test is it?" I asked, afraid of the answer.

"*Batey*," he answered, and after several long minutes of mimicking by his men, I was made to understand that it was a ball game played on a court of some kind.

I explained what I understood to the men, who were agreeable to the challenge. But Pinzón, ever the one to look out for his crew, wanted to know more details of the agreement. Could we expect guides to lead us to where gold was, or would we wander aimlessly until we found it? And what would happen to us if we lost, which was highly likely, seeing as this was not our game? Would we be killed or eaten, as our guides had warned us? Would that be our punishment for going off on our own to find gold?

'If you win, we will give you guides to find your gold," the chief said. And to think that just about then the men of the *Santa María* were being given gold leaves from a crown by a chief who only wanted bells and trinkets in return.

"But if you lose," he said, "you must leave this place and never come back."

CHAPTER SEVENTY-THREE

The following morning, we were awakened at dawn to be led to where we would play the game of *batey* with the natives. Most of us were groggy and not in any condition to do anything of the like. Despite Pinzón's warnings to consume in moderation if we hoped to have a chance of winning, the men had given in to their desires, gorging themselves on meats, fish, beans, nuts and fruits which we had no words for yet. For example, we feasted heavily on a sweet orange and starchy food known as *batata* that sat heavily in our bellies that morning. To make matters worse, women had come to us and offered the men all sorts of gifts after the meal, and many had stayed the night to keep us company.

The natives played all sorts of instruments as we marched through the forest. Besides drums and primitive flutes, children walked along shaking dried-out gourds, so that the seeds rattled. I asked one little girl what this was called, and she said that they were called '*amaracas*.' Her older sister was playing a larger

358

instrument made of a large gourd with three strings pulled over a carved-out hole and tied around both ends. As she plucked at it with her fingernails, I was reminded of how long it had been since I'd been able to play a Moorish guitar for the dancers of Triana, or the African drums in the land of the Bolama, and a wave of nostalgia washed over me.

After about a half-hour's walk, we arrived at what seemed an immense court. It stretched at least a hundred paces from end to end, and looked just as wide. We felt impressed by the tall stones surrounding it, as well as the artistic designs of *zemis* marking each corner. All of the gods looked angry to me, as each either kicked its feet or stuck out its tongue.

Some people had arrived early from the village, and we noticed ruefully that the men who were to be our opponents had already been practicing with several brown balls and jumping up and down and doing other exercises to prepare for the challenge. In addition, there must have been close to a thousand people who had come out to watch the showdown.

A great cheer went up when we arrived, and this took us by surprise. How was it that they were cheering for us? Was it good-natured, or were they simply glad that the games were about to begin?

As the noise died down, we were told to sit down at a place on the side of the court that had been especially reserved for us. Soon, the crowd became silent, and a well-decorated man wearing feathers and red paint entered the court. He looked grave, and stood silently before he scooped up a bit of sand and a few pebbles from the court. He held them level with his head as he chanted some words, then turned and swung around quickly, sending the chaff all across the center of the court. The crowd cheered, and the man smiled as he strode quickly away.

He must have been a priest or a medicine man, I thought, and he must have just blessed the court.

Next, a group of two dozen or more women entered from both sides of the court. The men of our crew gasped, as these were many of the maidens who had just spent the night with them, and had vanished before dawn. Not only were we surprised to see them, but, to our amazement, they were almost completely nude, wearing only a bit of white cotton cloth about their waists. They each carried a frond from a palm tree, with which they coyly covered and uncovered their bodies. They began to dance, weaving this way and that, and it was all so lovely that for a moment, we forgot about the game we'd come to play and lost ourselves in the beauty of the dance and the dancers. They seemed to be praising the sky and the earth, and they even turned and gave a dance to their king, who was sitting on a litter held by four men, with a woman beside him. I would later learn that this woman was his great and powerful sister, Anacaona, the wife of Caonabo. She was a very wise woman, I was told, and I resolved then and there to try to win her friendship. I learned that the dance they'd just done was a religious dance called an "*areyto*," and that most of the women who'd been dancing were wives or concubines of the king.

The women finished their dance and laid the branches they'd been holding at our feet. There were twenty of them, the same number as the men of our group, and they each gave one of us a branch, which we took as wishes of prosperity and goodwill.

Next, another group of women and children came out onto the court and lined up on opposite sides. They played in what we assumed to be a demonstration of how to play the game, and we watched, trying to learn what it was that we had to do.

The game itself wasn't very difficult. Using whatever part of the body one chose except the hands, one had to keep the ball in the air once the other team tossed it into the air. Some of the children were quite good at this, as one boy of about twelve years demonstrated by a deft kick that sent the ball flying. A middle-aged woman rushed forward, however, and struck the ball with her shoulder, which sent it just over the line in the middle of the court, scoring a point for her team. The game continued for a while, but soon the children and adolescents pulled ahead and beat their mothers, aunts and grandmothers.

The game was out of twenty points, and took about twenty minutes.

I wondered how long *our* game would last.

***

We lined up on the far side of the court, where the women had just played. It felt like a bad omen, but we had no choice — the chief himself indicated that we were to go there, and his courtiers led us there personally.

The other team lined up on their side, and naturally there were twenty of them to match the twenty of us. Soon, a boy came out onto the court and handed us one of the balls that we'd seen played with in the previous game. To our amazement, it bounced up and down when we hit it.

Next we were fitted with stone belts and cuffs for our feet and arms, which had cotton swaths to hold them to us. Confused, I asked what these were for, and they explained with gestures that the belts and cuffs were to help us hit the balls. The other team wore them already, so we decided that it wouldn't be a bad idea to follow their example. Besides, a lot of wealth was at stake.

The boy who had given us our belts told us that we could strike the ball and send it first to the other side. We decided to let captain Pinzón go first.

The sound of a flute-like reed came from the side, and we took this to mean that the game was about to begin. The chief nodded at us from his litter, so Captain Pinzón threw the ball as hard and as far as he could toward the other team. The other side jumped into action, and one of the young men rushed forward to hit the ball back to us with his left foot. The ball flew through the air and landed on our side well in front of García Hernández, the dispenser from Palos. The crowd cheered loudly at this victory for the Tainos.

Our men had not even left the line where we'd begun. Captain Pinzón, barely controlling his anger, said, "All right, men, spread out all over our side, as they've done. Come on now, some in front, some in back, let's go, lads!"

We tossed the ball again, and another man came forward and hit the ball with his head. This time, however, it was a high ball with a long arc, so we had plenty of time to react. I saw that the ball was coming directly at me, so I called that I could get it, and put my arm out to deflect the ball. I hit it, and I felt a surge of satisfaction until I saw a Taino man rush forward and kick the ball easily back onto our side, where it hit the ground. The crowd cheered once again, and I saw that two rocks had been placed on their side of the stone barrier.

This time, Diego Bermudez of Palos threw the ball and one of the young Indian men rushed forward to try to hit it with his foot — but the angle at which he approached was wrong, and the ball skidded off to his left. We breathed a sigh of relief. We had finally won something!

Next it was my turn to send the ball. I tried to decide who on the other team didn't look like he was paying attention, and in fact, I did see one young man who was staring at nothing at all. In a second, I made my decision, and I threw the ball toward him. He turned and hit the ball with his elbow, but it went high and landed well before the line. We had another small victory.

So we continued playing, but try as we might, the other team would not make the same mistakes twice. It was, after all, *their* game, and they were very good at it, and had doubtless chosen the best players. When we'd finally earned six stones, for example, they'd won ten, and we had to surrender the initial throw.

***

We lost the game, of course. We knew we would, but we tried as well as we could.

When the opposite team had twenty stones, a young man came out onto the court playing a large drum. He was followed by many of the townspeople. Upon closer inspection, I realized that he was playing on a big sea-tortoise shell.

The people were still gracious and kind to us even though we'd lost. They invited us back to their village and fêted us all over again, serving us more food than we could possibly eat. They even gave us some gold before we left the following morning, and this was more than what we found anywhere before meeting up again with the others near where they had made the settlement from the wood of the *Santa María*. I was surprised by the fact that the people of the victorious village still traded us lots of gold for our worthless little trinkets.

We spent the few weeks or so traveling up and down the southern coast of *Bohío* — Colón had dubbed it Hispaniola or "the Spanish Island" when he saw its green mountains — before turning back and traveling up the western side of it again. We met up with the rest of the fleet in January, and we were surprised to find out exactly how good the settlement looked. The chief Gucanagarí had allowed — in fact, had helped, them to create a town there, which the Admiral called *Villa Navidad*, since they'd crashed there on Christmas. This, of course, had been after they'd had weeks of trading and interaction with the people of that region, and had been adored everywhere they went. The gold and adoration of the people had softened Colón's anger for the time being, so it had been weeks since he'd run someone through with his sword.

When Colón strode aboard our ship as we docked near the fort, however, he was not in good spirits. He called the Pinzón brothers treacherous villains, and blamed the rest of us for going along with them. And what was our reward for our greed? He demanded. Were we rich? He then insisted that we give him all our gold and surrender any of the other goods we may have found to him, as he was Viceroy and the queen's personal representative in any lands he claimed in her name. In his ranting, he seemed to blame everyone and everything but himself for problems that had arisen.

It probably wasn't the best time, but I'd grown weary of putting off the conversation concerning my reward and silk jacket for far too long. "When am I to be compensated for being the first to spot land, sir?" I asked when he'd calmed down a bit.

"You weren't the first to spot land, you stupid grommet!" he growled. "*I* was that man, not you."

I stood there dumbfounded, trying to decide what to say.

"And don't think you're going back with the rest of them on this voyage," he went on. "I need you to stay with the others in Villa Navidad, as chief interpreter."

CHAPTER SEVENTY-FOUR

So it was that I was rowed back to the little settlement as I sat numbly considering what this would mean.

It was better than going back home to Spain, wasn't it? What did I have to go back to, anyway? The only people who'd ever meant anything to me were gone, and I was a defrocked criminal in my land. I might as well stay here, I reasoned, and see to it that the Tainos were treated with as much respect as possible by my people. Still, I hated that I was obviously being left behind so that my reward could be denied me. I had entertained a vague idea of collecting it and trying to slip away in Sevilla and head for Venice or Rome, but that now seemed quite impossible.

Another problem, of course, was that Colón had staffed his flagship with men who only wanted two things: gold and women — and they didn't care how they got them. They were mostly men with an almost complete lack of morals, and a fearsome lot to boot, armed with swords and lances that they were supposed to use only for the defense of the fort.

Maybe that's why it's no surprise that when the Great Admiral came back the next year the entire group, with the exception of me, had been massacred by the Tainos.

***

We sat in silence as what had just been said took time to sink in.

I became good friends with Guacanagari soon after my arrival. The *cacique* had been delighted to meet a new Spaniard he'd not been introduced to before. We spent hours getting to know each other those first few days, and he appeared impressed finally to meet a Spaniard who could speak Taino — by that time I'd learned enough to be fairly fluent — and he asked me all sorts of questions about my land. He told me all about Colón's visit, and how he'd been put off by certain European habits. When asked to explain, he said he'd been perplexed by the constant insistence on finding gold, even during the most solemn gift-giving or welcoming ceremonies that the various Taino chiefdoms had prepared. Also, when the Taino had given so generously of themselves — as when they'd rescued the crew and all their possessions from the *Santa María* on Christmas Day — the Christians had shown little or no gratitude toward their hosts, whom they dismissed as mere servants. Also, they seemed too attached to their property, the *cacique* went on. When they were asked for things, they clung to them instead of giving them freely, which was the Taino way.

I learned that Guacanagari was a very well-respected chief. He was not one of the major chiefs of the island, but sometimes I thought he hoped to become one, and this was why he'd ingratiated himself so toward Colón. He'd had visions that indicated we would come, and that we would change the way of life on the island forever. This is part of the reason why I imagined he'd organized elaborate gift-giving ceremonies on the deck of the *Santa María*, and why he'd tried to chase away other chiefs who wanted to meet and curry favor with our Admiral.

But now, because of the way our men were behaving — they'd gone on a rampage of killing, robbing, and raping — the chiefs of the island had gotten together to decide if we should be eliminated once and for all, since they thought that no good could come from our presence. I could tell that Guacanagari was in favor of sparing our lives, but I was unsure why, and wondered what part in his master plan I played.

"They're considering killing you all now," he said to me finally that night. "It's being decided. Perhaps we can think of something. I hate to think of what your *cacique* would say if he came back and found his men slaughtered."

I didn't like the thought of that, either, although I doubted that our 'great admiral' would shed many tears should something happen to *me*. Back in Spain, he'd already begun spreading rumors that I had fled to Tangiers to live among the Moors, and that I had abandoned Christendom forever.

CHAPTER SEVENTY-FIVE

Guacanagari took a wooden cup and drank from it. He then took a bite from some of the crunchy dry *cassavi* bread and a bit of the pithy yucca from the baskets of food that had been laid at his feet, as well as the meat, which was the main course. He smiled and bowed and offered up a silent prayer to his personal *zemi* for whom this feast of sea turtle was being given. I'd seen that, here on the coast, the Tainos of this island kept large weirs where the animals were bred and raised for food.

Before eating, we'd all gone through a purifying ritual in which I'd been sprinkled with dust by the local *bohiti*, or medicine man, "he who knows the wisdom of both the plant and spirit world." We'd watched many of the young women of the village perform *areytos* as they sang holy songs and celebrated the past exploits of the *zemi*, known as guawanayuki. Once, the year before, the *cacique* had interceded on the people's behalf to save them from a *huraca'n*, or the "center of the wind" that the Tainos believe the Lady of the Winds sends each year. The *zemi* had listened to his plea, and his people had been spared. This feast was well-timed, it seemed, as they held one each year to thank the *zemi*. But they could also hold one to ask for help in other matters. On other days, they'd give thanks to their supreme god, Yocahuguama, or the long name of 'Yucahu,' the god who they believe brings them their daily yucca.

Now it seemed that they wanted to know what was to be done about *me*. As I said, it had been decided by some of the other caciques of the island to kill the other Spaniards, but Guacanagari and some of the others had grown fond of me and hoped to spare my life. After all, as they'd learned from the Lucayan guides with the smashed flagship, I was the only one who had tried to convince my fellows to treat the people of the Indies well.

The chief stopped chewing and pronounced the food good and safe to eat. With an exclamation of joy, the people began to help themselves to the feast and soon the sounds of drinking and eating could be heard from all corners of the chief's great thatched, rectangular feast-house. I couldn't help thinking how different this was from how it had been in Spain, with the king having a commoner taste his food to make sure it was safe before he partook. Here, apparently, the *cacique* was seen as more of a protector than a tyrant.

It seemed that the entire entourage of Guacanagari's court was there: his first wife, Gwakawudi, as well as many of his concubines and other wives. His medicine man was there, as well as his

370

advisors and extended family and others from the upper class of Tainos, known as the *nitaino*. I thought of how this stratum of society was like my father, a member of the noble class, although many of his friends were *hidalgos*. The lower class, who were known collectively as the *naboria*, were like serfs or commoners and were the ones to work in the fields raising food for the *nitaino*. I was able to visit some *naboria* homes, and I'd always been greeted warmly by smiling women and men who offered me something to eat from their pots of peppers, sweet *batatas*, and fish. Needless to say, I was sometimes painfully reminded of my own youth in Sevilla and the class system that so defined my family's status and position. The son of the chief even had a tutor as I'd always had, although this tutor seemed to care much more about the instruction of the future *cacique* than my tutors, except of course for Father Sebastián, had ever cared about me.

I tried to explain to Guacanagari what it had meant for me to be a monk back in Spain, and he took it to mean that I was a *bohiti*. "I guess that's one way of looking at it," I said, thinking about all the elaborate cleansing rites which would have made Father Hojeda seethe with inquisitorial rage. Guacanagari asked if I had some female spirit as well as male spirit in me that made me a *bohiti*, I made a grimace of disdain at this idea. But the chief explained that this was far from an insult among the Taino people. In fact, those with both were considered special and holy in their society, and were never ones to pick up a lance, hunt or even farm. I was about to explain some of my duties as a monk, but before I could do so, the door of the hut

371

was thrown open and a young man with several guards walked angrily into the room. This caused a sensation, as you can imagine, since this is a sacrilege that can be punishable by death among the Tainos, especially during a feast for a chief's *zemi*.

Several of the guests had moved out of the way of the man who strode purposefully toward the chief, his two guards following closely at his heels. I shot a worried expression at Henyasey, the medicine man, as the *cacique* stood up to face the intruder, who wore a crown of feathers and a dangling human mask, made of *guanin*, around his neck. I was surprised to see him wearing a coarse brown cloth around his midsection, which was more than most men of his caste wore. His dress reminded me of the way Behecchio had adorned himself during our ball game several weeks before.

"How dare you invite an *ari* to dine with you in honor of your *zemi*?" he demanded, pointing at me. The word '*ari*' means 'foreigner' or, more accurately, 'invader.' It was certainly not the kindest word he could have found to refer to me, and this bluntness was very rude, to say the least.

Chief Guacanagari held his ground. "O-Rodrigero is my guest today as we implore the wisdom of my *zemi*. In the days to come, we're going to need the wisdom and power of all our *zemis* as we decide what to do with the *Guamikena* in our midst. I see nothing wrong with *that*," he said. Then his look hardened and he said, "How dare *you* come here uninvited and interrupt our feast? I should make you to drink poison manioc for this."

"You want *me* to drink manioc?" he said with a dismissive laugh, referring to the poison in the cassava juice that can kill if it's not properly filtered out before bread is made. "Why should *I* drink poison when it's *you* who's letting the enemy come among us, plotting our destruction? You old fool! You probably think you can use this to make yourself a powerful *cacique* instead of the little man that you've always been."

The old man didn't say anything for a long moment, and I wondered if the younger chief had struck a nerve with what he'd said. He put a finger to his lips in thought, and then said, "Look, Guarionex, these men — they're sure to come back soon with many more in their number. They're a reality that we must face, and so it seems wise to deal with them in such a way that won't incite their wrath—"

"*No!*" shouted the younger man. "You've always been so afraid of a fight! This is *our* country, and they can't take it from us unless we don't fight them. You can't just trade us to the *ari* like so many seashells to the Lucayans!"

"What would you have me do, then?" asked my friend, striking the pole that held up the roof of his hut with the palm of his hand. "Would you have me risk the death that awaits our people if we kill this group of men? You were not here to see them using their logs of fire that can split a tree with one single shot. And with their lances, they can stab and kill three men at once. You don't know what they're capable of, my boy. So don't call me a fool for not angering the giant that is the kingdom of—" he turned to me, and seemed to grasp for the word. "The *caciazgo* of Castile.

373

Why anger the kingdom of Castile when we might trade with them and make peace with our brothers across the sea, as my *bohiti* advises?"

"We can't make peace with men who know nothing of manners or of what is right," Guarionex said, glowering at the medicine man. "Did you know that they have crossed the river Yaque and are poised to enter the territory of Caonabo already? And did you also know that they've been breaking down grass doors and stealing from people's homes the entire way, as well as taking any women they find in their path?"

I groaned inwardly when I heard this. Why couldn't the men behave themselves long enough to befriend these people? Now they were probably going to kill us all in retaliation. I decided to go to them as soon as I could, as I'd seen a large group of them come trooping home to the fort as I'd been trying to sleep in a hammock of one of the chief's guest huts the previous evening. Maybe they'd listen to me if I explained the seriousness of the situation.

"The older chief extended his hand to the young man and softened his voice. "Give me a little more time, and let me work with Rodrig-ero here." The younger man looked at me fully for the first time, and I saw a look of recognition on his face. I hoped that he'd heard of my skills as an interpreter, and that he would honor Guacanagari's wish to try for peace through me.

"Very well, Father," he said, taking the man's hand and kissing it before bringing it to his chest. "I'll stall the wrath of Caonabo and the others as long as I can. I've even got a group of Ciguayans who met with

374

some more *aris* to the east who said they attacked them with bows and arrows before they fled. The fools took them for Caribs." He gave a dismissive grunt, then paused, and looked about him. "But pray you get a strong hold on those men soon, or disaster will surely befall us before this moon is up."

Guacanagari's son then turned on his heel and strode out of his hut, his two guards never far behind him.

CHAPTER SEVENTY-SIX

I took another piece of green *cohoba* and put it into my mouth, between my molar and cheek. I began to chew a bit, but the *bohiti* motioned to me that I shouldn't do this. We were seated on grass mats in the cacique's own *zemi* shrine, not far from where the feast had been held earlier that day. The *bohiti* had performed another cleansing ceremony on me and the chief, and we now sat in silence expecting a trance that would help them to communicate with helpful spirits — spirits which would tell us what to do. Incidentally, this was the sort of thing the Tainos used to do often, although sometimes they'd put sticks in their throats to vomit or sit sweating in fire-lit caves to induce hallucinations so that they could be more receptive to messages from their *zemis*.

Guacanagari's *zemi* was a small triangle that sat on a wooden stool. It was bigger, however, than some of the ones that had wide, funny eyes and leering mouths that farmers and pregnant women used. He often courted it for help after a special bathing ritual that is important for the Taino elite. Some of his wives and concubines had bathed me as well, in a small red mangrove-filled lagoon, so that I'd be able to participate in this ceremony of prayer.

The *bohiti* began softly to hum, and soon the chief and I were both chanting as well, although I wasn't conscious of having begun. Soon, my entire body felt alive with a strange buzzing sensation that began on my lips and moved down to my shoulders and then to my arms and hands and legs and toes. My head began to feel light, and I feared I might faint. Yet still I hummed, and I kept on humming.

Soon, I began to see a vision. I was at the head of a river — yes, it was one of the rivers near the village — and I saw myself riding a big animal in the water. It was one of those great beasts that we Spaniards in our ignorance had thought mermaids, but the Tainos call *manitees*.

I saw myself riding one of these manitees as we entered the river. I saw Taino fishermen with their spears who came for us — but my animal guide was too quick, and we dashed away. As we sped up the river, I felt us approaching an entire army of Taino soldiers. Sure enough, I looked to my left and there on the bank was a group of archers with longbows and arrows shooting at me. But once again, my manitee was a deft swimmer, and even though I thought the river couldn't have been very deep here, we kept on going. Soon, I saw chief Guacanagari and his son, Guarionex, poised on the edge of the water. Each man held the other, and I could tell that if one of them let the other go just a little bit, they'd both fall into the water and be swept away by the strong current — or they'd have their heads bashed in by the sharp stones. This reminded me of how Esther had once saved my life.

Finally, my manitee and I came to a rest in front of a large fort. It was Villa Navidad, of course. My animal came to a stop, and I got out onto the shore.

The Tainos were behind me, and advancing quickly — but I knew what I had to do. As I slowly lifted my eyelids, I saw the cacique and the medicine man looking at me expectantly.

After a moment, they nodded to me, and then got up and walked out of the shrine.

**

"Look, you've *got* to try to understand me," I said to the men that night. "They mean to kill us. They think we're becoming too much of a threat."

"So what?" asked Pedro de Lepe, as he speared another sweet *batata* with his knife and stuck it into his almost-toothless mouth. "We can take 'em if they try to attack us. What're they gonna do, attack us with those little sticks and rocks?" As he laughed, the other men joined in.

"Remember, there are only thirty nine of us, and thousands and thousands of *them*," I said. "And they do have those sharpened sticks, and some of the Indians off to the east have big bows and arrows. From what I heard tonight, Admiral Colón and the Pinzóns already had a run-in with them when they sailed that way to go home, and now they're itching for a fight."

"Who cares? We've got crossbows and bombards, and they'll work unless it starts to rain," said Diego de Harana. His opposition was bad for my case. Most of the men deferred to him as their captain now, since it was Juan de la Cosa's failure to obey orders that had doomed the *Santa María*.

"Why do they want to kill us *now*?" asked Antonio de Cuellar, a sailor from the Bay of Biscay. "I guess you weren't here for all that talk of us bein' from heaven and gods and all that. Besides, they're afraid of us. I fired the bombards the first day we were here, and you should've seen the little buggers scatter like flies!"

I had finally learned how to work the weapons, placing the heavy, stone ball inside the shaft, and had even gotten used to the smell of powder, saltpeter, charcoal and sulfur. One only had to touch the end of a flaming stick to the hole in back to fire them. I hated using bombards, though, for the noise they made and for their notorious inaccuracy.

"They scattered like flies!" Antonio repeated. The men laughed again, but I was becoming more and more impatient.

"Look," I said, trying not to lose my calm, "perhaps if you behaved a bit more like gods and less like depraved thieves and fornicators, the Taino could respect you more and hate you less—"

"Hey, my *pinga*'s got to get some action with these Indian girls!" yelled Alonso de Morales, one of the grommets I most despised for his crudity. "It's so bleedin' easy — you just grab 'em and show your knife, and nobody gives you any trouble and you can

379

do whatever you damn well please with 'em!" To this, many of the other men cheered in agreement.

"Yeah, and it's so easy to break into their homes whenever we show up in the forest," said Rodrigo de Escobedo. I was surprised to see the mild-mannered scribe speak this way. "They don't even bar their doors here, and never post guards or keep hounds. All you do is break down the door and you can take whatever you like with nobody stopping you."

"Please," I said, trying one more time to contain my anger. "If you keep this up, they're going to kill us all, and I mean in a few short days. They've already got an army ready. Besides, what you're doing is *wrong*. Remember, Jesus told us to love our fellow man. It's unchristian to take what isn't yours."

"You know, I'm getting awfully sick of you," said Pedro Gutierrez, the former courtier. "How do we know *you're* not plotting against us with the savages?" He slammed his tankard down on the bench where he'd been sitting and got up, moving toward me and brandishing a knife. "You'd *like* us to be weak. I bet you can't be trusted, and that you're *trying* to get us killed!" Some of the other men grunted their agreement, and some others had gotten up as well and were coming toward me.

"What are you talking about?" I edged backwards. "I'm trying to help you — *us* — our cause. Don't you want what we do here to be a success? What if they kill us all tonight as we sleep?"

"How would *you* know?" Pedro asked. "It's not like you've been planning on sleeping here much. Why, you've been the guest of the chief there every night since we've arrived. How convenient if you've been helping them plot an attack on the fort some night." His face looked sinister in the light of the lantern, almost like a demon's face, mocking me.

If they really thought I was plotting with the Tainos, I wondered why they thought I would warn them about what would happen to them in the next few days. What purpose could that possibly serve?

I felt myself grabbed from behind, and before I knew it, three men held me tight as another forced my hands into a rusty pair of shackles. I writhed as they snaked a length of chain around my hands and ankles. "You don't know what you're doing!" I cried as they led me away, down to the storage shed. "You've got to listen to me! They're going to kill us! You've got to change what you're doing right now, or else!"

The men just sneered and spat at me. "Take him down and throw him by the supplies where he won't be able to bother us," Juan de la Cosa ordered.

It was the last time I saw him — or most of those men — alive.

CHAPTER SEVENTY-SEVEN

"So it wasn't long after then that the fort fell, I presume?" Bartolomé asked.

"No, it wasn't long. It was the following night, in fact."

***

The sun had just set, and I'd watched it from the small window in the supply shed next to the fort. My stomach growled, since the men had neglected to feed me, and I was mad with thirst. I think they hoped I would die, and then they could be rid of me. They said they would have returned to Spain and not been left to rot here among the savages if it hadn't been for me. Never mind that they never would have made it home if the mutiny had occurred. The supplies wouldn't have lasted nearly that long.

Caonabo had attacked earlier before the rainstorm and killed some of the men, including Guitierrez. There were now only Diego de Harana and perhaps ten others who were left to defend the fort.

For the first time, I was glad that my friends William and Luis Torres had gone back to Spain.

I heard the sound of shouting from within the fort, and I heard my countrymen shouting an alarm. Many of them had been asleep, so they had to be woken up and made to man their stations.

"I've been hit!" yelled one of the men, and I couldn't tell whose voice it was. "They're shooting arrows at us!"

"Fire the bombards," I heard Juan de la Cosa say. "Get your swords ready, boys!"

"Where's the saltpeter?" One of the men cried, and I knew that they hadn't prepared for this attack, despite my warnings.

Outside, I began to hear the cry of the Tainos as they began their renewed attack. They whooped and gave a fearsome war-cry, and I was happy to be in chains in the storeroom and not outside to meet their fury.

I heard them approach the fort, and the men shouted and ran about frantically. A fire broke out somewhere — I could smell its acrid smoke and see the flames sprouting up through the fort, although from where I was sitting I couldn't say where the main fire was. I heard one of my compatriots fire a bombard, but this only seemed to make the Tainos angrier, as I heard another, fiercer war-cry come from every side. This final cry was so intense that my skin became gooseflesh and I balled up like a baby.

Before long, I heard men screaming. I would learn later that the male and female warriors had broken into the fort and begun stabbing with their sharpened sticks and spears. I also learned that they strung several vines and tobacco chords together, which they used to strangle some of the men. I think it must have taken several of them to kill each Spaniard, as someone would have to hold each one down as the ropes were put around his neck as he struggled. This isn't to say that the men didn't put up a valiant fight — on the contrary, in fact. I know for a fact that they killed at least as many natives that night as there were Spaniards, which isn't a small feat considering how vastly outnumbered they were. Even if the bombards were slow to be readied and fired, swords and knives needed only to be pulled from their scabbards to be instantly useful — and deadly.

But the battle was hopeless for the Spaniards, as you can well imagine — and it was over before it had started. Soon, the screams and yells in Castilian ceased, and a victory yell went up from the Taino warriors.

I shuddered. What was to be done with me now that the Spaniards had been defeated? How much could I count on the goodwill of Guacanagari?

The door of the shed opened after a few minutes. A Taino man, whom I recognized as the fierce Juatinango, stood before me, his face streaked with blood. He wore the look of a man who lusted for more carnage, and was jubilant to have found another victim for his lance. Only he didn't carry one of the sharpened Indian sticks, but a bloodied Spanish sword stolen from one of my fellows.

Much later, I reflected on the fact that while I

seemed only seconds from a brutal death, my enemy Colón was being celebrated at the court in Barcelona for his amazing discovery.

I looked again at Juatinango. Anger flashed in his eyes, and he lunged toward me. I closed my eyes and said a prayer, knowing that this was the end. I heard a cry and I readied myself for a painful death.

He was stopped by a shout from the doorway. I opened my eyes.

It was Guarionex.

The man came over to the warrior and spoke quickly to him. After a moment's hesitation, Juatinango gave the chief his sword. After a command from Guarionex, he walked out of the shed, shooting an angry look backwards as he did so.

The chief came to stand in front of me, and then crouched down to look me in the face.

"Do you want to live, O-Rodrig-ero?" he asked, taking out a piece of vine long enough to strangle me with. I shrugged, feeling that I'd seen so many brutal things in my life that I honestly wasn't sure I wanted to see any more. Besides, what did he have in mind? If it was some kind of torture, I'd rather be killed right then with the vine and spared the suffering. I'd already had one of my thumbs broken in the stinking prison of Sevilla, and couldn't stomach the thought of more pain.

"I'll let you live, but only because you're not like the others, the ones we had to kill tonight," he said after a moment. "But if you're to be spared, there's something you're going to have to do for us."

"What's that?" I asked, fearing the reply.

"You'll find out soon enough. But first, you've got to come to my *zemi*'s shrine with me and stand in front of my people. I've got an important message for them I want you to recite."

CHAPTER SEVENTY-EIGHT

It was about a year later, and I lay crouched in the tall grass by the side of the river Yaque. I couldn't believe what I was seeing as I lay beside the footpath we'd used for months to convey messages about the new settlement. Could Colón really be doing this?

He rode out in front, perched on a spotted gray mare, an animal which, incidentally, caused the Tainos to cower in fear during those first months, thinking that the men riding astride them were some kind of half-man, half-beast monster. Colón was the only one to ride something so impressive. Since he'd been sick before the beginning of the second trip to the Indies, he'd not noticed that the twenty lancers had bought nags after they sold their good Arab chargers, pocketing the difference.

He was leading an expedition of at least three hundred, and if one were to include the hundreds of adoring natives marching behind them, there must have been at least five hundred souls together that day. The Spaniards marched in military formation — they were men of the royal militia, I reckoned, and some *hidalgos* from the Order of Santiago. I looked for my brother Ricardo, but decided he would be too old to be among them. The men marched behind a well-formed cavalry which Colón was leading personally, and there were helmeted, armored and chain-mailed men with banners of the green cross, much like the ones that had been raised over the last Moorish citadel not two years before and the one the admiral had planted in the sands of San Salvador. The men fired bombards into the air and the forest, shattering the silence that had reigned only half an hour before. As if this were not enough, loud trumpets sounded and echoed throughout the valley with obnoxious fanfares, and vicious, sleek hunting dogs snapped and barked at the nervous Taino. The trees and mountains of the *Cordillera del Norte* stretched behind and above us, and behind us lay the valley the Spaniards would soon name the *Puerto de Los Hidalgos*. It was a great plain of more than eighty leagues long by thirty.

My mind raced. If they were able to penetrate this far so soon without supplies from the motherland, how soon before we would be completely overrun by them? How could the Taino ward off the dogs being used to attack their best warriors?

Guarionex turned to me with a pleading look in his eyes. In the past few weeks, I'd seen him change from a confident, arrogant warrior to a worried young man. "What are we to do now?" he asked in a low voice, hoping we wouldn't be discovered and that we'd be able to beat a hasty retreat once the men passed. "What do they want? Why are they doing this?"

"I don't know," I said, shaking my head. It was supposed to be my job to know the Spaniards and their ways, and to advise Guarionex and the leaders of the resistance on how best to deal with them. But in the case of Colón — well, one never knew what went on in *his* mind.

For example, when he'd returned a few months before, in November of 1493, I was sure that he would attack Guacanagari and his town of Guarico when he found out what had happened to *Villa Navidad*. But he'd accepted the *cacique's* explanation wearily and with a nod, and accepted more offers of food and hospitality. Thinking back on it, this was probably not so strange, as he was doubtless tired and low on supplies after having traveled to many islands before returning to Hispaniola. The Admiral must have decided that he could use as many native allies as he could win in this part of the world, and Guacanagari was only too happy to oblige, much to his son's anger and dismay.

It hadn't been long before the Spaniards had founded Marta, which the admiral soon renamed Isabel in honor of the queen, about fifty leagues to the east, on the river Bajabonico.

The name for the spot was perhaps not the best, as our queen had been born under an unlucky star. This was just a short distance away from where I'd been living with Guarionex, on the border of the chiefdom of his cousin, Mayobanex. This was a good site upon which to found a colony, my spies told me, as there was lots of good water and space for mills between the two rivers there. In addition, the cliffs provided good protection, as well as a grove of trees that was so thick a *hutia* couldn't have fit through them, much less a man. In addition to a fortified house for Colón, they'd also built a church, a hospital, a storehouse, and quarters for soldiers and officers. They'd been able to pack earth into blocks to build walls coated with lime plaster. Within days of the town's founding, gardens had been planted and the Tainos from all around — or those who hadn't been mistreated by the rogues of Villa Navidad, at any rate — paid them curious visits and brought them many gifts of food and bits of gold. Word had spread that *caona* was what these strange people from the heavens really wanted.

Those who had seen the strangers up close came to me in Guarionex's camp posing many questions during those weeks after the founding of Isabel.

"Why are so many of them sick already?" asked one young man who had been to see the seventeen ships of this second expedition bobbing in the harbor. "Many were just lying about, and your *bohitis* were speaking softly over them, holding those crisscrossed sticks of wood over them."

"I hadn't heard that so many were sick," I said truthfully. I wondered if it was like the bad air I'd experienced in Africa.

"What are all those strange animals they have with them?" asked one girl as she thoughtfully nibbled on a turnip. "Some of them look like big *hutias* and *coris* — but they're bald."

"Oh, those are probably pigs," I answered. "I think they also brought some goats and cows, to milk and to fatten for their meat, especially if it takes time for growing crops. We keep them enclosed back in my country, much as you chase the *hutias* from the woods and keep them in fences when the forests are burned."

"But we have all the food we could possibly want here," she countered. "With the *conuco* and the fruits of the earth and the parrots and iguanas we pluck from the trees, who could need anything more?"

"I think the *ari* have different tastes than you," I said with a laugh, remembering Captain Pinzón's grimace when a man at the feast of Behecchio had brought him a barbecued iguana. He had grandly placed the meal in front of Pinzón, expecting him to eat it with gusto. The captain had gingerly picked it up and taken a few bites, but had soon broken down and jumped up to empty his belly under a big shady *guama* tree, much to the hearty laughs of our hosts.

I didn't know how the little colony planned to start growing crops at the beginning of the dry season. Were they all going to die of starvation before finding a way to eat? I didn't want them to succeed, but I didn't want them to starve, either.

"Why do the Spaniards smell so badly?" asked one girl who'd gone to visit some of the soldiers in Isabel, and was less than delighted by their hygienic practices there.

"I guess they haven't yet learned to use the seeds of the *Guayacona* tree for soap. Maybe you should tell them to use that, or show them how."

"I don't understand what those big, noisy animals are that they ride about everywhere," said one *siani*, or senior married woman. "How do they make them obey?"

"Those are called horses," I said, thinking of how my brother Ricardo had once been a fine jouster, always unseating, and sometimes seriously injuring, his opponents as he guided his stallion effortlessly and without reigns against other sons of the nobility. "Horses have to be well-trained and taken care of with just the right amount of love and grooming. If this is done, they will grow to love their masters and will never falter." I thought of the Romany, and how they spent long hours brushing and riding the horses they sold at their fairs, and felt a twinge of nostalgia.

Stop it, I told myself. You have no home to go to now. You're nothing but a wanderer, the last of your tribe — the lost and lonely tribe of Benjamin, meant to wander the world all alone, like the gypsies.

But at least the gypsies had each other as they wandered, I thought sadly. Who did *I* have to tell my stories to?

CHAPTER SEVENTY-NINE

"So, why is it that those little *zemis* look so funny?" I asked Guarionex one day as we were sitting by the Yaque River.

"Why do you think them funny?" he asked with a snort. "Do you think those little statues of the Virgin aren't funny to us?"

I couldn't see how Mary could be seen as funny, but I tried to see his point.

"Look at this," he said, scaling the bank to a conuco mound that some *naboria* had been harvesting earlier in the day. With a thoughtful look on his face, Guarionex hunted around in the rich, black soil, his arm in almost up to his shoulder. "Ah ha!" he said, and triumphantly pulled out a small, tri-corner statuette. "See this?" he said, showing it to me. "It's Yucahuguama, buried to make the harvest come."

I peered at the little *zemi*, and tried to imagine how it could make such a thing happen.

"See here, look at his little ears," he said, turning the *zemi* on its side and showing me the

393

designs of his patterned ears that I hadn't even seen. "This is where we can put on the *guanin* earrings, which shows his nobility."

"Yes, but what about that wide mouth — and those eyes!" I said with a chuckle. It looks like he's screaming or giving birth."

"Well, he is, in a way," Guarionex said. "See, look at the horn rising out of his head. He's pushing the crop — a gift from the gods — out through his head after he eats the earth and the sun and water himself for a while. That's the way it works, and then we get to eat. See, it's the place where land, water, and people all come together."

I looked again at the little statue, and, indeed, I could see how it looked like it was working hard to sprout a harvest for his people. I felt a twinge of guilt for having made fun.

"O-Rodrigero," he said smiling, "you have a lot to learn about the world and all those who live in it. There is magic all around, and the world is full of *zemis* of one kind or another. We give of ourselves and live from this together. You'll see, I hope, before it's too late."

CHAPTER EIGHTY

"So, you were there to see the conquest of the island of Hispaniola," Bartolomé said, making a few more notes in the margins of the book he'd written on the Great Admiral's journal. "It's odd that he'd only wanted a trading post at first, and then when that failed, he wanted a beachhead. I guess he really *did* think this was a part of Asia."

So far, all of the information his guest had given Bartolomé seemed to match up with what he had been told. Only, of course, Rodrigo had quite a different perspective than Admiral Colón had. Still, Bartolomé enjoyed hearing this other viewpoint, and had listened especially carefully to some of the facts that he'd conveyed to him about these early days. Unlike Colón, his guest wasn't trying to make things seem better than they were to serve his own purposes.

"Yes, but you don't understand, Bartolomé," Rodrigo said once more with a sigh. "Please close that infernal journal of yours this very minute. I'm not telling you all of this so that you'll have more details for your book. This isn't supposed to be purely an intellectual exercise for you. You're missing the point."

"Pardon me," Bartolomé said with a shrug. He placed the book back on the shelf.

***

During that time at the beginning, the Spaniards were dazzled by the vegetation. The greenery, the maize, the mohogany, the ebony, the silk-cotton trees — it used to be so breathtaking. The forests I saw reminded me of what I'd seen in Africa, as they were so humid and full of lizards and insects, and all along the mountains there were tall canopies of green in the wet, wild woods. Sometimes, if we swam out in the sea, I noticed the rich reefs where little needle-nosed fish darted back and forth before my eyes. Up by Lake Neiba, the salty one by the Bahoruco Sierra, I used to sit and watch big caymans sun themselves on the cracked, brown banks between feedings and, to my amazement, large, pink birds that hunted for crabs in the mud. And everywhere I looked, I saw orchids and other flowers that were red, blue, and all the colors of the rainbow.

But it was all to be devoured or destroyed, you know, and Hojeda's men began it by ruthlessly extorting money and taking unwilling girls as concubines.

***

It had now been more than four years since I'd first spotted land from the *Pinta*.

I placed my hand to the girl's forehead one more time. Her fever had subsided, but the sores that covered her small body were still there. I somehow felt sure that this one, at least, would make it. I offered up a prayer to God for her, and said another to the Taino earth goddess, Caguana, just in case.

I sighed as I finished the prayers. I felt so tired, and an incredible urge to sleep washed over me, which I fought with all my strength. I'd already administered last rites to many people that afternoon, and I needed to keep going for the sake of many others. Still, I was glad to think that at least one of my charges was going to make it. There had been a few cases of recovery that gave me some cause for hope, although this was a hard thing to come by for the Tainos in the days following the Admiral's return.

"Rodrigero," a voice behind me said. It was Guarionex, and he sounded worried. "I need to have a word with you, my friend."

I'd never told any of the Tainos my other name. I know that this must seem strange, but by the time of the destruction of Villa Navidad, I guess I'd just decided that since the Taino knew me as 'Rodrigero,' or sometimes 'O Rodrigero,' there was no use in confusing them without reason. Besides, I decided, I'd spent most of my life deceiving others in one way or another. Why change now?

I stood under the wide, palm-thatched canopy of Guarionex's house, and the late afternoon sun was still bright in my eyes. He looked at me and his face softened a bit. Still, there was a look of fear and humiliation there that had not been there when I'd first met him at Guacanagari's feast four years before.

"What's going to happen to my people?" he asked, reaching out to me with a trembling hand. His other hand clenched tightly his *zemi* necklace, which, like your Juanito's protective amulet, showed a small man baring his teeth out of anger and protectiveness.

"What's going to happen to us?" he asked again, this time more softly than before.

It's true that these had been brutal years for the Tainos. After the admiral's *entrada* — he'd wanted to make such a show of himself, as always — we'd tried our best to sack one of his forts, the one called Santo Tomás. Things had gone well, at least at first. Another *cacique*, Caonabo, had led the attack and I'd told the chief and his men all I knew about Spanish military and culture, and what they could reasonably expect from my countrymen. I apologized for my lack of more precise knowledge in this moment of need, but I was after all only a humble *bohiti* whose life had been spared only by the grace of Guarionex.

It had been an interesting process, what I went through to become one of them, considered just as Taino as anyone — and a member of the *nitaino*, no less. I'd had my flesh scarred and these markings put on my face and back, and I'd had to fast and wait for visions. Besides the gods of the sun and moon, who the Tainos said emerged from a cave long ago, I was visited by the snake of the water goddess. Then the angry red bull of Sevilla came to me time and time again, like when I was in Africa. This was strange because a spirit guide was supposed to come to me, but the Tainos could make nothing at first from my descriptions of the red bull, as this is, of course, a European, and sometimes African, beast. They had a better idea after livestock from Castile began to arrive in Isabel.

I didn't participate directly in the raid and this was mostly out of fear of being recognized and dragged back to Isabel in chains, and then having to deal with the admiral or his brother once again. I needn't have worried, though. When the seventy men of Santo Tomás reached the settlement, hunger, disease and discontent far outweighed the talk of one man they may have thought they saw in the fracas.

Colón, who was most unhappy with the way his colonists were faring, made a rash decision based on his anger toward the Indians for the raid. It was then that he decided to send that tyrant Alonso de Hojeda — a cousin of the prior of the Dominicans in Sevilla — into the Vega Real. I knew him a little by sight, and scrupulously avoided him and his men whenever they were out in the bush, where we were crouching, waiting and wondering what was to come next. He and his men were to "strike fear and terror" into the countryside and help the men become better acclimated to the tropical environment. Colón still claimed to harbor dreams of discovering the land of the Great Kahn, and I assume he thought that battle-tested men would be the best kind to take with him when he did this.

In any case, it wasn't long before the restless grumblers of Isabel were pillaging all across the mountains of the *Cordillera Central*. Santo Tomás fell easily enough, but that didn't stop the soldiers from pushing further and further east and south, hungering always for the lands of Caonabo and their legendary streams of gold and pearls.

I was there the night that this *cacique* was tricked into becoming the Spaniards' prisoner. We'd had an evening of turtle meat and *cassavi* bread, and some of the young women had just performed a few *areytos*, praising and praying to the *zemis* of Caonabo and his ancestors.

Guarionex and I both knew that something was about to happen that night. We'd just been to see Guacanagari, and I'd been allowed to act as the official *bohiti* after the feast was done and the dances performed. We'd sat in the chief's shrine and hummed and sung and chewed *cohoba* together, hoping for some trances that would guide us, with the help of our *zemis*, to make the right decisions. We had foreseen trouble.

Guarionex and I had similar visions that evening, and Guacanagari, although he hadn't had our vision, agreed with our interpretation. I'd seen a tribal gathering at Caonabo's *caney* home in the Maguana region, the one that was ambushed by the soldiers. I'd seen the *cacique* drinking out of a cup and talking about how he'd bested the Spaniards militarily at Santo Tomás. My *zemi* spirit guide, the one I had finally accepted was the red bull, showed me everything in my vision. It showed me *quebasa*, which is a fruit the Taino believe they eat in the afterlife, and the belt Caonabo wore of spun cotton, with shells, gold and animal teeth woven into the green and red fabric. Sure enough, when I arrived at the feast, he told me that the design was of Gwaptowagi, his personal *zemi*. In any case, the thing that I saw that day, and Guarionex and I had both seen in our visions only rarely, was the very thing I dreaded the most: a black cloud over his head, which meant certain disaster. I tried to warn Caonabo of the danger, but he'd have none of it on a day of feasting and dancing. I fled in terror and dismay when a group of Spanish soldiers suddenly appeared at the door. I was still mortally afraid of being found out.

"*Turey, turey*," the Spaniards cried, kissing his hand and holding up the adornments which were, they claimed, a gift from their *gwamiquina*, or chief, which they wanted him to try on.

Caonabo demurred, or so my sources told me later, because he had such a bountiful feast before him, and besides, who were these men to interrupt such an occasion? But, yes, the Spaniards could stay if they wanted to dine with them, if they were hungry. Wouldn't they prefer to eat instead of putting on this gift from the sky? Besides, they hadn't even taken any of the ceremonial ablutions or cleansing herbs one should always take before such a meal.

"So, let us bathe, Brother, and straightaway," Hojeda said, the snake that he was. "Let us bathe and then we'll put on this *turey* from the sky. It's a special gift for you from our *cacique*, the admiral."

The great Caonabo was on a horse being spirited away to Isabel before I knew what had happened or would have been able to warn him. How was he to know that the *turey* — the "gift from the sky —" had been a pair of Biscay handcuffs which had been polished to look like glowing silver? Or that he was to die en route to Castile, still a prisoner, in the hurricane a couple of years later in 1502?

It wasn't long after then that the orders were given for the tributes to be given to the Spaniards by all the Tainos. Everyone was to provide a hawksbell of gold dust or, if they were not able to do so because of where they lived, they were to provide an *arroba* of cotton each. Of course, many tributes of *conuco* were extracted instead, as things were going from bad to worse back at Isabel. Hunger and sickness-due, it was thought, to the humidity and the diet of this strange land, caused ever more deaths, and starvation always loomed as an ugly probability when supplies were late in arriving from Spain. Colón, who was even worse an administrator than a navigator, was having a more and more difficult time proving that his venture was profitable. To make matters worse, Isabel was leaking men and beasts faster than the *Pinta* used to move on a windy September day. Men were running off to the forest to do as they pleased and dig up *conuco* plants before they could be harvested, sometimes long before they were even ripe by Taino standards. As if this weren't bad enough, they spread disease and misery wherever they went, and the Tainos seemed to have no resistance to the pox or measles we brought with us. So, in short, the people whom I'd grown to love and serve over the last four years were being killed off by hunger, murder, and European pestilence faster than I would have ever believed possible. It was enough to make me curse the land where I'd been born, and decry the gods who hadn't sunk our scurvy-ridden ship before she could ever bring the message back to Spain.

402

"I don't know *what's* going to happen," I said, taking Guarionex's hand in mine, and kissing the *zemi* he held. "I wish I knew, but all I know is that I'm very afraid."

CHAPTER EIGHTY-ONE

The little green tree frogs — the ones the Tainos believe are the tree spirit of the earth — were not singing their song of "coquí, coquí" that night in the ceiba trees. There were too many people around — thousands of people in fact, and all of the frogs had been frightened off, and were singing somewhere else.

Soon, the people began to yell, "Give us back our *caciques!* Give them back!" Of course, the few Spanish guards up on the ramparts of Concepción de la Vega didn't understand what they were saying down below on the ground. They exchanged worried looks, however. It was not difficult to guess what the Tainos were so upset about.

I'd tried to warn them, but my efforts had been in vain. I hadn't even been able to get to Guarionex in time, and none of my messengers had made it to the other settlements in time, either.

Two days before, I'd been told by some of Guarionex's spies that the men of Concepción de la Vega — now the strongest fort in the strife-ridden

Vega — were up to something. None of them had been seen entering or leaving the fort for quite some time, and some of the men had become suspicious.

They'd decided that I should be sent into the fort to gather information.

"I, um, I've brought some *cassavi* bread from Isabel," I said to the guard, who looked me over doubtfully. I hoped against hope that he couldn't tell that I hadn't spoken Castilian in almost four years except to give language lessons to Guarionex. "I cooked it this morning in the…kiln."

I cursed under my breath as I heard myself say this. I'd heard about the kilns they had at the doomed town, and they were made only for bricks, not for bread, which they extorted from the Indians.

The guard frowned. "Why would they have any more bread than we've got here?" he asked suspiciously. He was right to be skeptical; in the midst of a famine, why would gifts of food be sent about by an unguarded old man? I was lucky to have been taught to gather roots by the *bohiti* of Guarionex's village, and that there had been enough *cassavi* bread among the spies to provide a reasonable excuse for my entry into the fort.

"This is excellent bread," I said breaking off a crunchy chunk and taking a bite before waving it under the man's green Galician eyes. "I'm sure a man who's served the queen as *you* have and worked hard to pack the walls of Isabel deserves to fill his belly a bit, no?"

Soon I'd found myself standing near a rickety table upon which a map of the surrounding chiefdoms was displayed. I felt both ashamed and impressed that the Spaniards had such a map while the Tainos and I had never thought to make up something like it.

"All right, do you all know where you're going now?" asked Roldán, the rebellious *hidalgo* who was to lead the group of about thirty. "According to our sources, the *caciques* don't post guards outside their doors at night, so they should be relatively easy to capture. But just to be safe, make sure that each man brings with him both a gun and a dagger. Is that understood?"

There were murmurs of agreement from the men.

"Good," he said. "Well then, let's have a look at the map so that each group knows where to go."

I had already gotten a few suspicious glances as I stood in the background looking like a Moor as I covered as much of my face as I could with a handkerchief. I noticed Hojeda studying my face with a look that told me that he was racking his brains in an attempt to recall where he'd seen me before. I tried to think of a way to sneak away, but I knew I would be noticed. I resigned myself to remaining there, listening to the plot with a look of feigned indifference until the men were ready to split up and execute it.

"Are you ready, men?" Roldán yelled.

"Yes!" they cried in unison. I should have yelled this like the others, but was feeling too overwhelmed to do so.

Soon the gates were thrown open, and we were released into the night, the teams of men racing off down the paths to the homes of the *caciques* they were to capture.

I felt a hand reaching out to grab me then, and I dashed to the left, suddenly full of fear and rage. What would they do to me if they caught me, or knew who I was? Would I burned like a bungle of twigs?

I ran to where some of Guarionex's spies were lying in wait for me at the side of the path. "We've got to warn them," I said, out of breath.

"Warn *whom*, Rodrigero?" the group of spies asked me, confused.

"The *caciques*. All of them hereabouts. They're out to capture them tonight," I gasped.

But despite my best efforts, all fourteen of the *caciques* of the region had been caught before word could be sent that trouble was afoot. And now here were perhaps five thousand men and women gathered outside the walls of the fort brandishing spears and a few firearms — I had taught some of Guarionex's men to use them, and they'd learned well. In addition, there were some Ciguayans who'd already shot their arrows deep into the wood of the fort. It was good to have them there, as the Spaniards had been afraid of them ever since the run-in in the Bay of Arrows during the original expedition. I wondered how afraid the Spaniards must be, as even I was surprised by the response mounted by the Tainos to this latest aggression.

Soon, the *adelantado* and son of the Viceroy, Diego Colón, appeared at the top of the fort flanked by about a dozen of his guards who pointed their weapons menacingly at the crowd below, daring anyone to make a threatening move.

"Your *caciques* will be released to you," he said in halting Taino. My God, I thought — I spoke better than that after only four weeks here.

"The *caciques* will be released, but on one condition," he continued in his horrible accent. "They must cooperate fully in delivering all of the tributes their subjects owe us. Otherwise, they'll all be killed tonight."

I was shocked. For one thing, he referred to all the Taino as subjects — "naboria" — of their *caciques*, which showed a complete lack of understanding of how their society worked. The *naboria* were the lowest, laboring class who were mostly engaged in agriculture, hunting, and the raising of turtles. Furthermore, I didn't see how any more tributes could be paid to the Spaniards. As if it weren't enough that the Tainos' food was stolen and their farming completely disrupted, they were still dying of disease and exhaustion as they tried in vain to gather enough gold to avoid losing a hand or a foot. Of course, those who tried to escape were hunted down with dogs and killed in the woods and the mountains. The admiral had filled several caravels of gold and parrots which he had sent to Spain, but this didn't quell the rumors of corruption or the tongues at court who demanded a royal inquest into his behavior as governor and viceroy of the Indies. A delegation for an audience with him was even then being assembled in Toledo, I heard later.

It was obvious to me that the Colón family was becoming desperate.

"From now on, King Guarionex is to coordinate the deliveries of tribute as well as the labor of the mines," the *adelantado* concluded, casting a nervous look at the bewildered crowd below. "You are all to follow his orders if you wish to avoid further bloodshed."

King Guarionex? Since when had he been anything but one *cacique* among many?

CHAPTER EIGHTY-TWO

By late 1496, the population was in a very rapid decline, and the island had become so beaten into submission that The admiral could march across it almost completely unescorted.

Guarionex and I stood once again under the verandah of his *caney* house, this time overlooking the valley of the *Vega Real* on the eastern side of the mountains. I noted with sadness that he had aged quite a bit in the last few years. This wasn't surprising, I suppose; he'd been a young fighter, then a disheartened *cacique*, then a rebel leader by default after Caonabo's capture, and, finally, the coordinator of tribute deliveries and labor to those who had murdered, starved, and enslaved his people.

He had had enough.

"I can't stay here any longer, Rodrigero," he began. "I'm sure you know why...it's all too much now. I can't do this any longer."

410

I nodded. This didn't come as a surprise to me. He'd done his best, and we'd done our fair share of fighting. I'd also made sure that much of the tribute and food had been sent to the most vulnerable of his people. The Spaniards were so desperate for anything they could get that they never noticed a little missing here or a little extra manioc poison there. But the years of threats and violence and witnessing the torture of his people at such a close range had taken their toll.

"I'm going north to the land of the Ciguayans," he said with a note of finality. "Mayobanex has said that he'll take me in, and my family as well. I'm no longer of any use here. There's almost nothing more they can squeeze from us. I doubt anyone will care very much that I'm gone."

"And what about *me?*" I asked. "Where should *I* go?"

The man studied me for a long moment and I felt very self-conscious of my Spanish identity and my red hair, which never fails to amaze Taino children who reach beneath my brown cap to play with the graying strands. How could he help but hate me, I wondered. But then, how *could* he, after all we'd been through together?

"O-Rodrigero," he said, turning to go back into the *caney*. "Rodrigero, my friend, you do as you please," he said, closing the grass door behind him.

***

He was wrong about one thing. The Spaniards not only cared that he left — they were furious over his leaving them in the lurch.

You see, they'd grown so used to dealing with him that they couldn't fathom the idea of trying to collect from someone else.

So it was that, once again, violence consumed the countryside. It's amazing that so many Tainos were left by that time, now that I think of it.

Diego Colón became obsessed with the idea of catching the "renegade" *cacique* when he learned of his escape. I guess he reasoned that, since his clemency had spared his life, as well as the lives of eleven of the other thirteen *caciques*, they owed him perpetual loyalty. Unfortunately for him, the Tainos didn't see things that way.

So it was that the *adelantado* marched through the area north of the *Cordillera del Norte*, burning still more *conuco* crops and sacking villages, demanding that Mayobanex hand over his former "vassel." I still can't believe what fools they were. It was stupid to waste valuable crops and land while making more enemies of the people of that region. And they were fools on the other hand to think even for a moment that one Indian on the entire island would betray another to a Spaniard, after everything that had happened. Fear and hatred had taken root in the hearts of so many people, and I wonder how many times I myself was almost killed for who I am, despite all that I did to help.

For all the differences of languages and everything else, I was pleasantly surprised at how the Ciguayans took Guarionex in and treated him like a brother. I drifted up there to see him not long after his departure, once I could be sure that the tributes would still be collected during my absence and delivered to the garrison at Concepción. For all their warlike ways, I was pleased to find that the Samana peninsula, which had not been attacked as often as the middle of the island, was full of dances and sweet, gentle laughter. After two days there, I almost had a hard time believing that these had been the people who had attacked the ships with arrows soon after I'd left the *Pinta* in 1493. And to think that we'd thought these proud people were flesh-eaters like the Caribs! True, they made strong and flexible bows, and used cactus fiber to string them and shoot arrows to defend their land, but that didn't make them natural or bloodthirsty killers.

Before long, one of the *adelantado*'s messengers arrived to announce that Mayobanex was to hand over his guest right away, or else fear the wrath of two hundred men accompanied by horses, weapons and dreaded hunting dogs.

The Ciguayan leader heard the news calmly and soon called a gathering of his people on the main plaza and ball-court of his village so that he could put the question to them for a unanimous decision.

"No!" they cried when he asked whether to send the guests away to meet the wrath of the Spaniards. "Never send them! They're our brothers and sisters!"

"We shall not betray the noble Guarionex," the chief told the messenger. "He's a good man who taught my head wife the finest *areyto* of Magua, his village."

One thing to understand about the Taino culture is that the dances are so sacred that the

413

teaching of one, from one ruler to another, is more valued than all the gold in Castile in their eyes.

As can be expected, the *adelantado* attacked and immediately the Tainos began to resist in any way they could as the Spaniards ravaged the land. I did what I could to help, but it never felt like more than a drop in the sea compared to what was happening around me.

And soon, twelve neatly disguised Spaniards crept into the Ciguayan camp and ambushed the chief's family, taking them prisoner back to Concepción. Guarionex gave himself up not long afterwards, bewildered by the fact that the Spaniards had pursued him so far.

Mayobanex died in chains in the prison at Concepción. That brave man died alone and hungry in an unlit cell, and his only crime was that of hospitality.

CHAPTER EIGHTY-THREE

"And you know what happened to Guarionex, don't you, Bartolomé?"

"Yes," the priest said, remembering well the day he'd arrived in the newly founded port of Santo Domingo. Bartolomé thought again of what he had seen that day, and of the horror of it. He closed his eyes and leaned back, remembering it all.

Later that day, when he had walked into one of the huts that served as a disreputable tavern for the governor and his men, he'd heard them discussing a letter of warning from Admiral Colón that was mocked openly by Ovando.

"Your Lordship," Bartolomé began, addressing the governor. But Ovando was too busy with the letter to pay him any attention.

"The great cheat says there's to be a tempest on the eastern side of the island," he said, stroking his chin and trying to contain a laugh. "He wants us to tie down all the moorings of the ships in harbor and refrain from sending other ships forth for a few days."

415

"How decidedly *convenient* for him!" crowed one of Bobadilla's friends and Guarionex's jailor. "He'd stoop to nothing to stop bad reports of him from being sent home, no?" said another man with a sneer.

"What makes him so sure there's a tempest coming, anyhow?" asked another man, the son of a nobleman from whom Bartolomé's father had borrowed money when he was a child. "What do you think, Bartolomé?" he asked, turning toward the future priest. "You're a smart man, *Licenciado* Las Casas," he said, addressing him with the usual title of a man who's had the benefit of a university education. "Wouldn't you agree that this is a weak plot from that damned Italian to try to put off the inevitable?"

Surprised, Bartolomé said nothing. How was he to know what was written in the man's heart? He was sure only of one thing, and that was that one of the grommets on his ship from Sevilla had said that it was sometimes possible to detect an oncoming storm — or *hurrica'n*, as the Tainos called these monstrous tempests — by the shape and the form of clouds high up in the sky. And who better than Colón to know of such things? And besides, what harm would a delay of two or three days do? He voiced this concern, but the governor laughed and called him a fool who should stick to Latin and the clerical work to which he would be assigned.

Ovando would soon regret his haste in dismissing the Admiral's advice. Just hours after the three ships departed, a horrible *hurrica'n* came swooping down from the northeast which sank two of the ships of the group. Only the ship containing the Admiral's gold ever made it to Spain, which caused people to fear him as a magician.

"I remember that day as if it were yesterday," Bartolomé said to Rodrigo, thinking again of when he'd seen Guarionex being led to the ship. "He looked so sad, so defeated, chained up like an animal bound hand and foot. And with Anacoana murdered, and her daughter and granddaughter under that intendant, Mojica…"

Rodrigo was silent for a long time, his hands together under his chin, watching his host, almost as if in prayer.

"It didn't take you long to get used to the Indies, though, did it Bartolomé?" he asked in a knowing way. "If I remember correctly, you were Ovando's right hand man for a while as he butchered the followers of the brave Hatuey. Besides Xaragua, they were the last part of the island to fall under the yoke of the white man."

Bartolomé clenched his fists as he thought of that time, and of all that happened. "I hoped to be able to win some souls over for Christ," he said, trying to keep his composure.

"And you thought you could do it by murdering innocent people?" The old man stared piercingly at Bartolomé, and the priest looked back, unable to believe what he was hearing.

"What are you talking about?" he asked, sitting straight in his chair.

"Does the name Juan de Esquivel mean anything to you?" Rodrigo asked, studying Bartolomé's face with a look that burned itself into his soul. "How about knives? And carnage? And butchery?"

"Stop!" Bartolomé yelled, leaping to his feet. He began to sweat and his hands clenched. "Stop it! I don't want to hear about — how did you know? Who *are* you, you devil?" Suddenly, before he knew what he was doing, he had him by the smock and had shoved him against the wall.

"Tell me who you are, you whelp of Satan!" Bartolomé snarled.

He suddenly realized what he was doing, and he let him go. He sat down hard beside his guest, and put his head in his hands.

"How did you know about that?" he asked again, finally looking up. This time, his voice was a barely audible whisper. "Who *are* you, Rodrigo? Have you been watching me my entire *life?*"

The old man just looked at him without saying a word, and the tears came again to Bartolomé's eyes. He began softly to sob.

"So many of them," he said, after a while, his voice hoarse and choking. "There must have been hundreds and hundreds. It was my first mission, and they told me I was to help put them down. I was just along to absolve the men of whatever they did in the name of the crown and The Lord. And all they had was knives with them, since all the gunshot had already been used..."

Rodrigo moved closer to Bartolomé and placed a hand on his shoulder. "I know, Bartolomé. I know, I saw the aftermath. I'd been wandering through the spurs of the mountains near the Baoruco

418

range when some runners came up and told us. We went there as fast as we could, but it took us days, and it was too late to save anyone."

"And we *did* butcher them. They didn't think that they'd need my help, but they said they didn't have enough men. Some of Esquivel's men locked them up in one of their palaces when they were waiting for us to dine with them — what do you call those houses, the fancy ones? *Caney?*"

Rodrigo nodded, not saying a word.

"And then we butchered them. I mean, we locked them up and then he sent us in with the knives. Oh God, it was horrible. I still hear the screams when sleep flees from me at night. That's why I keep a taper by my bedside."

"I know." The old man took Bartolomé's hand in his. "But you've got to remember it all. An attempt to forget it won't help you. You've got to remember what happened, and let the memory transform you into something better, something more pure. You've got to remember and draw strength from the knowledge it unlocks."

"Who *are* you, Rodrigo? Or Benjamín, or whatever the hell you—"

"Shush," the old man said with a whisper. "My tale's almost done."

After a while, he ended the day by saying something Bartolomé would never forget: "One thing that Father Sebastián taught me is that we should never spend too much time worrying about the past. The past is like a book whose pages are thrown into a river that we never see again, even if we remember

419

what's written on them. It's a useless thing, mourning the past. You have to turn to the present to fight for a better tomorrow."

CHAPTER EIGHTY-FOUR

By the time the Higuey had been put down, about the only place rebels could take refuge was in Xaragua, in the land of Behecchio and his much-loved wife, Anacaona, the mother of Higuemota — the one who married that brute, Guevara. She's the one I had seen that day by her brother's side during the match so many years before and I had vowed to befriend.

I had been seen by more and more Spaniards in those years, and my red hair and broken thumb had allowed some people to piece together the mystery of my identity. Someone eventually did tell the Colón family, and Governor Ovando put a bounty on my head because of my help in planning raids for the Indians who, as you well know, were dying off in droves. Sooner or later, the Spaniards were going to have to find someone else to work on their accursed haciendas and dig in their damnable mines. We had an extensive chain of messengers and spies. They ranged from the humblest house-slaves of the governor to the old conuco-farmers and sons of the chiefs — but it wasn't enough. Our resistance movement was dying almost as fast as the Tainos themselves.

So I suppose I shouldn't have been so surprised the day I met an African on my way to the river.

I stood there, unable to believe it. Was I imagining this, or was he really there in front of me?

I stepped forward and the man took a frightened step backward. And why *shouldn't* he have been afraid of me? He'd been captured, put in chains and kept on a ship for months before arriving here, I presumed, and then somehow managed to escape. Now here was a wild-looking white man with red hair who was dressed as an Indian. God's teeth!

"Hello," I said to him tentatively in Wolof, remembering with some effort the bit of that language which Kinjay had taught me so many years before on the deck of the *María Luisa*. I remembered that this was the *lingua franca* of the region surrounding the great Gamby River, in any case.

"Hello," I said again, but the man just looked alarmed. He took another step back, and seemed about to run away.

It was then that I saw the tribal markings on his cheeks. My heart leapt as I ran to him and embraced him with a kiss on the cheek, yelling the familiar morning greeting of the Balanta.

The man darted away from me, and sat crouched by a tree. Slowly, without taking his eyes off of me, he reached down and picked up a spear from the ground next to him.

For the first time, alarm overcame my excitement, and I raised my hands high to show that I was not going to hurt him. "Don't worry, I'm a friend," I said. "I won't hurt you." How ironic it would have been to have lived through all that I'd lived through only to die at the hands of a man who could be the cousin of my friends from Bolama!

The man came closer to me, and put the point of the spear to my chest. "Do not do that," I said gently. "I'm a friend. A friend of the Balanta from the Island of Bolama. A friend of Winnoke, and of Firofa — and of Kuja, the rice-gatherer."

He lowered his spear then, and sat down hard on the ground, a blank look of disbelief on his face. I decided not to say or do anything that might upset him any further, eyeing the sharpened point of the spear once again.

"Mandinga," he said, pointing to himself. Then, he seemed to think about something for a long time, and he looked like he was going to cry. Then, he opened his mouth, and began to speak in very broken Balanta.

"I...I stolen from near Bolama island...as a boy. Small child. Never working, small boy only..."

His eyes rose to meet mine, and I nodded.

We both knew what it was to be very far from home.

***

It wasn't long before I brought the young man to see Behecchio, and more important, his sister, who had inherited what was left of her husband Caonabo's *caciazgo* in the center of the island.

423

The chief was so excited to see the young man — whose name, I'd learned was Gweriko. She got down from the litter upon which she'd been riding — as far as I know, she was the only ruler to still be carried around that way by 1503 — and she went to him and put both her hands to his face, and felt his woolly hair. "He's so beautiful," she gushed.

Her *bohiti* was quickly summoned, and we were cleansed with his ceremony in order to partake of a special feast. I wasn't invited to act as *bohiti* because Anacaona was quite attached to the man who'd been serving her for years. However, I was invited to the feast, as I was to serve as the man's interpreter.

Some things never change, I thought.

CHAPTER EIGHTY-FIVE

"So, where is Gweriko from, exactly?" asked the chief once the barbacued *hutia* had been blessed and the guests were eating the food hungrily. The sound of smacking lips and the licking of fingers could be heard among the normal feast-chatter.

"He's originally from the Bolama people, in Africa," I said. Realizing that this would mean nothing to her, I added, "It's not so very far from where I myself am from."

I thought of the weeks I'd spent at sea, and of the *malaria* I'd had back then, over twenty years before. It may have been easier to say then to explain, but the land of the Bolama was *hardly* near Castile.

"But he looks nothing *like* you or the others," Anacaona said, looking from Gweriko to me, and then back again. "How can that be?"

"Well," I said trying to clarify, "it's on the same side of the Ocean Sea, but Castile is still very far from Africa."

"Do you have the same *cacique*?" she asked, studying her new guest. I realized that she must have assumed he was a king because of the "gw" sound at the beginning of his name.

It was a good question, I thought. But as far as I knew, Spain had limited its Colonial aspirations to the Indies. Now, Portugal on the other hand...*that* was anybody's guess. I spoke to Gweriko, and he told me that, although the Portuguese did deal in slaves and conduct their own raids, the Mandinga had not yet been conquered, and the Balanta, true to their name, were a people who would resist as long as possible.

"No, we don't have the same rulers, although the Mandinga have been attacked by the white man, much as the Tainos have been," I said.

"Is that so?" she asked, leaning back on her stool. She looked at her guest with renewed interest now that she realized they shared a common enemy.

I grew excited as I realized the importance of what I was saying. "He was brought here against his will, a slave like so many sons of this land who labor in the mines," I said excitedly. "And there are others, a whole shipload of them. We could free some of them and ask them to help us fight! The Mandinga are warriors — most of those caught were captured warriors from their tribal wars. And I speak Balanta, like Gweriko here does."

"Yes," Anacaona replied, "but only a bit. And only because he was captured as a boy. What was it that they speak again, O-Rodrigero?"

"Mandinga, Ladyship," I replied.

"Well, then," she said as a smile tugged at the sides of her mouth. She looked at her guest once again, "I think that you'd better start working on learning Mandinga. And quickly! We'll need all the help we can get from these people."

***

And so I began learning yet another language — and at the age that most men are grandfathers! I could scarcely believe it, but it just goes to show you that you're never too old to try something new. Father Sebastián always used to say that the day a man stops learning is the day he starts dying. I believe that now more than ever before. And now, as I am about to leave this world, I can say with confidence that I speak a dozen languages.

Before long, the Tainos had freed over a dozen of Gweriko's Mandinga compatriots. You should have seen the looks on their faces as they realized that the Spaniard who'd been guarding them could not only speak a bit of their language, but wanted to take them to meet a group of rebel Tainos who needed the same man to make Mandinga words. It was even more of a surprise to learn that I wanted to help them to resist their former captors. It seemed like too much for them at first.

Soon, we were holding meetings in which we were plotting strategy. Some of the Mandinga were learning Taino fairly quickly, and sometimes the two sides used bits of the Castilian they both knew to get a point across. This was especially true for weapons and such that were only known because of the Spaniards. At other times, they'd say something to Gweriko in

Mandinga, who would try to think of a Bolama or Balanta word that they hoped I would remember and be able to say in Taino. In the face of such confusion, you can imagine why games of gestures were often used, especially at first.

The experiment was a huge success, as Anacaona had suspected. Before long, we were attacking forts and settlements, as well as mines and haciendas all along the center of the island. Morale improved and foodstuffs were won back — and I think that we may have begun to reverse the rate of population loss in that part of the island for a few months. At least fewer people were swallowing poison manioc or jumping off cliffs during that time of great hope.

Things were looking better all the time, and you could see the difference in people's faces. Anacaona herself had taught some of the Mandinga her most precious *areytos*, and some of her favorite maidens had become the wives of our new comrades. The Africans also taught *us* some of their dances, and made ferocious masks painted with all sorts of colors for some of their more impressive displays.

As if this were not enough, there was an added surprise in store for Anacaona and her brother Behecchio. Some of the Spaniards living in this western part of the island were, not unlike myself, renegades who were opposed to the autocratic rule of Santo Domingo, the new Spanish capital. Ex-soldiers and guards themselves, many of these men were also instrumental in helping the warriors learn how to attack the fortresses at their weakest points.

It was several years, however, before the time that two men, Guarocuya — the boy you protected after the Xaragua massacre whom the Franciscans renamed Enriquillo — and Hatuey, emerged as leaders of this ever-weakening movement. I remember the night they first met, like Lorenzo and I had once long ago. They were fast friends by the end of an evening of strategy for which I'd been simultaneously interpreting about five languages for a raid of Bonao and San Cristobal. Before long, they'd built up a system of messages and codes that would allow them to fight the Spaniards for years to come. Wherever they went, the people of the island cheered and wept and offered them food, drink and, if they needed it, shelter from enemy guns and lances. We were nomads, superstitious and fearful, not wishing to come into contact with the tight crowd of Spanish steel and the fire of the harquebuses and cavalry charges. This resistance movement was all we had, it seemed.

But it was not to last. Governor Ovando, as well as his successors, wouldn't have it, this disruption to the mining or the challenge to their power. Before long, preparations were being made for Ovando to make an official state visit to Xaragua, where he was to meet Anacaona tête-a-tête for a feast. It would have to be with her anyway, as her brother had died and she was the most powerful *cacique* on the island after that.

"It's a trap," I tried to tell her as she practiced her *areyto* that afternoon, one that she hadn't danced since her girlhood. "You've got to *do* something. At least keep a group of guards nearby, just in case. Please, to be safe?"

"O-Rodrigero," she said, stopping the graceful movements and straightening her ceremonial belt, the one with the pattern of her own personal *zemi* woven into it in vibrant reds and oranges. She placed one hand on my cheek and said, "my dear friend. I can't have guards here while I'm entertaining for a feast. What kind of signal would *that* send? What kind of a thing is that to do, you man of no faith? What would my *zemi* say to that?"

"My lady, with all possible respect, I had a very disturbing vision this morning about—"

"You're *always* worrying about something," she said with a gentle pat on the shoulder. "*My* bohiti didn't say anything about such a thing."

"That's because he's a coward," I snapped. The time for mincing words was over. Every bit of my being, every corner of my reason and intuition told me that disaster was about to strike.

"Nonsense," she said, beginning to dance again. "The Spaniards see the power that we possess and are finally ready to sit down and negotiate like *people*."

CHAPTER EIGHTY-SIX

A long time passed before the old man said anything. Just when Bartolomé thought he had drifted off to sleep, a violent cough took him, and he made horrible retching sounds. His host brought him a bowl and a cloth, but he pushed them away. Bartolomé saw that there was blood in what he'd expelled. Worried, he decided that he didn't need to be told the rest of the Taino story that night. He remembered clearly how Xaragua had been overrun by three hundred men, and how over eighty *caciques* had burned to death that night immediately following the most regal of Taino feasts. Legend has it that their cries of agony could be heard all across the Valley of San Juan, as they echoed and resounded off the cliffed walls — and that their ghosts can still be heard there on dark, lonely nights.

The last *caciazgo* of Hispaniola was crushed when Anacaona was hanged the morning after the feast like a common thief outside the city walls.

***

Bartolomé came back to check on his aged guest just before daybreak. He'd been ranting and raving in his sleep about Esther, Lorenzo, the gypsies, Kinjay, and Anacaona. He'd finally stopped an hour before sunrise — but it was then that the priest had become worried about him, and had not been able to sleep himself. He set the taper down and lightly knocked on his door. "Come in," said the raspy voice from within.

He opened the door and went in, afraid of what he might see. But instead of a gruesome sight, all he saw was Rodrigo, sitting comfortably on his pallet, the blankets pulled tightly under his chin.

"Today is the day, Bartolomé," he said. "Today I'm going to leave you. It won't be long now."

Bartolomé didn't say anything for a long moment, as he tried to comprehend what the old man was telling him. "Is there…anything I can do for you?" he asked, a lump forming in his throat.

"Yes," he said. "Help me outside. I want to lie in a hammock and watch the sunrise one last time. That's where I'll tell you the end of my story."

Bartolomé helped him up, and they slowly made their way outside. The air was cool and fresh, and the priest reflected that it had been years since he'd been up this early, before even his slaves awoke to prepare for the day.

He placed the old man in the hammock — it had now become *his* hammock — and Bartolomé stretched out in the other one. The sky off to the east was a tawny shade of pink and gray over the far, blue reaches of the sea, and Rodrigo now had a perfect view of where the sun would soon come up.

"I guess there's not much more to you tell you, Bartolomé," he began. "About life in *this* part of the world, at least. You've been here for a dozen years yourself, and you know as well as I do how things went from bad to worse after 1503."

"Yes, I know," Bartolomé whispered, thinking back on all the old memories he'd tried so hard to banish.

"What do you remember about when you were a boy, Bartolomé?" Rodrigo asked.

Bartolomé was surprised by the question. "I don't know," he admitted. "I was always afraid during thunderstorms, like all children. I remember the queen, the Giralda, the bullfights, market days. Usual things for Sevilla, I guess."

"What do you remember about your family?" he asked.

"I remember my father as a thrifty and hardworking merchant. He always loved me and showed me all the wonders of Sevilla. He loved me more than life itself, I sometimes think."

"And what about your mother?"

"I *do* remember a maternal presence, but it's only in occasional flashes," Bartolomé said. "She died when I was very young. And besides, I was often ill as a child, and there are entire parts of my youth that I don't remember at all."

"Give me your hand," Rodrigo said. The priest paused, then reached out to the old man. "Now, please know that what you are about to learn will come as a great shock to you, I have no doubt."

Bartolomé said nothing. Rodrigo took a deep breath, his throat sounding as if it were full of phlegm.

"You are Pobea," he said. "The son of Ostelinda."

"*What?*" Bartolomé said, snatching his hand away, as if from a burning log. "What are you *talking* about?"

"It's very simple, my friend. *You* are Pobea. Most of the women and children were killed that day in Triana all those many years ago. It was no surprise to us, we who knew it was coming in some way or other. I made a promise to your mother — Ostelinda — long ago, as she lay dying in that wagon we shared, that I would look after you, and that you'd grow up to be an admirable man, a redeemer…just as the fortune-tellers predicted."

This was too much. Bartolomé sat down on the ground by the hammock, feeling like he had been struck across the face.

"It's true," the dying man whispered. "No sooner had Triana been attacked than I heard that one small boy had been saved by the old priest of Santa Ana. The boy — you — knew where there was a secret entrance, and the priest took you in while the carnage went on outside. I'm sorry to tell you all this, but a middle-aged widower and a distant cousin of Esther — the man you would come to know as your father — approached the church months after the massacre upon my urging. He went with the intention of taking in the six-year old boy to have as his son, but you were a shadow of your former self. It was as if you had died the day Triana was destroyed, and only the outer shell of you had somehow survived. You didn't talk for months, I heard — you just sat and stared about with no expression. But the old man loved you so dearly! He'd lost his wife to the Inquisition — their entire families were *conversos* — and he'd always wanted a son, and somehow, he nursed you back to life. In the end, the only way he'd been able to wrest you from the priest was to threaten him with exposing his sins and the fact that he had fathered more than a dozen children in Sevilla and Triana himself."

Bartolomé still said nothing. He felt as if he'd been kicked by a horse.

"I promised your mother," Rodrigo said, his voice barely a whisper. "You're one of our tribe, you know. The gypsies, the wanderers, the slaves, the outsiders, the lost ones."

He didn't say it, but Bartolomé knew what he was thinking.

He was also a Taino now.

What Rodrigo had not said, did not need to say, was that, as Juan de Guzmán was his father, Bartolomé carried the blood of the Grand Inquisitor in his veins, as well as a bit of Rodrigo's.

"Pobea — Bartolomé — I'm dying. It is up to you to raise your voice for the salvation of these beautiful children of God...before it's too late. You can write, and can do it well. You have a special gift to convince people back in Spain. Just as your mother danced with *duende*, you can write with spirit, even better than Montesinos can. You can outbalance the evil in this world that your blood-father wrought, and a quill in your hand is mightier than a sword in the hands of any other man. Your real father, the man who raised you, was gentle and kind, and that is the sort of man you must be as well."

The old man was seized with a coughing spell, and he lay back in clear agony. Still, he seemed to fight the urge to succumb to silence. "That is why they sent me to you. You are the true voice of Christ in the wilderness. You're the best hope the Indians have."

Bartolomé finally found words to speak. "But, how? The Indians are being murdered by the hundreds every day. How can I possibly make a difference?"

Rodrigo seemed to struggle even more for his words. "I'll never forget what Esther told me once, a lovely thing from the Talmud. It was, "He who saves one life saves the world entire.""

Bartolomé sat for a long time, and the feeling of incredulity washed over him again and again like the waves of the Ocean Sea.

When finally he realized what had happened, the sun had risen. It was the most beautiful and soothing sight he'd ever seen. He felt cleansed, full of new spirit and purpose. He had not felt this way in years, or possibly ever before.

The old man lay cool and still in the hammock, a slight smile on his lips. His eyes were closed, as if he were in the middle of a peaceful dream.

He had died in his sleep by Bartolomé's side, and had never even made a final confession. Slowly, the priest did the only thing he knew to do under the circumstances: he folded his arms over his chest and prepared him for a Christian burial. As he did so, he felt a small lump on Rodrigo's chest. As he opened the man's hands and smock, he saw the ruby that Esther had given to him so many years ago.

He folded Rodrigo's arms once again over his chest. "*In manus tuas, Domine, commendo spiritum meum,*" he whispered.

"Farewell, my friend." Bartolomé fastened the ruby necklace around his own neck.

***

Bartolomé sat at Rodrigo's grave for a long time, journal in hand, trying to decide what it all meant. Here was a man who had spent his entire life being rejected, beaten, hunted, tortured and despised — and he'd come to Bartolomé to tell him all about it. But why *him*? Why hadn't he chosen someone else? Could he really write so well? And did being the son of a gypsy and a Guzmán really matter? He felt guilty for feeling a twinge of anger at the old man for telling him all of this and then dying so abruptly.

His house slave approached slowly, holding something in front of her.

"Master?" she said cautiously. "This came for you. A letter. From your uncle."

He took it and tore open the seal. He hastily read the following, which he had to read twice before its import fully struck him:

Dear Bartolomé,

Beware the man who has come to you. Contact a royal official at once, I beg of you, as this man is a dangerous criminal, and I shudder to think what he might do to you. In any case, let me now go right to the grain of what I wish to explain:

Once, when you were barely more than eighteen, you went to that man for lessons at the Dominican School, as your father was too poor to pay for university at that time. The monk taught you about everything-rhetoric, religion, logic, calligraphy, philosophy, but then the prior found out through his confession, that the wretch now known to you as Rodrigo is a sick man who had sinful thoughts for you, his young student, as well as for other men. He said you reminded him of a friend he'd once had long ago, in his youth. Although he was never able to touch you or corrupt you — we made sure of that — he was removed and was going to be burned for his sins. His life was spared when some of his powerful relatives intervened on his behalf to avoid a scandal. He agreed never to see you again and to undertake Admiral Colón's journey as an interpreter instead of meeting the purifying flames. Since you never seemed to wonder why you had to switch tutors, you may not remember the incident, and God knows we never reminded you of it — until now that you are in this unexpected danger.

Please don't be upset with us because of this secret, Bartolomé — we were only trying to do what was best for you under the shameful circumstances.

I repeat to you, dear nephew-do not make any deals or contacts with this sinful man, who is almost certainly a blasphemer or a sodomite, but contact a royal official at once and have him dealt with by the appropriate officials right away.

Your loving Uncle,
                    Juan de la Penalosa

HISTORICAL EPILOGUE

Following certain events of the spring of 1514, Bartolomé de Las Casas was to free his slaves and give away all his property. He was then to spend the next five decades as the Bishop of Chiapas, a humble Dominican friar, and a noted historian and chronicler. Most importantly, he was forever afterward a great humanitarian. He crossed the Atlantic at least seven times to speak with kings, church officials, and anyone who would listen to him about the abuses brought against the Natives of the New World at the hands of their often cruel and inhumane European conquerors. An indefatigable writer and activist, Las Casas was often a lone voice arguing for peace, compassion, and justice for all the peoples of the New World.